ABOUT THE EDITORS

LIZ GRZYB was born in the middle of a thunderstorm in Perth, Western Australia. She is the editor of acclaimed paranormal romance anthologies *Scary Kisses* and *More Scary Kisses*, the Orientalist pantomime *Dreaming of Djinn*, steampunk romance anthology *Kisses by Clockwork*, co-editor of paranormal noir anthology *Damnation and Dames* and *The Year's Best Australian Fantasy and Horror*.

TALIE HELENE is a musician and writer, from Melbourne, Australia. She writes poetry, fiction, and songs. Talie is horror editor for the anthology *The Year's Best Australian Fantasy and Horror* (Ticonderoga Publications); she was news editor for the Australian Horror Writers' Association for four years (2006–2010). She is a member of the SuperNova writers' group. Talie has a background in music journalism—especially extreme genres. She performs as a singer/songwriter, and has performed with many artists including The Tenth Stage, Wendy Rule, Saba Persian Orchestra, Maroondah Symphony—and is delighted to be collaborating on the new reincarnation of one of Australia's premiere Gothic Ethereal bands, Eden. For the latest updates, visit **www.taliehelene.com**

Also edited by LIZ GRZYB

Scary Kisses
More Scary Kisses
The Year's Best Australian Fantasy & Horror 2010 (with Talie Helene)
The Year's Best Australian Fantasy & Horror 2011 (with Talie Helene)
The Year's Best Australian Fantasy & Horror 2012 (with Talie Helene)
Damnation and Dames (with Amanda Pillar)
Dreaming of Djinn
Kisses by Clockwork

Also edited by TALIE HELENE

The Year's Best Australian Fantasy & Horror 2010 (with Liz Grzyb)
The Year's Best Australian Fantasy & Horror 2011 (with Liz Grzyb)
The Year's Best Australian Fantasy & Horror 2012 (with Liz Grzyb)

THE YEAR'S BEST AUSTRALIAN FANTASY & HORROR

~ 2013 ~

EDITED BY

LIZ GRZYB & TALIE HELENE

THE THIRD ANNUAL COLLECTION

THE YEAR'S BEST AUSTRALIAN FANTASY & HORROR

~ 2013 ~

EDITED BY

LIZ GRZYB & TALIE HELENE

T℘
℘℘
Ticonderoga
publications

for

Chuck Chainey-McKenzie
(L.G.)

For Adam Calaitzis
(T.H.)

The Year's Best Australian Fantasy & Horror 2013
edited by Liz Grzyb & Talie Helene

Published by Ticonderoga Publications

Designed by Russell B. Farr
Typeset in Sabon and Poor Richard

A Cataloging-in-Publications entry for this title is available from The National Library of Australia.

ISBN   978-1-921857-72-0 (hardcover)
       978-1-921857-73-7 (trade paperback)
       978-1-921857-74-4 (ebook)

Ticonderoga Publications
PO Box 29 Greenwood
Western Australia 6924

www.ticonderogapublications.com

10 9 8 7 6 5 4 3 2 1

The editors would like to thank Lee Battersby, Deborah Biancotti, Trudi Canavan, Robert G. Cook, Rowena Cory Daniells, Terry Dowling, Thoraiya Dyer, Russell B. Farr, Marion Halligan, Dmetri Kakmi, David Kernot, Margo Lanagan, S.G. Larner, Martin Livings, Kirstyn McDermott, Claire McKenna, C.S. McMullen, Juliet Marillier, David Thomas Moore, Faith Mudge, Ryan O'Neill, Angela Rega, Tansy Rayner Roberts, Nicky Rowlands, Carol Ryles, Angela Slatter, Anna Tambour, Kaaron Warren, and Janeen Webb.

CONTENTS

THE YEAR IN REVIEW

LIZ GRZYB & TALIE HELENE

THE YEAR IN FANTASY

Jonathan Strahan has had another successful year. He was nominated for a Hugo Award for Best Editor, Short Form and the Locus Award for Best Editor, and was awarded the Peter McNamara Convenors' Award for Excellence at the Aurealis Awards. His anthologies were nominated for a World Fantasy Award, a Locus Award and an Aurealis Award, and his *The Coode Street Podcast* was nominated for a Hugo Award and a Ditmar.

Australians were very well represented at the Hugo Awards this year, with Strahan's shortlisting for the Best Editor, and no less than four Australian or Australian-involved podcasts being nominated for Best Fancast.

Kaaron Warren and Angela Slatter had stories included in Paula Guran's *Once Upon a Time: New Fairy Tales*. Angela Slatter had a prolific year of international publications, being involved with Stephen Jones' *Fearie Tales*, *The British Fantasy Society Horror Anthology* and *The Dark* magazine, among others.

Thoraiya Dyer and Joanna Fay were two Australian authors included in Josie Brown's *Daughters of Icarus: New Feminist Science Fiction and Fantasy* anthology this year, from Pink Narcissus Press.

Alan Baxter had his short story "Not the Worst of Sins" published in *Beneath Ceaseless Skies* magazine. Anna Tambour's

"Marks and Coconuts" was published in *Postscripts* 30/31. Ian McHugh placed The Canal Barge Magician's Number Nine Daughter" in *Clockwork Phoenix* 4.

Gerry Huntman published "Dom and Gio's Barber Shop" in *Lovecraft Zine* #21, The Cutpurse from Mulberry Bend" in *Penny Dread Tales III*, and "In Arcadia" in Catharine May's *The Dark Bard*.

Lisa Hannett also placed a number of stories with international markets, such as "Another Mouth" in *The Dark* magazine, "The Coronation Bout" in *Electric Velocipede*.

Peter M Ball published "From Tuesday to Tuesday" in *Daily Science Fiction*. Tansy Rayner Roberts wrote "The Minotaur Girls" in *Glitter & Mayhem*. Trudi Canavan published "Camp Follower" in Jonathan Strahan's *Fearsome Journeys*.

NOTABLE NOVELS

Harper Collins supported Australian fantasy to a great extent this year, with many authors beginning or continuing series. Kylie Chan began her Chinese mythology-inspired Celestial Battle series with *Dark Serpent*, which was nominated for the Norma K. Hemming Award. Jennifer Fallon released the third book in her epic fantasy Rift Runners series, *Reunion*. Another Chinese link for Harper Collins this year was Traci Harding's *Dreaming of Zhou Gong*, which is set in ancient China. This is the first book in her new sf/fantasy Timekeepers series, which was voted in the "50 Books you Can't Put Down" get reading campaign. Duncan Lay continued from his 2012 novel *Bridge of Swords* with *Valley of the Shields*, the second in his Empire of Bones series. Felicity Pulman's *A Ring Through Time* is a young adult historical novel which was shortlisted for the Davitt Awards Best Young Adult Novel. Jo Spurrier's *Black Sun Light My Way* is the second instalment of her Children of the Black Sun series, and KJ Taylor continued her Risen Sun series with *The Shadowed Throne*.

Escape Publishing, the digital imprint of Harlequin Australia, has really expanded their Australian speculative romance offerings this year. Ros Baxter began her Aegira Chronicles with the quirky and very readable mermaid romance *Fish Out of Water*, Sarah Belle released fantasy romance *Hindsight* and Jennifer Brassel produced *Secret Reflection*. Jenny Brigalow started her young adult paranormal Nightshifters series with *The Children of the Mist*. Shannon Curtis began her fairy story-inspired Once Upon a Crime series with *Enamoured*. Alexis Fleming released the saucy paranormal *Hidden Fire*, and Juliet Madison published her time-travel fantasy romance *Fast Forward*. Nicola E. Sheridan released the erotic magical fantasy novel *A Warlord's Lady*, and Rebekah Turner continued her Chronicles of Applecross series with the second book, *Chaos Bound*. Jacquie Underdown had two magic realism romance books published with Escape this year: *Beautiful Illusion* and *The Paler Shade of Autumn*.

Pan Macmillan released the second in Juliet Marillier's excellent young adult Shadowfell series, *Raven Flight*, which won the Sir Julius Vogel Award for Best Youth Novel, and was nominated for the Tin Duck for Best Long Work. Jay Kristoff continued his Lotus War series with *Kinslayer*. Kristoff's Lotus War novella "The Last Stormdancer" won the Aurealis Award for Best Fantasy Short Story.

Momentum Books, the digital imprint from Macmillan, have continued to support Australian fantasy authors, bringing out a number of titles this year. Notables include Chris Matthews' debut novel, coming-of-age story *Mudlark*, and Adina West's *Dark Child: The Awakening*, which was released as five novella-length episodes before the omnibus edition was published in June. Momentum also published Dirk Strasser's *Eclipse*, the third title in his Ascension series, as well as re-releasing the first two titles in the series, *Zenith* and *Equinox*, which were originally published by Pan Macmillan.

Berkley Books continued publishing Australian and New Zealand paranormal romance. Kylie Griffin brought out the third in her demonic Light Blade series, *Allegiance Sworn*, which won the Australian Romance Readers Association Favourite Sci Fi, Fantasy or Futuristic Romance Award. Erica Hayes also released the second in her Seven Signs series, *Redemption*, following fallen angel Japheth and vampire Rose. New Zealand paranormal powerhouse Nalini Singh continued both of her series with Berkley this year, with Guild Hunter #6, *Archangel's Legion* and Psy/Changeling #15, *Heart of Obsidian*, which won the Australian Romance Readers Association Favourite Paranormal Romance Award. Singh also released three novellas set in her two paranormal worlds with Berkley, as well as a collection of her Psy/Changeling novellas and shorts, *Wild Invitation*.

Random House has had a lot of success with their Australian authors this year, with Allyse Near's *Fairytales for Wilde Girls* winning Best Young Adult Novel and nominated for Best Horror Novel in Aurealis Awards, and being shortlisted for the Inky Award, as well as for the Norma K. Hemming Award. Charlotte McConaghy began her young adult romantic fantasy Chronicles of Kaya series with *Avery*. Michael Pryor continued his young adult magical realism Extraordinaires series with *The Subterranean Stratagem*.

Allen & Unwin continued to support young adult fantasy series, publishing the first two new series. Amie Karfman and Meagan Spooner's sf/fantasy trilogy Starbound began with Aurealis Award-winning and Inky shortlisted *These Broken Stars*, and the first of Marianne Curley's new Avena series, *Hidden*, was released, featuring a stolen angel. Julie Hunt released her Children's Book Award-shortlisted novel *Song for a Scarlet* Runner, which was also shortlisted for an Aurealis Award for Best Children's Book. Garth Nix & Sean Williams brought out their third Troubletwisters title, *The Mystery of the Golden Card*.

Angry Robot continued to feature Australasian names, releasing Lee Battersby's sequel to *The Corpse-Rat King*: *The Marching Dead*, which was nominated for Best Horror Novel at the Aurealis Awards. New Zealand author Freya Robertson began her Elemental Wars series with the Sir Julius Vogel Best Novel Award-winning *Heartwood*.

Clan Destine Press published three Australian novels in the fantasy genre this year. Patricia Bernard began her young adult fantasy series M'dgassy Chronicles with *Legend of the Three Moons*. Dean J Anderson brought out steamy action paranormal *Unnaturals*, and Cheryse Durrant began her young adult paranormal Heart Hunters series with *The Blood She Betrayed*.

Hachette Australia released fantasy thriller *Lexicon* from Max Barry, which won Best Science Fiction Novel and was shortlisted for Best Fantasy Novel in the Aurealis Awards. M.K. Hume completed her pre-Arthurian Merlin's Prophecy series with *Web of Deceit*. Ian Irvine completed his Tainted Realm trilogy with *Justice*.

Fablecroft continued their focus on novels this year by releasing the long-awaited third in Tansy Rayner Roberts' young adult Mocklore Chronicles, *Ink Black Magic*, which was shortlisted for the Aurealis Best Fantasy Novel. Fablecroft also re-released the first two volumes of the Mocklore Chronicles, *Splashdance Silver* and *Liquid Gold*, as ebooks.

Through 47 North, Amazon's speculative fiction imprint, Mark Barnes brought out two volumes from his Echoes of Empire fantasy trilogy: *The Garden of Stones* and *The Obsidian Heart*.

Penguin digital imprint Destiny Romance released two speculative romances by their Australian authors, Peta Crake's paranormal *Revelry* and Bernadette Rowley's fantasy *The Lady's Choice*.

Rowena Cory Daniells concluded her epic King Rolen's Kin series with *King Breaker*, published by Solaris Press. Robert Hood's horror/fantasy novel *Fragments of a Broken Land: Valarl Undead* was released from Borgo Press (an imprint of Wildside Press), winning the Ditmar Award for Best Novel.

Tartarus Press published Nike Sulway's fantasy/science fiction novel *Rupetta*, which won the James Tiptree, Jr. Award, the Norma K. Hemming Award and was shortlisted in the Aurealis Awards for Best Science Fiction Novel, and the Crawford Memorial Award.

Garth Nix's amusing magical romance *Newt's Emerald* was released through Jill Grinberg Literary Management, and was shortlisted for Best Fantasy Novel in the Aurealis Awards. Joanna Fay continued her Siaris Quartet with the second book, *Reunion*, and the third, *Vow's Answer*, through Musa Publishing. *Vow's Answer* was nominated for a Tin Duck Award for Best Professional Written Work.

Neil Cladingboel released the final novel of his Erebus Equilibrium series, *Beloved Sons*, through his publishing house, Equilibrium Books. Equilibrium Books also released Karina McRoberts' first instalment of her Chelandra trilogy, *Chelandra*.

Crimson Romance, an e-publishing imprint of F+W Media, released TF Walsh's paranormal *Cloaked in Fur*. Prolific erotic fiction author Christina Phillips had two new speculative novels released through Ellora's Cave this year, the fantasy romance *Betrayed* (Forbidden Book 3) and the paranormal *Bloodlust*

Denied. Christian Baines released his gay paranormal romance *The Beast Without* through Interactive Press.

Bec McMaster released two steampunk paranormal romances in her London Steampunk series with Sourcebooks this year: *My Lady Quicksilver* and *Heart of Iron*. She also self-published *Tarnished Knight*. NZ author Summer Wigmore had her Sir Julius Vogel Award-nominated novel *The Wind City* published by Steam Press.

Grant Wales brought out a Noah's Ark retelling, *Man After His Kind* through Dragonfall Press. Shimmer by Jennifer McBride & Lynda Nixon is a young adult novel about a teenaged genie, released by Fremantle Press. Natasha Ewendt published her vampire novel *This Freshest Hell* through Lacuna Publishing. Kylie Sheaffe and Mel Tescho released inspirational fantasy romance *Believe* with Soul Mate Publishing.

Many self-published novels are starting to win awards and being included in shortlists. In the Sir Julius Vogel Awards shortlist in New Zealand, three out of the six shortlisted novels are self-published, and in the Aurealis Awards in Australia, three of the six "book" categories included a self-published book, and two awards were won by self-published works. As the information for the introduction was being collated this year, another interesting phenomenon was noted: that a large number of self-published works were listed as published by a company which turned out to be made up of the author. While there obviously continues to be a stigma attached to self-published works for this to occur, it seems that the awards are beginning to reflect more of an open door to non-traditionally published works.

Mitchell Hogan published his own novel *A Crucible of Souls*, which took out Best Fantasy Novel in the Aurealis Awards.

Andrea Host was another self-published author who made waves in the awards this year, with her novels *Hunting*, which was shortlisted in the Aurealis Awards for Best Young Adult Novel, and *Bones of the Fair*.

Two self-published titles were shortlisted for the Sir Julius Vogel Award for Best Novel. Sam J. Charlton's Palâdnith Chronicles Book 1, *Journey of Shadows*, and Sharon Hannaford's third instalment in her paranormal Hellcat series, *A Cold Day in Hell*, were on the shortlist.

COLLECTIONS

Ticonderoga Publications took the lead again in the number of single-author collections published this year, edited by Russell B. Farr. Cat Sparks' thought provoking science fiction collection *The Bride Price* won the Ditmar for Best Collection and also Best Short Story for the excellent story "Scarp". Sparks was also nominated for Best Artwork in the Ditmars for her cover of this collection, which was nominated for Best Collection in the Aurealis Awards.

Juliet Marillier's collection *Pricklemoon* won the Tin Duck for Best Professional Long Work, as well as being nominated for the Sir Julius Vogel Award for Best Collected Work and the Tin Duck for Best Edited Work. Stories from the collection won the Aurealis Award for Best Young Adult Short Fiction, the Sir Julius Vogel Award for Best Short Story, as well as being nominated for the Ditmar and Tin Duck Awards. Even the cover art by Pia Ravenari was nominated for two awards.

Kim Wilkins' *The Year of Ancient Ghosts* was shortlisted for the Aurealis Award for Best Collection, and the title story won Best Horror Short Fiction as well as being shortlisted for Best Young Adult and Best Fantasy Short Fiction in the same awards. The story was also shortlisted for Best Novella or Novelette in the Ditmars.

Jason Fischer's *Everything is a Graveyard* has many fantasy elements, but the stories sit squarely in the horror genre. Steven Utley's final collection, *Invisible Kingdoms* is another collection with elements of fantasy, this time more in the science fiction realm.

Twelfth Planet Press has continued to produce outstanding boutique collections from big names in Australian speculative fiction. Alisa Krasnostein edited two collections this year, Thoraiya Dyer's Asymmetry and Kirstyn McDermott's disturbing *Caution: Contains Small* Parts. Both collections were nominated for Best Collected Work in the Ditmars and Best Collection in the Aurealis Awards. McDermott's collection was nominated for Best Long Fiction in the Chronos Awards. "The Home for Broken Dolls" won Best Novella or Novelette in the Ditmar Awards, as well as "What Amanda Wants" being in the shortlist for the same award. "The Home for Broken Dolls" was also nominated for the Best

Horror Short Fiction Award in the Aurealis Awards. Dyer had her own share of successes this year, with one of the stories fro her collection, "Seven Days in Paris", being nominated for Best Science Fiction Short Story in the Aurealis Awards, and Best Short Story in the Ditmars. Amanda Rainey won the Tin Duck for her Twelfth Planet Press book covers.

Fablecroft's excellent collection this year was Joanne Anderton's *The Bone Chime Song and Other Stories*, edited by Tehani Wessely, which took out Best Collection at the Aurealis Awards and the Australian Shadows Awards, as well as being nominated for the Ditmar, and two of the stories from the collection were nominated in short story categories for both the Aurealis and the Ditmar awards.

David Conyers released a number of short fantasy/horror/science fiction collections this year: *The Impossible Object (Harrison Peel Files #1)*, *The Weaponized Puzzle (Harrison Peel Files #2)*, *The Uncertainty Bridge*, his Cthulhu collection *The Nightmare Dimension*, and *The Entropy Conflict*.

Kaaron Warren released a reprint collection of five of her dark fantasy/horror stories, *The Gate Theory*, with Geoff Brown at Cohesion Press. Andrez Bergen published his eclectic collection, *The Condimental Op* through Perfect Edge Books. Edwina Harvey released her collection, *The Back of the Back of Beyond* with Peggy Bright Books, edited by Simon Petrie. Anthony Sweet brought out his collection, *Simple Broken Things* through An Altered Aspect.

Jay Caselberg released his collection *Unnatural Conditions*, containing nineteen of his fantasy, horror and science fiction short stories.

ANTHOLOGIES

Jonathan Strahan brought out two fantasy anthologies this year: *Fearsome Journeys: The New Solaris Book of Fantasy Volume 1* which was nominated for a World Fantasy Award, and the seventh volume of the Night Shade Books compilation *The Best Science Fiction and Fantasy of the Year*, which was nominated for the Aurealis and Locus Best Anthology Awards. Strahan was also nominated for a Hugo Award for Best Editor, Short Form, and was awarded the Peter McNamara Convenors' Award for Excellence at the Aurealis Awards.

Fablecroft and Ticonderoga Publications both published two anthologies this year, and each had one reprint and one original anthology.

Tehani Wessely of Fablecroft released *One Small Step: an Anthology of Discoveries* and *Focus 2012: Highlights of Australian Short Fiction*. *One Small Step*, with authors like Faith Mudge, Deborah Biancotti, Lisa Hannett and Angela Slatter, explored new worlds with a deft touch. The anthology jointly won Best Anthology at the Aurealis Awards, D.K. Mok's story "Morning Star" was nominated for Best Young Adult Short Fiction in the same awards as well as being nominated for the WSFA Small Press Award for Short Fiction, and Tansy Rayner Roberts' "Cold White Daughter" was nominated for Best Short Story in the Ditmars.

2012: Highlights of Australian Short Fiction contained a number of award-winning and critically acclaimed stories from the year. It was nominated for the Aurealis Award for Best Anthology.

Ticonderoga Publications' original anthology for the year was Liz Grzyb's Arabian Nights-inspired *Dreaming of Djinn*. This title won the Tin Duck for Best Edited Work, and "Street Dancer" from the anthology won the Tin Duck for Best Short Written Work. The anthology was nominated for the Aurealis Award for Best Anthology, and various other stories were nominated for the Tin Duck Award for Best Short Written Work.

Liz Grzyb and Talie Helene's *Year's Best Australian Fantasy and Horror 2012* co-won the Aurealis Award for Best Anthology, as well as being nominated for the Tin Duck in Best Edited Work.

Stephen C. Ormsby brought out *Tales of Australia: Great Southern* Land with Satalyte Publishing, which was nominated for Best Long Fiction in the Chronos Awards. Sean McMullen's story "Acts of Chivalry" and David McDonald's "Set Your Face Towards the Darkness" were both nominated for the WSFA Small Press Award for Short Fiction.

Anna Caro edited *Regeneration: New Zealand Speculative Fiction II* with Random Static, which focused on the idea of adaptation, transformation and new growth. *Regeneration* was nominated for the Sir Julius Vogel Award for Best Collected Work, and its cover by Emma Weakley, won the Best Professional Artwork Award.

Simon Petrie edited CSFG's *Next* anthology, which combines stories from many of Australia's excellent short fiction writers, across all the subgenres of speculative fiction.

Guy Salvidge and Andrez Bergen co-edited the post-apocalyptic noir anthology *The Tobacco-Stained Sky* with Another Sky Press.

Issue 42 of *Griffith Review: Once Upon a Time in Oz* from Text Publishing was an interesting assembly of stories, as it was focused on fairy stories. Editor Julianne Schultz included both fiction and non-fiction pieces centred around the fairy tale idea.

Sophie Yorkston edited *Star Quake* 1, the anthology collecting the best stories published in *SQ Mag* in 2012. The anthology was nominated for an Australian Shadows Award.

New Zealander Freya Robertson published her own collection of short stories, *Augur and other short stories*, which included one story from Chris Robertson.

VISUAL

Shaun Tan's gorgeous new picture book *Rules of Summer* garnered critical acclaim this year, taking out the Chronos and Ditmar Awards for Best Artwork, and being nominated for Best Art Book at the Locus Awards. Tan was also nominated for Best Artist in the Locus Awards.

The comic *Burger Force* from Jackie Ryan was joint winner of the Aurealis Best Illustrated Book/Graphic Novel Award this year, alongside Tom Taylor and James Brouwer's Volume 2 of The Deep, *The Vanishing Island*, from Gestalt Comics.

New Zealand continued its involvement with fantasy in TV and film, with the second film in the *Hobbit* series, *The Desolation of Smaug*, being made. The film won many awards, such as the Saturn Award for Best Production Design, the CinEuphoria Awards for Best Costume Design and Best Art Direction, the Empire Awards for Best Male Newcomer and Best Sci-Fi/Fantasy film, the MTV Award for Best Fight. It was also nominated for Academy Awards, BAFTAs, and a World Fantasy Award, among others.

Return to Nim's Island, *Atomic Kingdom: Revolution* and *Goldie* were other fantasy films made in Australia.

PODCASTS

Australian podcasts did extremely well at the Hugos this year, with Kirstyn McDermott and Ian Mond's *The Writer and the Critic,* Gary K Wolfe and Jonathan Strahan's *Coode Street Podcast, Galactic Suburbia* from Alisa Krasnostein, Alex Pierce, and Tansy Rayner Roberts, and *Verity!* which Tansy Rayner Roberts is involved with, all being nominated for the Hugo Award for Best Fancast!

The Writer and the Critic and *The Coode Street Podcast* were also nominated for a Ditmar. *Galactic Suburbia* was also nominated for the Ditmar award and the Tin Duck for Best Fan Production.

Galactic Chat Podcast won the Ditmar for Best Fan Publication. Bruce Gillespie's *SF Commentary* won the Chronos Award for Best Fan Publication and was nominated for the Ditmar.

Ion Newcombe's *Antipodean SF Radio Show* delivers stories, news, reviews and interviews from the Antipodean SF Magazine.

MAGAZINES/WEBZINES

Grant Watson's blog *The Angriest,* where Watson reviews films, TV ad books, was nominated for a Chronos Award for Best Fan Publication.

Dark Matter Zine, run by Nalini Haynes, was nominated for a Ditmar for Best Fan Production. *Dark Matter* prints reviews, interviews, and blogs.

Aurealis Magazine is available electronically through iTunes and other formats through Smashwords. *Aurealis* released ten issues in 2013, combining fiction with opinion pieces.

Andromeda Spaceways Inflight Magazine released issues #57 and #58 in 2013. ASIM is available both electronically and in print through their website.

Cosmos Magazine regularly publishes speculative fiction edited by Cat Sparks, both in the print magazine (now available as an iPad app) and on the website. While these are primarily science fiction, some stories have fantasy elements.

Antipodean SF has continued to prolifically publish speculative fiction online, releasing monthly issues.

Review of Australian Fiction brings two stories from Australian authors every two weeks, and frequently offers speculative fiction pieces.

New Zealand webzine *Novazine* from Jacqui Smith brought out six issues in 2013, including short stories, news, reviews and trivia. *Novazine* was nominated for a Sir Julius Vogel Award for Best Fan Production.

INDUSTRY NEWS

Perth-based small press publishers Dragonfall Press closed their doors this year, after three years of operations. Their titles are still available through Smashwords, Tomely, and Amazon.

Solarwyrm Press, run by Jax Goss and Dominica Malcolm, is another new small press who opened in 2012 but produced their first publications in 2013. They run in a crowdfunding, cooperative style.

Crowdfunding is still a new area of exploration for Australian publishers and authors, as well as internationally. Some authors and publishers have been able to use it as the backbone of their business, whereas others' experiments in the area have not resulted in enough backers to successfully fund through this means.

THE YEAR IN HORROR

NOVELS

2013 had a very diverse range of horror novels published, and the borrowing of horror tropes by paranormal authors continued to blur the genre boundaries. Winner of the Australian Shadows Award for Best Novel was Marty Young's 809 *Jacob Street* (Black Beacon Books); the novel concerns a teenage boy and a seasoned bluesman who are drawn to a haunted house in rural Australia in the 1980s. Kent Hill's *Alien Smut Peddlers from the Future*, a bizarro western, was published by Strangehouse Books. *Black City: The Lark Case Files Book 1* (Gestalt Publishing) by Christian Read, introduced protagonists PI Lark and ex-librarian Scarlett, in a hardboiled gangwar context with occultism and witchcraft. *Bloodlust Denied* by Christina Phillips was published by Ellora's Cave; a Regency romance with light BDSM and horror tropes. The debut novel from Jason Franks, *Bloody Waters,* was published by Possible Press; a rock'n'roll Faustian deal with the devil—guitarist Clarice Marnier brokered not for chops, but for survival. K.C. Webb's *Body Jump* (Dark Wind Books) had homicide detective Susan Claw on the trail of a body jumping serial killer dubbed "the butcher". Adrian Scott's *Child of the Living Dead (The Sins of Mason Thurlow 1)* was published by Rebecca J. Vickery; a historical zombie saga set in Haiti. Adina West's dark urban fantasy *Dark Child* (Momentum) introduced Kat Chancer, a half-vampire/half-human hybrid pathologist. Matthew Tait's *Dark Meridian* (DM Publishing), set in the Adelaide hills, musician Adam Lavas confronts the supernatural gateway of the sinister Meridian House. *Dark Rite*, co-authored by David Wood and Alan Baxter, was published by Gryphonwood Press; an oldschool occult horror tale set in the tiny Appalachian town of Wallen's

Gap. Keri Arthur's *Darkness Unmasked (Dark Angels 5)* (New American Library) continued the story of half-werewolf/half-Aedh Risa Jones. *Deicide* (Rethink Press) by Tim Hawken concluded the Hellbound trilogy, with a finale in hell. Daniel Brako had arguably the tightest biography blurb/novel tie in—a clinical psychologist turned author, his debut novel *Doors* (Momentum) concerned a successful psychologist drawn into a murder mystery, who finds his own sense of reality challenged by the uncanny.

End of Dreams (The Immortal Destiny 1) by Kim Faulks opened a dark paranormal series; a young woman and a hard-bitten detective caught in a supernatural war. Allyse Near's *Fairytales for Wilde Girls* (Random House Australia) was billed enticingly as a "deliciously dark bubblegum-gothic fairytale". Bec McMaster published three novels with publisher Sourcebooks, all set in the same world, London's Whitechapel district in the late 1880s—*Kiss of Steel, Heart of Iron* and *My Lady Quicksilver*—concerning werewolves, vampires, and a clockwork army. Luke Keioske's *Her* (Severed Press) was a supernatural woman-scored rampage. Max Barry's *Lexicon* (Penguin) was a recoiling dystopian about "the power of language and coercion". D.L. Richardson self-published *Little Red Gem*, a comedy paranormal romance about a haunting. Demelza Carlton published two novels in her Nightmares Trilogy, Book 1 the *Nightmares of Caitlin Lockyer* and Book 2 the *Necessary Evil of Nathan Miller*. Dirk Flinthart's *Path of Night* (FableCroft Publishing) gave us the first installment in the Night Beast Series, set in Sydney using a hardboiled narrative style; Michael Devlin awoke in the morgue with new abilities, and hunted by a cabal of monsters. N.A. Sulway's *Rupetta* (Tartarus Press) concerned a clockwork woman, an immortal keeper of law and memory— invoking the European fantasy/horror tradition. *Secret Reflection* by Jennifer Brassel was published by Escape Publishing; a modern gothic romance between a dashing ghost and a beautiful skeptic. *Skin* by Kylie Scott was published by Momentum; a disturbing zombie apocalypse romance that blurs the line between BDSM and abuse. S.M. Johnston's *Sleeper* (Entranced Publishing) opened the Toy Soldiers series; a heart transplant recipient inherits nightmares and supernatural abilities. Antonia Marlowe's *Strange Bodies* was published by Not So Noble Books; a crime thriller set in the Blue Mountains of NSW.

The Asylum (Random House Australia), by the impressive John Harwood, is a gothic suspense novel set in late Victorian England, on Bodmin Moor, Cornwall. *The Beast Without* (Interactive Publications/Glass House Books) was the debut gothic romance from Christian Baines; vampire Reylan cruises Oxford Street gay bars for human companions, until one is killed by werewolf Jorgas. *The Beckoning* (Damnation Books) was a return to adult fiction by Paul Collins, with a dark occult horror; a lawyer attempts to prevent his psychic daughter being drawn into a sinister cult. *The Dark Lands (Valkeryn 2)* by Greig Beck, a far future dystopian where the descendents of canines are the dominant species, published by Cohesion Press. Greig Beck also published *The First Bird* (Momentum), the first in a three part eco thriller. *The Last Girl* (Allen & Unwin) by Michael Adams concerned a psychic teen protecting her little brother in a post-apocalyptic world. LegumeMan Books published the debut novel from Scott Tyson, *Topsiders*, an urban horror novel. Timothy Bowden's *Undead Kelly* was published by Severed Press; a zombie novel set in Melbourne of the 1880s, with convicted Ned Kelly taking on the undead.

The novella/novelette length "short novel" was popular both in collections, and as a stand-alone ebook format. Damien Broderick's "Quicken" novella in *Beyond the Doors of Death* was notable; science fiction concerned with horror territory, Broderick authored a far future follow up to Robert Silverberg's *Born with the Dead*, the 1974 Nebula Award Winning novella about a couple separated by unique circumstances—the husband alive, the wife one of the "rekindled dead". Steve Gerlach published the novella 'Darkness Burning' in *Autopsy II: Darkness Burning* (LegumeMan Books). Astrid Cooper published *Blood Immoral* (eXtasy Books), a rollicking paranormal with cat shifters and rogue vampires tangling in the city of churches. Clan Destine Press published a few stand alone novellas, with two on the darker side—*Rosalie: Fearless* by Anders, an erotic novella about a morgue worker who likes the quiet, and Mary Borsellino's *Loveless*, a vampire novella. Phil Cohen self-published *The Stony Streets of Hell*; a child journeyed to the underworld to bring back their parents. Evil Jester Press published *The Last Night of October* by Greg Chapman. Eleni Konstantine published the novella 'Snoop' as *Snoop Cases* #1 (Musa Publishing); a PI tackled a vampire and a gremlin. Ros

Baxter published *White Christmas* (Escape Publishing); a post-apocalyptic world overrun by ice vampires.

YOUNG ADULT AND CHILDREN'S HORROR

There have been a high volume of young adult and children's horror books for 2013, including many novels. H.Y. Hanna's *Big Honey Dog Mysteries 1: Curse of the Scarab* (Wiseheart Press) was a Nancy Drew style children's adventure using motifs of hieroglyphs and scarab beetles to unravel an Egyptian curse. A. Finlay's *Binding Darkness* (Unique Publishing) was the second installment in the *Shadows of Light* series, a dark teen ensemble drama peppered with spirits, bats, and crows. D.C. Green's *Monster School* (Ford Street Publishing) was targeted at younger readers; swamp boy saved from Mafia goblins by vampire, zombie and giant spider classmates. Martin Chatterton's *Mortified: Lost in the Sands of Time* (Random House Australia) concerned 10,000-year-old Mortimer DeVere and his sister, Agnetha, who confront zombie-mummies while exploring Egypt during the reign of Queen Victoria. Natasha Ewendt's debut novel *This Freshest Hell* (Lacuna Publishing) was a Young Adult vampire story with two teen girls discovering the supernatural. Jenny Brigalow's *The Children of the Mist* (Escape Publishing) was a Young Adult paranormal; two best friends, a teen-wolf and vampire, are caught between feuding families in the Scottish highlands. Sue Whiting's *Portraits of Celina* (Walker Books Australia) presented a Young Adult tale blending vengeful haunting with paranormal romance. Cheree Smith's *Shadow Embraced* (Dark Cherry Press) introduced wayward teen Scar as she ventured into an underground "fight club" of vampires, werewolves and witches.

At novella length there were many more YA and children's works, many of which were also illustrated. Deborah Abela's "A Transylvanian Tale" appeared in *Ghost Club 3: A Transylvanian Tale* (Random House Australia). 'Bewitched' by Colin Thompson, a children's comedy with horror tropes set in Transylvania Waters, was published as *The Floods 12: Bewitched* (Random House Australia). *The Grimstones 4: Music School* (Allen & Unwin) continued the series by author Asphyxia, with another Gothic fairytale adventure for protagonist Martha Grimstone. The anthology *Stories for Boys* (Random House) included Bill Condon's

"The Ghostly Foot". The Eerie children's 10+ series from Penguin Books Australia, penned by "S. Carey", proliferated in 2013 with titles including *Game Over, Graveyard Watch, Hunter and Collector, Killer App, Swarm, The No Bodies, The Night Prowler, The Specular, The Trunk, Thriller,* and *Tiddles.*

COLLECTIONS

Everything is a Graveyard by Jason Fischer, edited by Russell B. Farr (Ticonderoga Publications) collected fourteen stories ranging from horror to fantasy to bleak absurdism; three stories were original to the collection, the titular story is a road warrior epic during the drop bear apocalypse, and "L'Hombre" and "When the Cheerful Misogynist Comes to Town" are both surreal dark fantasy. Kim Wilkins published *The Year of Ancient Ghosts* (Ticonderoga Publications) edited by Russell B. Farr, opening with a fabulous horror novella from which the collection takes its name, as well as four short stories. The fantasy tale "The Lark and the River" was also original to the collection.

The Twelve Planets series from Twelfth Planet Press continued with two more excellent volumes, both edited by Alisa Krasnostein; *Caution: contains small parts* by Kirstyn McDermott, featured four unflinchingly confronting horror stories, the titular tale, the novella length "What Amanda Wants" and the utterly harrowing novella "The Home for Broken Dolls", and the intertextual "Horn"; *Asymmetry* by Thoraiya Dyer also collected four stories, opening with the horror offering, the very fine werewolf story "After Hours".

David Conyers was prolific in his themed collection releases with *The Impossible Object (The Harrison Peel Files* 1) including the novella "Driven Underground" ; *The Weaponized Puzzle (The Harrison Peel Files* 2*)* with a novella length title story; *The Nightmare Dimension* featuring original stories "The Dream Quest of a Thousand Cats"; *The Entropy Conflict* including the titular tale original to the collection.

Jenny Blackford published a chapbook of cat poems *The Duties of a Cat* (Pitt Street Poetry) which included the dark, weird poem "Something in the Corner". *The Bone Chime Song and other stories* by Joanne Anderton (FableCroft Publishing) included the post-apocalyptic "Fence Lines". Kaaron Warren published an electronic collection of five previously published works, *The Gate Theory* with Geoff Brown's Cohesion Press. Andrez Bergen released *The Condimental Op* (Perfect Edge Books); this included the new story "Revert To Type" about a haunted typewriter. David Kernot self-published *The Early Years* collection. *Keep Off the Grass* from Michael Le Page was a self-published collection including three new stories "Attack of the Karma Pigeons", "Thick Skin" and "Windows to the Soul". Dayle R. Grixti released *Nobody Can Scream and other stories* (Really Blue Books). Daniel I. Russell published the *Tricks, Mischief and Mayhem* collection with Crystal Lake Publishing; the collection included one exclusive story "Linger" which engaged so energetically with popular culture and music, it inspired awe for the music publisher permission fees alone. Marija Elektra Rodriguez published the collection *Masquerade and Other Stories* (Huntress Ink), offering twenty-nine tales spanning Gothic horror and paranormal romance genres.

Anthony Sweet published *Simple Broken Things* (An Altered Aspect), a collection of three short stories, predominantly fantasy, although "Tunevalve Blues" notably incorporated voodoo. C.M. Simpson self-published *Short Stories & Poems from* 2012, which included one dark fantasy and one paranormal/urban horror story; this very prolific author also published a number of stand-alone ebooks containing single stories including the novella *Death Comes in Bone*, and she boasted a prolific 2013 YA output as nom de plume Carlie Simonsen. Meg Mundell published *Things I Did for Money* (Scribe Publications), which had decidedly surreal and nightmarish moments. Jay Caselberg released self-published collection *Unnatural Conditions : Collected Short Stories* with the stories "Cuckooo", "Laughing Boy", "Magus", "The Axe", "The Tower", "Thunder Head" and "Verisimilitude" all original to the collection. David R. Grigg self-published *The Dark Lighthouse*, collecting forty three stories, with seventeen previously unpublished; the collection tended towards dark fantasy over horror.

ANTHOLOGIES

The Great Unknown (Spineless Wonders), edited by Angela Meyer, set out to "pay tribute to the undeniable cultural influence that American TV programs such as Twilight Zone and Outer Limits have had on our lives 'down under'." Gathering together authors from the speculative and literary enclaves, there were some darker and more macabre offerings, most notable Ryan O'Neill's "Sticks and Stones" (reprinted in this collection), Damon Young's "Art", Chris Somerville's "The Rift" and A.S.Patric's "Memories of Jane Doe". Other uncanny fiction from Krissy Kneen, Alexander Cothren, Kathy Charles, and Carmel Bird.

Canberra Science Fiction Guild published *Next*, edited by Simon Petrie and Robert Porteous. An anthology ranging the speculative genres, it included four horror tales, Claire McKenna's "The Ninety-Two", Janeen Webb's "Hell Is Where the Heart Is", Ian McHugh's "Vandiemansland", and Craig McCormick's "Ned Kelly and the Zombies", and a wry poem from Chris McGrane titled "The Cat and the Zombies". FableCroft Published *One Small Step: an anthology of discoveries*, edited by Tehani Wessely; dark stories featured were Kate Gordon's "Shadows" and "By Blood and Incantation" co-authored by power-duo Lisa L. Hannett and Angela Slatter. *A Killer Among Demons*, edited by Craig Bezant at Dark Prints Press was a very strong collection of paranormal noir with some dark and decidedly occult moments. Stories from William Meikle, Stephen D. Rogers, Chris Large, Greg Chapman, Alan Baxter, Madhvi Ramani, Marilyn Fountain, Angela Slatter, S.J. Dawson, and Stephen M. Irwin.

New Zealand publisher Paper Road Press brought out the substantial *Baby Teeth: Bite Sized Tales of Terror* edited by Dan Rabarts and Lee Murray, thirty seven stories from twenty seven authors from New Zealand and elsewhere; the book collected a number of awards, winning the Sir Julius Vogel Award for Best Collected Work, winning the Australian Shadows Award for Edited Publication, and scoring the Australian Shadows Award for Best Short Story for Debbie Cowens "Caterpillar". New Zealand writers featured were Debbie Cowens, Grant Stone, Paul Mannering, Lee Murray, Jack Newhouse, Elizabeth Gatens, Jean Gilbert, Dan Rabarts, Celine Murray, Jenni Sands, Sally McLennan, Matt Cowens, Eileen Mueller, Darian Smith, Anna Caro, Jan Goldie, Michael J. Parry, Kecin G. McLean, Piper Mejia, Morgan Davie and JC Hart. The book was a fundraiser for Duffy Books in Homes, a program providing free books to over 100,000 New Zealand children every year.

Tales of Australia: Great Southern Land (Satalyte Publishing) edited by Stephen C. Ormsby and Carol Bond, mostly collected magic realism and fantasy, but darker offerings were Lee Battersby's "Disciple of the Torrent", Sean McMullen's "Acts of Chivalry"and David McDonald's "Set Your Face Against the Darkness". *The Tobacco-Stained Sky* (Another Sky Press) was an anthology of post-apocalyptic noir edited by two Australians who also have stories in the book—the cyberpunk "In-Dreamed" and "We Are Not Afraid, We Serve" by Andrez Bergen and feverish dystopian "The Dying Rain" by Guy Salvidge. No outright horror, but certainly dark in tone. The book also featured Liam Jose's "The Holy Church of the Scalpel". Kalamity Press produced two monstery anthologies, *This Mutant Life: A Neo-Pulp Anthology* and *This Mutant Life 2: Bad Company* both edited by Ben Langdon; while there were no outright horror tales, the anthology collected an interesting group of emerging writers, which bodes well for future speculative forays. Kayelle Press published *Tomorrow: Apocalyptic Short Stories* edited by Karen Henderson, which leaned quite strongly towards science fiction albeit with a bleak outlook. Robert Hood's "Soul Killer" was published in *Zombies Vs Robots: Diplomacy* edited by Jeff Connor (IDW Publishing).

Star Quake 1 (IFWG Publishing), edited by Sophie Yorkston, is the "Best Of" anthology from *SQ Magazine*; Antipodeans featured included Daniel I Russell, Michael B Fletcher, and Mitchell Edgeworth. *Undead & Unbound: Unexpected Tales From Beyond the Grave* (Chaosium), edited by Brian M. Sammons and David Conyers, included the excellent "Romero 2.0" co-authored by the editors, and "The Unforgiving Court" by David Schembri. Conyers had a strong year, and also published "Playgrounds of Angolaland" in *Eldritch Chrome: Unquiet Tales of a Mythos-Haunted Future* (Chaosium) edited by Brian M. Sammons & Glynn Owen Barrass, and "The Road to Afghanistan" in *What Scares the Boogey Man* (Perseid Publishing), edited by John Manning. Sharyn Lilley placed "Caleb's Chair" in the *Blood and Roses* anthology from Scarlett River Press. Aimée Lindorff's "The Silent Door" was included in Pillow Fight! (Tiny Owl Workshop), a project pairing art and story in a textile art format, launched at the Brisbane Writers Festival.

Pete Aldin placed "Mud" in *Horrific History—An Anthology of Historical Horror* edited by Robert Helmbrecht (Hazardous Press). *This Is How You Die: Stories of the Inscrutable, Infallible,*

Inescapable Machine of Death (Mulholland Books) edited by Ryan North, Matthew Bennardo, and David Malki, included two very fine stories by Australians—"Blunt Force Trauma Delivered by Spouse" from Liz Argall, and "La Mort d'un Roturier" from Martin Livings. Peter M Ball published the YA ferryman tale "Tithes" in Canadian anthology *Coins of Chaos* edited by Jennifer Brozek (Edge Science Fiction and Fantasy Publishing), and Martin Livings also graced these pages with "In His Name". Alan Baxter placed the very creepy male-gaze story "A Time For Redemption" in *Urban Occult* edited by Colin F. Barnes (Anachron Press). Linda Brucesmith's "The 25th Caprice", a Paganini inspired tale, appeared in *New Ghost Stories 6* (The Fiction Desk) edited by Rob Redman. Crystal Lake Publishing's *For the Night is Dark* anthology, edited by Ross Warren, featured a number of Australians—G.N. Braun with "His Own Personal Golgotha", Tracie McBride with "Father Figure", and Daniel I. Russell with "God May Pity All Weak Hearts". Steve Cameron published "I Was the Walrus" in *After Death...* (Stony Meadow Publishing), edited by Eric J. Guignard.

Jay Caselberg had a prolific 2013; Caselberg published "Angelic" in *Halloween: Magic, Mystery and The Macabre* edited by Paula Guran (Prime Books); published "Collage" in *Dark Visions: A Collection of Modern Horror—Volume 1* (Grey Matter Press), edited by Sharon Lawson; published "The Track" in *The End of the Road*, edited by Jonathan Oliver (Solaris). Greg Chapman published "Like Windows to the Soul" in *Sex, Drugs & Horror* (James Ward Kirk Publishing). Simon Dewar placed "The Kettle" in *The Root Cellar and Other Stories* (Random House). John Paul Fitch published "Pyramid" in *Keeping the Edge: An Anthology of New Urban Fiction* edited by Alex Poppe and TC Clerkson, showcasing current and former students on Glasgow University's Creative Writing program. Jane Domagala published "The Tunnel" in *Dying to Live* (Diabolic Publications), an anthology of vampire fiction.

Mark Farrugia sold "The Emu in the Sky" and Tracie McBride sold "The Oldest Profession" to *Horror Library, Volume 5* (Cutting Block Press), edited by RK Cavender and Boyd Harris. *Demonic Visions: 50 Horror Tales*, edited by Chris Robertson included Rebecca Fung's "The Mile Low Club" and "Self Help" by Raymond Gates; the follow up anthology, *Demonic Visions:*

50 *Horror Tales, Book II*, also published in 2013 and edited by Robertson, included "Baby Hands" by Rebecca Fung and 'Contemporary by Proxy' by Raymond Gates. Rebecca Fung had additional publication successes with "Dresses of Fur and Fangs" in *Witches, Stitches & Bitches* (Evil Girlfriend Media) edited by Shannon Page, and "Tea Time" in *The Inanimates I* (Strange, Weird, and Wonderful Publishing) edited by Mary Patterson Thornburg. Raymond Gates published "All I Want for Christmas" in *O Little Town of Deathlehem: An Anthology of Holiday Horrors for Charity* (Grinning Skull Press) edited by Michael J Evans and Harrison Graves.

Lisa L. Hannett published 'Morning Passages' in *Shadows Edge* (Grey Friar Press) edited by Simon Strantzas; Hannett placed "Snowglobes" in *Chilling Tales: In Words, Alas. Drown I* (Hades Publications), a showcase of twenty Canadian authors, edited by Michael Kelly. Gerry Huntman published in a range of anthologies in 20013; "In Arcadia" appeared in *The Dark Bard* anthology (Indigo Mosaic); "Pretty Kitty" appeared in *Contrary Cats* (Indigo Mosaic); and "The Cutpurse From Mulberry Bend" appeared in *Penny Dread Tales Volume III: In Darkness Clockwork Shine* (Runewright). Dmetri Kakmi published "The Boy By The Gate" in *The New Gothic* edited by Beth K Lewis (Stone Skin Press); Fi Michelle's vampire tale "The Debt Collector" appeared in the same volume.

The Demonologia Biblica (Western Legends Press), edited by Dean M Drinkel, featured prominent Australian horror writers, with Tracie McBride contributing "Waiting for Eisheth—E is for Eisheth" and Daniel I. Russell contributing "The Love Revolution—L is for Lempo". Another prolific writer for 2013, Tracie McBride published in numerous anthologies; "Slither and Squeeze" appeared in charity anthology *Shifters* (Hazardous Press); "The Touch of the Taniwha" appeared in *Fish* (Dagan Books) edited by Carrie Cuinn and KV Taylor; "With Paper Armour and Wooden Sword" appeared in *Bleed* (Perpetual Motion Machine Publishing) a charity anthology where the profits aided children with cancer.

Suburban Jungle (Tasmaniac Publications) included two highly contrasting Australian horror stories—Kirstyn McDermott's "Partisan" where a female sexual assault victim connected socially and made choices to take her power back, and Daniel I. Russell's "Devolution", where a female narrator (along with her daughter) had options narrow until she was trapped in a rape crucible, in dreadful hopelessness. Intentional or not, the juxtaposition of the two tales was extremely interesting.

Thomas David Moore's "Old Souls" appeared in the themed anthology *The Book of the Dead* (Jurassic London), edited by Jared Shurin and published in collaboration with the Egypt Exploration Society, the UK's oldest independent funder of archaeological fieldwork and research in Egypt. New Zealander Lee Pletzers published "Ellen" in *The Best of the Horror Society 2013*, edited by Carson Buckingham. Tansy Rayner Roberts published "The Raven and Her Victory" in *Where Thy Dark Eye Glances: Queering Edgar Allen Poe* (Lethe Press), edited by Steve Burman. David Schembri's "The Black Father of the Night" appeared in *Eulogies II: Tales From The Cellar* (HW Press), edited by Christopher Jones, Nanci Kalanta and Tony Trembly. Angela Slatter's "The Song of Sighs" appeared in *Weirder Shadows Over Innsmouth* (Fedogan and Bremer), edited by Steven Jones. *Fearie Tales: Stories of the Grimm and Gruesome* (Jo Fletcher Books), edited by Stephen Jones, included two Australian contributors, Angela Slatter with "By the Weeping Gate" and Garth Nix with "Crossing The Line". Kyla Lee Ward's "The Character Assassin" appeared in *Schemers* (Stone Skin Press), edited by Robin D. Laws.

Kaaron Warren had a year of anthology publications more slanted towards fantasy genre, but there were some stellar horror stories— "The Human Moth" in *The Grimscribe's Puppets* (Miskatonic River Press), edited by Joseph S. Pulver, and "Sleeping with the Bower Birds" in *Shivers VII* (Cemetary Dance Publications), edited by Richard Chizmar, and the quietly suffocating "The Unwanted Women of Surrey" from Ellen Datlow and Terri Windling's *Queen Victoria's Book of Spells: An Anthology of Gaslamp Fantasy* (Tor). Marty Young published "The Frequency of Death" in *Fear the Reaper* (Crystal Lake Publishing), edited by Joe Mynhardt. Kim Falconer published "Blood and Water" in *Vampires Gone Wild* (HarperCollins), collecting four paranormal romance novellas.

MAGAZINES & JOURNALS

The Australian Horror Writers Association published two issues of

Midnight Echo Magazine. Midnight Echo #9 was edited by Geoff Brown, and featured notable contributions from antipodeans— "Black Peter" by Martin Livings, "From The Forebears" by Stephen Gepp, "The Fathomed Wreck To See" by Alan Baxter, and "The Road" by Amanda Spedding. *Midnight Echo* #10 was edited by Craig Bezant and included the winners of the annual AHWA Short Story and Flash Fiction competition—joint winners "It's Always the Children Who Suffer" by Alan Baxter and "Darker" by Zena Shapter, and the Flash Winner "Moonlight Sonata" by Tim Hawken. Other original fiction from antipodeans in this issue was "Stillgeist" by Martin Livings, "Blood and Bone" by Robert Mammon, "Exposure Compensation" by Alan Baxter, "Little Peace" by Rebecca Fung, and "Mother's House" by Greg Chapman.

Andromeda Spaceways Inflight Magazine (Andromeda Spaceways Publishing Co-op) published two issues in 2013; *ASIM Issue* #58 included Felicity Pulman's "Mirror, Mirror" and *ASIM* #57 included "Luminaries" by Jacob Edwards. *Aurealis Magazine* (Chimaera Publications) published six issues in 2013, not all of which showcased antipodean horror fiction. Notable issues were *Aurealis* #66 (edited by Michael Pryor) for New Zealander OJ Cade's "Burning Green", an extremely dark fantasy about fertility, loss and death, *Aurealis* #65 (edited by Michael Pryor) for Jason Franks urban grunge "Butcher's Hook" and SG Larner's confronting and violent "Poppies", and *Aurealis* #61 (edited by Stephen Higgins) for Sophie Masson's excellent ghost story "Restless". *The Review of Australian Fiction* published two short stories per issue, and a number of issues showcased dark speculative writers. Notable publications were "The Canals of Anguilar" by Lee Battersby in *Volume 5, Issue 5*; "Door Thread City" by Trent Jamieson in *Volume 5, Issue 4*; "Glasskin" by Robert G. Cook in *Volume 5, Issue 6*; and "Lost and Found" by Kirstyn McDermott in *Volume 5, Issue 2*. *Dark Edifice Magazine* (Dark Gaia Productions) edited by D. Robert Grixti published two issues—*Dark Edifice* #4 featured an apocalyptic tale by the editor, and *Dark Edifice* #5 included stories by antipodeans Jacinta Butterworth and Shannon Bell, and a rather fine dark poem from Brendan Sullivan. *Griffith Review* #42 (Text Publishing) edited by Julianne Schultz included a number of speculative tales, and the notable dark tales were "A Castle in Toorak" by Marion Halligan, "Snow White and the Child Soldier" by Ali Alizadeh.

Jenny Blackford had success publishing poetry in a number of journals in 2013. "Hungry as the Living Sorrow" was awarded second prize in the Long Form section of the Science Fiction Poetry Association competition for 2013, judged blind by the esteemed Jane Yolen; published on the Science Fiction Poetry Association website in September 2013, the poem concerns a strange amphibious pregnancy. "Liquid Pleasure", a cold and quietly sinister love poem to a water nymph, was published in the pagan literary webzine *Eternal Haunted Summer Issue #14*. Blackford's abstract homage to Bradbury "The Aluminium Apples of the Moon" was published in *Quadrant Volume LVII, #10*.

Krissy Kneen published "The Devil Smile" in *Island #135*, fiction editor Geordie Williamson. "By Desecration Rock" by Margo Lanagan appeared in *The Lifted Brow #19*. C.S. McMullen's "The Nest" appeared in *Nightmare Magazine #12* edited by John Joseph Adams. Fi Michelle's "The Kyne Extraction" was published by *Plasma Frequency Magazine #Issue 5*, edited by Richard Flores. Alan Baxter published the western vignette "Not The Worst of Sins" in *Beneath Ceaseless Skies #133*, the Halloween Edition. Steve Cameron published "The God Thing" in *Outposts of Beyond* (October 2013), edited by Alban Lake & Tyree Campbell, and "Best Served Cold" in *Disturbed Digest, Issue #1*, edited by Terrie Relf. Deborah Biancotti placed the elegant Gothic tale "All The Lost Ones" in *Exotic Gothic 5, Volume I* and Terry Dowling placed the awesome horror story "The Sleepover" in *Exotic Gothic 5, Volume II*—published by PS Publishing, both volumes edited by Danel Olson. Thoraiya Dyer's "Tintookie" appeared in *Kaleidotrope* (Summer 2013). "The Coronation Bout" by Lisa L. Hannett appeared in *Electric Velocipede #27*. Gerry Huntman's "The Wooden Tomb" was published in *Frostfire Worlds* (November 2013). David Kernot sold "Harry's Dead Poodle" to *Cover of Darkness Magazine* (White Cat Publications). "The Coming of the Drac" by Barry Rosenberg appeared in *Hungur Magazine #16* (White Cat Publications). "Monster" by Natasha Sampson was published in *Imagine: A Journal of Student Writing* from Deakin University, Geelong. Angela Slatter's "By My Voice I Shall Be Known" and Lisa L. Hannett's "Another Mouth" both appeared in *The Dark Magazine* #1. Angela Slatter's "The Burning Circus" was published in *The British Fantasy Society Horror Anthology* (March 2013) edited by Johnny Mains.

Pete Aldin sold the very dark pagan story "The Whipping Tree" to *Nightblade Fantasy and Horror Magazine Issue #23 Blodeuwedd*, and the noir flash story "No Good Deed" to *Bareknuckles Pulp No. 31* (Out Of The Gutter). "Lost Lake" by Greg Chapman appeared in the *Literary Mayhem* webzine edited by Peter D. Schwotzer. Robert Datson's "Shoe Shine" was published in *SQ Mag* #10, edited by Gerry Huntman. "Nip, Tuck, Zip, Pluck" by John Paul Fitch appeared in *Psychopomp* #4. "Rear View", a quiet ghost story from David R. Grigg, was published at the author's *The Narratorium* website. Gerry Huntman's "Dom and Gio's Barber Shop" appeared in *The Lovecraft eZine* #21. "The Curious Case of the Frozen Revenant" by Gerry Huntman appeared in *Railroad: Celebration Station*, edited by Tonia Brown. D. Robert Grixti published "Pretty Birds" online at his Dark Gaia blog. "The Skeleton in Her Closet" by Heidi Kneale, appeared in *Penumbra eMag, Volume 2, Issue 7*. Kirstie Olley's story *Emily's Typewriter* was published on her website. "Squeak" by Emma Osborne was published in *Daily Science Fiction* (July 25th, 2013). "Blue Swirls" by Guy Salvidge appeared in *Tincture Journal* #1. "Fusion" by Amanda J. Spedding was published at the Cohesion Press website.

GRAPHIC NOVELS

A Brush With Darkness (Milk Shadow Books) collected Dillon Naylor's early horror comics and experimental work, along with posters and CD covers for The Beastie Boys, Area 7 and Powderfinger, and Melbourne cult bands The Fireballs, The Fat Thing, and Satellites, and promotional graphics for the all-ages *Pushover* festivals of the 90s. *Savage Bitch* by S.C.A.R. (Steve Carter and Antoinette Rydyr) collected the cult comic-strip originally serialized in *Picture Magazine* (Australian Consolidated Press) between 1995 and 1997, as a complete full-colour graphic narrative; included are the two graphic adventures *Land of the Buku Buku* and *The Fury of Blood Bitch*, with a foreword by Stephen R. Bissette (*Swamp Thing, Tyrant, Taboo*) and a special guest spot by artist Dave Heinrich (*The Phantom: Ghost Who*

Walks). Zetabella published the graphic novel collection *The Lesser Evil, Omnibus Edition* by Shane W. Smith. "Zig Zag" by Andrez Bergen appeared in *Uncanny Adventures* edited by Jess Dubin (8th Wonder Press); thirty comic creators and twenty one genre-spanning stories.

FILM

The showcase event for horror films in Sydney, *The Night of Horror Film Festival*, was held again in 2013, including the festival awards. Antipodeans to take out award categories were the occult dysfunctional family feature *The Taking* (Dir. Cezil Reed and Lydelle Jackson) for the Independent Spirit Award, the Audience Choice Award: Best Australian short went to *P.O.V: Point Of View* written and directed by Benjamin Morton, and winner of Best Animation went to Gothic horror *Butterflies* (dir. Isabel Peppard). *Butterflies* was also honoured with the *Cinequest Film Festival* 2013 prize for Best Animated Short, and the Yoram Gross Animation Award at the *Sydney Film Festival* 2013. The Fantastic Planet Feature Film Award in the category of Director's Choice Award went to *A Dark Matter* (Dir. James Naylor), and the award for Best Female Performance went to Emma Lung (Crave). The Fantastic Planet Short Film Awards bestowed the honour of the Audience Choice Award: Best Australian Short to *Wolf At The Door* (dir. David Fairhurst).

Australian feature horror films completed in 2013 were *Lemon Tree Passage,* the directorial debut of David James Campbell concerning an urban legend about a haunted road of the same name in Port Stephens, and *Wolf Creek* 2 directed by Greg McLean and starring John Jarratt as fictional serial killer Mick Taylor. New Zealand feature horror films completed in 2013 included *Housebound* the directorial debut of Gerard Johnstone, and *What We Do In The Shadows* directed by Jemaine Clement and Taika Waititi, a mockumentary about a share house in Aukland occupied by vampires.

· · · · · · · · · · ·

REMEMBERED

Chrissy Amphlett, 53, Australian singer/songwriter, who thought "love was science fiction"; **Steven Utley**, 64, "internationally unknown" American SF writer; **Paul Williams**, 64, American writer and publisher; **Gregory Rogers**, 66, Australian children's book writer and illustrator; **Richard Matheson**, 87, American fantasy/horror Grandmaster; **James Herbert**, 69, English horror Grandmaster; **Jack Vance**, 96, American sf/fantasy Grandmaster; **Iain Banks**, 59, Scottish fantasist; **Parke Godwin**, 84, World Fantasy Award winner; **Frederik Pohl**, 93, US sf Grandmaster; **Joel Lane**, 50, World Fantasy Award winner.

THE
YEAR'S BEST
AUSTRALIAN
FANTASY

&

HORROR

~ 2012 ~

THE THIRD ANNUAL
COLLECTION

CAUTION: CONTAINS SMALL PARTS

KIRSTYN MCDERMOTT

Tim places the small wooden dog on the coffee table and checks inside the box a second time. No card, no note, nothing besides the dozen or so crumpled sheets of week-old *Herald Sun* that cushioned the toy during its journey through the postal system. Nothing to explain what it's for or why it's been sent to him.

"Maybe it's a joke," Linda suggests.

Grabbing the twine that's strung like a garrotte through the dog's neck, she pulls the toy along the tabletop. It has smooth wooden wheels in place of legs, painted a bright and glossy shade of red, and a brass bell on the end of its tail that tinkles with each movement of its multi-coloured, segmented body. The head bobs back and forth in a strange, jerky way that gives Tim the creeps. More like a mutant pigeon than a puppy. What sort of parent would buy their kid a toy like this anyway? What sort of kid would want one?

"There's no return address?" Linda asks.

"No, just mine." Printed in thick black capitals and Tim can't decide whether or not the handwriting looks familiar.

"It's sad."

"You think?"

"Yeah." She drops the twine and the dog creaks to a standstill. "Look at its sad little eyes, and its sad little mouth. Poor thing, I feel sorry for it."

Tim shrugs. It doesn't look sad to him; it looks . . . wrong.

"Maybe it got sent to you by mistake," Linda says. She turns back to her trashy gossip mag, to the photo spread of *Stars! Caught*

Without Makeup!, and shakes her head. "You should hang onto it, in case you have to return it. Might be some child's favourite toy got sent here by mistake, you never know."

"Yeah, maybe."

As Tim picks the dog up, meaning to put it back into the box, a patch of chipped paint on one of the wheels catches his eye. Not really chipped, now that he looks closely, more like bitten or chewed. A toddler with serious teething issues, with serious *teeth*, to gnaw away so much wood. He dumps the dog into its nest of expired newsprint, then closes the flaps on the box and kicks it under the coffee table. Stupid toy.

Later, after Linda's gone home, he'll take the whole thing out to the bin.

• • •

Four minutes past three in the morning, according to the red glow of his alarm clock, and Tim lies perfectly still in bed, his ears straining for a repeat of whatever sound it was that woke him. Nothing. He rolls over, reaches for the glass of water on the bedside table. Empty. He must have forgotten to fill it before turning in; never mind, he'll do without. But his tongue catches on the roof of his mouth and the more he thinks about not needing a drink, the thirstier he feels. At sixteen minutes past three, he swears and swings his legs over the side of the bed.

In the kitchen, light from a near-full moon washes through the window so Tim doesn't bother flicking the switch. Just fills his glass with tap water and stands in front of the sink, looking out into the backyard as he drinks. The lawn needs to be mown, but he can still see dozens of lemons nestling amid the grass like overripe hand grenades. Linda usually picks a few to share with the girls at her gym, but even they can't keep up with the prodigious output. Lemons. The most useless fruit in the world and he scores a yard with two trees full of the bloody things.

Not for the first time, Tim wishes he'd rented a townhouse or unit instead. Some modern, low maintenance prefab with concrete and pavers to keep Mother Nature at bay.

Behind him, a bell tinkles.

Tim jerks around. Water splashes over his hand and across the front of his shirt, and he swears again. Then he sees the thing sitting just inside the kitchen doorway and further words desert him.

Impossible—*impossible*—that the small wooden dog should be there, *right there*, where he would have had to walk past it, step over it maybe, as he entered the room. Not when he threw the toy into the outside wheelie bin just that afternoon, not when he lugged the very same bin out onto the side of the street, where the garbos will be coming to empty it in a few short hours.

Impossible.

Without taking his eyes from the dog, Tim reaches around and lowers his glass into the sink, wipes his hands on his pyjama pants. Unless . . . unless he only threw out the box itself. Linda might have rescued the toy without him realising, maybe hidden it somewhere as a joke. Tim frowns, tries to remember the feel of the box in his hands, the weight of it. Tries to remember if he heard the bell ring as he tossed it into the half-empty bin. He shakes his head. It doesn't matter what he remembers—the dog clearly couldn't have been in the box because right now he's staring at the damn thing with his own two eyes. Okay, so Linda took it. Put it . . . under the kitchen table? Where the vibrations of his own footsteps caused it to roll out? Sure, why not? Witching hour logic, but it's good enough for Tim, or nearly so.

He takes a step towards the dog but finds himself loath to touch it—not with his bare hands anyway—and he doesn't want to think too hard about why that might be so. It's just so creepy, all painted eyes and flat black stare, sitting there now, not so much motionless as . . . coiled.

Ridiculous, but still. Tim throws a tea towel over the toy before picking the bundle up with both hands, and finds himself almost relieved when it doesn't begin to wriggle within his grasp. His jaw clenches, anger seeping into his blood now as fear beats a shameful retreat. Damn Linda and her childish bloody jokes. He's not going to give her the satisfaction of even mentioning it.

Outside, his breath frosts the air. Tim jogs down the driveway to where his bin now stands beside those of his neighbours, a trio of patient old soldiers huddled shoulder to shoulder against the darkness. He lifts the lid and drops the wooden dog inside, tea towel and all. The muffled tinkle of a bell sounds from the depths.

"Good dog," he mutters. "Play dead."

• • •

The phone rings as soon as Tim arrives home from work the next evening. Groaning, he hurries into the kitchen, juggling keys, work satchel, rain-soaked umbrella, and a thin plastic bag of takeaway Thai which has been threatening to snap a handle ever since he picked it up. Only two people ever call him on the landline: his mother, who doesn't trust mobile phones; and persistent offshore telemarketers. He dumps everything onto the bench and reaches for the handset. The caller has a private number, which does nothing to narrow the field—his mother doesn't trust phone directories either; she hasn't been listed for years—and he considers just letting it ring out. But if it is his mother, she'll only call back in five minutes, and in five minutes after that, and in five minutes after that. Better to get it over with.

He presses the answer button. "Hello?"

"Is this Tim Jennings?" The woman sounds young and weary and possibly, vaguely familiar.

"That's me," he replies. "Who's this?"

"It's Anna Vidicci." A pause. "Melanie's sister, you remember."

It's almost instinctive, the way his guts tighten. *The Crane?* Why is the Crane calling him? It's been almost four years since he broke up with Mellie; what can her bitch of an older sister want from him now?

"Anna, hi. It's been a while." Tucking the phone between his cheek and his shoulder, he pulls the containers of Thai from their bag. The red chicken curry has leaked through the edges of its lid; coconut sauce drips across the bench, pools around his keys.

"Do you have a few minutes to speak?"

"Um, I'm kind of in the middle of something here." He rinses his keys beneath the tap, leaves them in the dishrack to dry. Grabs a handful of paper towels to take care of the mess on the bench.

"I have some bad news." Her voice is thin, its edges sheet-metal sharp.

Tim licks his fingers. "Look, can I call you back? What's your number?"

"Melanie's dead."

"What?" He couldn't have heard her right, she couldn't have just said—

"Last Thursday," the Crane tells him. "I thought you should

hear it from me. The funeral's on Wednesday, if you want to come. Sorry about the short notice, there were a lot of people I needed to call."

You were the last name on my list, are the words she leaves unspoken.

Tim closes his eyes, allows himself to slide down the front of the cupboard to slump onto the tiled floor. A handle digs into his back; he doesn't move. Today is Monday—four days ago, Mellie was still breathing somewhere. Still scribbling in those notebooks of hers as well, most probably, and talking to people who weren't there, and sniffing her food for traces of poison—but still breathing. Still alive.

"What happened?" It's a question he's not sure he wants answered.

"Melanie wasn't well, you know that. There were a lot of bad days, especially after you left. Thursday was one bad day too many."

He swallows, tries to ignore the accusation in her tone. "I'm sorry, Anna."

The way she speaks, the Crane always seems to be accusing somebody of something. He can picture her now, those pale lips pursed to a thin line, the furrows in her brow deepening to troughs as she *pecks pecks pecks* at the phone, determined to find fault, eager to apportion blame.

"Do you want to know about the funeral?" she asks.

Tim pretends to write down the details, repeating them back to her even though he already knows he won't be going. He can't see the point. It's been over with Mellie for longer than they were ever together and it's not like they bothered to stay in touch, not even on Facebook. Before tonight, he can't recall the last time he even thought about her. No, it would be stupid to go to the funeral. Mellie's family wouldn't want him there; the invitation is merely protocol.

"Thanks for calling, Anna. I'm sorry about Mellie, I really am." He pauses, tries to conceive a suitable condolence. "She was a special kind of person."

"Yes," the Crane says, and, "Well."

They exchange awkward goodbyes and Tim stands to return the phone to its cradle. Left lidless on the bench, the Thai curry has started to separate and congeal. Orange pools of oil glisten on its surface. He picks up a plastic fork, stabs half-heartedly at a large chunk of chicken. Pale and tender, the meat splits easily apart, dripping red as he lifts it from the sauce. The smell is thick and rich and close to nauseating. Tim puts the lid back on the curry and returns it to its bag along with the rice and the little parcel of deep-fried spring rolls, then shoves the whole lot into the fridge. He can nuke it in the microwave later, or maybe tomorrow.

Maybe tomorrow, he'll feel hungry again.

• • •

Friday nights, Linda comes over to eat pizza and watch movies. Sometimes she brings her overnight bag and stays the weekend but not tonight. Tonight the only things in her hands when Tim answers the door are a couple of new release DVDs, a six-pack of Mexican beer, and a small wooden dog.

"Starting a collection?" She grins, brandishing the toy like it's some kind of weapon. The bell on its tail jangles fiercely.

Tim takes a backward step. "Where the fuck did you get that?" It's the same damn dog—it can't be, but it is. He can see the scratch marks—the *bite* marks—on the front wheel.

"Hi *Linda*," she says, and pushes past him. "How *lovely* to see you."

"Sorry," he mutters, not really meaning it. He closes the door then follows her deceitful arse into the kitchen, tries not to look at the dog that sure as hell better not be looking at him from where it now sits on the kitchen table. "Just, seriously, where did the toy come from?"

"It was on the front steps when I got here."

"When you got here."

"That's what I said." She grabs a bottle opener from the top drawer, flips the caps on two of the beers. "You have any lemons inside?"

Tim shakes his head. "You didn't bring it?"

"How could *I* bring it?"

"Come on, Linda, a joke's a joke. What, because I never said anything about Sunday night, you thought you'd have another go? Okay, fine—you scared me a little. Happy? Wanna tell me how you did it now?"

She glares at him. "Whatever. I'm getting a lemon."

"No." Tim grabs her arm as she moves towards the back door, wrenches her back around to face him. Ignoring her startled yelp, the bright and sudden flare of shock in her eyes, he pulls her face close to his own. "First you tell me."

"Ow—let me go!" Her nails dig into his wrist. "I don't even know what you're talking about!"

Beneath the pain and the anger that contort her features, Tim glimpses a real and genuine bewilderment. She isn't lying, she really doesn't know anything about the stupid dog, and here he is manhandling her like some kind of Neanderthal, one hand squeezing her arm hard enough to bruise, the other flexing to an eager fist at his side. Horrified, he releases his hold.

"God, Linda. I'm so sorry." Meaning it this time, for what little he knows it's worth. "I didn't—I've had the worst week."

She snorts. "Oh right, you've had a *bad week*. No problem, feel free to take that shit out on me whenever you need to." There's a slight tremor in her voice and she's looking at him now like it's the very first time she's really seen him. Like it might be the very last.

"I'm sorry," he says again. Her expression doesn't soften at all and so he tries to explain—about the stupid dog, about the Crane and Mellie—but it doesn't make much difference. He's cold, she implies, for not going to the funeral; colder still for not mentioning his ex-girlfriend's suicide until now. Disconnected, is the word she uses, but he knows what she means. Cold. Heartless. Maybe she's right. Should he have called her after talking to the Crane, asked for her shoulder to cry on? Is that what the protocol is?

They order pizza, though he has to force himself to eat even two slices of his usual meat lovers special. Beer helps the doughy, clotted mess go down but it still sits like a lump in his stomach. Linda doesn't eat much of her Hawaiian either, and as the credits roll on the first movie, she gets up from the couch and slings her handbag over her shoulder.

"You're going?" Tim asks.

"Tonight's not really working out." She ejects the DVD from the player and returns it to its case. "Did you want me to leave the other one for you? It's due back tomorrow."

He shakes his head. Some American comedy about a Las Vegas bucks night gone wrong which Linda probably rented with him in mind—an attempt to balance out the dire vampire romance they'd just sat through—but he couldn't care less. "Take them both," he tells her. "I think I'll hit the sack early."

Her face stiffens. "I'll get going then."

Tim follows her to the front door. Is he supposed to ask her to stay, is that the game they're playing now? And is that because she wants to say *yes*, or because she needs to tell him *no* one last time? Doubt curdles anxious in his guts, a sensation old and familiar and decidedly unwelcome. This was how he felt around Mellie a lot of the time near the end—uncertain, apprehensive, forever trying to avoid countless unseen fractures in the ground beneath his feet, and all the while suspecting that this was exactly the way she wanted him to feel. No, he won't go back to that place, not with Linda. Not with anyone.

"Sorry about before," Tim says. "The thing with the dog. I shouldn't have taken it out on you."

"No," she replies. "You shouldn't have."

"I'll give you a call next week, then?"

"If you like."

Linda stands there, head tilted slightly to the side like she's waiting for him to make the next move, but Tim simply leans forward and kisses her on the cheek. If there's something to be said, *she* can damn well do the talking. He's done playing the psychic boyfriend game. Instead, he tells her to drive safe, then waits dutifully at the door until the taillights of her Mazda disappear down the street. She doesn't beep the horn like she usually does; he doesn't bother to wave.

Back inside, he wishes the house felt as empty and hollow as he does.

• • •

What Tim doesn't do is take the dog out to the bin with the cold, stale pizza the next morning. Because what doesn't get thrown away, can't come back to surprise him. For *surprise*, he absolutely doesn't tell himself, read *haunt*.

And when Tim invites himself around to his brother's place to watch the AFL match that afternoon, it's not because he can't stand to be alone in his own house for any longer than necessary. No, it's just that he hasn't hung out with Rick in a while, Rick and Sally, who's pregnant again—a girl this time, she tells him, a little sister for Liam who's going to be two this August, can he believe it?—and half a dozen of their football-mad friends who crowd around the massive plasma screen television, eating corn chips dipped in Sally's homemade guacamole and exploding into raucous cheers every time Hawthorn scores a goal.

Afterwards, when he drinks so much during the impromptu victory barbeque on his brother's deck that Sally confiscates his car keys and insists he spend the night on the sofa bed in the games room, it's not because he's leery about going home. That's also not the reason he tags along on their Sunday shopping expedition to the kiddie supercentre, holding onto Liam's hand while his parents bicker mildly about whether the colour of the Sports Deluxe twin stroller they're looking to purchase should be charcoal or champagne or a combination of both. And when Rick takes him aside after dinner to suggest that, while the weekend's been great and it's brilliant for Liam to spend time with his uncle, maybe Tim should think about heading off soon—just so Rick and Sally can have an evening to themselves, right little bro?—Tim certainly doesn't think of asking if he can maybe just crash for another night or two.

No, he doesn't think about that, not even for a second.

In the same way, he doesn't think about the fact that the wooden dog is no longer on the kitchen table when he gets home, or that it's inexplicably removed itself to the living room and is now perched on the end of the couch where Tim himself usually sits to watch television.

Tim doesn't think about the toy at all over the next week or so. He especially doesn't think about it while lying in bed in the dark, trying to sleep with his iPod speaker-docked and cycling on random, the volume turned up loud enough to cover any noise that might otherwise seep in from beyond his bedroom door. Which means that he doesn't hear the wooden scrape of wheels along an uncarpeted hall floor. Or the discordant jangle of a tinny, brass bell.

Tim doesn't hear these sounds every single night.

And he's fine with that. He's absolutely fine.

• • •

Until one sleep-starved morning, he shuffles into the kitchen for coffee and toast—not looking for the dog, never looking for the dog—and sees the boy.

Around the same age as his nephew, maybe a little older, but with dark brown hair instead of Liam's straw-coloured curls. Sitting cross-legged with his back half-turned, red-and-orange-striped pyjamas too baggy for his too skinny body, shoulders hitching up and down like he's playing with something on the floor in front of him, so real Tim can hear him breathe.

Tim sags against the doorjamb, a strangled gasp caught in his throat.

The boy pauses. That small, dark head lifts. Begins to turn.

Tim slides around the doorway, presses himself against the adjoining living room wall. Behind him, he doesn't—he definitely *doesn't*—hear the pad of bare feet on kitchen tiles. Not what he expected, not a *boy*, not a *child*. Maybe—not that he ever thought about it, because he doesn't think about it—but if he did—maybe it's Mellie, he might have thought, maybe it's something to do with Mellie. Not that she is *haunting* him—because that's impossible—as impossible as the toy dog which absolutely does *not* roll through the house in the middle of the night, which absolutely does *not* toll its fucking bell at all hours of the fucking night.

Breathing. Behind him. Beside him.

Any moment, he feels certain, any moment now it will touch him. Tiny cold fingers, tiny cold hands, reaching up to clasp his own, and a tiny cold face with a tiny cold mouth opening wide—

"Enough!" The strength of his own voice surprises him, propels him back around and through the door and into the kitchen.

The *empty* kitchen, or very nearly. Because in front of the sink, in the space where an impossible child absolutely could not have been sitting, are scattered a jumble of brightly-coloured wooden shapes. Tim picks up a red disc, runs his finger along the rim where jagged gouges catch at his skin. Most of the wooden pieces now bear similar marks. A piece of green dowel as thick as his finger has been snapped—*bitten*—in half. Torn from its body, the dog's head now lies on its side, one painted eye staring up in dumb accusation. Tim swallows hard. A trickle of sweat runs down the side of his face.

He wonders what else the boy might be capable of disassembling.

• • •

"How did you get this number?" the Crane wants to know when he calls.

"I remembered you were in real estate," Tim says. "Your mobile's listed on the company website, you know."

The Crane sighs. "What do you want?"

"Can we meet somewhere? I need to talk about a few things."

"We're talking now."

"Not like this, not over the phone." He wants to do this in person; he wants to see her face. "It's about Mellie. There's, ah—I have some questions."

"We didn't see you at the funeral."

"No, I—I couldn't get time off work."

"Really? Not even for a funeral?"

"I'm sorry, I know I should have been there."

The Crane makes a sound somewhere between laughter and a snort.

"Please, Anna. It's important."

Silence, stretching crisp and brittle-thin between them.

"Anna?"

"I have half an hour between open houses this afternoon," she says at last. "You can talk to me while I grab a coffee."

This time he does write down the address she gives him, some café way out in the northern suburbs. He'll have to leave work right after lunch, claim sudden illness or some kind of family emergency. Tim grimaces. Family emergency, right. That might only be halfway to a lie.

"This doesn't make us friends," the Crane is saying.

"I know that," Tim tells her.

"We've never been friends."

• • •

She hasn't changed. Tall and excruciatingly thin, the same beaky nose and stoop-shouldered way of moving that earned her the nickname in the first place—a snide sisterly baptism he eagerly picked up and ran with long after Mellie herself let it drop. Because it fit, because it was perfect. Anna the Crane, perpetually hovering around her younger sister as though Mellie was the last chick in the nest, fragile and still to fledge, the need for constant vigilance a given.

Turns out, maybe she wasn't so wrong about that.

Tim lifts his hand to wave at the exact moment the Crane spots him. She nods and marches over to the table where he's been sitting for the past fifteen minutes, an obligatory coffee growing cold by his elbow.

"I wasn't sure you were coming," he says.

"The open house ran late," she tells him. "There's a lot of interest in this area right now. I won't have as much time as I thought." A waitress materialises and she orders a large skinny latte with no sugar to go, hands over a five dollar note.

Her attitude pisses him off. She doesn't have time to talk about her sister, barely a week in the ground? Fine, he'll cut to the damn chase then. "Why didn't you say the funeral wasn't just for Mellie? Hoping to surprise me?"

"What?"

"You know."

"Tim, I really don't." The Crane reaches into her bag, pulls out a folded sheet of paper and slides it across the table. "Here. We had spares."

It's a memorial pamphlet, obviously homemade on a computer and printed off somewhere like Officeworks or Kinkos. There's a photo of Mellie on the front, skin too orange and smile too fake, listless brown curls falling half across her face.

"It's the best we could find," the Crane says. "You know how much she hated being photographed."

Beloved daughter of Rocco and Yvette, and sister of Anna.

No other names are mentioned anywhere. Tim frowns, bites his lip. The words he's been rehearsing all afternoon lodge stubborn in his throat; he can't bring himself to loosen them. Mellie stares out at him through tangles of hair, silent now, and forever. *What happened*, he wants to ask her, *what did you do?*

"You said you wanted to talk," the Crane prompts, her tone edged with impatience. "You said you had questions."

"Yeah." Tim takes a sip of his coffee, lukewarm and sugarless, but at least it moistens his mouth. "See, this *thing* has happened, this weird thing, and I thought it was to do with Mellie, that she maybe—I mean, did she ever, was there—you're her sister, you'd have to know, right?"

"What?" Lacquered fingernails tap briskly on the tabletop. "What would I have to know?"

He takes a breath, then plunges straight in. "Look, did Mellie have a kid? And did she—did the kid die as well?"

The Crane's eyes widen. "Don't be ridiculous."

But her gaze flickers, darting briefly away from his own before returning with twice the chill of winter. That's more than enough for Tim. "What aren't you telling me, Anna? Was there a kid, a little boy maybe?"

"This is insane." She pushes back her chair.

"Wait," he says. "I want to show you something." He reaches for the plastic bag at his feet, hauls it up and drops it on the table in front of her. "Look."

She doesn't move. "What's in it?"

"*Look.*" Tim turns the bag upside down, allows the pieces of wooden dog to fall with a clatter from its mouth. A red disc describes a lazy arc, then settles by the Crane's hand. She flinches as though it might bite.

"Where did you get that?"

"You know what it is? What it used to be?"

"*Where did you get it?*" she hisses.

"I think Mellie must have sent it to me," Tim says. "Before she, you know."

"Keep it then. I don't want the damn thing."

Their waitress returns with a takeaway cup and a fading smile, finds a space on the table for the former then quickly leaves. Tim waits until she's out of earshot. "It's a kid's toy, Anna. Who did it belong to?"

"No one," she says. "Melanie bought it, years ago."

"But why?"

"Who knows why my sister did anything?" She's leaning back in her chair now, arms crossed over her chest. "Put it away. Please."

He doesn't move. "What was his name?"

"For God's sake!" The Crane rises swiftly to her feet, scooping up her bag and the takeaway coffee in a single, angry motion. "I'm not listening to any more of this. You're worse than Melanie ever was."

"I've seen him," Tim says. "Little boy, kind of skinny, dark brown hair."

She pauses. An uncertain expression, some strange twist of fury and fear, flashes across her face. But it's too quick to catch hold, and she shakes her head, squares her jaw. "I don't know what you think you've seen, Tim, but Melanie never had a child." Her hand holding the coffee cup is shaking just a little. "You know, sometimes I really wish . . . "

"What?"

"Beggars and horses." The smile that twitches her lips could not be more broken. "I'm done with this, okay? Don't call me again. I'm *done*."

Tim says nothing, just watches her walk, shoulders more hunched than ever, out of the café and across the road to where a silver Honda coupé is parked. She sits in the driver's seat for maybe three or four minutes, head bowed over her coffee, motionless. He wonders if she's crying, if she's even capable of crying. He's never once seen the Crane with tears in her eyes. Finally, she starts the car and drives off to her next appointment.

He gathers up the pieces of dog and returns them to the plastic bag. The rattle of wood on wood is somehow comforting.

It sounds solid. It sounds real.

Mellie gazes up at him, orange and flat and far beyond reach. Only four years, and there's not much he can remember of her with any degree of clarity. He can't decide if that's wrong. "I'm sorry," he whispers, digging into his pocket for enough change to pay for the coffee.

Tim leaves the pamphlet behind on the table. He doesn't need any more baggage.

• • •

"I'm not really up for anything," Linda tells him. "I've got work tomorrow."

This phone call is the first time they've spoken since their aborted movie night, and Tim isn't even sure why he's rung her now. He doesn't want to go home alone—or *un*alone, or however the hell the situation back at the house could best be described— but neither does he have the headspace for being social. Linda seems the best compromise.

"We don't have to go out," he tells her. "I'll bring something over. You feel like Chinese or pizza?"

Linda sighs. "Let's not, okay?"

"If you're still mad at me about the other night—"

"Tim, just stop."

"What?"

She remains silent for a few seconds, and he can picture her rubbing at her forehead, at the twin creases that form between her eyebrows whenever she gets irritated or perplexed, or both. "Maybe we should just let things rest for a while," she says at last.

"Rest? What do you mean, rest?"

Another sigh. "This isn't really going anywhere, is it?"

"What isn't?"

"Look, you're a fun guy and you're easy to be with most of the time, but I think it's all starting to get a bit . . . *complicated*, and right now I'm really not looking for complicated. Sorry if that sounds harsh."

"You're dumping me?"

"Oh, Tim, please don't pretend like we ever had anything serious going."

He swallows. "No, I guess we didn't."

"Because that was kind of the idea, right? Nothing serious?"

"Yeah, it was."

Then she reminds him what a nice guy he is, really, and how he'll make some equally nice girl very happy one day if he ever decides to come out of his shell, lower the barricades, take down the walls—just not Linda, because Linda isn't looking right now—and her tone echoes the Crane's parting words.

Don't call me again. I'm done.

"You sound tired," Linda says. "Are you getting much sleep?"

Even after he hangs up on her, Tim can't stop laughing.

• • •

He keeps the bag of dog parts beneath his bed, right beneath the spot where he lays his head on the pillow.

On the pillow, and sometimes under it, those nights he definitely doesn't hear the pad of small, bare feet on the hallway boards outside his door, or the high-pitched keening that might be the cry of a child waking in darkness, or delight. Those nights he absolutely does not feel the subtle shift of the mattress at his back, or the tickle of breath over his cheek.

Those nights especially, Tim's eyes remain resolutely closed.

Because there is definitely, absolutely nothing to see.

• • •

Walking home from the train station after Friday night drinks with the guys from sales, Tim's half-blinded by a sudden flash of headlights, twice in quick succession. The car is parked out the front of his house, its paintwork pale and gleaming beneath the glare of the streetlight. He can make out the vague shape of a driver, but nothing else.

Tim pauses. The headlights flash again. Just once.

Cautiously, he keeps walking. As he approaches the vehicle, its passenger side window slides down with a low, mechanical hum and the interior light switches on. "Tim?" the Crane asks. "Do you have a few minutes?"

A mild sense of relief shivers through him. "I thought you were done," he says, annoyed. "Isn't that what you told me?"

"Please." She reaches over and opens the door, pushes it outwards.

"Uh, it might be more comfortable inside."

The Crane shakes her head. "I'd rather stay out here. No offence."

"Whatever." Tim slides into the passenger seat, pulling the door closed behind him. The heater is running on full; sweat beads along his hairline almost immediately. "How long have you been waiting here?"

"Long enough." Her lips press so tight together they turn white. "What you brought to the café the other day. My sister really sent it?"

"I think so. The box is long gone but the handwriting—what I can remember about the handwriting—I'm pretty sure it was Mellie's."

She sighs. "I suppose it's the only logical explanation. I turned our flat upside down this past week, you know, in case she had hidden it somewhere. Nothing, so it must be the same one."

"She was still living with you?"

"It was easier. Melanie was . . . problematic."

Tim isn't dumb enough to take that sort of bait. He simply nods and waits.

"She called him Jacob," the Crane says.

"The dog?"

"No." She glares at him, pointedly. "Not the dog."

Tim lets out a breath he didn't know he was holding. "There *was* a kid."

"No," she repeats. "I told you, she never had a child."

"I don't understand—"

"Here." The Crane reaches around to the backseat and retrieves a green canvas shopping bag, thrusts it towards him. It's full of toys—rattles, stuffed animals, oversized plastic Lego blocks—padded out with neatly folded baby clothes. "Melanie bought all of that, and more. I kept sending it off to charity shops, but she replaced it quicker than I could keep up. That wooden dog you have, that was the very first thing. She was hysterical when I donated it along with a load of other stuff. I had to go down to Vinnies the next day and buy the bloody thing back."

Tim takes a bright blue teddy bear from the top of the bag. "Why would she do that?" The bear stares back at him with eyes of empty glass.

"I used to hear her talking aloud in her bedroom," the Crane says. "Sometimes I even thought I heard someone talking back."

"Someone?"

"She called him Jacob."

Tim drops the bear back into the bag. "Why?" he asks again.

"Melanie wanted that child so badly," she whispers. "Sometimes I worry that maybe it would have been the best thing after all."

"Anna, you have to tell me what's going on."

"Why do you think I'm here?" She smiles at him then, that same broken smile he remembers from the café. "I'm so tired of keeping it all to myself. Maybe if I tell you, maybe I can start to let her go."

• • •

Tim closes the front door behind him, lets the green bag fall to the floor. He can't summon any hatred for the Crane, no matter how much he would dearly like to, no matter how much easier that would make everything. Because she's probably right. She was probably always right.

After you broke up with her, Melanie found out she was pregnant.

Why didn't she say something?

She didn't want you to come back just because of a baby.

You mean, you didn't want me to come back.

I did agree with her, yes.

You never thought Mellie and me should be together.

It's a moot point, Tim. You wouldn't have come back anyway.

Leaving the lights off, he feels his way into the bedroom, gets down on his hands and knees and reaches into the darkness beneath the bed. His fingers brush plastic, and he pulls the bag towards him. Wood rattles against wood; the sound is as close to comfort as he deserves.

Melanie wanted to have the baby on her own. She thought being a mother would be fun; she thought it would be fulfilling.

I bet you didn't agree with her about that.

Melanie could barely cope with being Melanie most of the time. How could she possibly bring up a child?

His toolbox is in the laundry. Nothing flash—he's never been much for DIY—but Tim finds a proper screwdriver among the assortment of Allen keys, along with an adjustable wrench and probably enough orphaned bolts and screws of various sizes to get the job done. Satisfied, he snaps the lid shut and takes the toolbox with him.

You should have told me, Anna.

Melanie didn't want me to.

I could have helped.

I'm sure you could *have. But the question is,* would *you have?*

Sitting cross-legged in the middle of the kitchen floor, Tim empties the plastic bag out in front of him. Dog parts scatter across the tiles. The little brass bell tinkles to a stop beneath the fridge. He uses the screwdriver to fish it back out, blows away the dust bunnies with a couple of forceful breaths. Holding the bell between finger and thumb, he shakes it, gently. "Are you there, Jacob?" he whispers and shakes the bell again.

What happened to him? How did he die?

I've told you already, Tim. She didn't have the baby.

But you just said she wanted him.

I convinced her otherwise. It wasn't easy.

You convinced her to . . .

She could always have had a child later. With someone who cared, someone who was serious about her and actually wanted a family.

You made Mellie get an abortion? You made her get rid of her baby—our baby—is that what you're saying?

Be honest, Tim. What would you have made her do?

The house is silent and still. Tim arranges all the pieces carefully on the floor, putting them in some sort of dog-shaped order so he can see how they're meant to go together. Most of the bits of dowel are broken. He uses electrical tape where he can, decides to substitute a couple of bolts where he can't. It's not like the toy needs to be kiddie-safe.

She called him Jacob.

He thinks about Mellie, whose face he can now only picture in the cast of that awful memorial photograph. She was always so anxious, so clingy, constantly needing to be touched, to be reassured that, yes, he loved her, yes, he thought she was beautiful. A need so hungry, not even the ghost of a child, summoned from frantic desperation and the smallest scraps of half-formed flesh, could begin to quell it. Maybe a real child could have. Maybe the Crane was right about that too.

Neither of them would ever know.

"I'm sorry, Jacob." Tim fits the dog's head onto its neck, makes sure the joint is loose enough to bob. "See, I'm fixing it for you, mate. I'm guessing it's your favourite, right, your very first toy?"

There's no sound, no change in temperature from one heartbeat to the next, nothing at all to indicate that the boy now stands behind him. Merely the calm, absolute certainty that he's there.

"Your mum loved you a lot, Jacob, she really did." Tim spins a wheel around on his finger. He should buy some sandpaper to smooth out the gouges, some red paint to touch up the damage. "But she was sick, you know, so sick she had to go away. And I think maybe that's why she sent you to me. She wanted to make sure there would be someone to take care of you."

Bare feet shuffle against the tiles. Closer, closer.

"It must have been scary, being in a strange place all of a sudden, without your mum." Tim tries to laugh. "Guess we scared each other pretty good, hey?"

A small face presses its cheek against his back. It's a curious sensation, the presence of a weight he doesn't so much feel as believe in. A tiny hand flutters by his ribs. Tim closes his eyes. He wonders if the boy will keep growing, keep getting older. If one day he'll be demanding Wiis and iPhones, or whatever will have taken their place in another ten years. If there ever will be one day.

daddy

Less whisper than vibration, this word he hasn't even dreamed of wanting to hear before now. It runs through him, beating a rhythm along with the blood in his veins, a yearning inexpressible and sudden and vast.

daddy

He can sense the boy standing right in front of him now, that unseen face leaning in towards his own, those tiny teeth bared in the sharpest of smiles. "I'm sorry, Jacob." A tear slips warm down his cheek. "I didn't realise, I didn't know who you were."

daddy

"I'm so sorry." Tim says, and opens his eyes.

BORN AND BREAD

KAARON WARREN

There was once a baby born so ugly her father packed his bags in fury when he saw her.

"Who did you lie with, the baker or his dough?" he called over his shoulder as he left. Already he was planning to surprise his girlfriend who always smiled when she saw him and asked for nothing.

"Only you!" the mother called back. She held her baby in a soft brown blanket, though she had to lean against the wall for support.

The baby was as heavy as a calf and the size of the award-winning pumpkin at the fair five years earlier, a pumpkin that had never been matched before or since. Yet the baby had slid out sweetly, like dough through a piping bag.

And yes, she was pale, pasty and fleshy.

"Don't leave her in the sun," Mrs. Crouch, the cruellest woman in the village said. "Or you'll have a loaf of bread for a daughter." (In her defense, her husband spat brown juice wherever he stood, beat her with a stick when he felt so inclined, terrified the children with ghost tales, and never, ever spent a dollar when a cent would do.)

Still, the mother loved the daughter very much, especially once she learned how to laugh. Chuckles bubbled out of her like the froth in fermenting yeast, and anybody close by couldn't help but join in. She was so gentle and sweet they called her Doe, and that suited the way she had grown to look as well, like well-risen dough waiting to be baked into bread or sweet rolls.

Children loved to make her laugh, because her whole body quivered with it and it was beautiful to watch.

Each night she and her mother would sit together and tell stories and jokes. Sometimes her father would visit. (Always at dinner time. Her mother was the most marvellous cook. Her pastry was like flakes of pure heaven.) And he would tell them stories of his journeys. His girlfriend was long-since departed, and he now travelled the world selling and buying clever items for the kitchen. He bought Doe's mother a gadget for lemons and one for eggs, he bought spices and seasonings that made the whole house smell delicious.

Neither of them hated him for his early desertion; he was, for the most part, a good man and they loved his stories and gifts.

Each night Doe's mother would stroke, mould, press, and knead her flesh, stretch and smooth it. Sometimes this hurt, but it also always felt good.

By the time Doe was eighteen, she had transformed into a beautiful, lithe young woman with a sense of humour, an infectious laugh and a vast storehouse of stories.

In short, she became marriageable.

She had no interest in such a thing, though. She knew she could not have children because those parts of her were not fully formed, and she saw no other reason to tie herself to one man.

Like her father, she enjoyed journeys, explorations, and with her mother's blessings and warnings, her father's financial help, she set out for adventure.

She spent ten years exploring the world, tasting, seeing, learning, becoming, loving. She ate damper, dinkelbrot, pain de mie, bagels, sangak, roti and pandesal. She learned how to cook each loaf, loved to watch it brown, hug it to her chest warm from the oven. And like each loaf, each lover felt different, because she could mould herself around them. Encase them. More than once a man wept after their lovemaking.

"Nothing. Ever. So beautiful." The words in gasps.

Each encounter left her dented and stretched. She could massage herself back into shape, but she missed her mother's gentle touch and the stories they shared.

One day, her mother contacted her. "Your father is buying me a wonderful gift. A bakery! I will make cakes people will want to keep forever and others they will eat while still standing at the shop counter and order another."

"Will you bake bread?" Doe asked

"If you come back, you can be the bread baker. My dear little Doe."

But Doe had changed. She felt as if all she'd eaten, smelt, and seen so much; all the men she'd loved, all the women she'd spoken with, all the stories and jokes she'd shared: all of this had altered her. Would her mother still love her?

Her mother sighed as they embraced, but there was no judgment, no disappointment. "I've missed you!" she said, and her fingers pressed and stroked until Doe felt ordinary again.

And she set to work baking the most wonderful breads for her mother's bakery.

• • •

All this is to explain how it came to be that Doe helped to fulfil the awful Mr Crouch's dying wishes and thus lay his cruel ghost to rest.

As he lay on his deathbed he said to Mrs. Crouch, "You have been a bad wife. Only this many times have we had relations." There is some dissention as to how many fingers he held up. "You owe me three more. After my death, you will lie with me three nights, or this village will suffer the consequences."

He lay back, then, and demanded bread. He loved Doe's tiger bread and chose that as his last meal.

Doe walked into his sick room. Even though she'd been warned, the stench was overwhelming. She knew the odour of yeast left to ferment too long, but that was nothing compared to this. She'd smelt dead animals in the roof drains and the worst toilets any nightmare could dredge up. She'd smelt a man who hadn't bathed for twenty years.

Nothing came close to the stench of this room.

She pinched her nose and squeezed to close her nostrils.

"Here she is, the beautiful baker," Mr Crouch said. "Come and knead me, darling. I am ready for you," and he weakly tugged away the covers to reveal his naked body.

She placed the tray of bread beside him and left the room.

It is said he choked on a crust; that was not Doe's doing.

They buried him three nights later. Fearful of his curse, the women of the town went to Mrs. Crouch, to help prepare her to go to his grave.

She said, "He was repulsive alive. I cannot lie with him dead. And you know he was a cruel man; he means to damage me. Destroy me."

She refused to go that first night. The next day ten fields were found withered.

She refused to go that second night and the next day the clinic for the unwell was burnt down. Many would have been lost were it not for the early-rising Doe and her mother, who sounded the alarm.

The villagers went to Mrs. Crouch to beg her to lie with her dead husband. "He will take the children next. You know he will," they said.

She refused. "He means to destroy me. Mar me for life, haunt me into eternity, kill me."

They turned from her, distraught but not surprised. She was selfish and cruel and didn't care about the rest of them.

"I am driven by bad fortune! All my life!" she called after them, as if that made a difference.

Doe had led a blessed life, really. Full of good fortune and windfalls.

She went to Mrs. Crouch, who sneered at her as she always did.

"My deepest sympathies," Doe said, and she held Mrs. Crouch close, squeezing until the woman made an imprint in Doe's soft body.

In the bakery, she mixed dough, let it rise, punched it down, shaped it, let it rise again.

She baked this bread hard and brown. She baked Mrs. Crouch with her eyes closed.

As the moon rose high, she carried the bread lady to the cemetery. It was light, as good bread should be.

She laid it on Mr Crouch's grave. "Darling," she called out. "Darling, I'm here."

Then she tripped away to hide.

At first, there was stillness, a terrible quiet that made her doubt her ears. Then a disturbance in the dirt, a writhing, then four nubs appeared, then eight, like pink growing tendrils of an unpleasant plant.

He rose up naked and fully erect.

He fell upon his bread lady, roaring, biting, thrusting, filled with lust and fury. Doe looked away and she thought, *I will tell her I understand. What woman could lie with this man and ever feel clean again?*

He fell upon his dough-wife, the Lady Bread, and his sweat, his juice, the dampness of the air, helped to dissolve the bread into a pale mush. He did not seem to care. He stood up, shook himself like a dog, then nodded and sank into his grave.

All at once, sound returned; the rustling leaves, the howling dogs, and Doe felt that she could leave.

• • •

In the morning, the only tragedy found was Mrs. Crouch, strangled with her own hands clenched around her neck, her eyes wide, tears dried in a map across both cheeks.

There was reward to be had though.

On clearing the Crouch's house, their secret fortune was found, and this was shared amongst them all. Not only that, but for a dozen years to come the crops grew tall and golden and brought good fortune to them all.

As for Doe . . . as her mother aged, they looked for a baker to take her place. One day he came to them, and Doe felt soft on the inside as she had never felt before.

His hands were warm and she could feel her flesh shift at his touch. He could mould dough like an artist and needed only four hours sleep a night.

All the village was happy for their Doe.

And that is all to explain why, each year on December the 21st, the villagers all buy the perfect Lady Bread, thus bringing good luck upon themselves and upon the village and all who pass through her.

THE SLEEPOVER

TERRY DOWLING

The only celebrity touch was the white stretch limo that took Jane Bastion to one of the side gates of Sydney's vast Rookwood Cemetery at the discreet hour of 11 PM. Those gates were quickly, miraculously it seemed, opened for the vehicle and just as quickly closed behind, showing that money can open doors in almost any world.

Eccentric millionaire visits grave of beloved father for solitary midnight vigil.

That was the official story if anyone raised a fuss, though Jane's sense of mischief added one more line. *Has friends over.*

That's where it all fell down. And as she watched the dark cemetery streets and lawn precincts pass beyond the limo's wide windows, she devised even more appropriate headlines.

Dead Meet the Living

Savini family tomb renovated for clandestine midnight soiree.

And less generously:

Ladies Only

The height of sacrilege and bad taste. Eccentric socialite Anabella Savini last night excelled herself by inviting eight of her friends to a special do in the recently cleared family crypt.

Cleared, that was the thing. What had they done with the eight bodies once interred there? Nine counting Anabella's father Tomaso, dead these past ten years. Relocating them might be legal, but was never really acceptable and rarely spoken of. The rumours had been worrying. Still, all would be revealed soon enough.

The limo moved into a newer section of dark tomb streets, finally stopped before the bronze door of one large crypt. The façade was featureless except for a dim amber memorial light to the right of that door. There were no architraves, no pilasters or niches, none of the urns, statues and photographs that marked the other tombs in the street. Either the renovations were incomplete or this was a new look for a new age. Austere. Minimalist. Stylish in the overpowering way the ancient funerary precinct of Djoser at Saqqara was stylish, though with one wonderfully discordant touch. A Portaloo was parked discreetly by the building's front left corner, no doubt a convenience hired for the evening's guests rather than left over from last-minute renovations.

How much money did it take to make this happen, Jane wondered yet again. Even as the chauffeur opened her door and helped her out with "Have a pleasant evening, ma'am," she went back to it. What favours, briberies, phonecalls? How did one begin to work this?

But after the mystery of the invitation, the insistence on a non-disclosure agreement and a ban on mobile phones, now the late-night pick-up, she was glad to be standing out in the night at last, despite the cool breeze and the macabre setting. Cemeteries had never bothered her overly much, though at 36 she was finding herself suddenly susceptible to the downright eeriness of Anabella's venue for this particular occasion, a little too keenly aware of her own mortality in the 30 down, 40-plus to go "wisening" that hits most of us once we reach age 30. Hair still dark enough, glossy enough, certainly, skin and muscle tone still good, but her favourite evening dress *was* a bit too snug, and her moderately high heels did have a dash of trying too hard about them. The mortal dreads pressed close.

Jane watched the limo pull away oh so quietly, heading back to the gates and the real—other real—world, all part of a brilliantly orchestrated fetch and deliver. *Full marks so far, Anabella.*

A cool wind blew along the funerary street. Trees rustled close by. Leaves scraped along the empty pavements. Jane drew her shawl closer about her shoulders.

Mid-autumn. Mild enough still, but time to be inside.

She approached the heavy door. What did one do, knock?

For it was so quiet, too quiet, just the wind in the trees, the skip-scatter-scrape of leaves.

It made her stop, kept her standing there, hesitating, wondering. Was she first to arrive (it was that quiet), the last (if so, where were the voices, the—dare she expect it—music?). Was she the *only* one to actually *be* invited? Though this *was* the family crypt. For all Anabella's quirks, her deserved reputation for con-jobs and frivolity, this event had to be important to her.

Jane did the logical thing then, the "Jane thing" as Anabella had once described it in the early days, back when it was still eccentric third-generation mining heiress meets acting sub-editor for the debut online issue of *Wellsprings*. She stepped a half-dozen paces back to the opposite side of the tomb street and simply took it all in.

The Savini crypt stood in a row of twenty or more tombs of various shapes and sizes in one of the circa-1960s sections of what was famously called the Sleeping City, facing another row of crypts opposite. Many of the vaults she could see showed the expected degree of opulence and ornamentation, but Jane confirmed that Anabella truly had—what was the best term?—uncluttered? neutralised? purged?—her family's vault. Already large before the renovations, the former architraves and pilasters had actually helped mask its true size, a building as large as a double garage at least. Now it loomed like a wall of Black Forest cake amid the meringues, with just that single heavy bronze door set above its doorstep, and the solitary eye of the amber memorial light burning to one side. And a Portaloo, for heaven's sake, a crucial concession to the living. You had to hand it to her.

Jane glanced up and down the street. The main cemetery gates were somewhere behind her to the west, the closer gates they'd entered by a kilometre away at least, and probably locked again by now. That was how these things worked in the movies and urban myths, people doing silly things in silly ways at anything but sensible hours. Well, she'd knock once on the metal door, just once, and be gone.

But when she raised her hand to pound on the dull metal, a proximity sensor activated a recorded male voice that was startling, deeply unsettling and comical all at the same time.

"Please come in—" There was the smallest hesitation as a digital menu was consulted. "—Ms Bastion. The others are waiting."

• • •

They were indeed. As Jane pushed the bronze door inwards and stepped through the opening, she found herself in a pleasantly warm interior lit by dozens of candles arranged in five standing and three elaborate table candelabra. Their light revealed eight smiling women seated about a large dining table covered with a white muslin table-cloth, laid with matching napkins, shining silverware and sparkling champagne flutes. Anabella Savini had spared no expense, and she sat at the centre of the group on the side facing the door. They had been waiting for her, and were clearly aware of her arrival ten minutes before. She could imagine Anabella even making fun of her caution. "Be kind now. It's the Jane thing."

Not surprisingly the crypt's interior had been masked to conceal its original purpose. Heavy floor-length drapes of rich red velvet covered the side and back walls, giving the impression of a *fin-de-siècle* orientalist's salon or a desert pavilion out of Hollywood antiquity. There were even two male servants standing silently by Anabella's chair, two well-built, slender young men wearing black bodysuits, white domino masks and white cotton gloves, poised in the act of serving canapés and topping up the champagne flutes. They had paused for her entrance. The faintest strains of Chopin's Piano Concerto Number 1 in E Minor could be heard and the air smelled wonderfully of spices and incense and the fragrances of a fine supper no doubt being warmed in hot-boxes discreetly out of sight behind the curtains.

Jane recognised all the faces, if only casually, from previous Savini gatherings, the parties and soirees that marked forever-to-be-unwedded Anabella's often louche, always fascinating and inventive lifestyle. Pretty faces for the most part or, at the very least, handsome, but allowably attractive every one.

To Jane's left as she stood with her back to the closed door, on one of the table's short sides, sat Candace Waygard and Claire Heymanns, the formidable, hard-edged ladies who served on the boards of two of Anabella's corporations as her "eyes and ears." She clearly wanted them seated together in plain view rather than next to her so she didn't have to turn her head this way and that to speak to them. On the short side to the right sat Anita Pike and Alana Goodrich, if Jane remembered correctly, while to Anabella's immediate left on the long side facing the door was Tory Mangan;

to Tory's right the dark-eyed fashion designer Seyer McNeil. Turned in her chair on the long side close to where Jane now stood, smiling up at her warmly, was Maggie Ardron. The empty chair next to Maggie was even now being pulled out by one of the young servants.

"Welcome, dear girl," Anabella cooed in the patently oversolicitous queen-of-the-world tone Jane hated most. "Now that our wonderful group is complete, supper can begin."

And so it did once Jane was seated alongside Maggie, her purse and shawl taken and her glass filled. The masked servants disappeared behind the curtains and returned with platters of small seafood vol-au-vent that were spicy, smoky and absolutely delicious. Two main dishes followed in leisurely succession, simple dishes really, easy to transport, easy to re-heat: a chicken casserole in a rich wine sauce and then a beef goulash that was sublime and left a smoky aftertaste that the vintage Moet matched perfectly. Small silver bowls of steamed vegetables accompanied each dish.

"Such largesse!" Alana Goodrich said, raising her glass in a private salute.

Anabella raised her own glass in return. "There is a point you reach, Alana, when you're wealthy enough that the connoisseurs and gourmands no longer presume to tell you which wines go with what. As the wisest Europeans have always known, "Olympus decides for itself and mortals scramble to allow.""

"Which translates as 'Money talks!'," Claire Heymanns said.

Anabella smiled quite mischievously. "As we shall soon see, I'm sure."

While the dishes were cleared and a dessert of profiteroles with King Island cream was being served, along with coffee and tea, Jane raised her glass several times as if to drink but only pretending, using the action to let her study her fellow guests.

They're all around my own age, she realised. No-one over forty but Anabella who—what?—had to be close on 55, but hardly more than that, despite her grande dame affectations. Candace and Claire were both 38, Jane was reasonably sure. Alana and Anita Pike, 37, Maggie and Seyer both 36 at least. Tory Mangan was the youngest at around 35. Jane was wondering if there was any significance to that when Alana Goodrich set down her dessert fork and broached a subject that had to be on all their minds.

"Anabella, I must ask. What happened to the—how shall I put this?—previous occupants? We've been dying to know."

Good on you, Alana, Jane thought. At least eight rellies disposed of, eight guests tonight. All a bit suss. The others had to have been wondering.

Anabella gestured with the back of one hand to the curtained section behind her chair. "I had hoped to spare you during supper but very well. Papa is behind this curtain here. The others are, well—" She indicated their surroundings, the walls of the crypt itself. "Let's just say they're still with us."

The table went silent as the implications sank in.

Anita Pike actually snorted into her champagne. "You walled them up?"

Tory Mangan giggled. "Anabella, how very Poe of you."

Anabella gave her throaty laugh. "Hardly, Tory. These old dears have been out of it a long time. No premature burials in this lot, though a few may have deserved it from what I've been told. No, look upon it as going modern, more like scattering the ashes, building a better tomorrow. They're earning their keep."

Maggie Ardron was shaking her head at the sheer boldness of it all. "You've made a literal House of the Dead out of them."

Candace Waygard's thin mouth was set in an approving grin. "You devil. You had them ground up for the mortar. Powdered rellies. It could start a trend."

"Only if you decide to tell, Candace dear. Naturally I'd prefer you didn't."

Tory Mangan giggled again. "Look around you, Ana. You invite us here and tell us this—us!—then expect us to keep it to ourselves."

"You'll do as you will, Tory love, of course, but you did sign a non-disclosure, and, anyway, telling would mean that you'd forfeit your chance at tonight's special prize."

"Which is?" Seyer McNeil asked. The designing mogul for Palifrey didn't try to mask her curiosity like some of the others.

"Aha, Seyer, it concerns the tomb's *remaining* occupant. The one remaining *in corpore*—what's the term?—*intacto*, *de facto*, *dura*? No matter. Something Latin."

The table went silent again.

"Your father?" Jane asked.

"Of course. My beloved Papa. Marco, if you please."

The white-masked, white-gloved factotum moved to the rear curtain, pulled on concealed draw-strings. The heavy drapes parted to reveal a single brushed-silver metal casket leaning upright at a slight angle against the tomb's rear wall. It had been dusted off, its anodised surfaces obviously polished for the occasion, though there was an indefinable quality about it that still suggested the passage of time: the ten years since it was last sealed.

The sight of an actual casket with its occupant inside had an immediate effect on Anabella's guests. Eyes glittered in the candlelight. Mouths opened in surprise. Anita and Tory actually had their hands at their throats, giving a distinctly Victorian or Edwardian cast to the whole thing, as if, like much of the vast boneyard around them, they were indeed more than a hundred years away from a world of Portaloos, stretch limos, propane hot-boxes and mobile phones.

Jane sat marvelling at it all. They were having a late-night supper in a crypt in honour of a deceased parent and yet many of her fellow guests seemed surprised to find his corpse present at the event!

"You didn't reduce *him* to powder then," Alana Goodrich said, and was probably the only person present who could have put such a comment so dismissively. "He's still with us."

Again, the implications set in. *Too fresh to grind down. Not desiccated enough.*

Candace Waygard braved the awkward silence as well. "You are totally unique, Anabella."

"We are all of us unique, Candace dear. I have chosen the eight of you to be here tonight both for your personal charms and for the very real esteem my Father had for each one of you."

I met the old lecher twice, Jane thought, just twice, barely spoke to him. She noticed that several of the guests wanted to remark on that as well.

But Anabella had raised her hand in another of her imperious gestures, one more suited to a woman twenty years her senior. "So let's move on to the special event of the evening. It is now 12:30, nearly one o'clock in the morning. I propose that each of you remains here the night and keeps my beloved Papa company in his new digs."

Tory Mangan raised her glass. "I'm game, if there's more of the bubbly! And so long as I can borrow the torch and use the Portaloo."

Candace was more composed. "Not much to ask, Ana. It's nearly one, like you say. I'm comfortable enough."

Anabella stood for effect. "Well, that's it, Candace dear. Not in your comfy rented chairs, I'm afraid." She made yet another gesture, proceeding according to whatever script she had devised for the occasion. The factotum to her left tugged at the cord for the curtains along the northern wall. The servant at the curtains to the right did the same. The concealing drapes slid aside to reveal eight identical funerary caskets, four along the northern wall, four along the southern, all the same split-lid kind used for viewing the deceased. They were propped upright in customised black metal frames that held them at a gentle twenty-five degrees from vertical. Their anodised metal shone wanly in the candlelight.

Anita Pike and Tory Mangan had their hands to their throats again.

"I don't believe you, Ana!" Anita said.

"Coffins!" Tory cried. "You can't be serious!"

Anabella seated herself once more. "But of course I'm serious, Tory, Anita. And they're caskets, not coffins. Coffins are wide at the shoulders, tapered at the head and feet. Caskets are rectangular like these. Don't worry, they're brand new, rented just for tonight, and really quite comfortable. And you'll notice they have mercy holes where your heads will be. You'll be able to breathe, I promise."

Jane studied the sinister shapes, saw that the upper section of each casket did indeed have a small rosette of perforations to allow breathing, which made her wonder at Anabella's use of the word "rented." Did people actually make caskets with breathing holes these days—mercy holes, she called them—if ever they had?

Maggie Ardron drained her glass and set it down. "Forgive me, Anabella, but why would anyone in their right mind agree to do such a thing?"

"Because, Maggie dear, I will give each of you who chooses to stay one million dollars in cash for participating. Not a bad fee for a five-hour sleepover. If only one of you agrees to do it, that person gets the whole eight million, provided they remain for the duration, until 6 AM. I'm serious. Two of you, four million each. Papa coveted each one of you when he was alive—you were his girls, if you like. It seems only fitting that we honour his memory in an appropriate fashion on this tenth anniversary of his passing."

"Encoffined," Anita Pike said.

Anabella gave her throaty laugh. "I swear, Anita, only you would use a term like that. Encoffined. Again, very Poe."

Alana Goodrich was far more direct. "People know where we are, Ana." The comment was so bold and accusing, so encompassing of their various misgivings.

"Of course they do, Alana darling. You're not going to be buried alive, I assure you. This is an indulgence on my part, keeping a promise in fact. One million for each of you when the caskets are opened at dawn. You each signed a disclaimer when you accepted my invitation promising that you would not bring your mobiles or divulge what took place here tonight. I will hold you to those agreements. I'd rather not have this on Facebook or in the tabloids."

"Will the caskets be locked?" Tory Mangan asked.

"For the duration, yes. I mean, Tory love, I won't be here myself. How will I know if you remain 'encoffined' as Anita so colourfully put it? You ladies are to spend the night with Papa, his sole companions, all tucked in together."

"What happens if we need to pee?" Anita Pike asked.

"One million dollars, Anita," Anabella said.

Tory Mangan set down her glass, frowning. "The door will be locked?"

"The caskets and the door will be locked until 6 am. But the tomb is well ventilated. The heating will be turned off, of course, all the catering equipment removed. No risk of carbon monoxide poisoning. But the caskets are well padded. Insulated."

Tory kept at it. "In darkness?"

"The candles should last the night, I'd say. But if not, yes, you would be in darkness for a time."

Seyer laughed lightly. "With just poor dead Tomaso for company."

"One million dollars, Seyer. With the added thrill of knowing that when you write your memoirs you can truthfully say you've been a bought woman at least once."

"What about these frames?" Anita asked.

"They're to stop the caskets toppling, of course. Can't have you being injured."

"So we'll be standing for five hours?"

"That's up to you, Anita dear. There's a small remote on a tether attached to the lid in front of you. You'll be able to reach it and retrieve it if it's dropped. Press the button and the hydraulic frame will lower your casket so you can recline for sleeping, raise it if you prefer to see the room for the duration. It's up to you."

The room. Jane smiled at Ana's choice of words. The vault, the crypt, the tomb more like it. Euphemisms were everything where death was concerned. The dead became the deceased, the departed. The language of sleep was used for death—"resting," "sleeping with the angels"—the language of death for sleep—"dead to the world," "no longer with us," even "crashed."

Anabella seemed to anticipate such thoughts. She clapped her hands to get everyone's attention, kept up the happy patter. "So, what's it to be, ladies? Those of you preferring to leave will be collected in—" Anabella checked her watch. "—fifteen minutes. No questions asked, no fee pocketed. But once you've decided, I want no changing your minds please. I'll leave you to discuss it and make your decision while I go and use the torch." She winked and stood. Marco opened the bronze door and handed her the flashlight.

Jane watched the group around the big table. All present knew better than to disparage Anabella Savini openly. There were no comments about mad schemes, lapses of taste and the private lives of those with way too much money on their hands. The wily heiress could be listening at the door, even recording it all. This was entertainment for her, theatre, spectacle, perhaps even a genuine and heartfelt ritual of love and devotion, however Grand Guignol.

Somehow the prospect of some of their company opting out and being returned home safely in the next ten minutes or so made Ana's request seem much less sinister. There would be witnesses; there *were* witnesses, family and friends, those who knew they were at one of Anabella Savini's do's, possibly had even more details despite the non-disclosures. The prospect of being free to go made staying easier.

"Hey," Tory Mangan said. "Ten thousand would have got me. A million nails it. And excuse that last comment. No pun intended."

Maggie Ardron was for it as well. "It's just five hours. If worse comes to worst I can buy a new dress. A new dress shop!"

Ten thousand probably would have bought Jane as well. She knew better than to let herself be a hostage to fortune this way, but it was a magic bullet moment in her life. Five hours shut away alone (though hardly alone) would pay off her mortgage, change her world in very significant ways. She didn't want to stay but, like the others, couldn't afford not to.

And so it went.

They all agreed to remain.

When Anabella returned and heard their decision, she actually clapped her hands in delight. "Excellent. Just the boys and me for the limo then. Can I ask you all to use the facilities outside, then Marco and Julian will tuck you in. You will be 'encoffined', you will hear the door close and lock, then you will tell each other bedtime stories to your hearts' content. It's up to you. You can lower your caskets and sleep or stay upright and awake, doing the Poe thing. We will return with a continental breakfast and your envelopes at first light."

One by one those who needed to do so went out into the tomb street and used the convenience while Marco and Julian opened the lids of the caskets to reveal plush, padded interiors of ivory, light-blue or rose satin.

Then, amid nervous giggles and goodnight kisses, the donning of shawls, wraps and jackets against the chill, Jane and the others stepped into their appointed chambers and settled themselves.

The bottom sections were closed and latched first, which was tactful, Jane thought, doing it in stages, letting them adjust to it, see the candles, see each other.

"Hope the old boy doesn't walk in his sleep," Alana quipped, causing more giggles and no doubt further pangs of unease.

Jane felt her heart pounding. We're going to be so vulnerable, she kept thinking. And we haven't verified any of the things we've been told, just accepted everything because of the money.

She was indeed letting herself be a hostage to fortune, breaking so many of her own rules.

But one million dollars!

As Marco and Julian moved quietly about the vault, removing the hot-boxes and the propane cylinders, the sound system and accompanying laptop, leaving the candelabra but taking down the drapes, next dismantling the table and carrying it out with the chairs, Jane felt the beginnings of panic. Anabella was over by the northern wall exchanging last-minute pleasantries with Claire and Candace while the place was cleared of everything but the caskets. The *nine* caskets.

But Ana would be leaving. That was the thing. Making jokes was easy. *They* would be staying.

Jane forced herself to breathe calmly. She could change her mind. She actually could, Anabella's insistence be damned. She could reach out right now and open the latches. Simply walk out. Who would stop her?

But a million. A million.

She stayed where she was, hating the greed that kept her there, hating her panic, her pounding heart.

The others had to be feeling it too: the helplessness of wanting the money, the growing dread of where they were, what they were about to do to get it.

And now Anabella was bidding them goodnight like any other dorm mum in that other world out there.

"Very well, ladies. Sleep soundly. We'll see you in a few hours."

Without another word, Marco and Julian began closing and latching the upper lids on the four caskets Jane could see. First Claire vanished from sight behind dully gleaming metal, then Candace, next Alana and finally Seyer McNeil. Then the men themselves disappeared from view as they turned their attentions to the caskets along the southern wall. Soon it would be Jane's turn, her final chance.

But a million. A million.

Marco was suddenly standing before her, smiling, eyes glinting through his white domino. "See you soon, miss."

"Marco—"

"Hey listen, just go with it. You'll be fine."

And the lid closed heavily, snugly, with such finality. She heard it being latched to seal her in, a sound no *living* person should ever hear.

She was in near-total darkness then, smelling the new, lightly perfumed satin, with just the rosette of, what?, at least sixty two-millimetre holes giving the most precious bloom of light before her, the barest broken glimpse of candle flames, the dull sheen of two other caskets. Whose, it didn't matter. All precious, so precious.

She heard a cheery "Goodnight, ladies!" from Marco or Julian, possibly Anabella herself for that matter—the padding muffled it— then there followed the dull boom of the bronze door being closed and locked, a Poe sound if ever there was one, another sound no living person should hear from *inside* a tomb.

Don't lose the key, Jane thought, then in the new silence found other things to trouble her, terrify her, truth be told.

We never asked to see Tomaso's body, she realised, leaning back in her casket, standing enclosed, encoffined, helplessly confined. What had she been thinking? *Not* thinking? None of them for that matter. Flattered by the invitation, the limos and the fine supper, the prospect of such wealth, all the attention, they'd never asked to see the ten-year-old corpse, never dared request it. Why would they, why would anyone?

But how do we know that other casket actually contains Tomaso's body at all?, she thought. That it's even locked? It was against the back wall, the eastern wall, right in her blind spot. Try as she might, pressing up against the rosette—the mercy hole, for God's sake, such a name!—she couldn't see it, could barely see anything.

What if it's all a joke? More theatre? What if someone, an actor, is waiting inside to climb out at the appointed time to deliver the next phase of Anabella's scheme? Though she'd seen no mercy hole on that casket . . .

"Hey, can anyone hear me?" a voice cried, impossibly distant, heard through the padded lining that covered all but the rosette. It might have been Tory or Anita.

"Jane here!" she called back.

"It's me, Jane. Tory," the small voice cried.

"Tory!" Jane called. "We can do it. It's just a few hours."

"It's me. Claire," another tiny voice said from across the room— the crypt—a thousand miles away.

"Candace, reporting in," a voice said, thin, so small.

"Alana, needing to pee already." Echo of an echo. "Sorry. Shouldn't have said that."

"Maggie here. Anyone got a spare teddy bear?"

"Seyer. Hi, everyone. Jane's right. We can do this." Small voices, all small, but shouting, obviously shouting in their separate prisons.

We're not going to be able to keep this up, Jane realised. We'll exhaust ourselves.

"Are you there, Anita?" Tory called, though it was a whisper, almost a voice in Jane's mind how it came to her. "Hey, Anita? You there, hon"?"

There was no answer.

"Must be asleep already!" Jane called back, to give what comfort she could. "Probably a good idea."

"Jane's right," Claire's tiny voice came. "We should sleep this through. Get it done as quickly as possible."

Jane heard a new sound then, hydraulics working.

"Assuming the horizontal position. Goodnight, ladies!" It was Claire again, had to be Claire. Ever practical. Looking after the crew and leading by example.

She heard other caskets activating then, moving down in their frames, taking a load off.

Not for me yet, Jane decided. I need to think, stay with this.

This isn't the Hilton. Someone has to keep watch.

The tomb became so quiet then, with some trying to sleep, the rest afraid to speak lest they ruin that blessed release for those already out of it. What did you do—speak or not speak? Those who wanted to stay awake were probably just standing there, forced into silence, without the one solace *they* needed most. Connection. Companionship.

It left Jane straining to see what little she could through the rosette, left her mind racing, imagining all sorts of possibilities, worst-case scenarios, everything from Anabella's limo being in a fatal accident to Julian thinking Marco had been sent to unlock the crypt while Marco expected Julian to do it, things like that.

Minutes crept by, seconds that felt like minutes.

Jane soon started imagining things—it had to happen—sounds other than the creaks and pops of metal cooling, stone and new concrete settling. Across two minutes or ten, twenty or sixty (how could she know?) there grew an almost hallucinatory intensity to everything: the feel of the satin, cool, soft and smooth against her fingertips and her cheeks, but too soft, moving a bit too much under her touch, the (surely) imagined smells of roses, then gas, faeces, human corruption. There were even moments of startling synaesthesia when she thought she could actually *hear* the flutter and dip of the candle flames in whatever eddies of air stirred out there, was sure she could *hear* seven other heartbeats drumming purposely in time with own, trying to synchronise. One moment she could taste vanilla, then cinnamon, the next iron and copper, as if her mouth were bleeding.

She was so aware of everything, of too much in fact, found herself devising aphorisms, litanies, truths of the tomb. One almost became a mantra.

Every time we wake the world is made again. Every time a reprieve, though we dare not admit it. We are all of us pre-death. It's the only status worth having.

However long these ramblings and wild imaginings took, in whatever time-frame they worked their subtle damage, the rosette became a mercy hole indeed, the source of all reality, all that was both good and terrible in this late-night world.

But soon all that settled too as her own fatigue settled her. It was late, well after one by now surely. What with the champagne, the food, the aftermath of the adrenalin rush, she soon found herself drifting. Lower the casket, she told herself again and again, let go, but snapped back to find that she was still standing, still leaning, drifting.

Then came an unmistakable sound in the self-haunting silence, unmistakable except that she was doubting everything now, needed it verified before she could be certain.

The sound came again, far off but distinct, a sound that wasn't the synaesthetic trickery of candle flames snapping and shuddering, granite blocks rasping and sliding, or worse, powdered relatives scratching, scratching, scratching in the walls, angry, restless and betrayed.

A casket opening.

It was. First the upper section, then the lower.

Jane froze where she stood, pressed one ear fiercely to the rosette.

Nothing. No-one called. No-one cried out. No-one else heard.

Or were they all doing as she was doing, standing in silence, absolutely still, eyes wide in terror and ears pressed hard against their mercy holes, trying to hear something, anything, above their own thundering hearts?

A casket had opened. Been opened. But from the outside or the inside?

God, no! Opened from the inside because never locked!

But who, who?

Cool businesslike Claire or equally ruthless Candace, Anabella's eyes and ears? Irreverent Alana Goodrich?

Tomaso?

Don't think it, Jane told herself. Never think it!

But who could it be? Who wasn't tucked in?

Tomaso!

But how—how could it possibly be?

We never checked, never looked. All of us hostages to fortune.

No other sounds followed. Nothing.

Just quiet candlelight. Just the room, the terrible room. Just the creeping terror and the doubt.

"Hello?" she cried, shouted with all her might.

There was no answer. No-one replied.

All asleep. All blessedly asleep. Lucky, lucky, lucky.

But not *all* asleep.

Tomaso.

Not possible. Simply not possible. An actor, surely. Or no-one. Nothing. Get a grip!

She almost managed. For then something passed in front of her mercy hole—a quick rush of shadow.

"Who's there?" she cried, locked up with terror. "Who's there?"

But again there was nothing, nothing.

The candle flames cut the dead air. The two caskets she could see caught the light, so much dull brushed silver.

Fucking Ana!

Then the candles flickered. They did. Quickly, suddenly. The tiny flames shivered, darted, trembled, became still again. A body wind. Someone had passed by.

A ghost wind.

Tomaso!

They'd never checked.

"For God's sake!" Jane cried. "Is anyone there? Can anyone hear me? Anyone?"

Silence. Silence.

Seconds rushing, creeping into minutes.

And again the candles flickered. Again someone had passed by, either that or they were becoming starved of oxygen, or simply guttering before going out. But no, no, Jane could see several of the thin white shafts, several steady flames. Plenty of time yet.

Someone passing then. Had to be.

Jane brought up her arms in the cramped space, first one then the other, and pounded on the padded lid. "Claire! Alana! Anyone! Who's out there! Answer me! Who's out there?"

There was only silence. Cool dead silence.

Then, suddenly, the room began darkening. The little blades of flame were being extinguished one by one. She hadn't noticed at first; it was happening so gradually, one flame snuffed out, then another. Being stolen away, bringing the dark.

"What's going on?" Jane shrieked, pounding on the lid.

No-one answered, and bit by bit, flame by tiny flame, the light fell away until there was total darkness at last, the darkness of the tomb talked about in stories, legends, urban myths.

And like any animal struck by too much fear, the right amount of terror, Jane became immediately silent, completely still.

It was the only way to hide, to stay small, unnoticed.

Draw no attention. Like fish in shoals, birds in flocks, insects in swarms, hide now! I'm one of eight, only eight, but precious eight. Quiet now. One chance in eight. Hide the only way you can.

She calmed, actually calmed. With nowhere to run, no other way to be, to go but into terror, she calmed, watched, waited. All she could do.

And she was rewarded unexpectedly. Her eyes adjusted enough to find scraps of light, barest traces through the mesh-covered filigree of the crypt's ventilation grilles, especially the one in her broken line of sight she hadn't noticed had been there all along, the ghost of a midnight blue square in the deepest black. It gave depth, distance to the world again, the tiniest sense of "over there" so it wasn't just "only here."

She eased, waited, protected. Listened.

Silence. Precious silence.

Let it stay.

Then, primed with cunning, wise with desperation, something else occurred to her, Anabella gesturing at their surroundings in response to Alana's question about the fate of the tomb's previous occupants. "They're earning their keep," Ana had said, and "building a better tomorrow."

Not in the walls, Jane realised, clearly, coldly, delirium on hold for the moment, panic at arms' length. *In the food*!

She couldn't be sure. Thank God, she couldn't. Her gorge began to rise at the thought of it. But the heavy sauces, the smoky aftertaste. All of them drinking generous top-ups of bubbly to cut through the taste. All drinking more than they might have. Not Poe, oh no. More like the ancient Greek legend of Atreus tricking Thyestes into eating his own sons.

All the while Ana eating selectively, knowing the safe dishes, pretending to drink even as Jane had pretended.

A sedative in the champagne too, just enough. That was why the others were silent, just herself left to keep this interminable vigil.

Jane tried to put it from her mind, controlled her gorge, worked to calm herself as best she could, listened, distracted herself by listening.

More seconds drip-fed into minutes, built slowest hours behind, dismantled those ahead.

Another sound! More than one.

Footsteps. She could hear footsteps. But soft, soft.

Someone *was* out there.

The synaesthesia was there too then, the slide and rasp of the brickwork, the scratch, scratch, scratch of walled-up kin, the smells of carrion and vanilla, old rose and cinnamon.

She stayed still, stayed quiet, tried to let it flow about her.

Play the game! Let it be what it is.

Then it happened. Her hydraulic frame activated, began lowering!

She hadn't pressed the button. The remote was in its cradle against the lid, but she hadn't pressed it.

Someone else! Someone else was lowering her casket.

Why? Why?

A more conventional death position. How you stacked a tomb.

She was finally horizontal, laid out on the floor.

Something covered her mercy hole then, snatched away the last of any other world but terror.

The air smelled of roses.

Panic and roses. Braving the darkness had made her think she could win, but there were too many roses. Too many.

• • •

"Wakey wakey, sleepy-head!" the voice came, and sunlight, the other world.

Marco was steadying her, helping her out of her casket, which was upright again. The door to the crypt was open. She could see part of a white limo parked out there.

There were others in that wash of light: Alana and Claire, Tory, Maggie, and, yes, Anita, thank God, shaky, soiled and millionaires every one. They were being helped out into the best day that had ever been.

Even now the piece of limo moved out of sight, and another pulled into view.

Jane tried to speak but couldn't manage it. She felt too leaden, too half-dead (but grinned at the thought of that) from nearly losing everything, everyone. They were safe, safe.

She tasted coffee, briefly, fleetingly, then slept in the limo all the way back to her apartment in Drummoyne, where someone, Marco it might have been, used her key to help her inside, then waited, assisted dutifully and respectfully, while she put herself to bed.

When she finally woke sixteen hours later, she found two envelopes on her bedside table. The first contained a cheque for one million dollars, the second a note from Anabella.

Jane dear,

Thank you for making the evening such a success. Should the pregnancy test prove positive, please contact me at once. There will be a further two million should you decide to carry the little one to term.

Forgive a daughter for honouring her father's final request. He really did love all his girls.

Anabella

Jane sat on the edge of her bed staring at the words until she no longer saw them, her mind filled with thoughts of anger in the walls and too many roses, of special meals and special needs and being a hostage to fortune yet again.

It was going to be an interesting week.

BLACK SWAN EVENT

MARGO LANAGAN

The first thing Dawn heard every morning was her brother stretching his wing. The soft whooping travelled down the hall and woke her from whatever doze or dream she lay in. Through the first bird-calls, or the wind hissing or the rain rattling or the traffic whining and rumbling on the distant highway, came the *whoop* and settle, *whoop* and settle, as Neddy worked the itch out, worked the cramp out, oiled the joints of the thing, before binding it to himself for another day of pretending it wasn't there.

He made no other sound as he stretched it, no groan or yawn. And he kept that room as neat as a pin, with nothing loose to fall or fly about. *Whoop* and settle. *Whoop-whoop-whoop-whoop* and settle. She would watch the wall, or the lightening ceiling, or her own clutter, the knick-knacks from her children that would be swept off and smashed by such wing-beats here, the yarn-scraps that would whirl into flight all colours. She watched their stillness, and listened to the air being struck and stretched down the hall, and felt nothing in particular, not any more.

· · ·

She had thought she must be sickening for something. She had not quite a headache, not quite an earache, not quite sinus pain. And maybe that last period eight months ago *hadn't* been the last after all. Was that what this feeling meant?

She got up early, troubled after a troubled night's sleep. The kitchen was cold but tidy; last night's casserole dish stood soaking on the stovetop. She got the jug boiling for tea, emptied the dish, turned on the hot water and put a fingertip into the first cold streaming.

She felt it then, very strong and unpleasant, in her womb and her bowel, in her thighs, something being torn up by the roots. Her hand snatched itself out of the water, and the dish thunked to the sink-bottom. The feeling stopped, just like that.

She stood breathing hard. The water twined down, warming. Slowly she brought her fingertip to just beside it. Yes, there was the ghost of what she'd felt, a dragging in her throat, a horrid anxiety in her guts. Her knees locked, ready should she put her finger in further.

She washed the dish, careful not to touch the running water. She towelled it dry, and bent and put it away.

Ned's footsteps sounded in the hall, his work boots, though he'd had no work in how long? She straightened and backed up to the cupboard as he came in. She must not greet him, must not speak. She knew this for a hard rule, and with that knowledge things began to come clear.

He saw the way she stood. "What's up?"

She put her fingertips to her mouth and shook her head. The water scrambled in the jug, coming to the boil.

"Are you all right, Dawnie?" he said. "Do I need to get you to the doctor's?"

The jug clicked off and she rushed to it, poured their tea. She brought the mugs to the table, snatched the calendar from the wall and a pen from the bench-top, and returned to sit, kicking out a chair for him. By mark and hand-sign she managed to tell him that she would not be going to little Josie's christening tomorrow, or the girlfriends' book club Thursday evening, that Phillip and Martha could not come to stay next weekend as planned and the whole family gather for dinner on Saturday night—and that Neddy must break this news to everyone.

"What'll I say, though?" he said after all this busy silence.

She shrugged and looked at him, made a motion of zipping her lips. *The boys will understand,* she wrote on the back of the calendar.

"It's not so much the boys I'm worried about," he said. "Does Martha even *know* about that stuff? You'll be really in the poo with her."

Phil might have to tell her, wrote Dawn. She sat back, looked at Ned levelly, sat forward again to write. *You know how important this is.* Her gaze fell from his eyes to the misshapen shoulder of his shirt.

"Don't muck me around, Dawnie," he said, very low, very hard. "We're both too old for that."

She put her hand on his, wishing he could feel her certainty. But he only looked terribly vulnerable, so sad and so old, her baby brother.

Well, he'd see, wouldn't he. She patted his hand, drank down her tea and got up from the table.

• • •

There'd been that one speaking glance. He'd cried out, as close to a human "No!" as a beak and swan-throat could shape; he had fallen back from her, and flung out his wings.

But Dawn had been exultant. Look at what she'd already done, her five brothers standing there! And Neddy was youngest and smallest, after all—perhaps the unfinished shirt would be enough. So she'd thrown it over him.

She had un-thrown it in her mind again and again over the years. It doesn't matter, the dream-crowd said, between cheers. With those other five handsome and whole, what do you need to prove? Finish it properly, girl; cast it then. The boy won't mind waiting, now that he sees you free. The boy can be a bird a while longer.

• • •

She knew exactly how much nettle to cut, for a sleeve. Ah, the smell of it! It was the smell of her youth, the smell of steadfast hope and solitude, out in the open, her urgency all the sharper for everything else idling, oblivious, around her—magpies gliding across the clear morning sky, rosellas flocking squeaking to a tree, Mason's cows tearing up grass beyond the fence there, a breeze flurrying the nettle-tops.

When she got back to the house, she found the old canvas wading-pool assembled, the hose lying in a couple of centimetres of water already, and Ned burrowing into the shed, bringing out boxes to make space to hunt deeper.

She sat by the pool, stripping the leaves off the nettle-stalks. One by one, the brothers who lived nearest came by to confer with

Ned, to speak to Dawn just to see for themselves that she wouldn't answer. Neville even hugged her, as if she were sick somehow. She acknowledged them but did not pause in her work, and Ned saw them off as quickly as he could, to dig some more in the shed. Her own children visited, bringing her grandchildren, and it was *very* hard not to speak to the little ones. Dawn smiled and kissed and hugged them, but signed that they must leave, that she was busy.

• • •

Seven children can create a world of their own, and a populous one. You can lose one brother to a job at the mines, another to the city or the next big town, and there are still plenty left. And each must get himself a wife, mustn't he? And breed up a storm of kids. Dawn had had her own four, two boys, two girls, so neat. What a whirl it had been, the babies, the schools, the sports, the get-togethers! This house had been the centre, of course; *she,* Dawn, had been the centre. If it hadn't been for her, they would all have been in the reeds raising cygnets, Gus liked to joke at a certain point in the evening. Not if Ned was around, of course. He wasn't totally heartless.

Neddy had had a wife, too, stringy little Adriane who must have thought she could do no better. He'd had a son, too, for a few weeks, born early but it had looked hopeful for a while there. Well, Dawn hadn't hoped; she'd known there was no point crossing her fingers for that one.

When the boy died, Neddy took it all on himself; he'd always been quiet, but his silence went denser, more complete. And all the wind went out of Adriane, too, as you'd expect. She looked around at them all, their houses and vehicles, recipes and hairdos, their kids running around reaching developmental milestones and bringing home trophies and yapping and crying. And the contrast must have been too much for her, just her and her flattened husband with the wing everyone pretended not to see, pretended didn't matter. All their unspoken pity finally got to her. She left, and Ned didn't go after her. She sent papers, and he signed and returned them. He sold their house and moved back in with Dawn, as her brothers always did when they visited, or were down on their luck.

• • •

Dawn spread the nettle stalks in the water in the early afternoon. Ned came out of the shed as she was pressing them down, the heddle from the loom in his hand. "Set her up in the lounge-room, I'm thinking."

She shook her head; he might need the lounge for hard-to-fend-off visitors. She led him instead to the lean-to at the back of the house, indicated with a wave that the two grandkids' beds could be stacked one on the other.

"You serious? You'll freeze out here!"

She took the heddle from him and propped it against the wall.

• • •

She must not have worked fast enough, all those six silent years. She had thought she could go no faster—she'd hardly had time to eat! Thin as a rail, she'd been; she didn't know how Jeff King had been able to see anything in that poor scrawny girl . . . But he had. Her mouth softened in a smile. Everyone smiled, memories of Jeff, but she most of all, of course. She'd had the best of him.

Right after the bird-business and everything coming right, her first period had started. She'd been sitting in a room full of girlfriends, butterfly cakes and laughter, talking nineteen to the dozen as she ran up her wedding dress, of creamy satin woven by some wonderful machine.

Your first? Cora had cried. *You lucky thing! I've been getting them for years, a week out of every month flat out on the couch with a hottie.*

Well, this has come just in time for Dawn and her hottie. Sylvie had grinned, pouring Saxa Salt thickly on the stain on the sewing-stool cushion.

Whip that skirt off, Dawn, said Jill. *Soak it in cold water. You got a belt and pads?*

Dawn had stared at her, mortally embarrassed by the whole business.

Of course she doesn't. Cora had snatched up her handbag. *I'll run down the chemist, shall I?*

Cora had gone through the change early, too, middle of her forties. The rest of them had pitied her then, but now they were all envious that she was done with it, the uncertainty, the insomnia, the dressing in layers—and the fear of old-hagdom, spilling at them like fog over the rim of the ranges. They joked loudly about it all the time, but that didn't make it go away.

• • •

In the night she went out, drained the pool and hosed down the stalks, filled the pool afresh. Even through the hose-plastic, even with gloves on, she felt the grab of the water. It took nothing from her, but oh, it wanted to. She paced around the filling pool, trailing clouds of white breath, and the blotched moon watched her, and she didn't speak a word to it, either.

• • •

Everything had been fast, crowded and noisy after the boys came back. *As soon as I have a minute*, she'd said to Neddy, *I'll sew up that last sleeve.*

No worries, sis, he'd said. *You've got a lot on your plate, haven't you?* He'd had a rare, slow smile that lit up the room. How long was it since she'd seen that smile? *And most of me's right, hey? I can manage one-armed for a bit.*

As soon as she and Jeff got back from Bateman's Bay she'd gone out to the gully and cut nettles, brought them home, stripped and retted and pounded them and spun. Queasy, she was, with the beginnings of her eldest, Charmaine. She had ploughed on, knowing in her heart that something important had gone from her, that her life was no longer quiet enough, or sad enough, to bring what was necessary to the weaving.

How embarrassed they'd been, she and Neddy, trying to fit the finished sleeve over the wing, cramming the feathers in, and neither feathers nor cloth firming up into flesh.

I don't understand, she'd said. *I never spoke a word to spoil it. I made it just the same as all the others.*

Neddy had put his hand on her shoulder. *Maybe they had to be made all of a piece, those shirts. It makes sense, sort of.* So anxious to ease her dismay, he'd been—and too young, then, to know how much he should mind for his own sake.

And he'd hidden the wing away in shirts with the sleeve turned inside out. He wouldn't let her sew up the armholes—he held out that much hope, at least. So just the shape of him reminded her, the shoulder too wide and too shallow, the back too rounded on one side, but no worse than that scoliosis that all Dennis's kids were born with. The wing edge curved down his side and into the back of his pants. All that his nieces and nephews knew was that Uncle Ned didn't go swimming. He'd lost his arm in a threshing machine, was the story the grown-ups spun them. *Don't ask him about it. And don't stare.*

. . .

All through the days of retting she maintained her silence, kept to it as if the old rule still applied, that Ned would die if she spoke. Cleaning and spinning the fibres, she never so much as hummed a tune to herself. The telephone rang, and if Ned was out she didn't answer it; the doorknocker sounded, and she sat motionless until the person went away, or if they were one of her blustering family and came around the back, wanting her to chat, wanting her usual noise, she sent them packing with a note.

Ned sometimes stood at the lean-to door, watching the sleeve creep into being. Everything he wasn't saying pressed against the back of her neck, but she didn't shoo him away. He had a right, didn't he, to watch and worry and hope there? Besides, she was more than occupied with her work, with the thread that was being spun from her and laid down in the fabric with the back and forth of the shuttle. She didn't remember this feeling from before, of being *expended* this way, from some deep store.

She measured the sleeve length, then went out to find Ned. He was on the front veranda reading the Saturday paper, pretending to be interested in the doings of the world. She knelt beside him and pressed the metal end into his armpit where his shirt seams crossed. Her thumbnail on the tape lay halfway down his shirt cuff. "Nearly there, eh?" he said softly.

She went back to the lean-to, wove, measured again and began the shaping; it all came back to her across the decades. She was that girl again, determined, lonely, with the whole town against her, in the dark before the day when everything would crash and burn for her. This flow through her fingers was all she had, its sureness, its grace, its knowledge of the shape and size of each brother's body.

She passed the shuttle through for the last time and snipped the thread. She took the piece from the loom and sewed in the hem of the cuff, left the threads loose at the armhole end, took fresh thread and sewed the inside seam from cuff to armpit. And then it was completed, as grey as clouds, as soft as smoke.

As she sat with it across her lap, a car came along the road, and she raised her head to listen. Yes, it was slowing, and turning in on the gravel at her gate. She stood up and took the sleeve through the house, impatient for an end to this, ready to speak now, to come back to life; she hoped the visitor wasn't some stranger who would require hiding from.

She pushed the screen door open; the low autumn sun gleamed on the veranda boards. Ned was out of his chair. "It's Phillip," he said, but she had seen that. "They've come anyway, when I asked them not to. Shall I tell him to—"

He saw the sleeve and stopped. She gestured that he should take off his shirt. "Here? Now?" She nodded. Warily he pulled the shirt-tails free of his trousers.

Phillip killed the engine as Ned undid the first button. Car doors opened. "Aunty Dawn, Aunty Dawn! Uncle Neddy!" cried the kids strapped into the back seat. Said Phillip, "No, you stay *right there*, Nathan."

Dawn hadn't seen the wing in years, but it was exactly as she remembered it. That corner of Ned flowed seamlessly from man to bird. The first feathers were hardly more than glitters in his skin; the muscle and bone adjusted millimetre by millimetre as human chest gave way to feathered wing. Young Nathan, running from the car, stopped on the frost-burnt lawn to stare. Dawn stared herself, and Phillip and Martha stared, at the reality of Ned that he alone had lived with all these years, binding his secret to his side to protect them all from the sight, from the impossible sight.

He cast a glance of dismay and shame across his nephew, his brother, his sister-in-law, the other children open-mouthed in the car. Tears stood in his eyes as he turned from them, jabbing the wingtip at Dawn; feather whispered on feather, and the trailing edge rustled.

"Come on, Dawnie," he said. "Make this right for me."

She threw the sleeve over the wing as she'd thrown all those shirts years before, wildly, almost carelessly, the crowd silenced around her. It filled with air as it flew in the sunlight; it landed and sank away into the shining dark feathers. She had known it would. The loose threads of the armhole knitted inside him, rippling the feather-sketched flesh of his shoulder. When they were done, this arm would plump out to match the other one.

She looked to Ned's face, to reassure him or to be reassured herself. One of his tears fell, but the emotion behind it had passed;

he was busy now with all the changes being worked on him.

They amazed him, those changes. He lifted his slow smile to Dawn. His eyes were bright blood-stained gold, with pinprick pupils.

"Oh, Neddy! But I didn't mean—"

"It's all right, it's all *right,* honestly—" And then words were beyond him to form, as his mouth reddened, flattened, lengthened out of his face. Black feathers sprang flat across his cheeks, fanned out on his forehead, and in the next moment he was wholly swan, a cob the size of a man, wings out, grey webbed feet paddling above the sunny veranda-boards, the shoulder-mass of him sunk and spread into the shining belly, the long black neck kinked to keep his elegant head clear of the veranda-rafters. Martha exclaimed, but Dawn had no voice to spare; hands to her cheeks, she only gasped in the air that the vast wings huffed her way.

The change complete, Ned shrank to swan size. He fitted his wings in against his feathery body, and the *cosiness* of that, the tidy self-satisfaction, turned Dawn's next gasp into a hoot of laughter. From the car came the tiny voice of her niece: "Wow, Uncle Neddy turned into a *bird,* Daniel! Did you *see?*"

The swan lumbered to the edge of the veranda. It spread its wings, tipped out over the flowerbed, and after brushing the lawn grass with its breast-feathers, rose over a quailing Nathan, and Phillip who flung up his arms, and began a great circle out along the drive, over the fields and cows, the sheds, the dam, the stands of gum-trees with their loose heads of leaves.

Dawn went down the steps to the grass. Nathan ran up and clung to her, and she held him at her side while the long-necked bird passed trumpeting over the house and the lawn again, and began another circle.

"Can you change him back?" said the boy.

"I don't know, Nathan." The three little ones were out of the car now, and all seven faces swung as one to follow the swan's flight. "Do you think he wants to be changed back?"

"Yeah," said Phillip, "would *you* want to be a person again, if you could do that?"

Martha turned, baby Daniel in her arms. Phillip's head was tilted back to watch the swan fly over. But Dawn saw the look his wife gave him, and the shock in Martha's face, the betrayal, pierced her to the very heart.

HELL IS WHERE THE HEART IS

JANEEN WEBB

Tell me who invented the human heart. Tell me, and show me where he was hanged.

—LAWRENCE DURRELL

The man in the immaculate Saville Row suit was talking at her, his words spilling across his polished desk in her direction. Each phrase held some new horror, the deep-down visceral gut-wrenching *personal* horror of words like terminal, and transplant, and urgent. She felt paralysed, trying desperately to focus through the shock. His lips moved again: "Mrs Hardcastle, Penelope, would you like someone with you through the rest of this consultation. It often helps. Is that your husband in the waiting room?"

Penny nodded, numbly. The surgeon patted her shoulder encouragingly as he stood, moving past her to speak softly to his secretary. Penny was not encouraged. She stared through the window at the park below, where other people were going about their lives. She barely noticed when John, his face frowning deep with concern, eased into the seat beside her and took her cold hand in his.

The surgeon went on, his composed, professional voice grating on her nerves. "I believe in being honest upfront about these things. In the long run, false hope is much more damaging than plain truth. And I believe these final tests I'm ordering will confirm my opinion that Penelope's situation is dangerous. All the indicators tell me she will almost certainly need a heart transplant in the very near future if she is to survive."

"How soon," said John. His voice was hoarse with worry. "How long have we got?"

"There's never an exact answer. But we are talking weeks, not months. I want to re-admit Penelope into the hospital as quickly as possible. It is absolutely essential that the heart is monitored constantly, and that the patient is rested and fully prepared for the procedure as soon as a suitable donor organ becomes available."

The conversation went on, the surgeon drawing diagrams and explaining procedures, roughly sketching out incision lines and insertion points on office notepaper. The consulting room smelled of disinfectant, and soap. Penny was trying hard to concentrate. She felt as though the men were discussing a technical problem, a problem in pipes and valves that happened to need replacing. Not Penny. Not her body.

Her husband was speaking again: "Forgive my asking, but how many of these transplants have you done?"

The surgeon spread his hands wide. "You don't want to know how many," he said wearily. "I lost count a long while back. By all means seek a third opinion. All I can do is assure you that this is routine surgery for me. There are never any guarantees."

John shrugged. "For you, this happens every day. For us, it's new territory. It's traumatic. We need to understand what is happening here."

"Of course. And there will be a whole support team looking after Penelope. I'm just the first step in the process. I'll give you some literature, put you in contact with our special psychologist, make sure you both have a chance to meet the rest of the surgical team. The safety net is there for you both, and for your family, John. You won't be alone."

They rose, shook hands. The surgeon said: "Let me know what you decide. If there's something you want to go over, any point you need clarified, just call."

He walked them to the door.

Despite John's comforting arm about her shoulders, as they left the consulting suite Penny felt very, very alone.

• • •

When she awoke in her narrow hospital bed, the world seemed far away. She seemed to have been transformed into some strange fleshly machine, a machine whose purpose was unclear. There were wiggly green lines on a monitor screen whose pulsing lights confirmed her existence. The machine hummed gently, its needs fed by the tubes that snaked in and out of her body at various points, monitoring vital signs, carrying blood and saline and God-knew-what else.

A tired-looking man came softly into the room, sat himself down wearily beside her bed, gently took her cold fingers in his warm hand, careful not to disturb the taped needle that dripped measured painkillers into her veins. His creased face looked slept-in, as rumpled as his suit. With him were two pale children, radiating anxiety. The girl clutched a drooping bunch of flowers from the downstairs charity shop.

"It's me, Penny. John. Your husband. Will and Emma are here. Your children. Can you hear me?"

She nodded, lifting her head a fraction from the pillow.

He squeezed her fingers. "Look. Emma has brought you flowers. She'll pop them into a vase for you."

Emma fiddled with the blooms, obviously glad of something to do.

"Mother sends her love." John turned away briefly, depositing a plastic bag in the closet. "Your clean pyjamas are in there, if the nurse asks."

His monologue dragged to a halt when Penny did not respond. John's need of her was clear as he gently buried his face in her dark hair, hiding his tears from his children. He sniffed, blew his nose, then kissed her lightly on the forehead.

Penny managed a weak smile. "Don't worry," she said. "I'll be alright."

She lapsed back into her drugged doze after the effort of acknowledging her visitors. She knew them, of course, but it didn't feel right.

The feeling still wasn't right when she finally returned home.

The new heart did not make that little skip the old one always had when John took her in his arms.

She wept her frustration, feeling miserable and disconnected.

John was patient. "You've been through a huge trauma, love," he would say. "Let's just give it time."

So she let him love her, feeling warmth, appreciation, sympathy, and companionship when he was with her, sometimes even desire.

But not love. The new heart did not love him, no matter how much she willed it.

It was months before she realized it loved someone else. Someone she didn't know. Someone she'd never even met.

And it meant to have him back.

• • •

After a dreary convalescence, the day came when Penny returned, thankfully, to her job at the bank. The tedium of customers worrying about their small holdings seemed like bliss after her boredom at home.

On Friday afternoon her friend Cassie caught up with her in the tea room. "Come on Penny. Let me take you for drink. We'll celebrate your release back into the world. Everyone shows up on Friday, and they'll all want to catch up with you."

Penny hesitated, twisting her scarf in her fingers. "I don't know that I'm ready for crowds."

"Nonsense. We'll just go for one drink. The *Heartache*'s just next door, after all. It's not as if you have to go out of your way or anything."

"John will worry if I'm late."

"So phone him. Leave a message. He'll understand."

"Okay. But just one drink."

"Great. I'll meet you in the foyer at five."

• • •

They rode up in the elevator with a chattering group of colleagues to the top floor of the plush *Intercontinental Hotel*, where the *Heartache* bar was popular with city employees. Throughout the week the sleek cocktail lounge furnishings and spectacular view over the city made it a favourite pickup spot for the well-heeled and terminally single. But on Friday nights Happy Hour was thronged with black-suited bankers and insurance executives swapping stories of this week's ups and downs, exchanging hot tips and office gossip. The five o'clock rush to nowhere.

Penny was enjoying herself. She was the centre of curious attention. She was ordering her second glass of Riesling when Cassie tapped her on the arm.

"Don't look now," said Cassie, "but we're being stalked by the head-office wolf."

"Who?"

"Grant Simpson. Hot-shot broker. Corporate Accounts. Private clients. Thinks he's God's to gift women." She giggled. "The women he dates mostly want to give him back! A new girl for every party—no-one sticks around long enough to go out with him twice."

"Is he really that awful?"

"Worse, now that his wife died. Poor Anne, she adored him. God knows why. He cheated on her every chance he got. He was always on the prowl. She didn't deserve to be treated like that, and now she's dead. And," she added significantly, "he was driving."

"Car accident?"

"Intersection smash. The passenger side was hit. Anne was killed outright. Broken neck. He walked away without a scratch. There's no justice in the world."

"You'd think he'd die of guilt."

"Fat chance. Brace yourself, Penny, here he comes."

The man closing in on them was stylishly, fastidiously turned out. A wolf in wolf's clothing: suit by Armani, hand-made snowy fine linen shirt set off by a Hermes dark patterned silk tie, shoes by Gucci. He was a real fashion plate. His thinning, sandy-blonde hair was cut boyishly short, parted on one side so that its ends flopped deliberately over his forehead to set off his ice-blue eyes. He should have been handsome, but the effect was too calculated to be convincing. His open features were overlaid with complacency, a sneering self-regard that Penny loathed at first sight.

The heart skipped a beat.

His advance was downright predatory. Penny felt frozen, trapped in the headlights of his intense regard as he moved in on her.

The heart was beating faster.

"Hi Cassie. How's business with the middle classes? Who's your lovely friend?"

Penny tucked her corporate-logo scarf tighter about her neck, suddenly self-conscious about her surgical scars.

"Hello Grant. This is Penny. She's married."

Penny smiled weakly.

"Grant Simpson. Pleased to meet you." He was standing too close, his Poison after-shave using up all the oxygen. He held out his hand, shook hers for a beat longer than protocol permitted, smiling engagingly.

Penny looked down, flushing slightly. She noticed the engraved initials on the stylish Dunhill cigarette case and lighter he'd placed carefully on the bar.

"That's nice. What's the U stand for? Unusual?"

He sighed, dramatically. "Everyone asks that. Might as well get it over. My father was a Civil War buff, and with Simpson for a surname, he just couldn't resist naming his son for his hero. Read it with an imaginary comma: Grant, Ulysses S. It was hell at school, but I learned to fight real quick. Respect through skinned knuckles, grudge matches, and long hours in the gym." He posed for her. "Anyway, I think of myself as more the original Ulysses type, always up for a new adventure." He leaned closer. "And my best friends call me Gus."

Penny smiled again, finding it suddenly difficult to breathe in the thickening atmosphere.

"Gus. We had a tomcat called Gus once—short for Asparagus. The most exotic name the kids could think of at the time."

He swallowed hard at the implied comparison, recovered immediately to say, "You have children then?"

"Two. A boy and a girl. Teenagers now."

"Charming." He lowered his voice. "You look like you could use some air. What say we go somewhere quieter . . . "

Penny looked around quickly for her friend. "Sorry, Gus. Cassie, we have to run. I promised I'd be back by seven," she said brightly. She took Cassie by the arm and steered her firmly in the direction of the door. "I can't believe I was flirting with that creep!" she said.

"How much wine have you had?"

"Just the one glass." Penny blushed. The heart was still racing. "Is he really as bad as the gossips say?"

"He's worse. Heartless. I used to find Anne sobbing her heart out in the Ladies. She really loved the bastard, and he treated her like dirt."

Penny sighed, willing her heartbeat to slow to a calmer rate.

The ride home was uneventful.

• • •

Next Monday morning when she arrived at the office there was a single red rose on her desk, with a card bearing one word—Friday.

Penny spent the rest of the week in an agony of indecision, listening to the argument between her head and her heart. Her mind rehearsed the overwhelming evidence against anything so foolish as a comfortably married woman getting involved with another man, especially one who was everything she despised, especially one who was already the mainstay of city gossip. The heart did not listen. It just felt warm at the thought of him.

The heart won.

Next Friday, she was in the *Heartache* bar at five past five. He was totally self-possessed as he strolled over to where she sat fiddling with her drink, took her hand, and bent to whisper, "Let's get out of here."

She did not resist.

His apartment was close by, one of those new inner-city warehouse conversions where mellow old timbers clashed horribly with brushed stainless steel fittings and too-bright feature walls. Very trendy. Everything was in its place, neat and cold and closed up tight.

"Come in," he said. "Champagne's on ice."

His arrogance was breathtaking in its casual presumption. He moved to kiss her, and Penny felt suddenly like meat being steered towards a marble slab.

The heart skipped a beat.

"I can't," she said.

"Of course you can. That's why you're here."

Her throat constricted. She could only nod her assent.

He peeled away her clothing, obviously fascinated by her scars. He ran his tongue down the purplish-red length of the long gash that started at her breastbone, tracing the slightly raised welt of the healing tissue. "It's weird, this transplant stuff. How does it feel, having part of someone else inside you?" He grinned at his rehearsed *double entendre*. "Apart from the usual, of course."

"It's just a muscle, Gus. Nothing more. The surgeons are wonderful technicians, but that's all it is. A spare parts replacement service."

He reached for her, pulling her down upon the bed.

Penny closed her eyes, her heart beating wildly at his embrace.

He was an expert lover, though what surfaced of Penny's mind regarded him as a bit too clinical. He focussed on his technique, turning her this way and that, putting himself through his paces, bringing her to an aching climax beneath him. It was soon finished.

They sprawled in the rumpled sheets, sated. His pillow talk was desultory, almost bored. Penny caught him sneaking a look at his watch.

She rose, collected her clothes, headed for the bathroom. There were fresh towels laid out. Confident bastard.

When she returned, he had dressed in jeans and a fresh shirt, ready to go.

He grinned at her. "Well, that was fun. Where would you like me to drop you? Home? Back at the bar?"

"No thanks. I'll make my own way home from here. It will look less obvious."

He laughed. "Maybe."

She moved closer to him, reached to kiss him. "Until next Friday, then?"

His smiled vanished. "No. Of course not. You can't imagine we'd want some kind of involvement, Penny. One to a customer, that's me. It's not as if we were in love or anything. We're just two consenting adults, having a bit of mutual fun. End of story."

He paused, considering. "Truth is, I just wanted to try it with a transplant person, that's all. I'm sorry if you imagined it was something more. I thought you'd feel the same about me—novelty value."

Penny could not prevent the tears that welled up, reddening her dark eyes. She fished a crumpled tissue out of her blazer pocket and dabbed at her nose. The heart was beating wildly.

"No," she said. "I didn't realize. I should have."

His eyes were colder now. "Oh stop it, for godsakes," he said. "You're not hurt. You remind me of my wife. She was one of your bleeding-heart organ donor types—always going on about the greater good and social responsibility and all that. There must still be bits of her around everywhere—cornea, kidneys, lungs, heart . . . "

Penny felt a chill feather up her spine.

"When did she die," she said.

"Last April. Why?"

"What date, Gus?" Penny's mouth was dry, the words an effort.

"What does it matter?"

"It matters. What *date*?"

"April 9th. Why? What's so important?"

"The date of my transplant, that's what."

The heart was beating erratically now.

Incredibly, Gus was laughing. "Well I'll be damned. This is great. Two women at once." He tapped her chest. "Hello in there, Annie. Did you miss me?"

Penny pulled away, appalled. "We don't know for certain, Gus. It could just be coincidence. It just freaked me out, you know?"

"Well, coincidence or not it's a hell of a trip!"

Penny grabbed her bag, bolted for the door, slammed it after her. She hailed the first cab she could find, and collapsed into the back seat, crying hysterically, her heart beating a-rhythmically now.

"You alright, love?" The taxi driver sounded concerned.

Penny managed a strangled answer, "Fine, really. Just had a bit of a shock. I'll be alright soon."

By the time she reached home she'd dried her tears, but the heart still hurt, and there was an ominous tightening in her chest. She paid the driver, walked unsteadily to her front door. Emma opened it.

"Mum, you look awful!"

"Thanks. I'll just lie down for a while. I'll be okay. A difficult day, that's all."

Emma looked doubtful, but left to make her a cup of tea. When she returned, Penny was curled up in pain, clutching her chest.

"I've taken my pills," she said. "They don't help. Call the emergency contact number for me, Emma. I think I'm going to need the hospital."

Emma dashed for the phone.

• • •

Penny was much worse by the time she was wheeled into the hospital. Her surgeon was there, his expression concerned. His diagnosis was instant.

"Rejection. Let's move, everyone—she hasn't got much time."

Rejection. The word resonated in Penny's mind as a needle slid into a vein, and she lost her last, tenuous hold on consciousness.

She did not re-awaken. Ever.

• • •

Upstairs, in Recovery, Calypso Jones was drifting into post-operative awareness.

Her new heart felt all wrong, somehow.

BOWFIN ISLAND

ANNA TAMBOUR

5 Nov, Fri

"sublime but commanding! poss see me immed" Hear texted, possibly trying to warn me off because he followed that immed w "poss prefer gdd tour italy?" I seriously don't think he meant the 'commanding' to be a come-on.

When I found him yesterday, he said that what I asked for was impossible. Something about the locals mustn't be after the tourist pound, and there's only one possible place to stay there anyway, and it's only got one room, and it's booked years ahead, and it costs more per night than a sensible person would . . . No reasonable person would . . . besides, there are plenty more places in the North Sea, and why not pick someplace warm and sunny anyway blahblahblaaa.

He's an odd duck, so out for my safety that it's a wonder he doesn't try to sell me a tour of my flat so I don't run the risk of leaving home. But he knows what he knows. I found him in the outer reaches of the Web, almost like he didn't really want to be seen, let alone be an agent. Hear Outer The Way Travel. But then, most clients have web presences before I work on them, that look like they don't want to be seen.

Someone was literally watching my back when I repld YS! NO! B thr! Then I might have screwed up someone's web page, working on two at once, Margate Council's Incontinence Support site & the Smoking Bum Cigar Lounge. I was THAT anxious the opportunity wouldn't slip away before I could seize it on my lunch break.

Luckily, Hear was only a block away, though my bum still hurts from slipping in the rain. That rain must have stopped anyone else coming. He was all alone. I don't know what people are coming to these days. A drop of precipitation, a bit of wind, and they're all inside, only giving their thumbs exercise.

He raised a hand and nodded and motioned me to the chair, but it was a full 2 minutes of anxious waiting for me, while he worked away on his keyboard. I would have said something, but my little mistake of adding Man About Town gents cotton protective pants with concealed waterproof liner to the menu list of the Smoking Bum and pasting the Hoyo De Monterrey Epicure #2 in the Council's IS Bladder and Bowel links stayed my tongue.

Finally he finished and frowned at me. He looked like Mum whenever she saw that I was going out to play. Where's your nicky-tams, she'd say. She never understood why a string tied around your leg just under the knee won't keep your trousers out of the mud. And when in uni, I bought cycling clips, she was downright obnoxious with her Oh now, Mister size 11 boots. You see that I've been right all along but too proud you are, to admit it! and her raised eyebrows and teeth clicks at the extravagances of those clips, followed by two sentences: How long d'you expect your money to last? As long as a piece of string?

I never got a chance, nor did I try to say that my pair of Ice Toolz Plastic Trouser Clips with reflective Scotchlite Strip was only £3.50. *Only*, she would have said, like a gust of wind fit to king-hit the chimney—for my lashout of £3.50 was 100 times, no, an infinity of multiples of what two pieces of string cost, since she even washed and saved the string that held the paper on fish-wrapping.

All my personality comes from Dad, so how could either of us feel guilty for, after she died, throwing away without discussion, her most treasured possession, the framed wallpiece that her gran had embroidered back in prehistory—I can see Great Gran now, embroidering with one hand while with the other, she is darning with cord that lasts, the toes of socks, all the while not letting her feet be idle, those that whip up stinking mounds of neeps and tatties that are, of course, not meant to be eaten for pleasure.

'Caution will seldom guide ye wrang' said the thing on the wall. I never did understand my parents' marriage. I did see Mum's mother once, and she was the opposite of what Mum's gran must have been. She wore more makeup than the Harlequeens who played the pub down the street when I was so young that I thought them beautiful, in a scary way. She had the kind of voice those men were trying to ditch. If you closed your eyes, however, the huskiness did have a certain 40s Lauren Bacallishness to it. The fag hanging off her lip didn't. Mum didn't approve of her, and she conveniently died suddenly of some complication, I think a truck.

So this agent had that look on his face, that *Mum* look. Then he added, "Dreams don't make good trips, but bad trips last forever. It is my professional responsibility to advise you against peradventure."

I hadn't noticed before, but he even sounds like Mum, and on his desk is one of those tourist plaques, probably made in China, but he must have bought it because it flattered his ego, "There's nane sae deaf as them that winna hear."

Without turning around, he pointed to the poster behind him. "Mr Hear," I said, "I must be back to work soon, so please, no games. Don't let anyone Scotch ye might mean something to you, but it's beans to me."

"T'other," he said, jabbing his thumb back to the left.

"See Skye afore ye Die"? Not worth reply.

Then he put his hands on something on his desk that he turned my way: a garish tabloid brochure fronted by a group of t-shirted girls looking ready to shag anything.

I stood up and took off my anorak. Now, staring at him from my t-shirt were the words, 'Twitch and Tick'.

"Bowfin," I said.

"A penny saved—"

"Is a 500th of a cup of coffee," I said. "Now Bowfin. Or Mars."

"All that money," he said, as if my spending it would hurt him. There was something positively Calvinistic about the douchebag. He was, in short, getting on my tits.

"A young man like you should be saving for—"

"There's nae poackits in a shroud!"

He smiled grimly. "Single?"

"Of course."

"Then," he said, "I can offer you from Friday the seventh, three days at Puddock House."

Whoa! That, as this diary shows, is only 2 days away.

"Only because of a cancellation due to premature death. It'll be filled—"

"Book it!"

"It'll cost—"

"Book it!" I screamed. My thumbs tingled with intended tweets: eat yr hrts out! Bowfin Is! Try 2 find on map! 1 Siberian Chiffchaff

I was fucked if I was going to miss this chance. I'd already stuffed the opportunity of going to Sula Sgeir back in May and possibly sighting the Red-necked Phalarope, and I lost my lunch one hot day in June when Geoff Pingly tweeted: South Uist flck of 127 btG.

NO ONE is gonna get between me and the possibilities on Bowfin Island. That place that I'd never heard of before Hear, but couldn't miss once I knew. Sure, he's a pain in the arse): but isn't that why good destinations, like good travel agents, are well-kept secrets:)

Not but he's weird! And here's the strangest part of that strange encounter, the thing that stopped him trying to put me off. My comeback. "There's nae poackits in a shroud."

Hell if I know where that came from. It was like, coming from someone inside me, someone I've never met let alone listened to. I might as well have been speaking in voices. But then it's the same when I'm writing code. My programming skills always seem to come from some unknown computer inside me. It's a crowded house in there.

I shouldn't complain. Hear's insides might be filled with caution-preaching vicars yearning to be mums—but inside me, I've got, atop the bank of supercomputers, some yelling hairy Scotsman with a wild sense of adventure that matches mine, and hey—he's human!

Meanwhile, at work:

The office has an automatic dobber-in on every galley-slave's chair that counts the seconds that a bum isn't pressing on it, working. You might as well have electrodes wired to your skull. Pressure pads sense just which muscles are tensing up, so the system aces the status quo, plain vanilla CCTV in all its costs. No one has to watch this. You just get shocked if you're deviating, and it's nothing light. After a treatment of this, a man's balls feel like cold falafels. And the system feels wetness just as well, so

Felicity Quimper, after her alarm went off for jumping out of her chair, went out and got a supersize Hot & Sour Soup that she took back to work and threw into the little room filled with servers. Defending herself later, she supposedly said that she thought it was an invasion of her privacy to be shocked for having thoughts. Her defence would have only cost her more money, what could she expect? She had committed thoughts during work hours.

I don't know why I wrote all that down. Maybe just for vanity. Will my next place of work be hopelessly behind the times technologically? Fat chance. The only thing that stays the same is that progress just changes the way slaves are punished. But then, that's in the office. One thing I love about twitching is that we tick off our subjects. We're in control. And there's not a damn thing the birds can do about it. They exist, so that we tick. Off hours.

During work hours, struggling is as effective as a wren caught in a net. Order me around, I say. Just pay me heaps. I'm lucky that I can work with my brain tied behind my back. I'm so good at my work that I skill up without having to work at it. If only it weren't all so BORING! I do suffer from interminable terminal boredom. But isn't that the scent of an office? Oh de ZZZ. Not that my smell is like the other galley-slaves who pong of fear, justifiably scared as rabbits in a fox coven. They're all so eminently imminently expendable. Not me. It must be my competence. Always ooze confidence! It would be nice though, to sit in a workchair and merely be passively observed ruining sight and spine and any sense of being human.

Anyway, I got back an hour late and tossed a hot moist bag already looking like it was made of waxed paper into Cooper's lap. THAT stopped him mid-yell, momentarily. He shouldn't complain. He loves samosas. Then I ignored the galley-slave corpsicles cracking their neck bones as they tried to watch yet keep their glute maxes and all their other little bum glutes absolutely dutiful . . . while I cleared out my desk and left, warbling over the alarm as effectively as a Hume's Leaf W trying to best a screaming plover.

The pay there was as usual, more than I'd put in a bank. And somehow I don't think I'll get a rec fr there. And I just spent my savings on the trip. But we're only alive once, some of us. The rest aren't alive at all.

As for those who are working without pay, Great Gran, since

you must be hard at it making yourself useful up there in your unheated heaven, here's a job to get on with:

Embroider it in red.

Every job's shite.

And since you must have a carpenter up there, too, please get it framed. Ta! And tally-ho, if you're looking, Mum!

6 Nov Sat

Exhausted already. 6AM London to Glasgow flight inexcusably delayed 5! NOTE FIVE hours by snowstorm somewhere. No snowstorm in London. No one fed us anything while we waited, the plane food was an insult, and the rest of the trip so far is a blur. It's 3am, and I'm supposed to be trying to sleep in a freezing cottage built of stone and romantically roofed with straw, like some effing fairytale. My head feels like a pummelled steak from the interminable howling wind.

I got here by degrees. A ferry to one island, then a wait with no time given to when some boat would take me to the next place, so I couldn't get anything to eat or have a decent crap, but three hours of that and the ferry pitched up, only something that took me to the next island. I thought it was someplace named Muck, but I think I thought that because I read some funny article about the Laird of Muck. Anyway, wherever it was, was just a stop along the way. Someone met me yet again, don't ask me how they knew. And then I was taken on a fishing boat to this place.

This journal smells of chunder. The fishing boat rolled like half a lemon in a punchbowl. I was the only passenger, said the captain. Yes, he called himself the captain. He tried to make the journey pleasant, plying me with slices of white bread. I tossed each overboard when he wasn't looking. Couldn't keep anything down, even though there was hardly anything in my stomach.

This journal makes me gag now. I shouldn't have tried to write in it on that tub, but I had to keep my head down, couldn't look at the flipping horizon. Cleaned up what I could then with the only thing I had, the sleeve of my anorak. The captain was bloody useless. He offered to toss buckets of water over me, and kept saying, "You're bowfin." I know I'm going there and so does he, but it's a bit rich, him treating me like luggage. I had to tell him to fuck off. The journal's been washed by rain since, and some of the pages are stuck together, but I can't throw it away, not after all I've put in it! When I get to Puddock House, will tell them to desanitise it somehow. With what I've paid, they should have a slave who could lick it clean. Part of the big adventure!

Somehow, just writing this makes me feel better. Can hardly feel fingers, it's so cold here. Light is from candle stub, must go.

7 Nov Sun

I hate boats.

8 Nov Mon

IOAM

The worst trip I've ever had ended last night when I was rowed to a beach the size of a g-string, and left. I didn't know how long I'd be waiting there in the pitch black with only the sound of waves to keep me company, but was vomiting too much to demand an answer. Finally, a few minutes or an hour later, someone came. I expected, for the money I've shelled out and the exclusivity, a porter who'd also climbed Everest and cowed everyone with his yachting skills at Cowes. He would, of course, carry me to Puddock House and deliver me to the tender attentions of my personal butler, who would have my bath ready. God, I stunk, and never want to see a slice of white bread again. Even the thought of white bread makes me retch.

Puddock House!

It's no old manorhouse. It's just a stone cottage, no bigger than a cell that someone would get housed in if he broke into a convenience store.

Its heat is a fireplace.

Bath: tin tub.

Cold water, or water from sleeve in Aga cooker.

At least that's what Macman says.

I thought that Agas were only decoratively archaic, like gas fires with ceramic logs.

He says this one needs fuel, and there isn't any I can see. There is in place of a basket of coal or logs, a basket with clumps of dirt.

This place should be called Siberia's Siberia.

Macman is a scream, if only I were warm, fed, clean, and watching him on a screen.

He's full of stories. Here's one:

It's said, he said, *There's nae poackits in a shroud*, so that is why every man on Bowfin Island was buried with his everyday clothes on, even if they are bloody, torn to buggery, or mockit in the crotch as would give you the dry boak.

Oddly enough, I understand him, even to the dry boak. And it's eerie that he used that line about the shroud. He couldn't be taking the piss out of me, but I do suspect that he used it because he heard that I had when explaining my extravagance to the first captain on this journey. Nosey parkers, they're all fascinated by everything about me. So along with me, the saying has been passed on along the line of people I've had to interact with.

I must make do with the man. He's all I've got. Besides, if I pause to think anything less than good of him, I don't think I'll be able to last until tomorrow. This place is

9 Nov Tue
10 AM

First the good. There are birds here that I wouldn't have believed, even in my wildest. The place is a bloody twitcher's paradise. Yesterday as I was writing this, a Siberian chiffchaff flew into a bush not three yards away. I stress here that this was not a 'possible Siberian Chiffchaff'. It didn't call. Grey and olive above, it had a very Siberian-like head pattern. It was, I stress, no straightforward collybita. Definitely not the common. It also has quite a lot of yellow across the breast. It was also unbanded! I would say with certainty that it was a definite sighting. Of course I dropped this journal, and I was trembling as I dug in my pack for my virgin Outer Hebrides Bird Checklist. It wasn't there! Bugger! I must have left it home. There was nothing for it. I would have to make one up in the journal. An annoyance, but that was only the lead up to the main show! Imagine how prophetic my imagined tweet had been: *eat yr hrts out! Bowfin Is! Try find on map! 1 Siberian Chiffchaff*

I don't think I've ever been so excited, so I fumbled reaching back into my pocket, and had to stand up. By then with all the commotion, the bird had long ago flown off, but it had served its purpose. Anyway, my phone wasn't in my back pocket, but then I remembered that I'd put it in my anorak, but it wasn't there. It wasn't in my pack. I ran back to the hovel and it wasn't effing

ANYWHERE. Macman was peeling potatoes and I asked to use his, but he said, What phone?

NO PHONE! For the whole time I'll be here. And here I just had the best sighting of my life, and it's gone to waste!

I wanted to choke Macman, but instead, I must be civil. It's torture, but he heated the water and washed my clothes and wiped my anorak down and made a pretty good stew, and—unbelievable, but it's true, sleeps in Puddock House too, on the other side of the room, a hellish blessing. More about 'Puddock House' later.

The torture continued. I went outside to cool off, and as soon as I got there, a male Dotterel pitched up. Then a female Ring Ouzel teased me, and flew off. A Ring Ouzel! Here! I was so upset that I tromped off and within five minutes, saw a spectacular pair of geese, as unbanded as everything here. I felt a sense of choking, I was so excited. But I didn't know for sure. If this was a pair of Bean Geese, that means that I was the first person to sight one south of North Uist in 20 years. But I had to check. It would be awful if I twitched Bean and they were, say, Richardson's Canadians, which sounds ridiculous but all of a sudden I was uncertain about everything. It was all so extreme!

So I dug out my Birds of Scotland, only to find—an apple. That's it. An apple. Oh, and The Source, my waterproof-covered journal where I store my passwords and a lot of code I've written. It's my stone-age backup, the only place I trust to keep these things safe, and now I remember. I took it with me so that if my flat is broken into, no one steals it. And here it was, able to slip out of my pack. I could have lost it at sea along with my phone while I was spewing my guts out over the side, or when I was shitting over the side (did you know that small fishing boats don't have loos? It should be illegal).

So HERE I AM. i cant twitch, i cant tweet. i might as well have stayed at work for all the good this crazy waste of time has been.

Tomorrow can't come soon enough. I dread the return trip, but soon it'll be history. In the meantime

2PM

Macman is useless. I told him that he didn't wash my stuff enough. They stink. He said, *You're* bowfin.

I had to walk away, because I couldn't afford giving him my mind. He's unbalanced enough. Still, I was fuming. He had no excuse, treating me like luggage. I mean, on that boat, the 'captain' had a bit of one, and I can even laugh now at the image of someone like him getting laid out as a mattress for telling a passenger "You're LAX."

But say there's another explanation, some New Age slop—"Be one with Bowfin. Om." I reckon Macman will spout that on the day he takes to dreadlocking his ear tufts. So he's not only useless but inscrutably mad.

Still, I can't get the smell out of my nostrils. A mix of vomit and something sweet, that kind of sweet of something dead. Nightmare sweet. I can't get it out of my nose.

3PM

Darkness is coming soon. I finally got Macman's name. It's Peasgood. I don't know the spelling, but it's Mr Peasgood. And he's got a sort of sense of humour. Remember what I told you, he said, when he saw me trying to scrape away the smell from my bare arms. He led me to an area where he said the smell came from, a very stony place where he repeated his story of the inhabitants having been buried with their clothes on. The ground was practically all stone with a covering as thick as an op-shop's Oriental carpet. He picked up something and told me to open my hand. It was, he said, a vertebra. !!!!!

The smell he said, comes from all those bodies. It's come and never gone away, though they were buried here that many years ago. I couldn't get out of him WHEN. That's why this is Bowfin Island, he said, and the penny dropped. Stinking Island!

Does that explain the sounds last night? Puddock House felt alive in ways I couldn't bring myself to say here yesterday, but I never before thought I'd ever be glad to have a roommate who's an old man. If it weren't for Mr Peasgood, I might have died of fright. There isn't room in the place for rats, but all night it sounded like the walls were streaming with rats. The place is made of stone. It's impossible.

Now that I know where the bodies are buried. Now that I think of the sounds, they were like fingernails, long toenails. I wouldn't sleep alone if I was told that I could live forever, and with no need to work again, if I only slept here alone for one night.

I asked Mr Peasgood why the people hadn't been buried in the deep dirt here. He was horrified at the thought. That's peat, he said. We need it to burn. So that's the big Oxo cubes of dirt by the stove.

Did I say before that he has a pet? A huge toad! It can't be native.

He talks to it.

A MONTH LATER?

Snatching a moment to say something for posterity here. I've learned how to make a fire in the Aga. I'm learning how to cut peat, and make a stew. Actually, cook it. I've also learned how to cook porridge. As for Mr Peasgood having a pet toad that he talks to, the toad is actually giving him instructions. I know how that sounds. I can only tell it like I see it. I can't tell you what the toad says. You couldn't cut his accent with a knife. You'd need a giant's cleaver.

Which leads to the birds.

When I'm not doing chores, I'm allowed to watch the birds. I've never seen so many. Some small bird with a red breast and short tail was singing this morning, and it was so beautiful in the way it tilted its head up and wagged its tail when it hit some notes. The birds here are fascinating. They do the most interesting things, and their songs!

Last year I downloaded Birdsongs of Britain thinking it might help me spot. It was useless. Now I know why. Some bird with, say, a red breast and a yellow cheek is gonna look the same each time you spot it, but its voice isn't like a ringtone. It's unpredictable, and I think, moody. Sometimes after the rain, you'd think it's won Lotto. But the same bird can also sound petty, lonely, frightened, morose, and I swear, horny.

At dawn and dusk, that's when I love to listen. Those are always busy times for me, when I should be setting the fire then or boiling water, or other chores, but instead of dobbing me in, Mr Peasgood always smiles indulgently, sometimes offering up a saying. He's got so many. My favourite is Listen at a hole, and you'll hear news o' yoursel. Aye, he has an accent. It's not like Mum's, but then I don't know what Mum's was, exactly. She was always vague, born in Glasgow but then she says she moved around. She must have, to meet Dad. I've lived in well-heeled London suburbs all my life—didn't know they were 'well-heeled' till I went to work and talked with other galley slaves—and Dad was plain vanilla pom.

So Mr Peasgood sounds a bit thick, but understandable. I had to literally pull up my socks here, learning how to dress. He's always wearing his tweed jacket, every rip always neatly darned. No stubble allowed here, though no electric shave. "Twitch and Tick' is now a cleaning rag. Shirt tails that are seen get dipped in salt water before being shoved down my underpants against my bare bum. As I said before, I learn fast, so that only happened once.

He's something of a stickler, but you have to be to live here. And about another thing, like everything else that I couldn't believe at first, but learnt soon enough that he was absolutely right: Bowfin Island only smells to foreigners. It's lucky for us that they never come here. I expect I'll find it enough of an interruption when he gets his half-yearly delivery of oatmeal and his few other treats. He asked if I wanted more paper, another journal that I can write in, but I don't really see the need any more when this is full. It is an affectation, isn't it? After all, who will care to read this, really? I wouldn't read yours, whoever you are if you read this sometime somewhere in the sometime future.

I'm grateful and kind of amazed that Mr Peasgood didn't just murder me or something for intruding upon him. It was unforgivable, what his nephew did, even if Hear did it out of caring, a sense of responsibility. So what if a man chooses to live someplace you wouldn't? So what if he likes the dead more than the living tweeting chirping never-shutting-up masses? So what if he wants to live in a place that smells so bad that you have to get used to it to bear it. No one tries to stop people spending their working life, which is, like, all their life, in hair and nail salons, or reeking restaurant kitchens.

So what if Mr Peasgood is getting old. He's got so much company here that he will never be alone.

And dropping me on him wasn't exactly charitable, was it?

Luckily, he's a good sport. My invasion of his personal space has been treated by him with more grace than I've ever seen in an office.

The dead are less accepting, but he's been there with me all the way, by my side.

I had no idea till yesterday that he also intervened on my behalf, saying that I shouldn't be put to death, that I wasn't a hostile invasion force of one, and did not seek to claim this Duchy for my own. I found out all this when I was formally brought before the toad. I was told to kneel. I did, of course. The toad didn't say a word to me, but no one could stand up to his look. He's got an eerie calmness, a majesty, that comes from, all I can think of is: assurance. He's never undermined by social networking, that's for sure. He has only these subjects under him, and doesn't seek for more.

I couldn't help but be awed.

Mr Peasgood could have been a great lawyer.

Spring

Just before I toss this into the sea for who knows who to find, I must say how happy I am that I've proved myself. Laird Puddock has appointed me Assistant Chief Minister!

Oh happy days!

As Mr Peasgood says, Let the dunlins sing!

I must ask him what a dunlin is, but there's only so much time in the day.

A CASTLE IN TOORAK

MARION HALLIGAN

The bouncer was cute. I gave him a wicked smile, he frowned, looked us up and down slowly, and let us in. I knew he would. We looked good, our clothes were right, we were young and pretty. Me more so than my sister Annie, who's younger than me, everybody says so, about being prettier, but she doesn't mind, I look after her, and make sure she's dressed properly. That's my career, clothes, or will be, and she's going to help me.

And then it's not that big a deal. It's a new *in* place, but hardly crowded with celebrities. I thought I saw Lara Bingle with some hunk, and maybe that was Miranda Kerr, but no, just someone with the same eyes-too-wide-apart face. Of course it was very dark, hard to see anything at all. The lighting cast strange flaring shadows, you wouldn't have known your own family.

Annie and I usually go out on Friday nights. We allow ourselves one cocktail, the most glamorous and extravagant they've got, and leave it at that. We don't binge drink, and don't waste money, either. We rather like the kind in big round glasses with cream in them as well as exotic liqueurs, then it's as though you are having dessert as well. We make the drink last, taking small luxurious sips, and see what happens. Sometimes we dance with one another, sometimes some guy asks us, it's nice sitting over an amazing cocktail and wondering what will happen next.

Annie saw the guy first, standing against the bar, with a head of curls and a tiny goatee beard. I looked at him, and he came over. Would you ladies permit me to join you, he asked, in a posh voice, and we said, Why not.

It all started from there. He wanted to buy us another cocktail, but we said we only ever had the one, and he said, How elegant. He did have a rather funny way of talking, old-fashioned, as if he belonged to another era. He gave us his card, and said he would like to see us for coffee the next day, so we arranged to meet at Caph's, late in the morning after we'd been shopping. In the bright light of day he was very colourful, with his reddish curls and beard, his bright blue eyes, his pale clothes. We knew from his card that his name was Frederick Barbour. We used to have an uncle Fred who was lovely, so that seemed a good omen, somehow.

He was very polite and not at all pushy. His manners were lovely. At first we didn't know which of us he was interested in, he included both in any suggestions he made, but gradually it became clear that it was me he cared most about. It's you, Cat, of course it is, said Annie, and I did feel pleased. But at first the three of us went around together. He was an IT specialist, he said, had his own business, but he was more interested in talking about his family history than in his present circumstances. He told us he was descended from Frederick the Holy Roman Emperor, that Frederick called Barbarossa, which you know, he said, means red beard, and you can see it persists til this day. He pinched his little red goatee. Got excommunicated by the pope and walked barefoot to Canossa, and waited in the snow until the pope relented. Do you have a title, I asked. Oh, mobs, he said, King of Germany, King of Burgundy, King of Arles, not to mention Duke of this and that and Holy Roman et cetera, but what's the point, these days. They're all out of date. Plain Frederick Barbour does me.

He was really very handsome. And very romantic. And kind. After a good while he asked me to marry him, and I said yes. We planned it for the end of the year, when I would have finished my fashion course. I didn't have anybody to talk to about it. No parents. There was a stepmother somewhere, but we hadn't seen anything of her since our father died. She was the worst kind. Didn't quite dress us in rags and put us to work in the ashes, but just about. Favoured her own horrible children. When she was little, Annie called her *that stepwoman*, which I thought was marvellous, and we always thought of her like that. We escaped when we were sent to boarding school, a good one, we flourished there. That was the good thing our father did for us.

Frederick gave me great wads of notes and told me to buy a wedding dress and a trousseau. He didn't actually say so but I could tell from his attitude that he always had plenty of money, that's it for you, I suppose. But I wasn't going to buy the dress, I was going to design and make it for myself. For a graduation project we had to do a cocktail dress, and that's what it would be, I didn't want the full meringue. And I'd design something for Annie too. I wasn't going to have the usual hideous bridesmaid business, as though the mean bride thinks she will look better if her attendants have ugly dresses. Annie was also interested in fashion, she was at the beginning of the course, and we were going to go into business together. I'd be the designer, mainly, she'd do the books, she's clever like that. She was an excellent seamstress, too, we both were, we were famous for our exquisite handsewing. We were going to sell our clothes under the label Annicat; Annie's idea, and brilliant I thought. She said she was sorry her name had to come first, but that was the only way to put them together.

My dress was very classical, with a scooped neckline and tiny sleeves, a fitted waist and a bell-shaped skirt. Plain, plain, just my figure and the ivory silk taffeta perfectly cut. I don't care for strapless dresses on brides. They make their flesh look ugly, either too bulgy or too skinny. Annie's was similar, in silver grey, very flattering. I am fair, she is dark. I spent money on shoes, and silk underwear, a pashmina shawl and some honeymoon outfits.

I could tell Frederick liked my dress by the way he looked at me, his gaze somehow moist, and yearning, and a bit breathtaken. He put his hand out and reverently brushed my shoulder, and I knew he liked the modesty and the understated sexiness of my appearance. We went to Port Douglas for our honeymoon, and I was so glad we had waited to be together, we had a suite and hardly came out of it except to swim in the pool sometimes. We flew back to Sydney and moved into his apartment in Elizabeth Bay. Annie and I had had a tiny flat in Potts Point, and Annie stayed on there. Early in the new year, Frederick said we would be moving to Melbourne. I wasn't happy at leaving my sister behind but he said we would take her with us, he had a house there, quite big, we could all live together and she could transfer her fashion course to Melbourne. I suppose most new brides feel like me, that life with this new husband is just wonderful, that he makes everything so clear and easy and such a delight. Annie was quite keen on going to Melbourne, but she found a tiny place to live near the college, and came to us mainly for weekends. I was back to designing, mainly drawing, but I was turning some designs into actual clothes. I was working on a collection for the next summer, that would keep me busy enough. Frederick suggested we rent a shop and sell them through that but I thought that was too big an enterprise for this moment, it would be better to sell into some boutiques and get a name first, and then when Annie was ready we could think about a shop. It's a big job, a shop is.

Frederick's working hours were erratic, sometimes he was off for long days and I only saw him at night, sometimes he had time to spare and we lived a life that was another sort of honeymoon, going to galleries and out for lunch and shopping. He loved shopping, loved buying us things. His house was a '30s mansion in Toorak, with towers and crenellations and a row of machicolations across the front, a kind of castle really, but it wasn't furnished in period style, thank goodness, but with wonderful timeless modern pieces. He said he wanted me to feel that it was mine, that I should buy things for it. He'd given me a credit card instead of the wads of notes, it had a $50,000 limit on it. I didn't expect to get anywhere near that. Sometimes we bought paintings, always choosing them together, and he paid. There were a lot of walls in the house, plenty of room to display them.

One day Annie said, You know, I think this house is a kind of reverse TARDIS. Bigger on the outside than the inside.

What?

She took me outside. Look, she said, how much house there is. I'm sure there are more rooms than we have been into on the inside.

The keys to the house were kept in a small mirrored cupboard in the hall. Not all of the rooms were locked. Frederick had pointed out the keys to me and said I could go wherever I liked. Annie and I wandered around, sometimes unlocking doors. There were bedrooms and sitting rooms, far more than we could use. Annie had a suite to herself. There was a nursery, decorated in lemon colours, everything was tidy and clean, a couple came in every morning and kept it like that. As far as I could see, we had been in every room. It just looks as though there should be more of them, said Annie. Optical illusion, I laughed, and she did too.

Annie liked to tease me about the titles. She'd call me *your majesty*, and say things like, which country are you queen of this week? Burgundy? Arles? I think you should be living in your palace in Arles, that would be good. It was a bit unfair to Frederick, who didn't ever boast of his family background. He liked it, yes, was proud of it, but in a tucked-away, taken-for-granted manner.

There was a framed picture in the house, a sheet of vellum from a medieval illuminated manuscript, of Frederick Barbarossa. Astonishingly like my Frederick. The pale heart-shaped face, the slender figure, the red-gold curls, the bright blue eyes. You know, said Annie, you know more about his twelfth century background than about the present one. What about his parents? Brothers and sisters? Where was he born?

He might be an orphan, like us, I said. I couldn't see that any of these things mattered much. I was very happy, married to Frederick. He was sweet tempered. Some people might think he was rather controlling, but it gave me pleasure to fit in with his wishes. He was so gentle and loving, there seemed no point in being self-willed or foolishly independent. He indulged me in everything I wanted. I was designing and making my clothes, they were much in demand, and I was employing some people to help me sew them. Think of opening that shop, said Frederick, who was very proud of me, maybe not immediately, but keep it in mind. Frederick set me up a website, and the clothes were photographed and displayed on that. Perhaps that's the way to go, I said. Could be, said Frederick.

I sold some of my clothes through a small boutique round the corner. Annie was on the point of finishing her course and was thinking what to do next. She managed to get a job in this boutique, so she could learn the trade at first hand; it seemed a good idea. She wasn't as keen on designing as I was, and learning management skills would come in handy when we opened the shop.

At about this time Frederick had to go to New York on a business trip. I thought he might have taken me but he said it would be too rushed, he wouldn't have time to look after me, I wouldn't enjoy it. When he came back we would go to Paris. I liked the idea of Paris. I'd never been out of Australia, and Paris was a dream of mine. Before he went he took the keys out of the mirrored cupboard. You know about these, he said, and now there's this—he showed me a small lacquered oval, with a series of numbers and letters engraved on it, not making any sense. This is the password to the big computer, he said, but I don't want you to use it. It's here, and it's safe, but you must never key it in.

So why leave it, said Annie when I told her, why not just hide it in a drawer somewhere?

Maybe it's a test, I said, like Pandora, or Eve. To see if he can trust me.

Huh, said Annie. Of course she is not the focus of Frederick's affection, the way I am, she is inclined to be a bit more critical, even though he has always been so good to her.

Still passing the test? she'd say, when she came to visit. It irritated me, rather. When Frederick came back he hugged me and we went to bed for the afternoon, as we sometimes did, it was lovely.

We booked our tickets for Paris, we weren't taking Annie, I thought she should make her own life, but before we went he had to make a quick business trip to Sydney. I took the rings of keys out of the cupboard and looked at the small lacquered oval. I wondered what would happen if I typed it in. I put the keys back.

Several times I did this, and then I thought, Why don't I just look. I always thought what Eve and Pandora did was important, it had immediate disastrous consequences but the result was finally immensely significant, bringing free will to the world and that. And there was no way Frederick would ever find out. I'd go in, look, and come out again. I was curious to see what he didn't want me to see.

I typed in the code and straightaway up came a film. Or maybe it was a video clip. Anyway, it seemed to be some sort of narrative. A beautiful pale woman lying naked on satin sheets, with fair curls tumbling about her shoulders. She smiled in a bewitching manner. Then a man came in. You couldn't see his face, but there was a flash of reddish hair, and that elegant white bottom, I'd have known it anywhere. He began to make love to the woman. That I recognised too, Frederick's loving foreplay, it was disturbing to see it on a screen before me, something that I thought belonged to me alone, and here was this other woman, luxuriating in his caresses. He entered her, and she threw her head back in ecstasy, then there was a faint pause and he put his arms around her throat and began to strangle her. Her eyes flew open and she choked, the music reached a crescendo, and as he came to orgasm she did too, in a kind of way, she convulsed and then went very still, her face twisted in an ugly mask. He walked away and left her dead on the couch.

I sat stunned for a moment. I had heard of snuff movies, of course I had, although people said they were fake, people didn't really die in them. But this woman was dead, I was sure of it, the ugly details of the soiled bed and her gaping face made that clear. I exited from the clip but that didn't work, it started playing over again. The more I tried to get rid of it the more frenzied it became, and then the screen started to flash as other women, but always the same man, went through similar motions, but with all sorts of variations. They cut back and forwards in a kind of frenzied fashion, and nothing I did could get rid of them. I looked for the cord to unplug it but it was fixed through the wall, I wondered about cutting it but thought maybe it would electrocute me. And how would I explain that to Frederick? I tried to do a force quit, tried to turn it off at the back. Nothing worked. I stared at this flashing screen in a panic. Telling myself to think, it was a computer, it must be possible to turn it off.

Now there was blood, red washes of it, and worse, I couldn't look any longer. And always the nipped waist and shapely buttocks of Frederick.

I took out my phone and called Annie, she's better at computers than I am. She didn't answer, I had to leave a message. I'm not sure what I said. Sex and death, maybe; did I use the word snuff? Something garbled and panicky. I put the phone back in my pocket and tried again to turn the infernal machine off.

Cat, what are you doing? It was Frederick, home early. I sat with tears pouring out of my eyes. Oh silly Cat, he said fondly, why? You make me so sad, I didn't think you would succumb, I didn't think you'd be like the others, oh, I am so sorry. He pressed some combination of keys, and the screen went dark. Come, he said. And took me to the bedroom, tucked me up under the doona, soothed me, but I was still panicking. He brought me a sweetish drink, and I must have gone to sleep. When I woke up he was lying beside me. I felt quite at peace, the images seemed a long way away, vaguely disquieting but somehow not immediately concerning. Frederick was naked, and so was I. He took me in his arms, his dear soothing self, and gently pulled away the doona. Something was worrying me. He stretched me out on the piled up pillows. A part of the panelling slid open, it seemed to be a door into a room I hadn't known was there. A man came out, carrying a large video camera. Frederick began to make love to me.

Well, you've gathered I lived to tell my tale. I did not become the unwitting star of my own snuff movie. When Frederick began to caress my drugged and languid flesh I could hardly move, but after a moment I was repulsed by his touch. That other woman's tormented face filled my mind. I couldn't move, hardly, but I could scream, and I did. Frederick put his hand over my mouth, and I bit him. I screamed again. But he was stronger than me, his slenderness was iron hard, underneath. I was helpless, and I thought I was doomed.

Annie had got my message, finally. She'd been at a party in the north west of the state, at the home of a girl she went to school with. One of those country places with no telephone reception. She came as soon as she heard it, driving down with the brother of the girl. He was a handsome brown farmery type called Sean. She let herself into the house and looked for me, running round the passages with Sean's hand in hers. It was very quiet, she said, I knew there was something wrong. Near my bedroom she saw a door hidden in the wall, leading into the room the cameraman had come from. It had been left open. She glanced in, through into the bedroom, and was transfixed by what she saw. By this time Frederick was trying to put a pillow over my face. My legs moved like a zombie's, she said. She dialled the emergency number on her mobile. Sean ran in and punched Frederick. He rose in the air and fell flat to the ground, his face pale, the hair on his head, face and groin shining golden red, his limbs splayed like a puppet. Apparently the cameraman said, Hey, watch it, mate, this camera's worth a fortune. He did his best to run away, but stopping to pack up his equipment. The police came, quite quickly, I don't know what Annie said but it got them moving.

Frederick had deleted all the stuff from his own computer, but there was another hidden room, in one of the towers, a kind of fortress, with a bank of computers. Lists of names of customers, the business was huge, international. Mainly online, but there were also some DVDs to be posted out. All in the trade name of Snuff/ Love. Frederick was tried for various murders, and convicted. All the money sort of disappeared, being proceeds of crime, but he had put the house in my name so I had that. I sold it and we opened a dress shop in Armadale. Our Annicat label. It did well. Annie proved a great businesswoman, and I was a good designer. The scandal could have helped. People came to stare, and stayed to buy.

THE SILENCE OF CLOCKWORK

CAROL RYLES

The knock was soft enough to not reverberate through stone or startle the rats. Nor would it alert beggars to the presence of Ruk's workshop amid the junk and debris of the abandoned catacombs. Ignoring it, Ruk knew it could only be Nell. Seeing as she was smart enough to unlock the door without a key, he concentrated on adjusting the steam conduits in the wings stretched out on the bench in front of him.

He barely heard the door open, barely heard her approach.

"Ruk," Nell said softly. "I have something to ensure that your wings will be more than a means of escape."

Ruk paused. Although some accident of birth had left Nell with the habit of twitching like a broken metronome, she was the sanest person he knew. She would not interrupt him unless it was important.

"I believe your wings will fly," she said. "But I fear their clockwork will be loud. You'll not have the benefit of stealth. Even at night."

Ruk put down his screwdriver. "I wasn't planning to attack anyone."

"I wasn't suggesting you were. But how will you prevent someone from attacking you?"

Ruk contemplated the wings—beautiful constructions twice the length of his height, a tapestry of copper-wire veins, tempered glass and leather pinions modelled on the aerodynamics of swan wings. When they were done, he would take them to the clock tower, strap them to his back and leave Forsham City to at last be free.

He rubbed his chin, admitting defeat. In his haste to get the job done, he'd refused to consider that the rattle of clockwork would indeed be a problem. "What do you suggest?"

He turned to find Nell already seated in his patched and re-stuffed armchair. Light from the jury-rigged gas lamp flickered over her face, making her blue eyes look as dark as the shadowed walls behind her. She twitched her nose like a nervous mouse, but looked confident nevertheless, leaning back with the disrespectful grace he'd always admired in her. She tossed a lock of hair from her forehead, sniffed, grimaced and then eased her feet out of her grime-streaked boots. Resting her legs on Ruk's table next to his teapot and cups, she crossed her ankles to reveal tights worn thin at the toes and the ragged frills of knee-length bloomers beneath her skirt.

"Ah, my aching legs. I walked miles to find the parts I needed for this." She dipped into her shoulder sack. "For you. Designed by yours truly."

Ruk raised his eyebrows.

She proffered it in her gloved hand: a brass motorized joint. As always when she dealt with clockwork, her twitching eased. "Silent clockwork," she said with undisguised pride. "I suspect it won't be difficult to replicate. However, I'm giving it to you and you alone."

Ruk stared at it, afraid to take it, knowing that if she sold it elsewhere it would bring ten times the price he could offer. "How much?"

She grinned. It struck him that her determined gaze reminded him of a woman he used to know—a shifter like himself. But that was in the days before most shifters turned demon. The memory hurt so badly he looked away.

"You can have it without payment for now," she said. "Workmanship such as this is priceless, don't you think?"

"I can't accept it. I'd be in your debt."

She laughed. "My, my, for a shifter you're uncommonly ethical."

Ruk bristled. "I'm human."

"I suppose you are, seeing as you're trapped in the shape of one." She gave in to a bout of blinking. When she was done, her gaze seemed all the more determined. "I'm told it's why the rest of your kind turned demon. You'd prefer to be animal, but your human sensibilities will no longer fit."

"Animals are simpler," Ruk snapped. "Human emotions swing from elation to grief at Fate's whim."

"It's more than that," she said wistfully. "Look at me, for instance." Her shoulder twitched, almost brushing her ear. "Even my ma didn't want me."

"Because you twitch?"

She shook her head. "No. Long before I was conceived, my ma decided she didn't want children. A trader's wife from Cornica told her the best way to prevent that was to insert a pebble into her womb to fool her body into believing she was with child. But my ma didn't like the idea of using a pebble, so she inserted a piece of clockwork instead. The silent sort—an old family secret—so it wouldn't keep her awake at night. That's why I twitch. It's in my blood."

Her left eye gave up blinking. She let out a series of clicks with her tongue. Wrinkling her nose, she tapped her forehead again. "When I formed in my mother's womb, my brain grew around the clockwork. It's why I'm expert at tinkering."

Ruk stared at her, unsure if she'd told the truth or had spun a tale to glorify her impediment. Whatever the case, it didn't matter. If her uncanny story bought her respect instead of ill treatment, then she had every right to use it.

"The problem is," she added. "People judge us by what they see. They value us for what we might bring. I'll not sell the secret of my clockwork because once I do that, I'll have nothing left. But I'll gladly give it to you because you treat me as an equal. I trust that when the time comes, you'll understand enough about humans to use it wisely."

Ruk did not know what to say. He did not believe her trust in him was justified. Even so, when he examined her clockwork he knew that the genius in her handiwork would help him. As she stood to leave, he offered her all the money he had.

She shook her head. "I heard once that shifter magic can be used to heal. Can you still do it?"

"All lies, I'm afraid."

She frowned and removed the glove from her left hand, revealing a grimy, blood-stained bandage. "It needs stitching, but I won't stoop to the butcher."

Ruk gently unwound the bandage. The slash in her palm was deep, already festering. She flinched as he cradled it in both hands and sent her a brief surge of magic. His reserves were low, as they usually were in this body he wore, so he tried not to use too much. When her skin grew warm beneath his, he pulled away.

"Fascinating," Nell breathed. Her wound flowed like liquid. Its edges merged into a scar that faded and disappeared.

"Do not forget that I'm now human," Ruk said softly. "You must not tell anyone this happened."

"You have my word." Nell froze. From the fear in her eyes, he could tell she was about to screech, like he'd once heard her do in the streets. He guessed she was trying to fight it, but soon it would get the better of her. Like her twitching, it was not something she chose to do.

He caught her in his arms and pressed his hand over her mouth, letting her screech into his palm so outsiders wouldn't hear. It surprised him how sweet she smelled. His heart skittered having her close to him. He almost felt more human than shifter. How thoroughly he could lose himself. How close to allowing the cycle of emotion and madness to start over . . .

She fell silent. He let go of her and stood back apologetically, the back of his neck prickling.

"Thank you," she said, blushing. I don't know what come over me. I've always stopped that from happening down here."

"My magic, I suppose. It must have unsettled you."

"Maybe. Last week the physicians heard me. They want to lock me up. My boy, Lucian too. They believe we're possessed by demons."

Ruk swallowed against a burst of anger. "Demon's arse you're possessed!"

"Those men! They call themselves physicians, but act like fools. They're arranging to listen for our clockwork. But they won't hear it because it's silent." She tapped her forehead. "If you could use your magic to help me, would you do it? At all costs?"

He stared at her, sensing a bargain, not sure if it was the kind he should agree to. Nell wouldn't cheat him, that much he knew. But she was, after all, human. And humans were notorious for cheating themselves.

"Only if it's all you have," he said at last.

She smiled. "Do you know what angels are?"

"I've heard of them."

"I suggest you shape your wings like theirs. You should let people see that you *are* one."

• • •

It took Ruk weeks to add Nell's silent clockwork to his wings, but he decided to forgo the angel shape. It reminded him too keenly of humanity and of how he could never return to the pure simplicity of being animal again. With time, he supposed, he would learn to accept that. At least for now he could find comfort in the catacombs, the drip of moisture down the walls, the innocent foraging of rats, the echo of footsteps; but he missed the sun. The dimness had turned his skin sickly. He'd already cropped his hair in preparation for his first flight. Now he needed only to wait for a perfect breeze, a clear sky, a half moon and perhaps a chance to thank Nell and invite her to watch him leave.

• • •

Nell let herself in as usual. She stood blinking in a strip of gaslight in his living alcove, her dark hair dishevelled, her boots sodden, the bottom of her skirt damp and reeking of sewerage. Her son— Lucian—stood beside her, looking barely five years old and not the eight she had claimed him to be. His blue eyes stared out from beneath a mop of ginger bird-nest hair.

"We need your help," Nell said.

Ruk turned abruptly away, unable to bear the desperation clouding her face. "Nell, I'm sorry. I can't."

"Please. You're all we have."

"I'm not yours. Besides, why not ask the boy's father?"

"He doesn't have one."

Ruk almost added that human business was for humans and that shifters could not risk being caught up in it. But then Nell let out a soft grunt. Ruk stiffened at the sound of flesh and bone thudding against the bare stone floor. He expected Lucian to cry out, but heard only the low hiss of the gas lamp.

Reluctantly—supposing that Lucian's silence meant he had known too much grief already—Ruk turned around.

The boy stood unmoving, his mother sprawled at his feet. He swallowed, took a deep breath. His left eye twitched rapidly. "She . . . took . . . poison," he stammered. He dropped to his knees, stroked his mother's cheek. "She said you're an angel. Please . . . bring her back."

Ruk knelt at Nell's side. He put his hand over her heart and found it no longer beating. "I can't. My magic's only strong enough for skin and bone. I can shift flesh to make it heal, but I can't restore life." He stood. If he allowed himself to give in to emotion, there would be no getting over it.

Lucian rammed his fist in his mouth and shuddered. His grief was silent, but no less terrible to witness.

Ruk turned away. He paced, allowing himself fury because fury was easier to control than despair. Why in Fate's name had Nell killed herself? Now her son's emotions would endanger him. Was this her bargain? That he should look after her boy? How could he fly now?

He turned back to Lucian and contemplated him, wincing at the stoop of his thin, boyish shoulders. "If the physicians wanted to lock her up, why didn't she simply flee Forsham?"

At first Lucian stared at his feet. Then he looked up, sniffed, blinked, his eyes sunken like the eyes of a small animal hunted to exhaustion. Ruk wondered if Nell had inserted clockwork in her womb before conceiving like her own mother had.

"Lucian," Ruk said softly. "Can you hear *your* clockwork?"

Lucian looked away.

"You can tell me the truth. The physicians are my enemies too. If they knew of my existence, they'd . . . "

Shuddering, Lucian wrapped his arms about his chest. At last, in a low voice he said, "No, I can't hear it."

"Ah . . . " Ruk rubbed his chin. "If the physicians can't hear it, they'll believe your mother was lying. They'll say your twitching is caused by demons."

The boy looked at him, eyes wide and glazed.

Ruk fought down a surge of temper. Why hadn't Nell explained? He would have helped her for this. "Lucian, you may stay here if it will keep you from the physicians' asylum. But soon, I must leave. Shifters should not live with humans. Your emotions . . . They're as good as poison for us."

Lucian held his gaze, his eyes wet. "My mother said . . . "

Ruk held up his hand. "Stop. Nell hardly knew me."

Lucian froze as if Ruk's harshness had purged the next twitch out of him. He lifted his chin. "My mother said you would help."

The words stung, bringing with them emotion that threatened

to spiral into demonhood. To protect himself, Ruk blanketed it with laughter that came out harsh and cruel. What could a shifter do? To date, his best way to survive humans was to avoid them. What good would a child be except to keep him grounded?

Forcing down anger, he gestured for Lucian to follow him. "I want you to see what your mother gave me."

Lucian's face blenched. "I'm not leaving her. Why won't you help?"

Ruk sighed. "I don't know how. I can only show you her final triumph."

"No!" Lucian threw himself over his mother's chest. "I'm not leaving her."

"As you wish." Ruk turned away. Softly, he made his way out of the alcove. Before closing the door, he turned back to see the boy sobbing silently over Nell's ruined body, a dim silhouette in gaslight.

Ruk's heart clenched so painfully he wanted to flee.

• • •

His wings were light, even wrapped up in blankets to avoid damage from the impending journey to the clock tower. As Ruk gathered them up, his sense of freedom did not give him the simple joy that it should have. It was Lucian's fault. Damn Nell. She'd given Ruk the means to escape. Now she had taken it back.

He lowered the wings carefully onto the bench. He looked about the workshop, at the junk strewn against the walls, the discarded machine parts and the original piece of clockwork that Nell had given him all those weeks before. He'd pulled it apart to glean its secret, then reassembled it soon after to keep as a memento. It occurred to him that perhaps its true purpose was to remind him of something else.

His heart leapt. "Sweet Nell. You guessed I was the only one who would understand."

He pocketed the clockwork, squatted in front of his toolbox and ran his hands over the tools. Nell's death was still fresh. Although he could not bring her back to life, perhaps if he worked quickly, he could help her.

By the time he'd gathered courage enough to return to her, he found Lucian spread out with his head on her chest. Gently, Ruk soothed him with a warm surge of magic and waited until he drifted into sleep. He picked him up, taking care to not let his head loll, then carried him to the armchair and covered him with a blanket. The boy did not stir, but with his eyes closed he looked too much like his mother, and far too vulnerable.

Keeping his emotions distant, Ruk knelt at Nell's side with his back to Lucian, shielding him from what he was about to do. He took up his drill, then held it over the exact spot where Nell had tapped her forehead when referring to her clockwork. He pressed the bit into her cold flesh and turned it, grateful that the dead did not bleed. Hands steady, he made ten small holes in her skull, forming a circle the diameter of a teacup.

Next, he took up the fine string-saw he used to cut automata skin, threading it through two holes at a time, sawing through bone until the circle fell free to reveal the surface of Nell's pale, convoluted brain.

As suspected, he found not a skerrick of clockwork.

Just to be certain, he probed deeper with a screwdriver, twisting it back and forth through soft, yielding flesh. Nell's blue eyes stared up at him, unblinking, approving.

Ruk leaned back on his haunches, wiped his forehead, surprised to find it damp with sweat. "Damn the physicians," he muttered. "Damn every one of them."

Holding his breath, he used a dessertspoon to scoop out a small section of Nell's precious brain. He placed it in a cup, then promptly hid it in his toolbox. Reverently, he took the silent clockwork from his pocket and eased it into the awaiting hollow, pushing it into place until its silver dome shone like a sunken carapace at the centre of her forehead.

He paused, his hands shaking. Damn humans. They'd be the death of him.

For a long while, he could not bring himself to move, could barely draw breath. Nell's face was too motionless and too pale. He would give anything to see her twitch again. Perhaps even his wings.

He was about to replace the circle of skin and skull, when a hand clutched his shoulder and struggled to pull him away.

"Leave her alone!" Lucian demanded. "Don't take it out."

Ruk held him firmly yet gently back. The boy sank to his knees, covered his face and sobbed.

With the fingers of his free hand, Ruk closed Nell's eyes. He fitted the circle of skull into place and sealed the skin with a surge of magic. The wound healed, faded and disappeared. Ruk breathed a sigh of relief.

He turned to Lucian. "I'm not taking her clockwork out. A long time ago, your mother asked me to check that it was really there. Now when the physicians look for it, you need not be afraid. You'll know they'll find it. They'll believe that you have it too."

Lucian's eyes glistened. He touched his forehead.

"It'll protect you," Ruk assured him. "It's what she wanted."

• • •

As Ruk climbed the clock tower, he hoped that Lucian and his new guardian would meet him at the top to watch him leave. When they did not, he supposed he should at least take comfort that, when the physicians had dissected Nell, they'd believed her clockwork was hereditary. "Her son has every chance of becoming a genius tinkerer," they'd said. "We'll ensure he has access to training."

But the price . . .

As always with humans, the price had been too high.

Ruk raised his arms. His steam pistons hissed, barely audible above the mechanical hum of the city below. His wings opened out and their leather pinions rustled as soft and silent as their clockwork. He leapt, soaring skywards, alone on the breeze, leaving Forsham and Lucian behind him.

THE RAVEN AND HER VICTORY

TANSY RAYNER ROBERTS

I recognised the woman in the poem. Perhaps no one else would have done. My name (for once) was not present, carefully couched in floral language or complex metaphor. There was no Victory or raven-haired Viceroy, no grey-eyed Victoire in russet skirts, not even a sly dig at Victoriana.

Still, I knew that the woman in the poem was me. The woman in the poem is always me.

• • •

I first met Ida May at a charity dance benefit for war widows and children. My aunt, Mrs Grayson introduced us, as young ladies with something in common. "Victoria, my dear, have you met Miss Midas of Baltimore? She's a writer, like yourself."

Miss Ida May Midas was an intense sort of woman, not pretty, with a pronounced brow and twitchy fingers. She wore brown, a striking gown if rather out of fashion, and she spoke in bursts, not used to polite company.

"Mrs Grayson exaggerates," I apologised. "I pen the social pages in our local paper. Hardly a celebrated poet like yourself."

Miss Midas gave me a dark, almost angry stare. "But you want to write. Real words. Real stories. You have a passion for the craft?"

I was unaccustomed for young unmarried ladies like myself to talk about passion, or indeed much of anything. "I have a great desire to write history," I found myself confessing. "But no one will let me do that, will they? I suppose I'll teach."

"You can do better than that," said Miss Midas, and something inside me unfolded like a crepe paper rose.

• • •

It was a mistake, I know that now. A scandalous, ridiculous mistake. And yet I hardly noticed it at the time, hardly thought about anything except the light in Ida May's eyes as she explained a particular story of genius, or took apart some lesser work with scathing, critical words.

We went about together for weeks, arm in arm. Visiting museums and tea houses, talking of history and politics and all manner of grand things. Words, all words. We filled the world with them. And then, in my aunt's garden at the end of a long and vibrant day, we dropped the pretence that we were merely girls being chummy with each other, and I let her kiss me.

Her mouth on mine was warmth and sunshine, even as the light faded in the garden. We clung to each other like trembling leaves, and then parted. I wanted nothing else in the world so much as her, that night, in my arms.

I opened my eyes for a moment and saw the lawn behind us flare up for a moment in so many colours that I was dazzled, and afraid. The world was all of a sudden a daunting and overwhelming place. So I ran from her.

It has been many years now, and I am still afraid.

• • •

Ida May sent me letters at first, scolding me for cowardice and scorching me with all manner of rebukes. Sometimes she enclosed downy white feathers in accusation, or dried flowers that fell to powder in my hands.

Every letter made my skin prickle with fear, for with it would come a dreadful portent of some kind. Draughts might blow suddenly behind my neck, or water might drip through the ceiling to wet my hair. Once, the fine Persian rug beneath my feet unaccountably burst into flames, and smouldered for hours no matter how much we soaked it with water.

After that, I left my mother's house for college, determined to train as a teacher and to leave my fears and Miss Midas long behind me.

She found my address soon enough, and though she no longer bothered to write whole letters to taunt me with, she continued to send feathers and flowers and occasional locks of her hair, each of which tormented me anew with small but impossible horrors.

If this was love, I wanted none of it.

• • •

Eventually, the letters stopped arriving. I learned to breathe again in a world without magic. There was a gentleman who courted me for a short time, though we parted as friends before our names were joined upon the tongues of our acquaintances. He was not for me, nor I for him.

Then in the third year of my studies, before we were released as qualified women of the world, there was Amy.

We were both so coy and bashful that I am sure no one knew that our friendship had turned to romance—even we were slow to admit that to ourselves. But we both loved poetry, and read it to each other in the spare hours, blushing all the while.

She read me one that she had cut from the newspaper, of a raven-haired princess in a magical land of many-coloured grass, and was surprised that it made my hands shake.

"Why, I thought of you when I read it," said Amy, so startled at my reaction that she forgot to blush. "Because of the title, see? And your hair is so lovely and dark."

The poem was "Victory," by I.M. Midas. It was the first of many. I should have known that nothing would quiet her pen. She would never release me from the burden of that single, fleeting kiss.

I could never kiss Amy. I did not fear society's condemnation so much as a woman in my position should, perhaps. My fear was wilder, that again I might ignite that dreadful power that had sparked between myself and Miss Ida May Midas.

My love for Amy was so much more than what I had felt so briefly for Ida May. Surely our kisses would set whole forests aflame. It could not be risked, and I could never tell her why.

• • •

The years passed. My friendship with Amy turned into a long and heartfelt correspondence as we taught in different schools, in different towns. Her letters soon became more friendly than passionate, and eventually I learned that she had chosen a conventional path, accepting the hand of an earnest young gentleman called Edward. I had never expected otherwise. She was too pretty to be a spinster.

Meanwhile, I.M. Midas grew in reputation, her dark and threatening mode of poetry capturing the imagination of the time. She moved to Boston and then New York, taking up with a bohemian set that only added to her literary stature.

One poem, about the ill omen of a raven, was published in over twenty newspapers across the country and for one brief season made Miss Midas a household name.

I found myself in that poem, as I always did. The raven croaked its chilly message to a woman who searched for victory in dusty old books, who craved a career as a historian (something I myself had ceased to yearn for years before now). A woman who desired to be forgiven by her lover.

Nevermore indeed.

After that, I.M. Midas was often referred to as "the Raven," even in my small circles. There were a few poets and book enthusiasts in my little town, and we met sometimes to read to each other while taking tea. Mr Oswald, who ran the library and the post office, took a particular delight in the words of "Mr Midas", and would regularly clip poems out of the newspapers to share with us.

"Ah, listen to this one, Miss Grayson," he said one afternoon as our little group sat in my schoolroom with cups of tea and slices of fruit cake. "You will appreciate it, I think."

It was not a poem, but a very short story, about poet dying for lack of beauty, and the lost love who had broken his heart.

"Why is Mr Midas always so sad?" complained Lucille Woodvine who was an excellent seamstress and quite pretty, but not especially bright.

I closed my eyes, and listened to the end of the story. The poet died, and only then was allowed to return to the land of many-coloured grass he had visited once in his youth, the single time in his life that he had ever been happy.

I would not crack. I would not. This was no more seductive than the letters or the feathers. Ida May had found another way to torture me for the choices of my past, and I would not go to her.

• • •

As Christmas approached, our little reading group received word of a new literary journal, The Stylus, edited by none other than I.M. Midas. I rejoiced in this news for I truly believed (I wanted to believe) that if Ida May received the acclaim due to her for her best and most powerful work, she might finally let go of the idea that our never-was love was such a great tragedy in her life.

I did not have to subscribe to the periodical, because Mr Oswald had already done so, and was delighted to go over the contents with the group. I did examine the crisp pages with great curiosity, I must admit.

There was a poem by Midas herself, and many other pieces she had chosen from favourite writers and friends—some were beautiful, some banal, and all quite wretchedly bleak.

Ida's poem was about me. Of course it was. The poems are always about me. This one for once made no playful pun about my name, not even a discreet letter 'v' placed somewhere noticeable, and yet it contained all of the elements I knew to recognise. The woman, this woman whom the poet loved, had a "classic" face, "queenly" stature, bright eyes, a musical voice, a pallid brow and curly dark hair.

Even when she did not name me, the Raven was still writing about her mythical Victoria, a woman she had constructed upon a few dim memories.

It was the article published at the back which made me tremble. It was a biography of I.M. Midas, poet-editor of the Stylus. A short piece, certainly, but one that was utterly false and scurrilous. No longer was Miss Midas merely writing under a name that implied she was male. Now she had actually allowed a piece to be written which stated her male identity as a fact. Ignatious Melville Midas had a Harvard degree, parents, enjoyed shooting and fishing, all artifice. A wife, by God, "his" helpmeet and muse, the raven-haired Mrs Victoria Midas.

Ida May had claimed me after all, woven me into her imaginary history of a celebrated male poet with a devoted wife.

As I consumed this news, smoke began to pour from the pages of The Stylus, and the journal burst into flames. Mr Oswald shouted, and Miss Woodvine screamed, and there was a great to-do with water and blankets.

I was not burnt, which they all claimed was a miracle. But I was indeed broken.

The very next day, I bought a train ticket to New York.

• • •

"Mr and Mrs Midas" lived in a tall, narrow house in tree-lined avenue of a wealthy district. I had bought another copy of The Stylus at the train station, so as to neatly copy the address on to a slip of paper I could keep in my pocketbook, though I was careful not to read anything else of the journal lest I cause further inflagration.

I stood upon their steps for a very long time before I gathered my courage enough to march up and ring their bell.

A maid answered, a shy girl in a crisp uniform with a cap pulled down upon her face. She bobbed and ma'amed and led me to a drawing room so full of books that I had no doubt I was in the right place.

"I should like to see," I said, and hesitated on the words, for no, I was not yet ready for the confrontation with Ida May. "The lady of the house. Mrs Midas."

The maid stared at me, quite startled, and I was equally startled to see her face. She had such bright eyes, and a brow that could only be described as pallid. It was like looking into the mirror I had owned ten years ago. She could have been me. "Yes, Mrs Midas," she said quickly, and fled.

What was I to make of that? For as I waited, I had a creeping suspicion that she had not been agreeing with me readily that she would fetch her mistress, but instead she had addressed me as her mistress.

No, that could not be.

A housekeeper came next, a stout and comforting woman, though again I had that quiet shock of recognition. She looked so like my aunt, or perhaps myself once I reached the age of my aunt.

"Mrs Midas, welcome home," she said in a voice that was certainly not my own, though I struggled at first to recognise it. "May I bring tea? Or would you prefer sherry at this hour? Mr Midas was sorry not to meet you at the station, but he will be along for supper directly."

"I am not," I said, and there was something wrong with my voice, too. It was deeper, more sardonic, and yet dreadfully familiar. "I am . . . " But what could I say? I was Victoria Grayson, unmarried, a schoolteacher, a lover of women? Mrs Midas was a Victoria too. "I am afraid . . . "

That, at least, was the truth.

The door rang, and the maid answered it again. I heard her speaking to the master of the house in the hallway, and he answering her, both in that same voice, the one I heard in the mouth of the housekeeper and of myself.

"Hello, darling," said Ida May, as she entered the drawing room. I had half expected her to be dressed as a man, all frock coat and tails, but she was dressed as she always had when I knew her, in a respectable brown linen dress and jacket.

"Where are we?" I demanded. Her voice spilled out of me, that rich sound. I was not myself any more. My clothes had changed, and my corset was tighter. I could feel myself stretching to fill her vision of me. She thought I was taller, more slender, and thus I became. "What is this house?"

Ida May Midas smiled at me with that angular face of hers, and took my hand. Gently, she led me to the window and drew back the curtains. The trees that lined the avenue outside were glowing gold with a sunlight that came from nowhere. As my hand shuddered in hers, I saw threads of bright and many-coloured grass spring up in the middle of the street.

"It's not a house," she said serenely, her fingers encircling my wrist like a trap, sprung. "It's a poem."

ALMOST BEAUTIFUL

ANGELA REGA

There are whispers of what happens when a mortal man copulates with a woman of scales and I serve as evidence to their tale. I tell my sea witch mother not to worry about my grim marriage prospects. I tell her all men are as shallow as the marshy lagoons that surround our island and can never know love unless it begins with physical beauty.

My mortal cousin, Isabella, is as beautiful as sunrise against a Venetian grey sky and unlike me, betrothed to be married. She preens herself like a vain caged bird, puffing her chest out and singing songs for anyone who'll listen. And I know that some women, too, are just as shallow.

The only thing Isabella didn't compete with me for was my wish to join my father's guild and become a glassmaker. She had laughed so much she hiccupped when I told her my wishes.

"Women don't make looking-glass! They use it to admire their reflections."

Then she laughed and didn't offer me an apology. I knew her meaning was to rub salt into my wound.

I was named Quasibella, 'Almost Beautiful' by my father, Giacomo, for my hare lip and fish tail. It begins from the back of my right thigh, separating into an appendage behind my knee and growing more obtrusive when I'm wet, nervous or angry.

"Let her be apprenticed to glass." My mother, who understood my urgency, had begged my father. She knew my prospects of marriage were not good; a skill would provide me with an income.

My father flatly refused.

Since time immemorial, many mermaids and sea witches of varying degrees of fin and scale have lived in our Venetian Lagoons. Brides of the Doges, they collect the rings tossed by the Magistrates in the water symbolising the marriage of the city to the sea. So vain some are, my own mother's mother traded her to my father, Giacomo, for a small Murano looking glass mirror.

Murano became renowned for its glass and mirrors and both have been in demand by mermaid and mortal women ever since. Still, my father wouldn't let me learn the skill of making them.

"I want to make a mirror that will show the beauty of heart of a woman," I'd said to my father.

"The only beauty a man and a mirror appreciate is physical beauty," he'd answered.

Marriageable age was passing me by, as was my patience. And what should a part mermaid daughter do when her father disagreed? Should she skulk or scream? Cry like a child and take to her bed?

I did what most scaled women do when they need time to think. I took a bath.

I didn't need to heat the water nor perfume it with lavender like so many noble ladies would; I am a cold-blooded creature, after all. Instead I hauled the water straight from the lagoons itself and sat in it. Cold like holy stone. The smell of brine and salt, the taste of old fish bones, was comfort for me.

"Don't spend too long in the bath!" my mother called out from behind the door.

"Father stops me from becoming a glassmaker because I'm a part mortal woman and you want to stop me from my bathing because I'm part mermaid!"

The doorknob turned as my mother tried to enter but I had bolted the door from the inside. "Quasibella, don't play with sea magic," she warned. "Long baths are no good for you."

I submerged my head, wishing I had gills like my full blooded sea witch mother. I had always done my best thinking underwater.

A masked messenger in a gondola came that night, and beat at our door with his oar. I lit a candle stub and followed my mother and father down to the antechamber that opened directly onto the water. The gondola had night lanterns made from delicate fishbone and the messenger wore a cloak of sea grass. He had a letter addressed to my father in black squid ink, sealed with emerald wax that shimmered with mermaid scale. It was unmistakably the seal of the Underwater Senate.

My father took the letter, fumbling as he opened it, his fingers stiff in the cold night air. "It's from your kingdom," he whispered to my mother.

"The seal . . . " my mother gazed at the letter and snatched it out of my father's hands, "it's an older version of the seal." She narrowed her eyes and looked at me.

I shrugged and avoided her gaze. But I knew what influence my mother's Underwater Kingdom had. The annual ceremonial marriage of the city to the sea meant that many mermaids were the rightful heirs to the maze of lagoons surrounding Venice and our island, Murano.

Father ushered us inside to read aloud the letter's contents:

Dear Sir,

The glassmaker guild's secrets leak like the chapel walls that let in the lagoons when it rains. Spies have come to Murano in the guise of merchants and have stolen our glass and mirror making recipes (only for them to be replicated in Holland, Spain and England).

What beauty is there in our glass if others can easily mimic it? For Murano to be unparalleled in glass and mirror making, the guild should forever keep its secrets. From this day forth, no glassmaker shall leave the island.

The Guild must recruit only the best apprentices. No strangers shall come to the island without special permits. Secrets shall be kept and more shall be contrived. No more ordinary glass or ordinary mirrors can be produced.

Let that be the task of the poor imitators. He who produces extraordinary glass shall be richly rewarded.

His Excellency, Turri, De Fiume Freddo
Doge of the Underwater Senate.

"What other glass inventions can there be?" My father had paced the floor of our foyer. "Already I make crystalline glass, and looking glass mirrors. Your uncle makes cobalt glass and lattimo."

"Apprentice me to glass! I will create a mirror to show the true beauty of a woman's heart, not her face!"

"Only men are apprenticed to glass. And cover that tail!" he snapped.

I lifted my skirt to hide my half-formed tail and limped outside, slamming the door behind me in protest. The lagoon was filled with an ebony emptiness that night; ribbons of silver lapped at the bridge nearest our door. I took off my shoes to feel the water on my feet and thought of the home that belonged to my mother, but not to me. I'd wiggled my scaled toes, letting the water seep between them.

When I looked down into the water, I saw my hare-lipped reflection gazing back at me.

"Even the spirits of the water can only show what brings me shame!" I cried and my tears fell into the water. Their salty brine mixed with the Murano waters and I heard a call that came from deep below. It had been a long time since I'd heard the voices of my underwater family but perhaps the letter had brought them to the surface.

Drink me . . .

I couldn't waste any time. So many years since I'd heard the voices of my mother's home . . .

Drink me . . .

I knelt and cupped my hands, cradling the water to drink then coughing at the water's bitterness and foul taste. There was no time to hesitate. I'd heard the voices of the spirits of water reflection. I was destined for a life of spinsterhood without skill or art. My father would never let me learn how to make glass and my looks would never allow me to know love and marry someone who would look after me.

But I was more sea witch than woman; I knew the secrets of the spirits that live in the reflections on water.

So I captured one for myself to marry.

I hauled myself up the narrow stairs and to my room, the nausea making me shiver and ache. "Mother?" I whispered and knocked at her door. My mother had lain awake knowing that I had left in anger. She came to the door and grabbed my shoulders to keep my shaking body steady.

"I've drunk a spirit of reflection. There isn't much time to perform the magic."

Mother helped me to my room and poured some cold water from my bathing jug into a shallow tub.

"Hurry," I whispered as she took off my outer dress.

Mother undressed me and laid me in the shallow bath of cold water.

My stomach churned and cramped. My mother went to my fruit basket and found the garlic, unpeeling it with her fingers. Then she rubbed the pungent cloves up and down my naked spine, uttering the spell to draw him forth from my body. Her old language rolled easily off her tongue.

I heaved. To bring forth a water spirit is a painful process; I'd seen it done before, by my own mother conjuring up lovers for the nuns in the same canals that expelled their sewerage. I gagged as emerald-green bile trickled down my chin, but I didn't stop. A chance for love, a livelihood, was worth a little suffering.

Finally, there was a gurgling sound as I regurgitated a sausage-shaped sac of glutinous jelly; first a toenail cut through the grey membrane and then the shape of a fist protruded. Mother wiped the green fluid from my face in satisfaction. I'd birthed a spirit of reflection! For me to marry!

"You see!" Mother exclaimed. She washed him clean with damp cloths until his eyes were shiny and his lips were wet for me to kiss. I uncurled his arms and legs from around his body and rubbed the same garlic cloves on his naked spine to lengthen his body. "I have brought forth a man to love me," I said.

"You need a future!" There was a look of resolute satisfaction on her face.

I sobbed and reached out to my mother.

"Not me, now, hold him. *He* is your husband. Father will apprentice him."

"I want to be apprenticed!"

My mother continued, speaking to the spirit-man. "I name you Venerio. You will live here and marry my daughter," she said, "You will take on an apprenticeship, spirit of reflection, and become the greatest glassmaker that Murano has ever known and care for my daughter!"

Venerio was beautiful. His eyes were grey green and had movement in them, like water. His skin was pale, like moonlight. His hair was long for a man, long brown tresses that were tangled with seaweed. Mother used her bodice dagger to cut his tresses short like my father's. I picked them up, held them close to my nose and inhaled their perfume of salt and the open sea.

Even though I had sworn never to use my mother's magic, my father clapped his hands in delight at what I had done and my reasoning.

"You are a genius, daughter!" He said to me. "For what better mirror maker could there be, than one who is reflection himself?"

On our wedding night, I shivered in excitement. What would it be like to be loved? To have a man to caress and hold me? I lay on my bed, my hair undone, my arms outstretched out on either side of me.

He came into the room and lay next to me, gazing into my face. I puckered my lips to kiss him and he puckered his lips back. I sat up on my knees on the bed, and he moved to do the same. Facing each other; I could see my reflection in his eyes, I lifted my hand slowly up to caress his chest; he did the same and touched mine. He reflected back the love and desire I felt.

That night, as we lay in each other's arms under a blanket of filtered moonlight, contentment welled in my heart. I would not be a glassmaker but at least I would be married to one. At least, regardless of my looks, I would have a companion, to whisper secrets to and sing songs about the Mediterranean with. Even if he had been my own creation.

My father understood Venerio's true worth—near the furnaces. Made up of water, he could withstand more heat and toxic salts than any of the other apprentices. I watched him work at the ovens. While the others coughed at the nitrates and the soda ash, his watery substance washed it away. He was a spirit of reflection. Made of water. Transparent and cold.

Meaningless until someone gazed into him.

There was a staccato knock at the front door. From the whistles that rose to my bedroom window from the Glassmaker's Canal below, I knew it was my cousin Isabella.

I descended the stairs to our foyer, lifting my skirts so they would stay dry. I should have put my small passarelle down, so that she would not wet her feet when entering our antechamber, but my disdain for my mortal cousin stopped me. Even the recent fire in her father's workshop that had reduced her family to poverty was not enough for my heart to warm towards her. Her presence was enough for my mermaid scales to start appearing on my legs, making them itch.

She stepped inside and, without waiting for my invitation, proceeded up the stairs to higher, dryer ground in the living room, perching herself on our divan.

"What brings you here?" I sat in the armchair opposite and shifted uncomfortably in my seat.

"Why haven't I met him?"

I smiled sweetly; there was no point taking time to answer. She was obviously here for the news of my hasty marriage to an apprentice glassmaker.

"Married so quickly! Any scandal I should know about?"

My tail whipped at the wet hem of my gown. I smoothed my dress down to conceal it.

"No scandal." I scratched at my legs and tried to change the subject. "Surely, you must be getting excited about your own wedding now."

Like a twittering canary, she divulged the details of her nuptials. It was to be a loveless marriage but one that would provide wealth to her family.

I rose from the chair and took the keys from the table to take her to the furnaces.

Isabella followed me behind, up the narrow staircase and down the main corridor.

"I don't mean to be rude, Quasibella," Isabella said, a smile forming at the corners of her mouth, "but you're very lucky to have found a husband."

"All daughters, part mermaid like me, or full blooded mortal like yourself, need good marriages for their livelihood," I answered and continued walking ahead, my limp more profound now that my tail had grown. All daughters, it seemed, in her opinion except me.

"Tell me everything! How did you meet?" She hurried behind me down the narrow stone corridor.

"The guild has been sworn to secrecy, Isabella," I answered, "and that includes information about new apprentices."

We walked on; the silence cutting between us, the floors were dry on the first storey of our home, its labyrinthine passageway leading us to the furnaces.

It would take only ten minutes to arrive at the glass-making furnaces by foot but I was already tired. It wasn't the silly banter of my cousin that made me so; my recent use of sea magic had aged me. My shin bones ached, longing to return to full flesh and scale, and I was short of breath. Still, I had been content for the first time since I married Venerio. We had all been happy for these past few weeks and I had not even argued with my father about being apprenticed to glass. For once, I felt equal to all the daughters of Venice, even to the featherbrained mortal cousin of mine that flapped about in her prettiness behind me.

"Quasibella! You aren't listening to me!" The shard sharp voice of my cousin shattered my reverie, bringing me back to the present. "I was telling you my future husband will hold a ball to honour my beauty!"

"We must make you a special wedding gift then, at the workshop," I said and continued walking. Her looks were her only talent.

"We?" She laughed. "Quasibella, you can't make anything!"

"I mean 'they'."

I smiled sweetly and continued on, beckoning for her to follow.

We arrived at the door that led to the workshop. The heat emanating from the furnace enveloped us. Isabella wiped the sweat from her upper lip with her sleeve.

"Would you like to return to the house?" I asked, "It is even hotter once we go inside."

"I want to meet Venerio. Not a peep about it and then a letter to say you're married! Before me!"

She pushed in front of me and walked in towards the ovens. Venerio was sweeping the embers from the floor, his shirt unbuttoned, and his face red from the heat.

"Venerio?" Isabella cooed. "We haven't had the pleasure of each other's acquaintance?"

Venerio didn't look up. Being a spirit of reflection, he didn't respond to words or commands. He was taught glass by being shown and copying my father's actions. He kept his head down, sweeping the stray bits of silica on the ground.

"Is he a simple fellow?" She asked me. "He doesn't answer me!"

"He's preoccupied with his work." I answered, my tail wanting to lash at her ankles.

Venerio *was* a simple kind of young man of limited speech and sometimes, I feared, empty of mind. Still, he was a good companion to me. Isabella tried asking some more questions but still he didn't look up. She laughed with her sharp shard voice and said that God made them and he paired them in two just like in the story of Noah's ark. Her eyes darted from him to me, indicating we were 'them'. I wanted to box her ears. Instead, I smiled. Let her say what she wanted. Soon, I would be of equal standing when Venerio invented glass to show a woman's true beauty and father would see my worth.

But when Isabella tugged Venerio's sleeve for attention and he finally did see her, he fell to his knees and kissed her dainty feet.

"Oh? Perhaps he's just deaf?" She giggled and put her hand out for him to kiss.

I held my skirt down as the last bit of tail whipped around my ankles. He was the spirit of reflection, as fickle as any man, and admired vanity when it gazed into him.

"You would have chosen me, of course, if you had seen me first. Am I not the fairest of all Murano women?" She said.

"You are the fairest, my lady," he said and gazed at her like a love struck pup.

I ran out of the workshop, my skirts flying behind me.

"Cover your tail!" my father screamed. I ran down the corridors, all the way back to my room and bolted the door. Breathless, I looked out the window. Sunset was approaching and the swallows circled the turrets in a mad frenzy. I realised that worse than no man at all, is to have one you love, and for him not to love you back. When did I start to believe the illusion that he loved me? I threw myself onto our marital bed, punching my pillow in frustration and cried myself to sleep.

I woke several times in the night, my head aching from crying and Venerio's pillow empty of his soft curls and face. Where was he? The window was open, allowing a wet wind into the room. I got up and bolted it shut.

Just before sunrise, mother knocked on my bedroom door, and without waiting for me to answer, escorted a bloodied and bruised Venerio into the room.

"I told you not to play with sea magic!" she scolded and pushed him towards me. "He escaped from your bedroom window last night, swam the many metres of lagoons until he reached Isabella's home. He climbed up into her room and your uncle found him there, gave him a hiding, then tossed him back into the water. Isabella was crying, said he would damage her marriage prospects. They cannot have her marriage prospects ruined since the fire at their workshop; it's their last hope of salvation."

I pulled the blanket up over my head and gritted my teeth to suppress a scream. Yes, they were poor, Isabella needed a good marriage, but she also hungered for love, she sought it and Venerio reflected it back.

Mother slammed the door leaving Venerio and I together.

"How could you do this?" I screamed and pummelled his chest with my fists. He didn't try to stop me but sat still, staring back at me. I stopped and looked at him. He wasn't angry. He didn't have a response. How could he when his very essence was shallow and without substance, meaningless unless there was someone to behold it? I had never gazed upon him with vanity but Isabella had, and it made him feel meaningful.

I had been fooled by my own illusion of love.

Finally, I begged my father to talk some sense into Venerio or else let me throw him back to the water from which he came.

"He is a good glassmaker," Giacomo said.

"He is a terrible husband," I said.

"He is a typical husband."

"I made him!"

"And you made yourself a wife! Infidelity is not uncommon. To be a good wife you must behave with dignity!"

My tail now stuck out from my skirt, thrashing at my ankles. I lifted it up under my skirt and walked across the cold floors and did what I do when I needed to think. I poured the cold Murano water into my tub for a bath and immersed myself.

Father was on an errand to pick up soda ash from a Persian ship at the main port. I had a few hours without his stern eyes upon me.

I walked the long corridors to the furnace and found Venerio near the ovens sketching a portrait of Isabella. When he saw me, he picked up his shovel and moved toward the lit furnace, as if he had been working all along. He's not that simple, after all, I thought. I squinted and drew from the anger in my tail to make Isabella's reflection appear in the fire. Her face jumped about in the flames, beckoning Venerio to help her. And the man made of water jumped in to extinguish them.

I'd watched the apprentices and Venerio long enough to know what to do. My hands shook as I crushed the crystal frit but I was determined. I'd made him from magic and I'd return him to water.

Solid water.

A mirror.

Better a widow than a woman scorned, Quasibella.

I was immune to his screams, his pleas for release as the steam hissed from his pores, his skin and bones liquefied. I threw the letter I had written under the guise of my underwater family into the fire, too, and used my last bit of magic to curse Isabella. I twined the two strands of Isabella's hair I had collected on her visit around a thorn-stemmed rose and threw them into the fire that made Venerio glass.

Two days later, I lay in my bath, ill from the pain and exhaustion only sea magic and spell-binding can bring. The muscles in my twisted leg had weakened and my tail had grown so long, it now dragged behind me, angry or not. I could not put any weight upon my feet. They itched and burned as the scales came through between my toes. Cold water was my only comfort.

Father came with another letter. This time, not written by me. It was from his brother.

Isabella's betrothal had been called off due to the scandal of Venerio's nocturnal visit. To avoid further shame, Isabella was to be shipped off to marry a widower with a baby daughter in Lombardy. The baby was known to be of a unique beauty and therefore considered a perfect match for Isabella to become her step-mother.

"So Venerio has fled to avoid my brother's wrath!" my father said, as though he had solved the puzzle of Venerio's disappearance. I let him believe it.

"Apprentice me to mirror making! Look at what I've made! It's in the armoire! Open it!"

My father cautiously opened the wardrobe's creaking door. Inside was a large, oval-shaped looking-glass mirror. He gazed into it and I stifled a giggle as my father jumped back as it spoke.

"What a fine beard, you have, Giacomo!" the mirror said.

"You've made a speaking mirror?" My father was incredulous. He let out a gasp of surprise and then began to dance a jig. "We will write to the Underwater Senate and get our reward! The fortunes such an invention will bring!"

"Apprentice me to glass," I pleaded. Father finally agreed.

We sold him for a fine price—a talking magic mirror that spouted empty platitudes to vain women. The widower bought it as a wedding gift for his new wife, Isabella, my cousin. I promised my father I would make extraordinary glass like the letter had asked.

Now I am a glass-maker. I make glass of cobalt blue and vermillion red, and mirrors that speak of a woman's beauty. As I hold the mirror that can reflect the true beauty of a woman, the beauty of her heart—I ponder my decisions and keep it covered.

After what I have done to Isabella and Venerio, I fear looking into this mirror. I keep it covered, afraid of what it might reveal.

STICKS AND STONES

RYAN O'NEILL

"False words are not only evil in themselves,
but they infect the soul with evil."

— PLATO

PAXZA'RAVRNAM'BABLLA'TOK

Early one morning in the summer of 2011, James Blackwood, Professor of Philology at the University of Newcastle, set aside the examination papers he was marking, and went out for a walk. It was a cloudless Sunday, and he strolled up the hill to the cathedral, waiting there for ten minutes until the hour. Although he was an atheist, he enjoyed the sound of church bells, and as he wandered away from the cathedral, he followed their pleasant echoes.

In a small side street, Blackwood stopped in front of a shop he had never noticed before. The walls were cracked and red paint was peeling from them like sunburnt skin. Even the graffiti on the side of the shop seemed ancient, resembling the symbols of a dead language. By the doorway, on a bench, an old man sat in the shade. Above him, printed on the filthy window, were the words A BADDON. Without the full stop, Blackwood was reminded of a sign on a cage in a zoo. The old man spat on the pavement from time to time, regarding the few cars and pedestrians that went by with barely concealed outrage, as if the world were his and his rights were being trampled on. Blackwood peered at a large cardboard sign taped to the door that read "Seller of Clothes, Food, Sundries" and was about to pass on when he saw that the last word on the list, very small, was "Books."

As he stopped A Baddon rose to his feet and went inside, and after a moment, Blackwood followed him into the darkness of the shop. Though it was a bright day, it seemed that the sunlight was hesitant to come in, as if it were afraid that the old man might charge it admission. The cracked windows were curtained with dirt, and across one of them, running diagonally, was a disgusting finger-written blasphemy that Blackwood, godless as he was, felt obliged to wipe off with his handkerchief.

On the wall to his left stood shelves of paperback books, mostly Westerns, and piles of old magazines that had the same discarded look as newspapers left on trains. Opposite these, hanging from nails, were racks of clothes, and teapots, pots and pans. Everything in the shop had a neat, handwritten price tag, and most of the prices had been revised up or down several times in red ink. The old man, Baddon, waited behind a dirty glass counter, watching him. "Good afternoon," Blackwood said.

"I was about to shut for lunch" the old man replied. He had a harsh Scottish accent that conspired to make even the most innocent word sound like a curse. "Just looking," Blackwood smiled. "Won't be a moment. Blackwood went to the bookshelves and cocked his head to read the titles. None of the books appealed to him, and he was about to leave when he caught sight of a broken-backed blue spine, which proclaimed in thick red letters: *Ten Terrifying Tales* by J.B Reid. Blackwood pulled the book from the shelf. It was a first edition printed in New York in 1938, and the yellow, brittle pages were almost falling apart. The cover showed an amateurish drawing of a woman shrieking in terror at a ghostly figure. She had evidently annoyed the old man for he had gagged her with the price tag of three dollars. It had been a long time since Blackwood had read a ghost story. He was glad to pay the old man and leave the shop before he found a price tag on himself as well.

DWIX'BITUD'SLEKDI'BERBOD'QADIV

Blackwood lived alone in a large L-shaped house on the corner of a busy street near the beach. He had been content there for many years, until a new neighbour had moved in, a rude, ignorant young man with tattoos on his neck and forearms. Often this neighbour played loud music until early morning, and Blackwood barely slept. But that night, after dinner, there was silence, and so Blackwood settled in bed and began to read the book he had bought at Baddon's. The first story had the promising title, "The Horror in the Darkness." Above the word "Horror," someone had written in red pen, "cliché." Blackwood tutted and flicked ahead to find that every page was similarly annotated. Blackwood disliked handwriting on books, considering it a kind of desecration. But after reading the first paragraph of the story, he found that he couldn't disagree with the judgement of the annotator, who had also circled it and scrawled, "Sheer hokum!" The story was so appallingly written that Blackwood only continued reading because of the amusing marginalia. Blackwood was proud of his knack at being able to guess the sex of his students, and even whether they were left or right-handed, from a sample of their writing. But the writing in the book puzzled him. Sometimes it sloped forwards, sometimes steeply backwards. It was usually very neat, but at the most juvenile sections of the book it would become messy and almost illegible, as if the writer had become agitated. Only the dark red ink and the heavy pressure of the pen remained constant.

Blackwood enjoyed the comments of the anonymous critic enormously throughout the first five stories, until he came across a rather odd note beside a lurid description of a Black Mass. "Not how this is done at all!" the critic had written, and underlined. For an instant Blackwood had thought the writer was talking of the Mass itself, but then he realised that he (Blackwood had decided it was a he) must be criticising the scene as a whole, which was badly conceived and absolutely without suspense. A few lines further down the page were written the words, "Stupid BITCH" in reference to the insipid heroine of the story. The comments became progressively ill-tempered after that, and Blackwood found them less entertaining. The only positive criticism he found were a few words in the margin of a story describing the summoning of an ancient, evil spirit; "There's something to this after all."

Blackwood couldn't agree, for this story was perhaps the worst of the lot. Still, he read to the end, as he had never left a book unfinished in his life. He had hoped the critic would have written a more extensive review of the book on the flyleaf, but there was nothing. Blackwood was about to lay the book aside when he noticed that the last page had, in fact, been ripped out. Considering the unseen writer's heavy hand, Blackwood found a pencil, and began to lightly shade the flyleaf, in case the writing from the missing page had imprinted itself there. After a moment he was rewarded with the ghost of a p outlined in lead. Childishly pleased, he continued shading with the pencil, and next revealed the letters a, x, z and a. It was gibberish. As he continued down the page, all he disclosed was five long lines of letters, making nonsense words. Blackwood squinted and stared at the letters, thinking that they might be anagrams, or a code. Tired, he was about to give up when he had the queerest feeling that someone was reading over his shoulder.

This was always a sensation he had particularly disliked, and it was for this reason he never read on a bus or a train. And yet, though Blackwood knew that his back was to the wall, he felt compelled to turn around and look. Upon the whiteness of the wall he saw the same rows of letters that he had been staring at for the last few minutes. At first, he thought this was simply an optical illusion. He was even satisfied with himself that he knew the scientific term; persistence of vision. But then all at once the letters began to move, like a mad optician's chart. The vowels and consonants re-arranged themselves on the blank page of the wall, so that they very quickly resembled nothing less than a face, with two o's for eyes, a line of i's for hair, an a for a nose, and a w for an angry mouth. Blackwood, thinking that he was overtired, went to blink away the letters, when the two o's blinked at *him*.

Blackwood shut his eyes. He had often thought that characters in ghost stories behaved as if they had never read a ghost story, and he wasn't going to make that same mistake. If, when he opened his eyes, the thing on the wall was still there, he would calmly but hurriedly leave the house and find a place where there were lights and noise and people. Slowly, he counted to ten, and opened his eyes. The words were gone. Blackwood laughed, and got up to put the book away on the shelf near his bed. It was only then that he screamed. All his dozens of books were leering at him, their titles unreadable, the letters transformed from familiar vowels and consonants into an alphabet of hell. Hundreds of strange red symbols that were somehow alive gnashed and tore and devoured and copulated with each other. Some signs resembled twisted serpents and others unnatural orifices, whilst others still appeared to be crucified men and deformed children. At this first glance,

Blackwood almost vomited. He felt as if he were looking at a bucket of maggots, or to be more precise, reading it, for the horrific symbols, though he couldn't understand them, still conveyed a sense of evil.

DAJUQ'SHROXNV'BLJPO'TODINALY'DEWH

Blackwood instinctively looked down, away from the books, and found that he was standing upon a newspaper, and that the headlines were crawling up his leg. He cried out and stumbled backward, kicking at the paper with his bare feet. The walls of the bedroom gibbered at him, but between the transformed books he could see the blessed white of the bathroom. Blackwood ran inside and locked the door behind him. Kneeling down and breathing heavily, he allowed his eyes to rest on the white tiles. Then he stood, and, turning around, caught sight of the shampoo bottle on the edge of the bath. Its list of ingredients writhed and suppurated until Blackwood, whimpering, threw a towel over it. Blackwood was grateful he was a tidy man; his toothpaste and deodorant were shut up in the drawer. He didn't want to imagine what their simple logos had been transformed into.

When he had caught his breath, he began to wonder what he should do. He couldn't get to the front door of the house for there were too many books in the way, and he knew that he couldn't face what the words had become. The bathroom window was too small to climb out of, but it faced onto the main road, and he reasoned that he could cry out for help. When he raised his head to the open window, he staggered back, sobbing. He had forgotten the advertising billboards across the street which now displayed sneering, hellish letters that were five or six feet high. At the sight of them Blackwood could no longer control himself, and he was violently sick in the toilet. He lay face down on the floor of the bathroom, exhausted, staring at the white tiles as if they might disinfect his sight. Finally, as an experiment, he began to draw the letter A on the mirror with soap, but he stopped at the end of the first leg, and smashed the mirror with his hand. The pain from the gash in his palm allowed him the clarity to gather his thoughts.

At first he tried to convince himself that he had had a stroke, and that this metamorphosis of words was some form of aphasia. But he knew, somehow, that while several of the letters he had seen resembled tumours and blood clots, they were not caused by them. Similarly he was certain that he was not insane, though of course he would think this even if he were. The transformation had begun when he had read the letters from the book, and turned around to see the thing made of words looking at him. The only explanation, then, was that the letters in the book were somehow cursed, and had possessed the alphabet. Blackwood spent the rest of the long night desperately considering what he could do. If the book had cursed him, he had no idea how to lift it, especially as he couldn't look at any other books to do research. All he knew about curses was that they could sometimes be passed on, and it was this thought he clung to as he spent a sleepless night lying in the empty bath. Fortunately the "H" and "C" on the taps had worn away long ago.

At dawn he shut his eyes tightly and opened the bathroom door. As he crossed his bedroom he tripped and fell against the bookshelves. He expected to hear the pages shriek at him, but the books simply thudded to the floor. It seemed the words would not harm him if he did not look at them. Blackwood knew that he had to find the book that had started it all, *Ten Terrifying Tales*. He was certain that it had fallen on the bed and he groped blindly for it. At last he found it under a pillow, and he forced himself to open one eye to make sure of it. A glance was enough—the woman on the cover was now screaming at the book's title, which writhed and leered at her. Blackwood almost screamed too. He ripped the flyleaf away and closed his eyes again. With bloodied shins he found his way into the living room, to his desk, and clumsily searched the drawers until he found a pair of old sunglasses. He put them on and slitted his eyes so that he could just make dimly out objects nearby and nothing else. Still he wouldn't risk looking directly at a book. Blackwood dressed quickly, and staring at the ground, went outside.

He hesitantly made his way to his neighbour's house, though at one point he was almost run over by a car when he stumbled onto the road avoiding a rabid cigarette packet. Blackwood rang the doorbell and waited, holding the torn page of the book to his chest. It was the first time he had felt glad that the man was in. There he was, with his habitual vacant expression, but mercifully wearing a long-sleeved shirt so that Blackwood didn't have to look at his tattoos of football teams and seemingly misspelled names that Blackwood assumed were his offspring

"What?" the man asked abruptly.

Noticing Blackwood's sunglasses, he laughed. The logo on the man's shirt winked at Blackwood, who said in a quavering voice, "I was wondering if you might help me. As you can see, I've lost my reading glasses, and have to wear these old things. My friend wrote me a message telling me where I should meet him today, and I can't make it out. Would you mind?"

The man scowled and snatched the page from Blackwood. He held it close to his face and looked it over briefly before muttering, "Can't read it."

"Please," Blackwood begged, "Could you look closer?"

The man stared at the paper a moment longer, his lips moving, and then he started. "I've told you before you silly cow, not to sneak up on me!" he roared. Glancing over his shoulder at the untidy hallway, Blackwood saw no one. The man spun around, dropped the page. Then he shouted something and sprang into the house, slamming the door behind him. Blackwood stooped and retrieved the flyleaf. Carefully, he returned to his own front door, stopping once to force himself to look up at one of the billboards across the road. The words were still capering and cursing and glaring at him, and Blackwood began to despair. Then he saw the e. It was very faint; the merest ghost of an e behind an obscenity that squirmed and tongued in front of it, but it was there. If the curse couldn't be passed on, Blackwood reasoned, then it appeared that it could at least be weakened. Squinting, he went into his house and fell into an exhausted sleep in the bathtub. An hour later he was woken by an ambulance siren, and eyes still shut he went to the window and eavesdropped on the commotion outside. They were saying his neighbour had gone mad, and had almost bled to death after cutting the tattoos from his arms.

XI'UCUMB'HIWPEQLO'UPQOJAJDFAH

The next day, Blackwood made two hundred copies of the flyleaf. It took him almost all day, for he had to shuffle to the library with his eyes half-closed, avoiding as best he could the nauseating litter, demented license plates and menacing things that infested the shoes and T-shirts and hats of passers-by. When he arrived, it took all his courage to go inside, knowing what awaited him there. Thankfully the photocopier was in an alcove near the entrance, hidden from the pulsating shelves of books. When he had gathered the papers together, he went out in the street and tried to hand them out. But few people would take anything from a bedraggled, trembling old man, wearing sunglasses in the rain. Those that did accept a paper only glanced at the first line before throwing it away, although one or two must have read the whole thing, judging by the distant screams Blackwood could hear, and the fact that he could now clearly make out the e and the s in the disgusting inferno of the Newsagent's sign. He walked the streets all day, but at dusk he still carried at least a hundred leaflets, and no more letters had become visible.

As Blackwood lay miserably in his bath that night, the only thing that prevented him cutting his wrists was that he could not bear to face the logo on his razor. He thought bitterly how all of this had come about through reading stories, and it was then that he had an idea. Perhaps people would only read the five lines of the incantation from start to finish if it was hidden in something else, like a short story. That was it! As soon as it was light, Blackwood would begin to write a story, or rather he would hire someone and dictate it, as he couldn't use a pen, or a computer. It may as well be a ghost story, he had read enough of them to write one, though it might appear somewhat old fashioned. Perhaps that was all to the good, for then the reader wouldn't suspect anything until near the end, when they had read the last of the cursed letters, and taken part of the curse upon themselves, and felt the eyes of the o's over their shoulders.

Uowhe'hiehih'dahzoz'bega
Now, look behind you.

AFTER HOURS

THORAIYA DYER

The thoughts you have before you fall asleep are unsaved files on a computer before a storm.

The blackout comes. The screen goes dark. You can't ever get back what's lost.

What am I thinking, right before a Change? I can't be sure. Maybe there's evidence of what I tried to do—sunscreen applied too late or the blinds half drawn. It hasn't happened since I joined the Air Force. Military life's very ordered. You don't forget what day it is.

I can see why Toby liked it. Even though it got him killed.

• • •

One hundred scrubs of the brush.

That's how many you're supposed to do. Nothing can make human skin sterile for long; the bacteria come oozing out of their hidey holes and recolonise your hands before you've even picked up a scalpel blade. But it's important to do your best.

I watch my boss, Bradley. He squirts a bit of chlorhexidine on his hands, squelches it around for a second or two and then rinses. He turns off the tap with his elbow. Without ever touching the scrub brush, he's snapping on a pair of latex gloves, grinning at me over his grey beard.

"Come on, Jess," he says. "We've got six dogs to do this morning."

I don't say anything. I'm a freshly minted graduate, one month into the job, while Bradley's been practicing for thirty-seven years.

Everybody loves him. He can spey a bitch in eight minutes flat. None of the dogs ever get infections. It's all about speed, according to him. Less time under anaesthetic. Less time with the abdominal cavity open. Less time searching around in there, doing unintended trauma.

Speed might do the trick for a rural mixed practice, but I want to be a specialist surgeon one day. I am methodical. Maybe that makes me slow.

By the time I get gowned up, Bradley's already got his spey hook around one horn of the dog's uterus.

"Here you go," he says. "Follow it down and bring the ovary out."

There's two things holding an ovary to the inside of a dog's abdomen. One of them is a ligament. You want to tear through the ligament with your fingers. The other one is an artery. You don't want to tear that one. If you tear it, you're in trouble.

Big trouble.

And when you're new to surgery, they feel the same. Like digging your gloved hand into a warm basin of spaghetti and grabbing two identical strands of it. You don't yet have the instinct for how much pressure to apply, or which direction to angle. Your heart's in your throat, wondering if you've pulled too hard. Is the patient's blood pressure normal? Are her membranes a little bit pale?

The ovary feels like ravioli in my hand. I pull. I stretch. It abruptly comes away. I bring it up towards the tiny incision that Bradley has made; an incision I feel is too small to properly examine the abdomen for an upwelling of blood.

Of course, Bradley doesn't have to do any examining, because there's never an upwelling of blood when he desexes a dog. He could do it blindfolded.

"Great, great," he says. "Here's the clamps."

He shepherds me through two more, then leaves me to do the other three dogs by myself while he goes off into the countryside to scrape some tumours off the eyes of half a dozen Hereford cattle.

The last dog is an enormous, overweight golden retriever. I search desperately through fat for the ovaries. Every time I think I've found them, my hand comes up holding globs of fat. It takes forever for me to clamp and tie them.

When I'm finally finished closing the abdomen, I look up to discover a stranger in the doorway: a short, heavily muscled man in army camouflage.

"Where's Brad?" the man asks.

"Out on a call," I say.

The man runs a roughened palm over his salt-and-pepper buzz cut.

"I'll wait in his office," he grimaces. "Black tea with two sugars."

He clomps off towards the office. I suppose he's mistaken me for a nurse, but then, I'm wearing a surgical gown. Maybe he's a mate of Bradley's, but this is a staff only area, and I sure as hell didn't go to university for five years so I could serve up black tea with two sugars.

I take a deep breath, count to ten, take off my mask and gloves and sit down at the computer to write up the surgeries.

• • •

The dog was new, they said. When they're new, they make mistakes.

They needed more dogs than they had. Their metal detectors were suddenly useless. The new IEDs had no metal or electronic parts. Instead of hacksaw blades coming together to complete the circuit, detonating the shell, graphite blades were used with ammonium nitrate. The Australian commanders had a choice between uncertified contractors and dogs who hadn't finished their training, and the troops were getting shirty with all the waiting around.

That dog should never have been there.

Well, by the time I'm finished with them, no bomb detection dog is ever going to make a mistake like that again.

• • •

Bradley arrives, out of breath, in his overalls, smelling of cow.

"Tia says Sergeant Scott is here. I came as fast as I could. Did you make him a cup of tea?"

"No," I say, looking up from the computer.

"Listen, Jess. The Air Force account is the most lucrative one that we have. If we lose it, we're out of business. We bend over backwards for them, okay?"

"Okay," I say. "I'll make the tea."

"No, no. I'll make it. I want you to go through the records of all the military working dogs we have on file. Put together an ice box with all the vaccinations that are due. I'm going out to the base in a couple of hours. You can meet me there after your consults."

When I look through the files, I find thirty German shepherds who've been given exemplary care. Their teeth are cleaned yearly under anaesthetic. State-of-the-art nutrition and parasite control is institutionalised. The dogs are fully immunised for duty in South-East Asia and the Middle East. They each have a service number, but their names are taken from defunct gods or warriors of legend: Ares, Odin, Ghengis.

All of them are undesexed males.

The handlers are almost all male, too, except for LAC Nadia Lucas. Her dog is MWD Ripper.

I try to imagine how it would be working with an entire squad of Sergeant Scotts, and salute Ms Lucas's fortitude.

Tia ducks her head around the corner.

"There's a poodle in consult one," she says. "Needs a heartworm injection."

When I go into the consulting room, the white standard poodle crouching on the table coughs nervously.

"Hi Nan," I say.

"Hello, dear," my grandmother beams.

"Hi Peppe," I say.

Peppe cowers.

I hold him gently while I examine him. He's got a dodgy heart. Through the stethoscope, the murmur is obvious, and his lungs crackle as he breathes with all the retained fluid in them. His pulse is pathetic and when I push on his gums, it takes forever for the pinkness to come back.

I don't say it, but I don't think heartworms could make his heart much worse than it already is. His teeth are terrible, too. Nan feeds him soft tinned food. There's great black and orange chunks of calculus around his molars.

"Nan," I say, "if bacteria get into his bloodstream because of his rotten teeth and end up in his kidneys, that could be the last straw for him."

Nan's expression turns miserable.

"It's my fault, isn't it?"

I tactfully ignore the question.

"He can't have an anaesthetic for a dental because of his heart," I say, "but I can try to crack some of that tartar off just while he's sitting there on the table."

She tries to hold him for me, but at the sight of the tartar removing forceps, Peppe goes berserk.

I talk quietly to him while I try to peel back his lips.

"Peppe, it's fine, everything is fine. I'm just going to scrape some muck off your back teeth. It's a little bit cold but it doesn't hurt. Good boy, Peppe. Good boy."

But it's no use. He's stressing too much, throwing his head around. I send him home with Nan before he can turn blue and keel over.

I wish the animals could understand me. I wish I could show them that I wasn't going to hurt them. And if I was going to hurt them, give them a needle or manipulate a sore joint, well, it would only be for a bloody good reason.

If only they knew, I could take so much better care of them.

• • •

I used to wonder about the last thoughts of the victims.

There's transmission. That happens to the strong ones. For the rest, there's the slow sickness and death. You can't tell from looking which one it's going to be. If you set out deliberately to make a human into a wolf, in all likelihood the only thing you're going to make is a human into a corpse.

We've all had our little slip-ups. You can't dwell on them. The important thing is, there's less of us, now. One day, there'll be none.

We're all pleased by that. Almost all. Someone will occasionally go on a rampage, but the Council finds them and puts them out of their misery. One new werewolf could be a mistake. Ten new werewolves, well, it's a death sentence, and that's getting off lightly, because where there's ten new werewolves there's a hundred dead humans.

Funny thing is, it isn't the wolf in them that makes the mad ones want to infect others. It's the human.

The side that feels loneliness like a kick in the gut.

I get that.

Shit, I miss Toby so badly.

• • •

The barking can be heard from the far end of the runway.

"They get loads of exercise," Tom says. "It's a big perimeter. We patrol the base with the ground defence personnel. Day or night. Rain, hail or shine."

I'm listening to the charismatic handler but not really hearing him. My knuckles are white on my seatbelt as he comes around a bend and floors the accelerator into the straight. The airfield is flat and grassy. Speed limit signs read one-tenth of Tom's current velocity.

"There's a stop sign," I say weakly.

"Oh yeah," Tom says. He swerves off the road to avoid the twin speed humps designed to force ground vehicles to stop and check for air traffic. The car shudders through the grass, crosses the perpendicular runway, hits the grass on the other side and swerves back onto the road.

Tom points at some buildings in the distance, outside the base itself.

"There's a vet surgery over there. Way closer than Brad's. We used to take the dogs there. Heaps cheaper, too. But the vet was scared of the dogs. Used to examine them from the other side of the room with his back up against a wall."

"Not very thorough."

"He was on holiday, one time. One of our dogs got bit on the face by a black snake. We took him out to Brad's. We couldn't muzzle the dog without covering up the bite. Brad marched right up to him and grabbed his head to have a proper look. Impressed the hell out of Sergeant Scott."

"I bet."

"He started sending all the dogs to Brad, even when the other vet came back from holidays. We had some mean dogs, then. Sure couldn't have used them for crowd control. They were vicious, mongrel things. The meanest one was Hurricane. He went in to have his teeth cleaned and Brad knocked him out for it. Only, Hurricane wasn't completely knocked out."

"What happened?"

"Oh he ripped a hole in Brad's stomach. Twenty-eight stitches they gave him at the hospital. We liked Brad before that, but after that he was a goddamned hero."

So that's what it'll take to impress Sergeant Scott. Twenty-eight stitches. Well, I'm not planning on getting bitten, but neither am I going to vaccinate any dog I haven't given a proper examination.

Tom pulls into the parking lot beside the kennels.

I carry the cooler with the vaccines and heartworm preventative over to the trestle table where Bradley's set up the paperwork.

The handlers bring their dogs out and form two lines. The barking doesn't stop.

"They're excited," Tom says, "because of the muzzles. They only wear them for two things. One of them is getting checked by the vet."

"What's the other one?"

"Attack training. When they practice on real people."

The first dog in my line is the only one that isn't barking. He's sleek, alert, and slightly bigger than the others.

His handler is a tall, dark-haired woman with John Lennon sunglasses and a peaked camouflage cap.

"This must be Ripper," I say. "Would you mind holding his head while I listen to his heart?"

"He won't move," Nadia Lucas says, loosely holding the end of the leather leash. I start to smile and tell her to do it anyway when I'm struck by the fact that Ripper is standing, unnaturally immobile, in the perfect show position.

He's wearing a muzzle. It can't hurt to try. When he moves, then I can ask Nadia to hold him.

I check his eyes, his ears and his lymph nodes. I part his thick fur and palpate his abdomen. I listen to his chest, take his temperature and feel his pulse.

Ripper doesn't move.

Shaking my head in wonder, I ask Nadia to take off Ripper's muzzle and hold back his lips so I can see his teeth. Nadia gives a little derisive snort before complying. Ripper's teeth are perfect. I give the injections and send them away.

"Nadia's brother," Tom whispers to me, "was in the infantry. Got blown up in Afghanistan last year. The bomb sniffing dog tried to pick up the IED. Nadia wants to transfer to Darwin to train bomb dogs but she's got to finish her basics here first."

"She's got Ripper trained pretty well."

"Nobody knows how she does it. It's not just Ripper. She can control any dog. Sergeant Scott won't pass her, but."

"Why not?" I hiss back at him, but then Sergeant Scott's at the head of the line with a dog that's straining towards me, hyperventilating, salivating and pawing at the ground.

"This is Stormy-Boy," the Sergeant informs me. "Son of the famous Hurricane. You heard about Hurricane?"

"Yes," I say. My heart gallops with the primal fear most people feel on confronting a snarling wolf, but this is it. I force myself to smile. This is my moment to show I can do the job.

Scott seizes the dog by the collar, getting it in a headlock while I make my observations. There's not much use trying to take Storm's temperature while he's overexcited. I pull on a glove and squeeze some lubricant onto a finger.

"You finished yet?" Scott barks over his shoulder at me.

"Got to check his prostate," I reply, seizing the dog's tail.

As soon as I insert a finger, Storm goes ballistic. It's all Scott and Tom can do to keep holding him.

"That's it, we're done," the Sergeant says.

"No," I say. "I haven't finished."

"You bloody well have."

"I'm sorry, but this is an entire male dog and he only gets checked once a year. He could die if he's got a tumour and it's been missed this time around."

There's laughter in the line behind Scott.

Wolf-whistles.

Bestiality jokes.

"For fuck's sake," the Sergeant says, bending back down to tackle the dog, whose whites are showing around its crazed eyes.

• • •

The new vet's so green.

Going through the motions like she knows what she's doing, but would she know an abnormality if she felt one?

Let's just hope she had good teachers that took her out of the lab and into the world. Because you can't work out what living tissue feels like if you've been taught with textbooks and virtual reality any more than a dog from outside the ADF that's been taught to retrieve mail packages full of drugs can work out not to bring a land mine back to its handler.

. . .

When all the dogs are vaccinated, Bradley claps me on the shoulder.

"Good job, partner," he says. "We've finished early."

Sergeant Scott comes up and shakes Bradley's hand.

"It wasn't easy or cheap, but we've implemented all your recommendations, Brad."

"I can tell. The dogs are in excellent condition."

"I'd like you to come out and give another talk on first aid in combat situations. We've got some new handlers that missed out on the last one."

"I noticed. The woman. Nadia? Pretty good, is she?"

Scott turns immediately sour.

"Women," he says, as though I'm not even there. "She'll be knocked up and out of the squad in no time. There's no point teaching them anything. They're gone before you know it."

I take the return ride to the surgery in Bradley's car.

"How was that, then?" he asks, full of good cheer.

"I don't think much of Sergeant Scott," I say. "Tom's alright."

"Give the Sergeant a break," Bradley says. "He hasn't been well."

"What's wrong with him? A carrot up his arse?"

"You could say that. He's got cancer. An osteosarcoma arising from the fourth vertebra of his tailbone. They can't excise the tumour and get clean margins without leaving him with permanent faecal incontinence and a high likelihood of recurrent infections."

"Oh," I say in a small voice.

"It was picked up on a yearly prostate check. Apparently his GP, a new graduate, missed it the first time around."

"What's going to happen? Will he try surgery anyway?"

"No. He said he'd rather die with dignity, though I don't think it's going to be dignified either way. They were looking at Tom for his replacement, but the kid keeps getting into drunken brawls at the local and being demoted."

I think: *That explains why he hates me.* Also, *Nadia should be the one to replace Sergeant Scott*, but there's no point even saying that aloud.

It's never going to happen.

• • •

News Flash: The old bastard's going to kick the bucket.

But I haven't finished with him yet.

He thinks he's keeping me back out of spite, because he's jealous of what I can do. In fact, he's still got plenty to teach me. A day's going to come when I'll want to teach others to train bomb detection dogs. Problem is, nobody but a werewolf has the skill of being able to put images direct into a dog's mind, to calm them down or stir them up just by thinking at them.

I need to know all of Michael Scott's little tricks, his devious ways, the things he feels so deeply in his bones that he's forgotten he ever had to learn them.

I've decided to take the chance. He's dying anyway, right? And if it doesn't work, well, I'll tell the others it was an accident. There's certainly no love lost between us.

• • •

The phone wakes me.

It's 2 AM.

The full moon hangs, huge, outside my window. I live in a unit above the veterinary surgery. It makes being on after hours duty that much more bearable. When people's cats start vomiting in the middle of the night, all I have to do is crawl into my clothes, sink a cup of coffee and stumble down the stairs.

The call centre connects me to the client. It's the RAAF.

One of the dogs is distressed, restless and panting.

I tell them to bring it straight down.

Fifteen minutes later, Tom lifts Ripper out of the back of the doggies' truck and sets him down on the paved driveway. He's unsteady on his feet. Neck extended, he retches uncontrollably.

"He's in a bad way," Tom says. "Nobody knows where Nadia is. Sergeant Scott isn't answering his phone, either."

The alert, obedient dog that I vaccinated at the base is gone. Ripper, despite trembling legs that won't hold him up, growls and lays his ears back as I examine him on the treatment room table. Tom holds the dog's jaw shut with one hand and hugs his chest with the other. He's got a weak, thready pulse and pale membranes.

"It's serious," I say.

"He got a clean bill of health yesterday."

I panic, wondering if I missed a life-threatening heart problem in my examination. All the dogs were barking and jumping around. Except Ripper. If any dog had been checked properly, it was Ripper.

"Put on the lead suit and gloves," I say. "I'm going to need him lying down on his right side on the x-ray table."

Radiographs clearly show the displaced, air-filled pylorus.

"It's gastric dilatation and volvulus," I say. "We mostly see it in big, deep-chested dogs like German shepherds and Great Danes. Plenty of room in there to move. The stomach expands and twists. Air can get in but it can't get out. A bunch of different blood supplies get cut off. I've got to get his stomach untwisted or he'll go into shock and die."

"Right now?"

"Right now. First thing is to see if I can get a tube down his throat and decompress that way. Then I'll go in and sew his stomach to his abdominal wall so it can't get twisted again."

He shuffles around a bit in his combat boots, starts to say something, decides against it, and then says it.

"You don't want to call Brad or anything?"

I do, in fact, very much want to call him. But I happen to know he's interstate.

"I'll need a nurse," I say, "to monitor the anaesthetic. I'll call Tia. But first I'm going to get Ripper on some IV fluids, get his blood pressure up a bit. You can help me place the catheter. Hold up his front leg."

"Brad doesn't usually shave the leg," Tom protests. "It takes ages to grow back and the boss doesn't like them to look sick when they're on patrol."

"Hair removal," I explain, mercilessly clipping a long rectangle of fur, "gets rid of a lot of dirt and bacteria, decreasing the amount of muck that's going to get pushed into Ripper's bloodstream when I stick the needle in. It also increases visibility for finding the vein, which will be flat and almost undetectable because of his shockingly low blood pressure."

"Oh, right," Tom says, brightening. "Just so I can tell that to Sergeant Scott. If he ever answers his phone."

• • •

The phone rings in his office but he doesn't get up.

He started to bandage the bite, but halfway through he keeled over on the couch in the staff lunch room, breathing deeply.

I sit back on my haunches in the open doorway. I howl at the painfully beautiful moon.

The dogs go crazy. I'm distantly aware of the danger. If anybody else comes, they'll be easy prey, unless I've got a thing for them, and I haven't got a thing for anybody, not even Tom. He looks too much like Toby, and he's done a tour of Afghanistan as well. Every time I look at him, I wonder why Toby got blown to hell and Tom didn't.

It's difficult to hold thoughts in my head. I let them drift away before an onslaught of scents and sounds: frogs in far hollows, machine parts being oiled and turned, boots in long grass. The small, sleepy, feathery smell of swallows under the eaves. The musk of the male dogs, their urine, the meat on their breath from the evening meal.

You don't Change for a while, you forget the clean, cutting enhancement of your senses. The joy of being alive. But the price tag is too high. I feel the thrill but then I remember that boy who followed me out of the club. All he wanted was my phone number. He was too shy to ask for it in front of my friends. The dancing had been frantic; I'd sweated most of my SPF 30+ away and forgotten to reapply it.

That boy was the same age as Toby when he died. When they both died. Maybe he had a sister, too, who loved him. Maybe she's hollow inside, like me.

The moon sets and I'm naked in the dark.

It's cold.

• • •

Nadia arrives first thing in the morning.

Sweeping past the staff only sign, she goes unerringly to the cage where Ripper is sleeping.

I follow her, bleary-eyed.

"What have you done to him?" Nadia asks.

"Surgical rotation and permanent gastropexy," I say.

At least, I hope that's what I've done. It was my first one and I'm not sure I've stuck the stomach on well enough. But I did my best.

Ripper wakes and whines and thumps his tail at the sight of his handler.

"Good," Nadia says. "That's good."

I'm startled by the praise. For a moment I wonder if she's talking to Ripper and not me.

"I'm sorry I wasn't here," she says.

"Tom was good with him. He should be able to go back to the base after he's finished that bag of fluids. I'll get the invoice printed out and give you a copy of the treatment record for Sergeant Scott."

"Sergeant Scott isn't well. I took him to hospital earlier this morning. I'll be looking after things until he gets out."

"Oh," I say uncomfortably. "I hope he's better soon."

"He won't be. You know a new grad missed his tumour the first time around?"

"Bradley told me," I say. "I suppose everybody makes mistakes."

• • •

It was a mistake. An accident.

When I came home from school, the big brick house was empty. Our parents were doctors. We didn't see much of them. Toby was six years older than me. He looked out for me. Cooked a mean mushroom omelette.

Wednesday nights were footy practice, though. He wasn't home. I got my bike out and went riding in the cul-de-sac with the other kids from the street. We rode on all the front lawns except for Mr Heery's, because he put a rope around it and put mean letters in our letterboxes if we went under it.

When we got bored we started daring each other to go under the rope. I went the furthest. All the way to Mr Heery's front door. It crashed open and he stared down at me, peeled-grape eyes in a pickled face with crazy white hair everywhere.

"Nadia Lucas," he said. "As loved and wanted as bird shit on a barbecue."

I ran away from him instinctively, springing over that rope like a gazelle while the others laughed and melted away to their houses.

My house was still dark. The street lights came on. I could smell onions cooking in the house next door. The full moon came up and I didn't go inside. I sat on the doorstep, holding the handlebars of my bike, getting angrier and angrier. I was loved and wanted. It was just that my parents were busy and important and Toby had footy practice.

— 187 —

I got so worked up that I decided to put bird shit on Mr Heery's barbecue. I scraped some off the top of our front fence with a steel kebab skewer, climbed under Mr Heery's rope, advanced up his manicured lawn and sneaked down the side of his house.

The tall side gate had a bolt that only opened from the inside, but my hand was small enough to fit through the wire.

When I opened it, a huge white dog knocked me down. It went for my throat. I stuck the skewer into its open mouth.

Mr Heery was brain damaged. His family waited two years before they pulled the plug and he died.

I should have died, too. Toby stayed in hospital with me for a week.

"You're strong," he said to me. "You'll make it."

And I did. In a manner of speaking.

• • •

It seems like déjà vu.

The shrill phone at 2 AM. The RAAF base on the other end. I think: *It must be Ripper. He's got another GDV. I did something wrong and now, a month later, the adhesion has failed.*

"Which dog?" I ask huskily, pulling on my clothes with the phone jammed between shoulder and ear.

"Oh, it's not one of the working dogs," Nadia Lucas says. "It's my dog. Mike. He's got a lump I'd like you to look at."

"What sort of lump? Is it painful?"

"It's not painful."

"Maybe you could bring Mike in first thing tomorrow."

Nadia's voice turns cold.

"No. He needs to be seen right now."

I hesitate. I recall what Bradley said about bending over backwards for the Air Force, even if this isn't a military working dog.

"I'll see you soon," I say.

I shuffle down the stairs and unlock the clinic, flicking on a few lights and eliciting a few plaintive whuffs and miaows from hospitalised snail-bait-guzzling puppies and overnight boarding cats. I check their drip lines and litter trays and pet them as I pass. One of the computers has to be booted up to give me access to the file.

Mike doesn't have one. Nadia's never brought him to us before.

I line a few things up in the consulting room. Clippers, for shaving the lump. Cotton balls soaked in alcohol, for swabbing it. A needle and syringe for aspirating some cells and microscope slides on which to spray them. A cigarette lighter to fix the cells onto the slides. Stains for giving them colour. Maybe I'll see bacteria. Maybe fat. Maybe cancerous white cells, the blood of a hematoma or the clear fluid of a cyst. I figure any dog of Nadia's will sit quietly while I take all the samples I need.

He explodes through the front door, heavy head fringed with brown and grey fur, yellow eyes gleaming. Nadia follows with the leash wrapped around her forearm, red-faced and thin-lipped.

I open my mouth to speak, but Mike launches himself at me. The leash snaps taut. His back arches. He lands on his side and immediately starts to roll, front paws scrabbling at his muzzle.

"He's going to get that off," I observe.

"Sit!" Nadia shouts, hauling on the leash. Mike's the size of an Alaskan malamute, but the stick-thin limbs, straight tail and long muzzle are all wrong. If I didn't know it was impossible, I'd swear he was a timber wolf.

"One moment," I say. I go to the surgery, where a thick, goose-feather quilt has been spread lovingly over the heating pads on the table, ready for a new patient.

When I get back to reception, Mike is still rolling and clawing at his face.

I throw the quilt over him and lie on the thrashing shape. Nadia gets the idea and joins me on the floor. I ease the edge of the quilt back so that his nose is poking out.

"Where's the lump?" I ask.

"On his tail," Nadia replies.

We switch places.

The lump is hard and immobile. That's not good.

"Can we carry him into the consulting room?"

"You'll have to sedate him."

"I don't know if a sedative will touch the sides, frankly."

"Then knock him out."

"I need his weight and his vital signs."

He is forty-three kilos with a heart like a horse. I give him an intravenous anaesthetic and between us we shift him to the consulting room table.

Nadia's phone rings.

"I have to take this outside," she says, taking her sunglasses out of her pocket, leaving me alone with the anaesthetised dog.

I shave the lump on his tail. I swab it and let it dry. When I insert the needle, the lump feels crunchy inside, like bone or calcium deposits.

The dog's head whips around. Its teeth graze my hand as I jerk back. The snap of his jaw still resounds in the room as the shaggy muzzle lowers itself back to the table, succumbing to the drug, eyes closing.

I stare at the shallow laceration across the back of my knuckles. I scrub the injury with iodine, thinking of Hurricane and Bradley's twenty-eight stitches. I've gotten off lightly and should have been more careful.

Still, I don't like to muzzle a dog while he's under. Gingerly, I replace the pulse oximeter probe on his tongue, waiting for it to read his heart rate and oxygen saturation levels before turning to the microscope slides.

• • •

I hang up the phone.

The night air has a tang. The temptress moon hangs in cloud-pillows. I go to the car to check the weather forecast. We've still got an hour. I slap more sunscreen onto the places where Mike's fur has rubbed it thin.

What could have been my biggest mistake ever has turned out just as I planned. Even if it was a bit tough to catch him and bring him in before the Council caught wind of him. I'll explain to him later what's happened and why.

There's no time for that now. I march back towards the clinic. No mistakes tonight.

• • •

"So chop it off, then," Nadia says.

I blink at her over the microscope.

"But I need the cancer to be staged by the pathology lab. I need to take a biopsy first. X-rays of the long bones. What if it's spread to the tail from somewhere else?"

"I can't afford all that," she snaps. "Just cut his tail off, will you? He's sleeping now, isn't he? I don't want to get charged for two anaesthetics."

"It's not like carving a roast," I reply hotly. "I can't do it here in the consulting room. I'll need a nurse to monitor the anaesthetic, if I'm going to surgery, and everything costs twice as much after hours as it would in the morning."

"I'm a trained vet nurse. I'll monitor the anaesthetic."

"You?"

"Yeah. I quit my job at the animal emergency centre and joined the Air Force when my brother was killed in action. So. I'll set up the rebreather with isoflurane and check the system for leaks, okay? Get going! I'm due back at the base in an hour. You've got thirty minutes to finish the surgery."

"You're joking," I say, but she isn't.

It takes five minutes for me to fill Mike up with antibiotics, get him intubated and get him properly positioned in ventral recumbency on the table. It takes another five minutes for me to get his tail clipped and prepped. Five more for me to scrub in.

"He's taking twenty breaths a minute," Nadia says, emptying a scalpel blade into my sterile instrument pack. "Heart rate's good. No blink. No swallow. Chop, chop!"

I make a double V incision in the skin distal to the transection site. The lump is attached to the bone, to caudal vertebrae IV. I'm going to remove number III as well, leaving number II and the levator ani muscle attachment intact, so there'll be no incontinence or herniation.

It takes me ten minutes to carefully dissect through the soft tissues. There are two big arteries to ligate and six smaller ones.

I use dissolvable suture material to tie off the median and lateral caudal arteries and veins. It's more difficult to isolate the smaller blood vessels.

"Bing," Nadia says. "Time's up, Ben Carson. You're not separating Siamese twins, here. Cut, damn it. Cut, cut, cut."

"I can't just cut," I shout at her.

She brandishes the cautery wand.

"Cut! Before I do it for you!"

I slash through the joint. The tail comes away. Without touching anything else, Nadia sears the six bleeding blood vessels until the bleeding stops. I'm aghast at the charred, dead areas she's created.

"Is that how you did it at the emergency centre?"

Nadia's already opening packets of suture material over my pack.

"Close it up already. And I don't mean plastic surgery. Just make sure it's going to heal cleanly."

I glare at her, but Bradley did say it was all about speed. I pick up the needle and forceps.

• • •

He changes back just as I'm tucking him into bed.

When I get home, I bury what's left of the tail in the back garden.

A week later, I'm handing my Amex over the front counter of the vet surgery when Bradley catches sight of me. He comes over to ask me about Sergeant Scott.

"How's Mike doing?"

"Pretty good," I say. "They did a scan and the cancer's gone."

"Gone? You mean shrinking."

"No, I mean gone. Tailbone too. Like they all just magically dissolved."

Most folks with tailbone problems don't have the luxury of turning into dogs. Even if they did, most folks don't know that the fused caudal vertebrae stuck on the end of a human sacrum has a direct anatomical equivalent in the dog which is much easier to access.

There are no werewolf vets that I know of.

• • •

Something is happening to me.

Peppe sits, calm and relaxed, on the table while I clean his teeth. Not just with the forceps but the scaler and polisher. Through the whining of the dental machine and the dampness of its cooling water spray, I extend to him my reassurance and, as pack leader, my insistence on compliance. He extends to me his trust.

When his teeth are clean, I scrub up for surgery. Without bothering about the scrub brush, I squeeze some chlorhex onto my hands and squelch it around for a bit.

It's all about speed, really. And I don't think I will go into surgical specialisation. I can do more good here, in a community like this one.

Besides, Bradley and Nadia are really good teachers.

THE BOY BY THE GATE

DMETRI KAKMI

It was a rainy night, and the four of us—Ross Orr, Geoff Hitchens, Rebecca Nagy, and myself—had gathered round the fireplace at Rebecca's home to stay warm and keep each other company during the longest and coldest night of the year. As happens at this sort of gathering, what with one thing and another, people began to tell ghost stories. Real ghost stories. Things that happened to them or to a close friend.

As Ross related a particularly gruesome tale about a driver who encounters a grey woman on a lonely country road, Rebecca shuddered and, excusing herself, went to the kitchen to fetch more of her excellent chocolate cookies. As a tribute to her culinary skills, they were devoured in no time, and the plate had to be replenished, together with cups of hot Belgian cocoa.

Next in line was Geoff with an unsettling story from his childhood. Between the ages of ten and eleven, he awoke every night to find a blond boy standing at the foot of the bed. Nothing ever happened. The scene merely repeated itself, night after night, until Geoff was used to the visitant and did not bat an eyelid when the phantom made his nocturnal appearance. In adulthood Geoff discovered that a child of the same description died in that room more than thirty years earlier.

Being the close-minded sort, I had nothing in the way of phantasmal visitations to offer, which meant I could pass the ball with relief to our hostess. Rebecca remained quiet for a minute or two. Then she raised her dark head and said:

"This didn't happen to me. It happened to a friend long ago, when she and I were in our last year of high school. If I hesitate it's because I'm not sure I have a right to tell the story to a group of strangers who didn't know her and can't possibly appreciate the seriousness of what happened to her at a young age . . . "

She trailed off, and her face clouded. Our murmured protests and encouragements were met with an inflexible silence. Rebecca's expression was eloquent. It said the story she was thinking of relating to this comic gathering was no mere light entertainment. It had obviously left a deep and lasting impression on her psyche.

"Come on, Rebecca, out with it," Ross, always the gregarious one, said. "It'll do you good to get it off your chest."

She smiled sadly. "I doubt that."

The fire crackled in the grate, and rain lashed the windows as we waited for her to reach a decision.

I studied Ross and Geoff as they sat in armchairs on the other side of the coffee table and saw that the high spirits had left them. Rebecca's disturbed mood pervaded the atmosphere and affected the entire company. It was as though the spectre of a dreadful past hovered over us like a stormy cloud. After some minutes, Rebecca stood from her seat beside me, threw a log in the fire, and said,

"If I'm going to do this, I'll do it properly. You see, I found out about it from a letter my friend Alice Kendall addressed to me before she . . . before . . . well, before it all happened. I don't think I could do the story justice if I told it in my own words. It's best if I read the letter to you, if that's all right . . . ? She was a talented writer; wanted to become a novelist." She cast questioning eyes round the room, and the three of us gratified her with a nod. "Excuse me a minute while I get it."

She was gone for about ten minutes, during which time Ross, Geoff and I contemplated our own thoughts.

The wind howled outside. The jacaranda tree hissed as it thrashed and tossed against the windowpane, the bare branches flung about like the arms of a demented skeleton. A part of me wished to be safely in the guest room upstairs, instead of playing silly buggers with adults who ought to know better. As I said, I am a cynic and very sceptical about supernatural occurrences. It was all I could do to stop myself from laughing or sneering at the circle of glum faces.

I was about to announce that I was going to bed when Rebecca returned with an envelope.

"Sorry, I had trouble finding it," she said, reclaiming her seat beside me. She opened the envelope and removed several sheets of thin, crackling, and somewhat yellowed paper. These were carefully unfolded and placed in her lap.

"Before I read Alice Kendall's words," Rebecca said, "I should tell you that all this happened at Port Fairy in the winter of 1986. It's a little town on the west coast of Victoria. Alice had gone there with her father, Barnaby Kendall. He was an academic, speaking at a literary conference. He had taken his only daughter along for a relaxing week at the seaside town. Alice's mother had passed away a year earlier." Rebecca raised her eyes and looked at each of us. Content with our undivided attention, she added: "And so to the letter. I'll leave out any parts that don't directly relate to the story."

She picked up the sheets and began to read in a voice that betrayed no emotion and yet provided the perfect accompaniment to the crackling of the logs in the fireplace and the shrieking of the wind outside. As she progressed with the tale, however, her voice gained a deeper, darker edge with rapid alterations in the registry of delivery. It mixed with the sound of rainwater gurgling in the drainpipes so that, by the time Rebecca finished reading, it seemed that we listened to a lament for the dead or a funeral rite. To this day, I shudder to think of it.

Dear Becky

On Friday night Dad was invited to dinner with people who are part of the literary festival. I had some stuff to do beforehand, so I promised to join him half an hour later. We are staying at a quaint place called the Merrijig Inn by the Moyne River. It's old and a bit run down but comfortable and it has heaps of atmosphere—you know the kind of place where crusty fishermen crashed for the night before going out to sea the next morning. Dad estimated that it'd take me about ten minutes to walk from the inn to the house where the dinner was on Regent Street, across the other side of town.

It was dark by the time I left. Port Fairy is a pretty town, with wide tree-lined streets and cute stone cottages tucked away in well-tended gardens. The thought of walking through the empty streets on my own didn't faze me at all. The guy at the reception desk asked if I'd be all right. I told him I was fine. The sky was clear, and a bitter wind prickled my skin. The air smelled of fresh brine and wood smoke, and there was a constant boom of surf coming from the back beach. It sounded like cannon fire. I stuck my hands in my pockets, hunkered down in my coat, and set off at a trot, virtually hopping from one distant streetlight to the next.

When I reached the centre of town, where all the shops are, I decided it would be quicker to cut through the churchyard at St. John's rather than walk the long way round to Regent Street. I know, famous last words. But it was so lovely and peaceful, and I felt so good and safe walking under the bright stars that I really didn't think anything of it.

I was standing on the nature strip, about to cross the narrow street and enter the churchyard, when I noticed something by the bluestone gate.

At first I thought it was a white balloon, hovering above the ground at about the height of a small child. Then I realised that what I took to be the light shining off white latex was, in fact, a face.

A boy's face.

I was startled at first and then intrigued.

He was incredibly pale and rigid as a statue. I was thinking a kid that young shouldn't be out on his own at this time of night, when I noticed his clothes. He wore an ill-fitting, old-fashioned jacket; heavy three-quarter length pants tucked in thick socks; and scuffed boots that were too big for him. His hair was dirty blond and messy.

Even as I stared at him, I could tell he was no ordinary boy. He was too still and vivid for that, as though he was some kind of high-fidelity projection put on freeze-frame. He even juddered a little at the edges, as though someone had paused a video. I was about to say Hello to him when he turned and not so much as walked but glided very rapidly behind the gatepost into the churchyard.

"Hey, don't go in there," I called. "It's dark." I ran after him, but he was nowhere in sight. He completely vanished. A quick search yielded nothing.

I didn't tell Dad. Next morning, straight after breakfast at eight thirty, I ran across town to the church, and there was the boy, waiting. In cold streaming sunlight that fell in dapples through the tree canopy, dressed in the same clothes, and standing at exactly the same spot, as if he'd been there all night.

The street was deserted; the houses closed up. I stood on the wet nature strip and studied his bloodless face. There was no indication that he saw me. The pale blue eyes seemed impossibly remote, as if he saw beyond this world into an altogether different plane. After a minute, in repetition of the previous night, he pivoted on the spot and disappeared behind the gatepost. Only this time, in daylight, I noticed something peculiar about the way he moved. It was as if he were a figure on a cuckoo clock, being shunted out on the axis of a mechanical arm and then whipped back again. It was alarming and frightening, too, because it robbed him of any humanity.

I searched the church grounds for a long time. There was nothing to find and, on the wide-open lawn, no place for him to hide. The church was locked so I couldn't make enquiries. A man stood smoking under a verandah across the street, but he didn't look like he'd welcome queries about peculiar children.

The important thing is, Becky, I wasn't afraid. Just puzzled. The poor thing looked so sad and lonely, and I wanted to help. I was convinced he was trapped on that spot for some reason, repeating the same action over and over again. For all eternity. Who knew how long he'd been there?

It was up to me to break the spell and free him.

At ten o' clock I went to a nearby bookshop and spoke to a woman with a black ponytail and beautiful silvery eyes. Her name was Jo. She was understandably perplexed by the story and said that, as far as she knew, no one had seen anything of that description in the churchyard. All the same, she picked a history of Port Fairy from a nearby bookshelf and leafed through it.

"Here," she said after consulting several dusty books, "listen to this . . . "

It turns out George O'Dowd, a fisherman, saw the boy by the gate in 1876. Marilyn McNally made the next sighting in 1916. The final recorded sighting was in 1946. The witness was Tony Wright, a war veteran who lived behind the church in Barclay

Street. In all cases, Jo read from the book, the witnesses reported that the boy ducked into the churchyard and vanished.

I asked Jo if there were any theories about who the boy might be. She read from the book.

"Many believed the ghostly boy was Davey Adair, a nine-year-old orphan who did odd jobs around town in the early 1860s. It was a severe winter. One night the boy sought shelter inside St. John's church. A heartless caretaker turned him out. Next morning, Davey was found frozen solid beside the Barclay Street gate. In death he received what was denied him in life. His young body was buried in consecrated ground just inside the gate."

"Here, look," Jo said and pointed at an ink drawing on one page.

At one stage the faithful were buried in St. John's churchyard. What is now a nice green lawn was once filled with tombstones, leaning every which way.

"What happened to the graves?" I asked Jo.

She shrugged. "The bodies were interred and moved to the Port Fairy Cemetery on the other side of the highway."

"Davey too?"

"Probably."

Despite the terrible story, I was thrilled to have found this much information about the boy. Now that I knew his name, I could help him.

"And I'm only the fourth person to see him," I said, trying not to sound too thrilled.

"I wouldn't jump to conclusions," Jo mumbled, her eyes still on the book. "They're only the sightings that were reported. There could be others that weren't."

Good point. "Well, thanks," I said, turning to leave.

"Not so fast," she said, grabbing my arm. "The book says that strange things happened to the people who saw the boy. I'd be careful if I were you."

"What strange things?"

She shrugged again. "Don't know. It just says, 'Strange and peculiar occurrences befell the unfortunates who witnessed the apparition.' Please be careful."

"You believe me, then?" I said to her with a smile.

"*Don't see why you'd make up a story like this.*" *She was a very practical woman, and I liked her a lot.*

That evening Dad had to attend yet another one of those endless dinners people are obliged to go to when appearing at literary events. This one was at the pub on Sackville Street, round the corner from St. John's church.

It was a bleak night, with the promise of rain. Dad and I were about to step into the warmth of the pub when I said, "Dad, can you give me a minute? I want to check on something," and before he answered I ran the few metres to Barclay Street and up to the church gates.

Davey Adair was waiting for me in his usual spot, as unnervingly still as ever. In the wan electric light that filtered through the thick canopy of trees, he seemed to be made of crackling frost.

I kneeled on the grass and stretched out my hands.

"Davey Adair," I said in my best voice. "My name is Alice. I'm your friend. Please let me help you, if I can."

There was no response or even a flicker of awareness. Except that the juddering round his figure intensified. Then again he pivoted on the spot like a mechanical toy on a spring and merged with the greater darkness behind the gate.

Disappointed, I ran back to Dad. I was at the corner of Barclay Street when I stopped and, for some reason, looked back at the church. Davey Adair's shiny moon-like face poked out and studied me from behind the bluestone wall.

"Good," I thought. "I got through to you."

When I reached my ever-patient father at the pub door, Davey stood at the corner of Barclay and Bank Streets, staring at me. Even though I knew he didn't mean any harm, it was a bit unnerving. His pupils looked as if they'd been painted on his eyelids.

"Who's the boy?" Dad asked.

"Oh, no one," I said, pushing him inside.

He gave me a knowing look and left it at that.

That was four hours ago, dear Becky, my bestest friend in the world. I'm now in my room at the Merrijig Inn, writing this letter to you. Dad is asleep next door. The rain is pelting down, and the gale coming off the ocean is enough to put the wind up Captain Ahab.

Becky, something has been scratching at the window for a half hour. I daren't look. The room is upstairs on the first floor. It can only be a branch from the big tree outside. Even so, I'm spooked.

Davey was on the street when Dad and I returned to the inn tonight. I caught sight of him as we came in the front door, and then I saw him again from my window. He stood under the streetlight on the opposite pavement, looking up at me. That little head tilted up. The pale throat exposed. The mouth moving as if forming words. But of course from this distance, I couldn't hear a thing. I must admit the idea that he followed me is freaking me out a bit. And then getting a glimpse of that mouth contorting in that awful way, as if he's forgotten how to perform perfectly normal bodily functions, gave me the serious heebie-jeebies.

I'm sitting at the small desk, wondering what I got myself into.

Becky, when the mouth opened, it was just a black hole that went all the way to the centre of his being. Poor thing. It started to rain, and the water fell into his open mouth as if it were a well or a bucket or something. He didn't seem to notice.

There's that horrible scritch-scratch of busy little hands at the window again.

Scritch-scratch; scritch-scratch.

It sounds like broken nails being dragged against glass. And it's driving me insane.

When I look up from the letter, I see over the well-made bed to the window with the pretty lace curtains gathered at the side. It's not a large room. It's quite small actually, built into the attic, with a dormer window, which is why I can clearly see Davey Adair floating, yes, floating one floor up, outside the rain-streaked glass. The hair is plastered to his forehead, and one hand reaches out to press the window. He reminds me of an abandoned puppy, begging to be let in.

All the same, it's a terrifying sight. And yet, for some reason, I feel so terribly sorry for him. My heart goes out to him. It almost breaks at the pitiful sight of him out there, alone and abandoned. He looks how I felt after Mum died. Shattered and lost and bewildered and in need of a friend.

Maybe that's what he wants, Becky. A friend.

If only his eyes weren't so lifeless. I'd fling open the window and say Come in, Davey, come in. I'll take care of you. You can stay with me forever.

His mouth moved again. I think he's trying to tell me something. If only it wasn't so black, like the coal chute at my grandmother's place.

All right. I've made up my mind. I've been sitting here for the longest time, trying to decide what to do. Now I know.

Hold on, Becky. I'm going to lay down the pen and open the window. I can't stand that scratching any more. And I must hear what he has to say. Hopefully he'll stop making that keening noise once he's out of the cold and in this warm, bright room.

I'm putting down the pen now, Becky. Wait for me, won't you? I'll be back in a tick . . .

Rebecca set the letter on the coffee table and looked up. There were tears in her eyes.

"She never came back," she said in a choked voice.

Ross leaned forward and said, "That's it?"

"Yes. She didn't finish the letter."

"But what happened to Alice?" Ross pursued.

Rebecca stared at the wall behind him and shrugged. "She disappeared. Hasn't been seen since. Next morning her father alerted the police. There was an investigation. Nothing was found, and, of course, everyone dismissed the letter as pure fantasy.

"The only sighting—if you can call it that—came late the next morning. A parishioner on the way to church found a pair of shoes embedded in the ground just inside St. John's gates. Turned out they belonged to Alice. Poor Barnaby Kendall returned to Melbourne with his daughter's suitcase and a pair of crushed, muddied shoes. He died not long after, believing he'd taken his daughter to her death."

"What do you mean 'embedded'?" Ross asked. For a sensitive man, he could be callous at times.

Rebecca sipped her cocoa before answering. "Just that. The shoes were half buried in the soil, toes first, like someone was trying to bury them."

Ross whistled between his teeth and said, "Or like something dragged her under the ground, and the shoes came off with the force of the impact."

Rebecca grimaced. "Don't. That's too horrible."

"There was no evidence in her room at the inn?" Ross relentlessly pursued his line of enquiry.

Rebecca shook her head. "The window to Alice's room was open. The rain got in and made a mess of the place. This letter was almost soaked through. The police said she'd probably run away with the boy her father had seen, but I don't know . . . She wasn't the sort. Studied hard, got top grades in just about everything. You know the type."

"You don't seriously think a ghost called Davey Adair took her," I put in.

"Well, what do you think happened then?" Ross called out. His eyes lit up as if he was about to punch me for daring to challenge what everyone appeared to accept without question.

"I don't know what happened, Ross," I replied. "I just don't believe she's being held captive by a bugaboo. And now," I said, gathering my cup and saucer, "if you don't mind, I'm off to bed. It's late."

Geoff, who had been quiet since Rebecca finished reading the letter, looked up from contemplating the embers in the fireplace. "I reckon we should all go to Port Fairy and see if the ghost is still there," he said.

"Well, if you do," I put in, "you go without me."

"I always wanted to," Rebecca said in a distant voice. "I was just too scared to go on my own."

Geoff saw his chance and grabbed it. "What self-respecting goth would turn down the opportunity to see a ghost? Are we going or what, team?"

"Count me in," Ross said. "I'll drive us up there tomorrow. It'll take about three hours in this crap weather."

"You don't drive," Geoff reminded him.

"Oh, yeah," Ross said. "You can drive then."

"I don't have a car," Geoff added.

"I'll drive," Rebecca offered in a frustrated voice.

And because we are and have always been a band of four, I was compelled to say that I too would go with them to a distant seaside town whose wide avenues and well-preserved cottages have seen more of life's beauty and savagery than most places in Australia.

Maybe the boy by the gate claimed his last victim in Alice Kendall. Maybe he still waits.

"If nothing else," I said to Rebecca, "you might find out what happened to your friend."

At that moment the window casement flew open with a crash, and all the wild restlessness and ruin of the night rushed into the civilized room. A gust of wind picked up the letter on the coffee table and hurled it in the fireplace. Everyone leaped to their feet with cries of shock and surprise.

"No, no." Rebecca jumped at the fire to save her friend's memento.

It was useless. The letter was reduced to ash in a matter of seconds. Feathery blackened pieces of paper floated up the chimney and disappeared. Geoff put an arm round her shoulders and pulled her away from the gutting flames.

It fell to me to close the window and return order to the room. I fought past the crazily flapping curtains and extended both arms into the feral night to close the wooden shutters. As I did so, ice-cold fingers locked round my wrists like shackles and long nails scraped my skin. Startled, I let out a yelp and leaped back. In doing so, I caught a glimpse of the storm-tossed garden and the thing Rebecca's letter had summoned to this house.

"What is it?" Ross cried. He pushed me aside and quickly closed the window.

Calm returned to the room as though a switch had been thrown. The curtains settled in their usual place against the wall. Rain glistened on furniture. A palm frond trembled in a corner. Rebecca wept against Geoff's shoulder, and Ross stood over me, asking why I had screamed.

But I couldn't tell him. For the life of me I couldn't . . .

Nor could I stop hearing that awful scritch-scratching at the window.

THE WAYS OF THE WYRDING WOMEN

ROWENA CORY DANIELLS

"Come here, Sun-fire." Druaric offered his hand, helping me off the bed, strangely gentle now the deed was done. *Sun-fire* was what they called me because I would not give them my true-name. They might have power over my body, but I wasn't giving them power over my soul. As a Wyrding-woman in training, I knew that much.

The three brothers escorted me to the great hall. Lohnan, the eldest took my right arm, Murtahg took my left and Druaric limped along behind. He was the youngest, the clever one who listened when their Wyrding-woman spoke. Marked by a clubfoot, if he'd been born a girl, he would have walked the Wyrding-ways.

First we passed the slaves and the household servants who all gawked at me, the captive who had the honour of housing their dead Warlord's spirit. Next we passed the sons' cousins and sisters, with their warrior husbands and children. Finally we passed the two eldest sons' wives and children. Clutching their toddlers and babes, the women watched me with barely concealed loathing. If the Warlord's soul cleaved to my unborn babe, my child would outrank theirs, so naturally they hated me.

I made the sign to ward off the evil-eye.

As the sons urged me on toward the clan's ancient Wyrding-woman my steps faltered and my stomach churned. I'd only been close to her once before, when she'd touched my belly to sense the new life-force quickening. Then I had been too frightened to move.

Now, her wizened face glowed with satisfaction. Incredibly old, mother to the Warlord himself, she had outlived all her children, had lived long enough to see her grandchildren produce children. Truly, she was so powerful that even her apprentices would be stronger than me.

When the sons had first captured me, I'd looked for girls with the Wyrding-signs but couldn't find them. Maybe they were like me, born with a caul. My Wyrding-sign was safely hidden under the hearthstone of my village's Wyrding-cottage. But I mustn't think about my home, or the way the sons had led their raiders into my highland valley, grabbing me because my red-gold hair caught their eye.

"Here is Sun-fire." Lohnan, the eldest, presented me to his Wyrding grandmother. "Wild-cat, more like. It took all three of us to hold her down but she did it, she inhaled our Warlord's dying breath."

And vile it was too.

Triumph gleamed in the Wyrding-woman's sunken eyes.

It was too much for me.

I sprang forward, slashing her forehead with my fingernails, drawing blood above her breath-line. It was the best way to protect myself from her power. The granddaughters screamed in outrage. Lohnan caught me and swung me around, holding my arms. Murtahg lifted his hand. I braced for the blow.

"No!" The Wyrding-woman's sharp voice stopped him in mid-swing. She looked pleased. I didn't understand. Then my skin went cold with fear as I realised I'd given myself away. She wiped the blood from her eyes with a smile. Her last three teeth stood like standing stones in the mounds of her gums. "An adept of the Wyrding-ways. This, I did not foresee."

I shook my head, but denial was useless.

The Wyrding-woman pointed to the long table. As Lohnan shoved me I looked down, unable to meet her penetrating gaze. Quick as a snake, she clawed my forehead. I gasped and bent double in shock.

"Lift her face," the Wyrding-woman ordered.

I had to blink blood from my eyes. She smiled and I knew she had negated any advantage I'd achieved by drawing blood above her breath-line. At every step I was outmanoeuvred. But I would not despair.

I would wait and take my revenge on all of them. It was the only thing that had kept me going. If we hill-people are good at one thing, it's holding a grudge.

"Behold the vessel of the Warlord-reborn," the Wyrding-woman cried as Lohnan lifted me onto the long table. A shout went up, a genuine cheer of triumph. They loved the old Warlord and why shouldn't they? He'd protected them from the other clans, making theirs the wealthiest and strongest in all the Wild Isles.

The Wyrding-woman nodded to Lohnan. "She must be naked when I fix his soul in the babe."

He was only too eager to strip me. Then she also clambered up onto the table. No apprentice came to help her as she produced her Wyrding tools from the deep pockets of her leather apron. Saying her chants, she made signs on the flesh of my naked belly and breasts with her oils. I recognised the protectors, rosemary and sage, by their scent.

With elaborate symbols to ensure my health and that of my babe, she stroked my flesh with her sacred feathers. I did not know the birds these feathers had come from. The customs of the coast-people were different from us hill-people, yet so similar it made me shudder, just as their language was the same, yet peppered with unfamiliar words.

Closing my heart and mind, I invoked the Wyrding-mother, begging her to make the babe shrivel and die or better yet, make it a girl with the Wyrding-sign.

When the ritual was over the Wyrding-woman stepped back and, with great respect so different from our ungainly struggle over the Warlord's deathbed, the sons helped me down from the massive table.

Of the Warlord's seven sons only these three had survived the raids. Lohnan, nearing forty, still waited for his chance to lead. Murtahg, ten years younger, seemed older because his face was set in a perpetual scowl, and Druaric. The raid on my village had made him a man at seventeen, late to this rite of passage because of his crippled foot.

Lohnan leered as he looked on my nakedness. Druaric swung a cloak around my shoulders. I felt strangely numb and feared the Wyrding-woman's powers were already at work, sapping my will.

She nodded to Druaric who sent a servant to fetch a zither. Everyone waited. Murtahg chewed on his pipe stem, all nervous energy. Ever practical, Lohnan's wife ordered servants to see to the Warlord's body.

Ensuring the Warlord's soul took root in my babe was only part of this day's work. They still had to send his old body to the next world. The Wyrding-woman watched her people, pale blue eyes sharp despite her age. Her clan boasted she'd seen nearly a hundred years of life and, looking at her, I believed them.

Averting my eyes with a shudder, I saw the servant return to give Druaric a beautifully made wooden box. There was a small hole in the middle and across this hole were strings of varying lengths. Sitting cross-legged, he placed the thing on his lap. I thought it odd looking, but when he plucked the strings I heard the Wyrding-mother's sweet voice and it brought tears to my eyes.

He sang of how the clan's Wyrding-woman had sent the Warlord's sons on a noble quest to win me—a raid that split the skulls of our valley's defenders and stole our sheep. He sung of how they had lain with me—raped me. It was no more or less than I'd expected. I was no shrinking virgin—we hill clans-people are a tough breed.

As I lay under the Warlord's sons I'd planned how I would kill each one. Slowly. Even the youngest one with the clubfoot, who had whispered that he was sorry.

He sang of how they had succeeded in saving their Warlord's soul—they had pinned me down on the bed and squeezed the air from my ribs just as the fierce old fire-brand rattled his last.

Then Druaric went on to sing of how I would deliver a healthy boy babe who would grow up to lead their clan to greatness. I felt their belief like a physical thing and that was when I sensed Druaric's power. He was *willing* events to come to pass. My gaze flew to the Wyrding-woman. She nodded knowingly. She might not have an apprentice but she had a grandson who could shape the world with his words.

The song finished and Druaric stood up, slinging his zither over his shoulder. It hung from a leather strap, impressed with symbols of power.

My heart sank. How could I defeat these two?

The clan moved out of the hall, across the yard, through the palisade and outer gate, down to the shore of the narrow, steep sided bay. As if in a trance, I followed, and watched as they placed the Warlord on his ship, along with weapons and food.

"Why . . . ?" I began then bit my tongue.

But the Wyrding-woman guessed my question. "If his soul does not take root in your babe we don't want him wandering between the worlds. His place in death's realm will be prepared just in case."

Three old slaves volunteered to go into the afterlife to serve him. Lohnan, Murtahg and Druaric strangled them while everyone looked on. They dealt so casually in death, it sickened me. At my old Wyrding-teacher's side I had dedicated myself to saving life. And, although I had survived so far, I was dying a thousand small deaths, losing my true-self. Standing there on the pebbly beach, I felt as if I was an empty shell.

Beyond the headlands, the sea was molten gold, lit by the dying sun. At a signal from Lohnan, the sail was set so that ship's prow faced west. I considered running out onto the wooden jetty, throwing myself into deep water. But it would do no good. Being born with a caul meant I could not drown. One of them was sure to jump in and drag me out. Then they would watch me even more closely. Instead, I would pretend to be filled with despair and choose my moment for revenge. I would find the killing herbs and then I would ensure the Warlord's last three sons joined him in death.

If the Wyrding-woman didn't realise what I was planning.

I tensed as Druaric approached, but he only sat on a wharf stone beside me with his zither. Hands that had just strangled the life from an old man plucked power from the strings. The clan took up the song, their voices rising and falling in an eerie dirge. I hated it, but I had to admit it was beautiful. Flames engulfed the ship as the outgoing tide carried it through the headlands. A bottomless well of sadness filled me. How could people who created such fierce beauty be so cruel?

Why had the Wyrding-mother forsaken me? The only explanation was that this clan's Wyrding-woman had a more powerful call on her.

When the song finished, Druaric sat with the zither on his lap. "You will be honoured, Sun-fire. You won't have to work until the baby is born. You'll have plenty of food and somewhere warm to sleep. If you use your wits, you can be the babe's wet nurse. Your position will be nearly equal to that of my sisters and my brothers' wives—"

"I will still be a captive." I glared over my shoulder at him. His eyes were the same severe, ice-blue as the old Warlord's. "Still a slave."

"What were you before?" he countered. "A wild savage scraping your food from the unforgiving hills, living in a single-roomed sod hut, lucky if you got enough to eat. Which is better?"

"Freedom!"

His gaze narrowed and he studied me thoughtfully.

I realised I'd revealed my true nature and I cursed my impulsive tongue. Like my true-name, a glimpse of my true nature gave him power over me.

· · ·

They locked me in the tower again. It was the only building made of stone in the stronghold. Five floors high with narrow windows, it was their last place to make a stand if the palisade's gate was breached. The door had barely closed on the sons' backs, when Lohnan's wife set me to work, mending her clothes. This was a calculated insult, for Wyrding-women do not toil like other women. Even if I had not been one of the Wyrding-mother's daughters, they should not have made me work; I carried the Warlord-reborn.

So I refused to do the mending. I refused to eat. For seven days I sat and brooded, growing pale and thin. In truth, I was plagued by constant sickness so going without food was no great hardship.

The Wyrding-woman was consulted. She had them plough a field that was lying fallow and told them I must walk it barefoot to draw strength from the earth. The brothers debated who should make me walk the field. Lohnan was eager to get his hands on me but his motives were impure. Murtahg wanted nothing to do with me since he'd learned that I followed the Wyrding-way, so it fell to Druaric.

I resisted every step of the way. Under the Wyrding-woman's watchful eye we trudged, me lurching and balking, him struggling with me and his clubfoot.

"Why do you make it hard for yourself?" he muttered, out of breath.

I refused to speak.

"You are not as strong as our Wyrding-woman."

It was true, but I wouldn't give up. I couldn't. We hill-people are a tough breed, we never give up.

Neither would he. He kept on doggedly, dragging me over the freshly turned soil so that in the end I had to walk or be dragged in the dirt. I chose to walk. But with each step an idea formed in my mind. Since my Wyrding-ways had been revealed I had seen respect in Lohnan's eyes and fear in Murtahg's.

"Each day as the babe grows, I grow in power," I told Druaric. He looked away. Good.

And it was true, as far as it went. With this babe I was growing in power. A Wyrding apprentice could not learn the deep lore until she had birthed her own daughter. Was my babe a girl? Perhaps this was the Wyrding-mother's plan.

• • •

Druaric must have spoken with the Wyrding-woman for she came to see me that evening. His uneven steps and her cane echoed on the stairs. By the time the door opened I was ready to face them.

"You think you are clever, Sun-fire." Her shrewd old eyes studied me. "But your knowledge of the Wyrding-ways is only a fraction of mine."

She produced an amulet from her apron, holding it in front of me. It had been made from familiar material, clothing that belonged to me. The cloth had been woven by my village and now it was stained with the blood of my struggles, which gave it power.

"This will counteract any spells or curses you might use to stop the Warlord's soul taking hold in your babe," she told me as she hung the amulet around her neck, tucking it inside her bodice next to her skin with a satisfied smile. "I have your measure, Sun-fire. You should fear me. In birthing a woman is at her most vulnerable. You'll need me to see you through it."

She was right. Terror cinched my stomach even as I raged at my impotence. How was I to settle my score with their clan? Revenge was the only thing that sustained me.

"You hate me," she said.

I did not deny it.

"I can live with that." She stroked the silver head of her cane, staring into its polished surface. "I have seen what the Warlord's death will do to our clan. By capturing his soul in your babe I have averted a battle for leadership. Without this babe our clan would be divided and tear itself apart. One day my children's children would have been slaves. Instead, with the Warlord-reborn our clan will become the greatest in the Wild Isles." She held my eye with the force of her will. "I will not be thwarted by a half-trained hill-brat!"

I refused to blink even though my eyes burned. We glared at each other. I fought to hold her gaze. She faltered and blinked before I did. Furious, she flung past me.

I smiled. It was a small victory, but it was mine.

She brushed by Druaric, forcing him to move out of the way. He bumped the mending basket.

"What's this?" His tone made her stop and turn on the top step by the door. He picked up a finely embroidered gown and his eyes narrowed as he recognised it. "Sun-fire is a Wyrding-woman, not a slave." He waved the dress at his grandmother. "You know how to stop this."

And he limped off with the basket, presumably to give Lohnan's wife a piece of his mind.

As his uneven steps echoed on the stairs, the Wyrding-woman's shrewd eyes returned to me. After a moment she beckoned. "Come."

I hesitated, but I was fed up with being shut away so despite my trepidation, I followed her. She led me down the tower steps, past another chamber and into the one below.

One look told me this was her Wyrding workroom. Filled with her tools, I felt its power close around me, cloying and oppressive. Much was familiar. Jugs and chests lined the walls, dried herbs hung from the rafters. There was a string of blue beads to protect against the evil eye and a snakeskin, fine as spiderwebs, to cure the bone-ache.

"Close the door, Sun-fire," the Wyrding-woman ordered and I did, torn between curiosity and fear. She thrust feathers under my nose. "What's this?"

I blinked. I could have pretended ignorance but pride would not let me. "Eagle feathers. To renew youth. You must have used them many a time."

She turned away, smiling her secretive smile. Taking a jar from the bench, she opened it to reveal dried foxglove. "And this?"

"Foxglove, also called dead-men's-bells, a poison."

She showed me another. "And this?"

"Fleabane, useful for putting in mattresses to kill bed mites."

She closed the jar and gnawed on her bottom lip. Then her expression cleared and she shoved something into my hands. "What does this tell you?"

I turned the child's leather ball over and over. She had not asked what it was, but what it told me. I cleared my mind and a vision came. "Blue bells."

With a hiss, she snatched the ball from me. I thought I saw fear in her eyes but the expression was gone too quickly to be sure.

She studied her shelves then sent me a sly look before handing me a small drum. "What child did this toy belong to?"

I held the drum, sensing great power. "This is no toy."

"Ha! Only half right. It is my Watcher," she revealed. "A faithful servant volunteered to die so I could have this drum made from his skin. If anyone tries to steal from me, the drum will sound."

I returned it with a shudder, which made her smile. How could the Wyrding-mother countenance power sourced from death?

"You are impressed with my Watcher," she said.

"I am surprised that you do not trust your own people. Our people would never have stolen from their Wyrding-woman."

"Slaves steal."

"We do not keep slaves."

"More fool you."

Again she studied the shelves, then shuffled over to get a jar. Without her cane her limp was much more pronounced and I realised she had a clubfoot like Druaric, though not as malformed as his. She unstoppered the jar to show me a fine powder. "What is it and what does it do?"

I sniffed. No scent. It could be anything.

"She does not know . . . " the Wyrding-woman muttered triumphantly. "But she should."

"My Wyrding-teacher died suddenly."

She resealed the jar and tapped the stopper. "This is powdered human skull, just the thing to quieten fits."

After replacing the jar on the shelf, she turned to look at me. "I will not have the mother of the Warlord-reborn belittled by the wives of my grandsons. I will take you for my apprentice."

I suspected she would dole out just enough knowledge to keep me docile, but my heart leapt at the thought of what I could learn, though I did not let her see this.

"You're as stubborn as the stone of the hills you were born in." She regarded me thoughtfully and seemed to come to a decision. "When I did the scrying and sent my grandsons out to find you, I did not see that you would be Wyrding-marked. Three girl children of my line were born with the Wyrding-sign but none lived long enough to train at my side. Now I see that the Wyrding-mother meant for me to teach you. What say you, Sun-fire? Will you put away your hatred and serve the Wyrding-mother as you have sworn to do?"

It was a tempting offer. I would be alert for lies or omissions on her part. She could not watch me every moment of the day. As her student I would find a way to rid my babe of the Warlord's soul. Serving the Wyrding-woman would give me access to all her herbals, including the poisons. Her grandsons would suffer as they had made me suffer. But to truly escape her, I would have to destroy the amulet.

All this went through my head in a blink. For now it suited me to train under this wise old Wyrding-woman so I inclined my head. "I will give the oath."

"Wise choice. We will prepare for the ritual."

I nodded. It would feel good to be walking the Wyrding-way again. *Like coming home.* This surprised me. Was she right? Was this what the Wyrding-mother had intended all along?

She tilted her head, sharp eyes on me. "You bear no signs, Sun-fire. How is it that you are Wyrding-marked?"

I smiled inside. Like my true-name, she would never know.

• • •

So I became the Wyrding-woman's apprentice; part slave, part daughter. Two moons passed in her service. Sometimes I pretended ignorance to test her and the few times her explanations varied from my teacher's it was only by a matter of degrees.

In all things I aimed to please her, to make myself indispensable and gain her trust. It was a game I played to win but one I could easily lose. For, in opening my mind, I opened myself. When I strove to please her, her approving words and smiles became my rewards.

I realised what was happening the first time she surprised a laugh from me. Sometimes, for a whole day I forgot that I was her captive.

But she never forgot. She always slept with the amulet around her neck.

Once a moon the sons would eat with the Wyrding-woman and make plans for the clan. They talked of uniting all the fierce people of the Wild Isles under one warlord and when they talked, it seemed possible.

More often, the sons came alone for there was no love lost between them, particularly the eldest two. Lohnan would sit and watch while I worked. He still hungered for me but he hungered for every woman, all the more if he could not have them. He talked of how, when their people gathered for the harvest feast, they would choose a leader to caretake the clan until the Warlord-reborn was old enough to lead them. He thought it should be him.

Murtahg did not sit. When he visited, he paced, chewing on his pipe stem, reeking of the weed that in other men induced good-natured laughter. In him, it seemed only to deepen his restless hunger. He claimed Lohnan was so fond of wine and women that his mind had gone soft like his body. And he was right.

The Wyrding-mother would say nothing, but the more she nodded and listened, the more they said, revealing the way their minds worked.

As for Druaric, I don't know what he thought. He never spoke of clan power. I guess he had power of his own. My favourite time was the evenings, when he came to play for us, singing their family's history while the Wyrding-woman dozed.

Soon I knew all the stories. I learned of the granddaughter, Druaric's older sister, who had been born with a Wyrding-sign that no one was aware of until it was too late. One day while playing with her ball, she was stung by a bee and fell to the ground screaming. In a panic, Druaric had run back to the stronghold to fetch the Wyrding-mother, but by the time they returned, his sister was dead amongst the blue bells. When I heard this, my heart contracted with sympathy and I looked down to hide my feelings.

Saddened by the memory, Druaric put his zither aside. It was so close I could have reached out to touch it. We had nothing like the zither in my village. Drums and pipes were our way of making music. I longed to see if I could coax the Wyrding-mother's sweet voice from it. "Keep playing, please."

"No more tonight." His voice caught.

Tears stung my eyes. I touched his arm. "I'm sorry. You could not know. Sometimes the Wyrding-sign is hidden."

"Like yours?" His hand covered mine, hot, dry and heavy with import. "I have seen all of your milk-smooth skin, Sun-fire, and I cannot forget it, but I did not see a single imperfection."

A wave of molten heat rolled through my traitorous body. "I was born with a caul."

"A useful thing." He nodded wisely. "Where is it?"

Sanity returned to me. "Hidden." And I pulled away.

• • •

Not long after that the brothers went off on another raid. They hadn't taken their ships reaving to the mainland this summer and it was too late to do so now, so they went raiding rival clans on their island. They came back laden with tribute, freely given, or so they claimed.

Later that day, I was grinding herbs when the three brothers came to see to the Wyrding-woman. Knowing Lohnan would try to catch my eye, I ignored them.

"So? Is the whole island ours?" she asked.

"Just as you said it would be," Murtahg said. "And—"

"The treasure was where you said it would be." Lohnan handed her a pouch.

She gloated as she undid the leather satchel. "Come see this, Sun-fire."

I didn't like the note of triumph in her voice. Steeling myself, I approached.

She showed me a small, translucent sheet of velum. No. A caul. *My caul!*

The whole world shivered.

"Catch her!" she warned. Lohnan needed no more urging to lay his hands on me. I tried to shove him away. He pinned me against his body, supporting me as my vision cleared.

"What is it?" Murtahg asked uneasily.

"Sun-fire's Wyrding-sign," Druaric said.

I glared at him and he had the grace to blush and look away.

Even though his betrayal cut me to the quick, I could see why the Wyrding-woman loved him best of all her grandsons. He was clever and loyal, placing his clan's safety above personal ambition. Reluctant admiration warred with my resentment.

"Say no more, Druaric. Knowledge is power," the Wyrding-woman warned.

Murtahg cursed. "It's not natural teaching him the Wyrding-ways. And you shouldn't be teaching this hill-brat. What if she turns on us?"

"I will teach who I choose, Murtahg. And the hill-brat is no threat. Her knowledge barely scrapes the surface of the Mother's Ways."

"Wyrding-ways!" He spun on his heel and marched out.

She ignored him, turning to me. "Now watch, Sun-fire."

I could not do other, as she removed the amulet and unpicked the stitching. Rolling up my caul, she tucked it safely inside.

"I may not have your true-name, girl, but I have this."

"It's mine."

"Yes. Now you are mine."

Despair and rage rolled through me.

Lohnan chuckled. "Eh, I can feel the fire in her. Let me have her. I don't mind if she scratches my eyes out."

"You're a fool, Lohnan. She's too powerful for you."

"She wasn't too powerful when I planted the babe," he protested.

"That was then." She dismissed him. "Let her go."

As Lohnan stormed out I realised that, despite what she'd told Murtahg, she needed my caul to keep me under control. I looked down, pleased with this new knowledge.

Druaric seemed to hesitate. I refused to meet his eyes, angry with him and with myself for I was doubly trapped by that amulet now.

"Go," the Wyrding-woman told him.

I waited only until the door closed. "I know how you found out about it. But how did you know where to look?"

She smiled, her last three teeth gleaming. "In a village the size of yours, where else would it be?"

Stupid of me. I had been a fool to trust Druaric.

• • •

Time passed. I enjoyed learning but felt Druaric's absence. He no longer came to spend the evenings with us. Every dusk I looked for him then had to remind myself of his betrayal.

I had been a prisoner for nearly four moons when the clan's metal worker delivered an object he had crafted for the Wyrding-woman. It was a perfect little bell strung on a piece of leather. She listened to the tone, then sent for Murtahg to bring his son.

When they came I recognised the lad. He was no more than seven and small for his age. But that was not why the others teased him. His words stumbled over themselves, harried by false starts and the more they teased him the worse his speech became.

"Murtahg and little Ciarnor," the Wyrding-woman greeted them. "Come, sit by me, Ciarnor."

Murtahg hung back, clearly uneasy with Wyrd power.

The lad approached and sat on a cushion at the Wyrding-woman's feet. She had earlier directed me in the mixing of a tincture. It was mildly alcoholic, sweetened with honey and contained a little of the powdered weed they smoked. A strange combination. Now she accepted this from me.

"Watch, Ciarnor." And she rang the bell.

His eyes lit up. "C . . . c . . . can I have it?"

"It is yours, but bells hold great power." She turned the bell over, poured a sip of the liquid into it and held it out to him. "Drink this."

He wrinkled his nose but did not complain about the taste, so the honey must have helped.

"Now ring the bell," she told him.

He turned it right way up and rang it, smiling at the pure tone. She nodded. "Now give the bell to Sun-fire."

His face fell but he obeyed, watching as I washed the bell and purified it. All the while I felt Murtahg's stare. By the time I had finished Ciarnor's blue eyes had grown glazed with the drug. I knew the signs; he was suggestible. If my old teacher had needed to perform a painful healing on him, she would have done it now.

The Wyrding-woman took the bell from me, strung it on a leather thong then leant close to tie the bell around his neck. "Listen to me, Ciarnor. From this day forward your speech will grow clearer. If you feel your words jamming up, ring the bell. Its pure tone will ease your tongue. Do you understand?"

"I do."

"See, it is working already." She beamed. Oh, but she was clever.

I watched her, torn between admiration and resentment.

"Off you go, Ciarnor."

"Wait, son." Murtahg put his pipe aside to study the bell. "Very well. Go."

The boy ran off, still a little stunned but happy.

"It is nothing but an ordinary bell. How can it work?" Murtahg demanded.

"Bells have great power. They banish evil spirits." The Wyrding-woman held his eyes. "There are many forces at work for good and evil. Perhaps you should look into your soul and ask why your only son's speech suffers. You say the words of devotion, but is your heart truly open to the Wyrding-mother? Here . . . " She dug into the deep pockets of her leather apron and pulled out a strip of leather. "I'll help you find your way back to the Wyrding-mother." Her gnarled fingers wove the ends together. "As I form this circle, so your life is formed. You spring from the Wyrding-mother and in the end, you return to the mother. Bend down."

Murtahg leant forward and she slipped the leather circle around his head. It was a tight fit and when he turned away from her to leave he did not look happy.

I noticed the pipe on the mantelpiece. "He forgot his pipe again."

"Leave it for now." She sighed and made her way to the work bench. "Do you think Ciarnor will be cured?"

I nodded.

"Because of the bell?"

"That," I said, "And because he believes he will."

My answer seemed to please her for she smiled and pointed to a small chest. "Fetch me that."

When I returned with it, she opened the lid and took out a fine cloth, unrolling it to reveal a perfect little silver bell, a pure white candle and many fine vellum sheets, sewn together down one side. I recognised the symbols on the front—Male opposed Female, Death opposed Life. I longed to turn over the pages to see how many more I knew.

Reverently, she showed me. "These are the symbols of the Wyrding-ways, my symbols. My candle to bring the light, my bell to banish the dark." Her finger, twisted by the bone-ache, tapped the vellum. "And the knowledge I have gained through my long life." She held my eyes. "All this can be yours, Sun-fire, if you will swear fealty to my clan. I will not live forever and we need a strong Wyrding-woman."

She meant it. I had won her over, but now that it had happened I realised she had won me, too. I wanted this so badly . . .

All I had to do was swear loyalty to the clan that had ravaged my valley, torn me from my home and used me as a vessel for their Warlord-reborn. We hill-people never surrendered.

Yet, I wavered.

One part of me argued that I could stay with her long enough to serve out the remaining years of my apprenticeship. Once I knew the Wyrding-ways I could go home to my valley. I imagined their joy when I returned as a fully fledged Wyrding-woman, versed in the deep, secret Lore.

But that was to forget the babe. It did not seem real yet. It had not shrivelled and died as many babes do in the first three moons, so the Wyrding-mother meant me to carry it to term. I was convinced that my child would be the daughter I longed for. But I did not want the Warlord's cruel soul twisting her nature. Before the birth I had to find out how to banish the Warlord's soul to save my little girl, and I had to reclaim my Wyrding-sign.

But for now . . .

I fell to my knees and spoke the words before they could choke me. Revenge was more important than being forsworn. "I swear clan fealty, Wyrding-mother."

She gave me frankly sceptical look.

"I do," I insisted. "For as long as it takes to learn the Wyrding-ways. Then I want to go home."

This must have satisfied her for that evening she left me alone in her private chamber for the first time. Feverish with haste I removed the foxglove jar from its shelf and took just enough to kill three men. Then I froze, waiting for the Watcher to sound. Nothing. That was odd. I realised her Watcher had a flaw; I had not removed the poison from the Wyrding-woman's chamber.

And now I had the means to exact my revenge. When I was ready, I would slip the foxglove into the brothers' stew. They would die and I would run away. It meant giving up the training the Wyrding-woman had promised me. Could I give it up for revenge? I examined this and decided I could. There were other Wyrding-women, ones who did not use death-power.

Besides, Murtahg and Lohnan deserved to die. I enjoyed imagining their death throes. As for Druaric . . .

Pain curled its hand around my heart with surprising intensity. Even though he had betrayed my trust, I could not bear to kill him. And I could not kill two, without killing the third and running away. Their deaths would be suspicious. Their wives would point to me.

Stunned, I put the foxglove back. How the Wyrding-woman would laugh if only she knew.

I had trapped myself.

• • •

The fourth moon of my captivity passed and the grain hung heavy in the fields. With the harvest came the farmers from the rich pasturelands, bringing a portion of their crops to their clan-leader as tribute. For several days there were reunions. And in the evening there was dancing, smoking of weed, singing and noisy couplings. But the revelry held a frantic tone for, come the feast, the clan's new leader would be elected.

Murtahg talked forcefully and loudly of what he would do if he led the clan. His men wove through the groups, urging his case. Lohnan's men spoke up, just as eager for him to take the lead. The supporters of the two eldest sons were itching for a fight. The Wyrding-woman had been right to try to forestall this.

I caught only glimpses of Druaric going about his business. And I refused to ask after him. First he had betrayed me then, as soon as he had what he wanted, he ignored me. I hated him, yet I could not bring myself to kill him. It was strange.

As the days counted down to the harvest feast, I watched the stronghold fill with clansmen and women. There was still time for me to slip away, time to retreat to the highlands and reach my village before the snows cut off the passes. But I knew, even though these festivities would have made it easier to escape, I wasn't going. I was weak. I had been seduced by the Wyrding-woman's promise of knowledge and by a sweet-voiced cripple who had betrayed my trust.

As yet there was no sign of the babe. My body was slim, though my breasts felt swollen and tender. This pleased the Wyrding-woman; it meant the babe flourished.

Then one day, as I labelled jars with Wyrding symbols, I felt a flutter in my belly. Like the wings of a humming bird, something barely brushed my senses. My babe had quickened. In that moment the child became real to me and my life narrowed down to a tunnel. At the tunnel's end was the agony of childbirth. Either I would die, or I would produce the Warlord-reborn in my daughter's body.

In that heartbeat I knew I could not be the clan's tool.

Tonight I would hit the old woman over the head, take the amulet and run. As for my revenge . . . It was clear now that I did not need to kill the three brothers. By leaving I would bring down the clan down. Without the Warlord-reborn, Lohnan and Murtahg's followers would tear it apart. This was a much better revenge. And it meant I did not have to raise my hand against Druaric.

A wave of relief washed through me. Tonight I would act.

"What is it?" the Wyrding-woman asked, sharp as always.

"Nothing," I lied, replacing the jar of lavender. "I gulped breakfast and now I'm paying for it."

"I can give you something for that." She mixed up some gripe medicine and I dutifully swallowed it, pathetically grateful for her thoughtfulness. I had to go without delay.

That evening Druaric came to the Wyrding-woman's chamber for the first time since he had betrayed the existence of my caul. My heart quickened for there was laughter in his eyes, and he could not keep the smile from his lips as he offered me something wrapped in a blanket.

I folded my arms. "I want nothing from you."

"Oh, take it," the Wyrding-woman muttered. "He's spent every night since the last raid making it."

Curiosity got the better of me. I took the object thinking it was light for its size and unrolled the blanket. My mouth dropped open.

He had made a zither, every bit as fine as his. The craftsmanship alone was enough to make me weep.

"Am I forgiven, Sun-fire?" he asked.

I wanted to refuse him but the words would not come.

"Here." He unslung his instrument and sat down, resting it across his lap. "Like this." And his fingers produced a bird song.

I did not want to accept his gift for it meant I condoned his betrayal. At that moment, I looked up into Druaric's eyes and saw his naked soul. My heart turned over. He loved me and I meant to leave tonight.

"What's wrong, Sun-fire?" the Wyrding-woman asked.

"No one has ever given me such a fine gift." I blinked away tears, letting her think I cried with joy.

Druaric laughed and hugged me. I did not pull away. Knowing I was about to leave, I revelled in the feel of him. The Wyrding-woman nodded, satisfied.

He released me, fingers going to his zither. "Watch, Sun-fire."

Truth be told, I was eager to learn. I joined him and so began the happiest, yet most painful evening of my life. After a while, the Wyrding-woman retreated to her bed in the alcove. As for us, we sat up so late discovering our shared love of the music that the cock crowed before we put out the candle. When I crawled under the bench to sleep on my pallet, I told myself one more day would not matter.

• • •

I slept all that day, missing the fight between Murtahg and Lohnan. The first I knew of it was when I entered the kitchen late in the afternoon in search of food. Instead I found the cook's assistants madly packing salted meat, skins of wine and rolls of cheese. From their chatter I learned Murtahg could have killed Lohnan but he hadn't, he had banished him. The eldest brother, along with his family and followers was sailing with the evening tide to set up a stronghold of their own.

Before he left, Lohnan came to get the Wyrding-woman's blessing. She gave him some of the sacred-hearth fire to seed his own hearth fire, and a shawl she had wrapped him in when he was a baby; these symbolised the luck of the household. When he complained that he did not have a Wyrding-woman of his own, they both glanced to me and I was glad that he could not take me.

With Lohnan gone, I thought the rivalry would settle down. Druaric was only seventeen and he didn't have a loyal core of followers ready to kill at his command. Besides, his place in the stronghold was different from Lohnan's because of his clubfoot and the power he had with words.

After the evening meal, Murtahg came to see the Wyrding-woman. She ordered me to prepare wine. Impatient as always, Murtahg chewed on his pipe stem and paced. Even from across the room I smelt the weed on him, coming through his skin as well as his breath.

Druaric sat in his usual place by the fire, plucking at the strings of his zither. He was composing another verse of their family saga, incorporating the new events. I heard snatches of it as I prepared the mulled wine.

The Wyrding-woman, worn down by her grandsons' feuding, had been bothered by the bone-ache so I added a little powdered snakeskin to ease her pain. As I did this, I realised I didn't want to hit her over the head. She was a hard woman because only a hard woman could control these headstrong men.

Like Druaric, she had slipped past my guard. I might not agree with her use of death-power but I liked and respected her as a practitioner of the Way. My head spun. The vengeance of the hill-people had motivated me since the day the brothers stole me from my people. Without it, I felt rudderless. I had needed it to make me strong.

Murtahg took his wine without a word of thanks, putting the pipe on the mantelpiece. "Now I learn that Lohnan took the metal-worker's best apprentice. I should—"

"Let it go. Let him go," the Wyrding-woman urged. "Your task is to care-take the clan for the Warlord-reborn."

Murtahg nodded but, from the look in his eyes, I knew he saw only the near future. It would take twenty years for the Warlord-reborn to grow up, and there wasn't much chance of Murtahg still being around then. Even if he was, he would be an old man of nearly fifty summers.

He grimaced and spat into the fire. "They whisper behind my back."

"Call the clan together tomorrow," the Wyrding-woman advised. "Give them stability and you will have their loyalty."

He nodded, draining the last of the wine. But, as he left, I noticed him glance at Druaric who was singing under his breath. With a sick lurch I realised Murtahg feared Druaric. I met the Wyrding-woman's eyes. She had seen it too and now she stared into the fire, troubled.

Druaric stood up and stretched. "I'm for bed."

I wanted to clutch his arm and warn him. But he wasn't mine to protect. No formal words had passed between us. I could claim him if I wanted to, for Wyrding-women take their lovers where they choose. But I hadn't lain with him last night because I meant to leave tonight.

Could I leave, after the way Murtahg had looked at him?

"Watch your back, Dru," the Wyrding-woman warned.

He shrugged this off with a smile. "I'm no threat to Murtahg."

She frowned as he limped off to his room above ours. Unlike the other unmarried youths he did not sleep in the great hall. The stronghold was packed tonight. Only the Wyrding-woman and Druaric had private chambers in the tower.

"Sun-fire, fetch me Murtahg's pipe," she ordered and I realised he had forgotten it again. She did not take it from my outstretched hand. Instead, she looked up at me, dread in her eyes. "What does it tell you?"

I knew what she feared. The same feeling closed in on me. It was an effort to clear my mind and then I wished I hadn't. Murtahg's hateful, hard-edged impulses filled me, circling like wolves around a new born lamb. One swift bite, tear out the throat, break the neck. "D . . . death."

She blanched.

I made to hand her the pipe but she shook her head; for all her talk of scrying, she did not have the Way of seeing that I had. "What will you do?"

She sighed. "I will do nothing until I have slept on it."

I cursed silently for I was hoping she would sleep deeply so that I could take the amulet. All the same, I felt sorry for her as she lay down in her alcove, only to toss and turn. I had to go tonight. Druaric's gift of the zither had convinced me that I could not stay. Not when invisible bonds threatened to make me his willing prisoner. What's more, with Lohnan gone the stronghold felt wrong, somehow.

It was lucky that I had dreamed the day away, for I had no trouble staying awake as I lay there on my pallet under the bench, listening to the stronghold wind down. Soon the revellers were in a stupor of wine, weed and exhaustion and the Wyrding-woman was blessedly quiet at last. This was my chance.

I was about to gather my things when the door creaked open. I recognised Murtahg by the glow of the hearth coals. One hand rested on his sword hilt. It was against clan law to wear a sword inside the stronghold. My mouth went dry with fear, but he crept past my bed where I lay feigning sleep. I wanted to run the moment he entered the Wyrding-woman's alcove. Another part of me wanted to spring up and warn her. I did neither; instead I listened.

"I'm not asleep, Murtahg," she said softly, and I was glad I had not tried to take the amulet. "Why do you come to me wearing your sword?"

"I come to talk sense."

"As you see it."

"No more twisting of words to suit your Wyrding-ways, Grandmother. You are not all powerful. I have eyes in my head. Get rid of Sun-fire before Dru can worm his way into her bed. With her at his side and him the stepfather of the Warlord-reborn, they'll undermine my power. Either you get rid of her or I will get rid of him."

I held my breath, waiting for her to defend me, even though I knew her loyalty had to be to her clan.

At last she let out a long sigh. "Much can go wrong while birthing. Druaric won't suspect a thing if she bleeds to death after delivering the child."

My heart turned to stone in my chest.

"Very well. But I will be watching. There are going to be changes, Grandmother."

He had called her 'Grandmother' again, denying her authority as the voice of the Wyrding-mother. Murtahg strode out of the chamber. I lay utterly still even after the closing door cut off the thud of his boots

In truth I was so stunned and frightened, I could not move. It was just as well because the Wyrding-woman came out with a candle.

I felt her observe me closely, but managed to keep my breathing steady. I must have been convincing because she muttered to herself as she opened a familiar jar. Only two days earlier she had had me crush hymlic then strain the pulp through cloth to produce this clear liquid containing concentrated poison.

Now she wept as she dipped the mouth piece of Murtahg's pipe in the jar. Tomorrow morning she would send a servant to return it. Soon after Murtahg placed the pipe on his tongue, his heart would falter to a stop. She did this not for me, but for the Wyrding-mother; her Ways had to be respected.

Replacing the pipe, the Wyrding-woman returned to her chamber. A soft keening arose as she wept her heart out. But I had her measure now. Her tears were for her failed plans. I was only a means to an end.

Cold within and cold without, I listened for her weeping to cease as she finally fell asleep.

Now, to take the amulet.

I crept into her alcove. It smelt of old woman and tired emotion. I knelt by her bed. The amulet had slipped out of her vest to rest on her shoulder. I lifted the leather strip that threaded through the loop and slit it with a soft snick of my knife, setting myself free. It was that easy.

Why had I waited so long?

I returned to the outer room and knelt by the glowing coals to take the amulet apart, removing its contents. The caul I tucked inside my bodice next to my skin. So soft and fine. So good to reclaim what was mine.

The rest of the contents, I studied. Salt, the purifier, was easy to recognise, as was the chip of iron, the protector, from a sky rock. But it was the circle of red thread that made my heart soar in triumph. This was thread from my hill clothes, woven into the circle to mirror the circle the Warlord's soul would make when it left his body and took root in my babe.

To be sure of my freedom I burned everything but the circle of red thread. I did not want to extinguish my child's life.

When in doubt fire is an excellent cleanser. However, it also concentrates power so I gathered the ashes and the hot sky rock from the little brazier used to prepare ingredients, meaning to throw them in the sea. Since water opposed fire I believed this would be enough to negate the Wyrding-woman's power.

Next, to deal with the red thread circle. It had been created to bind a body and soul, so I put the thread between my teeth and gnawed through it, breaking the Warlord's journey and reclaiming my daughter. Now the growing babe was all mine, for any child produced by a Wyrding-woman belonged to her.

"What are you doing?" the Wyrding-woman demanded.

I spun around to find her by the hearth. She lit a candle so she could see me clearly. Too late to dissemble, I displayed the broken thread then swallowed it to protect my child.

Her hand went to the amulet only to find it gone. Her eyes narrowed and I felt the power of her ancient will.

I was not ready for this confrontation.

Murtahg flung the door open and stalked in, eyes glazed with the weed, carrying his naked sword. Clearly, he had thought things over and he did not trust the Wyrding-woman's word.

The Wyrding-woman tried to bluster. "What are you doing here, Murtahg?

He did not answer, striding towards her.

Wyrding power lay in subtle threats, prepared treatments and manipulation of people, not in force. Still, she drew herself up to her full height. "Murtahg, I helped bring you into this world. Listen to—"

But he was not going to let her wear his will away with the weave of her words. He drew his sword arm back. She tried to dart past him. He caught her by the hair and ran her through. I saw the disbelief on her face as he let her drop.

He did not even wait for her to die, but turned on me. I backed up, arms lifting uselessly. Sweet Mother, why hadn't I run when I had the chance? Why hadn't I warned Druaric and run away with him?

"Come here, Sun-fire."

I couldn't move.

"Don't be afraid. I'm not going to hurt you."

I shook my head.

With a curse he caught my arm and jerked me towards him so that when I recovered my balance the bloody sword tip rested under my chin.

"The clan needs its Warlord-reborn and it needs a Wyrding-woman. But there are other Wyrding-women, Sun-fire. Cross me and I'll tell the clan you threw yourself off the tower. Do you understand?"

I swallowed and nodded numbly.

He let the sword tip drop then made to leave.

"Wait." I pointed to the mantelpiece. "You left your pipe."

He smiled and grabbed the pipe, tucking it in his pocket. "You learn quickly, Sun-fire."

Yes, I did.

The moment he was gone I peeped out the door after him. He

headed down towards the wing he shared with his family and supporters. I ran in the other direction, up the steps to Druaric's room on the floor above.

I threw open the door to see him kneeling by the fire, singing intently. "Come quick!"

He put the zither aside slowly, as if dazed, though he never smoked the weed. Stiffly, he came to his feet.

"Hurry, Murtahg's after you!"

Too late. Booted feet ran up the stairs, blocking our escape. Mouth dry, I backed away as Murtahg and four men filled the doorway.

"So," Murtahg muttered finding me with Druaric. "This is your idea of loyalty, Sun-fire."

"Don't speak of loyalty," I countered, pointing to his bloodied sword. "Not when you killed the clan's Wyrding-woman!"

"Brother, how could you?" Druaric whispered, shocked.

Murtahg's followers shifted uneasily, drawing away from him.

"Why . . . ?" one of them whispered.

"She was going to set these two up as clan-leaders," Murtahg said. Then, certain his own men would never turn on him, he took out his pipe, to chew on its stem.

How long would the poison take?

"Why weren't you born a girl, Dru?" Murtahg taunted. "Then I could have used you."

"You will not use either of us," I told him, stepping in front of Druaric. "The Wyrding-mother will not stand by and let the murderer of one of her servants go unpunished."

"The Wyrding-mother did not stop me." Murtahg grinned. "And I don't see her saving you." He nodded to his men. "Kill the hill-brat and the cripple."

His followers hesitated.

I pointed to Murtahg. "Wyrding-mother take this man. Make his heart race. Make his breath tight in his chest." As I described the symptoms of the poison, I saw evidence of its effect on him. His eyes widened in horror. "Make his fingers grow numb. Make his legs tingle. Make his heart falter." He dropped to his knees, hands going to his throat. The pipe fell to the floor. It had done its job.

I heard Druaric gasp behind me.

Murtahg's followers stared as he fought for breath; once . . . twice, then he pitched forward, face down on the floor.

I looked up at the remaining four men. "Put away your swords and the Wyrding-mother will not strike you down."

They hurried to obey.

I nodded to Murtahg. "In life he served the clan well. Let us honour him in death. Prepare him for death's realm."

This was familiar to them and two took his legs, while another took his shoulders. They shuffled towards the door. There they hesitated, looking back at us, unsure of me.

"Do not fear, the Wyrding-mother will forgive her children," I told them.

As soon as the door closed I threw the pipe in the grate and stirred up the fire, then turned to face Druaric. Did he fear me, too?

Graceful despite his clubfoot, he sat and took up his zither again.

"There's no time for this."

"Hush, Sun-fire," he said. "I must sing the way it will be. The greatest danger is panic, clansmen turning on each other to avenge old insults, tearing our clan apart, killing our people."

His people were not my people, but I listened as he sang of how we became leaders of the clan. He'd been singing like this when I came in to warn him. My skin went cold.

Truly, Murtahg had been right to fear him. How much more had he sung into being, here in the privacy of his chamber?

I heard the name he used for me and his words claimed me. I saw a vision of us leading the clan into a glorious future, safe from raiders and secure from want while I served the Wyrding-mother. Joy filled me, for she had never deserted me. This was meant to be . . .

Yet, at the same time, I knew my feelings were a product of his cleverly woven words. With great effort I sloughed off the effect of his power.

He smiled and stood, slinging the zither over his shoulder. "Come, we must reassure the clan, Sun-fire."

I was immune to his song. Could he tell?

"What is it? What's wrong?"

I read loving concern in his face. This much was not a lie. He opened his arms to me. It would be so easy to go with the song's seductive refrain, still echoing in my heart and body.

But I could not live as a slave, not even Druaric's. I took a step back. "You sang my love for you into being."

His eyes widened and I saw fear flicker in their ice-blue depths. "I sang to lure you. But only you can give your heart."

"I am the Wyrding-mother's servant. I serve no man. Murtahg was a monster but you . . . you sang him into—"

"No. I tried to sing him down but his soul was without music." Druaric licked dry lips. "Didn't you hear my words when you came in?"

I'd been focussed on warning him.

He put the zither aside. "Truly, Sun-fire, if you can see the weave of my song then I have no power over you." He swallowed. "The clan needs us. If we don't unite our people the other clans will turn on us, loot our stronghold, kill the men and take the women and children for slaves."

"It is no more than you have done to other clans, to my hill-people."

"Put aside your need for revenge," Druaric whispered. "It's a kind of poison. Look into your heart and tell me what you find."

Boots clattered on the steps as the warriors returned but still I hesitated. I could leave right now with my child.

"I am a cripple," Druaric said. "They won't follow me unless you are at my side."

It was true. To see the clan crushed and its people scattered would be sweet indeed but . . .

"Would you condemn the clan's children to slavery, Sun-fire? Little Ciarnor is innocent of his father's crimes."

The door swung open and I stepped across to join Druaric.

OLD SOULS

DAVID THOMAS MOORE

"It's weird. I honestly never talk about this sort of stuff, even with my friends."

She smiles at me, vulnerably, warmly, with a hint of a frown, genuine confusion in her eyes.

It's getting late. The sun's setting, somewhere out of sight behind the shops and terraces of whatever backwoods town it is I've got stuck in. The sky's deepening to that rich lavender colour it holds for maybe a quarter of an hour before the evening truly sets in. A few of the cars drifting past every few minutes now have their lights on. There's the beginning of a chill in the air; she's started to hunch her shoulders, and has taken to reflexively tugging her cardigan tighter every few minutes. I don't think she's even noticed, yet.

The table outside the coffee shop—Costa, AMT, something like that; the first place we found outside the train station—is cluttered with the detritus of a wasted afternoon. Wide cups holding drying teabags and the foamy dregs of lattes. An overflowing ashtray, and an empty Silk Cut packet. A battered old book that was too big to keep in my pocket. The scarf she took off when the sun was still out and has, for the moment, forgotten. Her notebook. Plates bearing the crumbs of the sandwiches we ordered an hour or so ago, when her stomach audibly gurgled. She laughed, then, easily and happily, and suggested, since we were showing no signs of leaving, that we get lunch. It wasn't a question, anxiously feeling out my intentions—*you do* want *to stay, right?*—but an admission of something we both knew.

That's over-romanticising a bit. She's bold, self-assured, but I'd be lying if I said there was no insecurity in her at all. She knows she wants to stay here with me, knows I want to stay in turn, but she doesn't know *why*—doesn't understand—and so she doesn't quite trust it. She's waiting to wake up from a dream. It would be more honest to say she's enjoying the moment and choosing to take me at face value, than that she doesn't feel any uncertainty at all.

We met on the platform, having both been kicked off the same train. There was a problem on the lines, something to do with signalling, and it had to be cancelled. Another train would be along. But no other train was forthcoming, and we got to talking. When it was clear we were going to be here for a while, I suggested a coffee. Initially we took it in turns to pop back into the station, try and get some sort of update on the situation, but we gave up on the pretence of trying to get home around the time we ordered food.

She's a writer, working as a proofreader for a company publishing text books. That was how she put it: "I'm not a proofreader that writes, I'm a writer that proofreads. Proofreading's just what pays the bills." She showed me some of her poems, and I smiled at the imagery. A vase, a bust, a stone nymph. "What?" she asked, not defensively. "Nothing," I said, earnestly. "They're very good."

It's been one of those long, rambling, winding conversations you can only have when you've completely connected with someone: intimate, familiar, frighteningly honest, ranging over every topic from work, to family, to sex, to books, to past relationships. Her hopes, her frustrations. We've sat side by side, eyes meeting and then looking away; tearing up till receipts, playing with our teaspoons; she touching my wrist once, me brushing her shoulder. We've people-watched and joked. An hour or so after sitting down, she phoned someone called "Babe" to say she'll be late and not to worry, and then put her phone away without explanation.

It's been one of those conversations that feel completely comfortable and completely familiar, even though you barely know the person you're talking to. One of those conversations where you feel like you've fallen in love, all in one day. It's straight out of a film. She's even mentioned Coward's *Brief Encounter* once, eyes dancing, smirking slightly.

It's tearing me apart. I don't think I can do this again.

• • •

I'm dying, and soon. A month or two, maybe a year. I've felt it coming, and I've been getting my affairs in order.

It's different for us; not surprisingly, I suppose. Not for us the gradual senescence that robs most men of half their lives, the creeping illness and eventual betrayal of our bodies. The day before we die, we're as strong as when we're born. Instead, we're visited with a growing awareness of the coming end, a feeling almost of doom. It's a gift, in a way—a chance to make arrangements, to ensure everything goes over smoothly—although it hangs over us, crouching over our hearts, just as it does everyone else.

That's why I was on the train. There's paperwork to be sorted out, payments to be made. Dying's a more expensive and complicated affair than it once was.

The thing is, even if I were—even if she were offering what I want from her . . . If she *could* offer what I need . . .

Well. It's too late. We won't have the time.

• • •

I smile back at her, and she sees something in my expression.

"What's wrong?"

"Nothing," I say, and fuss with my tea, add sugar. "It's just . . . " I have to look at her. I owe it to her. I can't retreat from her now, not after the time we've had. "This has been really nice."

She doesn't answer; cocks her head and gives me that slight smirk again, knowing, coy. She lays her hand on my wrist—deliberately, leaving it there for a moment before withdrawing it. I look down at her hand, back to her face. She's beautiful, really. Soft and expressive, with a smile that takes in her whole face.

"But"—how do I explain?—"eventually they're going to fix that fucking train."

She laughs, rips a page out of her notebook and scrawls on it. "I was kind of assuming this wasn't goodbye, to be honest." She hands the page to me: a mobile number, two names. "That's my name on Facebook," she says, pointing. "I don't like to be too easy to find." She shrugs. "We can keep in touch, and next time you're in Manchester, or I'm in London, we can meet up, have coffee again."

I nod, tuck the sheet away, flash her a grin. "Sure. Sorry, I was being silly."

• • •

All flesh is dust. Nothing lives forever. That's Maat. Even Lord Osiris died, and if the gods can die, then what recourse have mortals to complain?

If we cheat death—and can it be cheating, if we are following in His footsteps?—it's not by dodging death, but by returning on our own terms. Everyone returns—provided, of course, their hearts pass judgement—but most become lost when they do. The spark is gone, and with it the mind, the shadow, and the name are lost, scattered on the wind. The soul returns in new flesh, and cannot know itself, or recognise any other thing.

If you're properly prepared, the *ka*—the spark—and the soul are brought back together. And it's like a key in a lock, or one of those wooden puzzles they sell at gift shops around Christmas: bring those two parts together, and it all comes together. You're reborn in your own flesh, born an adult, with your own mind and your own name and your own shadow. It's just like waking up after a long sleep. We do it every human lifetime, with all the uncertainty that entails. Sometimes I have thirty years, sometimes near on a hundred, usually somewhere in between.

And death is . . . How to explain it, to someone who isn't one of us? For a time, all the parts of you are separated. The soul presents the heart to be weighed, while the mind sleeps, and the ka . . . waits. Regains strength. No part of you can wholly understand what's happening, without the other parts, and when you come together again, you can't properly remember. It's like a dream. You know you stood before Him, and His sister-wife; you know you were judged by His brother. But you can't remember what He said.

We've come together, those of us who are still around—a couple of hundred, I suppose; we're scattered, and can't always be reached—and talked about bringing back the practice, teaching people how to have eternity. Some of us say the knowledge should not be kept in our hands, and it would be Maat to spread truth and wisdom, while some way that the gods allowed our culture to be destroyed for a reason, and that it is Maat to respect their will. In the end, we always agree that it would be too dangerous to draw attention to ourselves.

And so I've met Christians, and Moslems, and Jews, and Buddhists, and people of all sorts of faiths, everywhere I travel, and I have been moved by their conviction, and impressed by their wisdom, and it breaks my heart to walk away from them knowing that they are, ultimately, doomed. Nothing but voices, whispering in the dust. But it's not my place to do anything about it, and I'm not sure I could change anything if I tried.

Not that it would help her. I lost her more than a thousand years ago.

• • •

What's written on the sheet in my breast pocket isn't her name. It's the name she knows, but it's not hers. She's used so many— Adrienne, Njèza, Elizabeth, Mawar, I forget them all—but her name, her *real* name, is Phoebe.

I met her in Greece, years after the homeland was lost. It would have been the fifth century, I suppose? I was already thousands of years old.

She was a farmer's daughter, but she'd come to Athens to be a sculptor's model. Even then, she'd had a fierce love for art, and she's always, every lifetime, been an artist, or worked with artists. She's a sculptress herself, usually, although she's also been a painter, and a composer, and other things besides. But her passion is to shape things.

It's much the same for me, I suppose. I was an architect, building tombs and temples in Abdju, in my first lifetime, which was why I was afforded the right to a tomb; and I've always been an architect, or an engineer—a builder, sometimes, if that's the only opportunity open to me. But I remember all my lives. I do it because this is who I am, what I know. She always seems to find her art again from scratch, one lifetime to the next. It's as though her soul remembers, even when her mind is gone.

She always seems to find me, too.

It took me a while to notice. I suppose I just thought I was drawn to people that were like her. But soul speaks to soul—it's something you become more aware of, when you've gone and returned enough times—and at length, I began to recognise her. We found each other, and we came together, again and again. I don't even know how she finds me, though find me she does.

We've not always been lovers. Sometimes she's been very young, when she's found me, sometimes very old. Sometimes, one or both of us has already been wedded. We've been lifelong friends, we've married, we've had affairs that have torn both our lives apart. I've raised her as though she were my daughter, and nursed her in her dotage.

It torments me. Every time, I recognise her; and I know that she recognises me, but she doesn't understand why. Always, there's this wonder to her, that she can find someone who understands her so well, and to whom she is so instantly drawn. Someone who fits. Always, when I see that hint of recognition in her eyes, that slight confusion, I'm filled with a sick hope: that she'll know me. That she'll be Phoebe, and she'll know me as she knew me then. I know it's impossible, that Phoebe's *ib*, her heart—her mind—is lost in the world, an echo of who she was, and that all that's looking out at me is her soul, as innocent and unknowing as a child. But I feel her soul call to me, and I can't help but hope.

I've told her, of course. She usually believes me. It speaks a sense to her, I suppose. But it's worse, then. She feels the burden of her past lives, an obligation to try and be the woman I loved, to be Phoebe. She rebels, which I understand—if she were to submit easily to that sort of tyranny, she wouldn't be the soul I know—and I lose her, or she wastes away, tortured by the history she can't remember.

I don't tell her anymore.

I've died for her. Been killed defending her, or avenging her. Fought with her brothers or husbands. In one instance, she killed me herself. Violent deaths are the most dangerous, for us. We're usually unprepared for it. Someone has to collect the body, see it conveyed to its tomb within seventy days. We tend to look out for each other, check in from time to time to see if it's needed. So far, thank the gods, one of the others has got to me every time.

I've rejected her before, for my own sanity. Fled her, reduced us both to shadows of ourselves. I can barely express how I suffer. I'm more conscious of what's happening, and can refuse it, in a way that—not understanding why she's drawn as she is—she's rarely able to, but don't imagine for a moment I'm any less compelled than she is. When people speak of soul mates, of destined love, they imagine it as an ennobling thing; but it's nothing of the sort. It's bitter, and it's oppressive, and it robs you of every simple and honest emotion.

I've raised whole cities, in my time, seen them spring from bare earth, sprawl out across miles, then wear away to ruins and dust.

I've sat on the hills overlooking Carthage's ruins—both times—and drunk sharp, sour wine to remember buildings I wrought. I've fought in wars that have, centuries on, shaped whole continents. I've met people who are now legends. In recent years I worked for both Wren and Brunel, if in a fairly minor capacity each time; today, fortunately, my skin colour is less of a barrier to working in my chosen field. But I look back and I barely see all of that. Just her, over and again through the ages.

• • •

I sit at that table, talking and joking, but there's a distance there now, and she feels it. I can't do this. I'm going to my tomb in a month or two, and I'll be gone, for a year, or ten years, or half a lifetime. I never know. But it'll be too long, and I'll lose her again. And I can't do it, to her or to me.

She's muted now, confused. We've touched one another, connected at a level she didn't expect, and now I'm withdrawing again. I don't want to, didn't mean to, but I have to. She gets her phone out again, checks her messages. Thinking about "Babe," and about getting back on a train.

My heart is leaden.

• • •

I'm going north to prepare. The body has to lie in its tomb, to re-enact His descent into Duat. Certain spells have to be set around the body, and the canopic jars have to be present. It doesn't have to be the same tomb as I was first buried in; it felt like taking a terrible chance, first time I tried that, but Meryetamun insisted she'd moved, and it had done her no harm. It came as a great relief to all of us, especially the way well-meaning academics kept pulling our resting bodies out of the ground. I've seen Tutankhamun's body, reinterred in his tomb, too late for the boy to make the return. We all loved him; he was beautiful, and always happy.

This time I'm using a lockup in Leeds, bought outright, with the best security and climate control money can buy. A couple of the others will be checking in on me every now and again.

The ushabti aren't necessary either, although they make life a little more comfortable in the underworld. I've left most of my old ones in Abdju, but I have a small box of them in my improvised tomb: a few servants, some tools and luxuries. Meryetamun went to bed with a crate of teddy bears, last time she went down. I've heard they snuffled about in Duat for a year or two, quite useless as servants, but caused something of a stir.

Aside from my tomb, I need to arrange for my current identity to "die" and for my disappearance to be explained. I need to create my new identity, have funds moved and documents created. I have the resources for all of this—I've become practised—but the wheels have to be set in motion.

• • •

Using the internet on her phone, she's confirmed that there's a bus service to get us both on our way again. We've a short wait. She's become brusque, cold. She orders another coffee and another tea, smiles breezily, starts talking about a film she's seen recently.

I miss her. Not just Phoebe, but already I miss her in herself, this proud, bold, warm, loving woman I met on the platform today. Sitting next to me, the scarf around her neck now, less tangible armour up around that, blowing on her latte and sipping it, and regarding me over the lip of the cup with bright, brittle eyes.

Blue eyes. Clear and open. Phoebe's had been dark. I actually think I like these more.

She's hurt, and she's not sure why. That I'm rejecting her, of course; that we've touched each other so and I'm closing up again. But she can't see why this stranger, this man she's just met, by chance, one autumn afternoon in a train station in the middle of nowhere, can have such a hold over her. She's angry with herself for caring that I'm leaving.

We talk for another fifteen minutes or so, on trivialities. The sky's turned nearly black, now, and the first few stars are coming out. By the time I stand to go—she'll catch the next one, she says; she wants to work on some poetry before she heads on—she's entirely fenced in again, as though nothing had happened. A rock has settled in my belly.

I shake her hand, smile mechanically, say goodbye. I use the name on the sheet of paper in my pocket, but my heart screams at her, *Phoebe*. She uses the name I gave her, the name of the identity I will kill in Leeds. On an impulse, I bend over and kiss her on the cheek before I turn to go.

POPPIES

S.G. LARNER

Screams punctuated the cold night air. Zahra clung tight to Adir, trembling as she buried her head in his shoulder. He tightened his embrace, whispered soothing words.

"If he finds out—"

"We're careful. He doesn't suspect. Besides, he's away." Adir stroked her long black hair. "I love you."

She was silent, listening to the distant sounds of death. An ugly cheer went up and soon after the night was still again. Zahra stretched out her legs and pushed Adir away before scrambling back into her clothes. He watched her with a smile on his face. Surrounded by moonlight-silvered poppies, she looked a goddess risen from the sea.

"He's back tomorrow," she said softly and rubbed her arms. "Adir . . . we must end this."

Adir got to his knees and stretched his arms out. He took her hands in his and kissed them.

"Go home. Sleep well. God give you the grace to endure my pig of a brother."

He heard her sigh as she turned and left him kneeling in the dirt. The opium poppies danced in her shadowy wake.

The sun was still sleeping when Adir climbed out of bed and dressed. He knelt and prayed for forgiveness, and for Zahra's safety. Then he left his barren house.

At this time of morning the village was peaceful. His breath puffed out in little clouds of vapour as he made his way through the narrow dirt streets, choosing the long way to avoid the village square. A newborn cried as he passed Sharif's house. He smiled but felt a pang. Zahra might bear his brother a child soon. A bitter thought.

The bakery stood still and cold until he lit the fires. He hummed as he kneaded dough and shaped the loaves. Some he left to rise; others were formed into flatbreads that he then baked on a hot stone. When the loaves were ready, he tossed them into the oven and wiped his floury hands on his apron.

Light crept into the bakery and he rolled up the shutters.

"Morning, Adir!" The cheerful salutation was followed by Hassan's ungainly form. Adir's teenage apprentice—an indiscreet boy, with no lack of friends—got to work, whistling as he swept the floor. "I didn't see you last night."

Adir rubbed his eyes with the back of a hand. "I felt unwell," he said. "These loaves will be ready in half an hour. I will be back in an hour, can you manage?"

Hassan nodded, his head bobbing precariously on his skinny neck.

Adir trod the well-worn path to his house; a small dwelling to the east of the village square. As he passed through the square, his gaze was drawn to a wooden post. It stood tall and solid in the centre of the square, the weathered wood stained dark by time and more ominous things. Its latest victim was gone, taken to the field of poppies.

He pulled his gaze away, but not before he caught a glimpse of a splash of red at the base of the post.

He cast a quick glance over his shoulder before taking a closer look. A solitary red poppy grew from the earth; a crimson cousin to the white opium poppies in the fields outside the village.

"That's odd," he said and reached out to touch it. A shadow passed over the sun. He shivered with the sudden cold and snatched his hand back. He looked around again and hurried to his house.

Once inside he splashed water over his face and scraped the stubble off with a knife. He sat down at his table and re-read his father's last letter. With a sigh he picked up a pen. He formed his letters slowly, with effort. Finally he threw the pen down and scanned his reply.

Dear Father,

In reply to your last letter: there is no one. I do not want to marry. Please come home soon. No good will come of this. We must go back to using sheep. You have to convince the Elders. Already the village is different. When you get back, you will see.

He grimaced at the painstaking scrawl. Writing was Sayid's talent, not his. Sayid was always the clever one; the one with the plan. That was why Adir, the eldest, was the village baker and Sayid, the younger, was the village's chief trader.

That was why Sayid was Zahra's husband.

He bent over the letter and added another two sentences.

Since you left there has been another. She was given to the crop that is due for harvest.

Adir folded and sealed his letter. He then threw his father's letter on the coals in his hearth.

As he stepped from his threshold a tiny black shadow accosted him. Deep-set black eyes studied him from above a stern nose. Wrinkles gouged deep chasms in her skin and spoke of a long life, hard won.

"Grandmother Junah," Adir said, bowing his head. The oldest woman in the village was not his grandmother, but she commanded his respect.

"Gambling is forbidden by our Lord God."

He looked up, startled. "I am a Godly man."

"You dice with the life of your lover. I am displeased." Her eyes narrowed. "You must leave her be."

Adir struggled to breathe normally. His eyes were wide. He smoothed his face. "Pardon, Grandmother, you are mistaken. I have no lover."

Her brows swooped into a fierce frown. "She is in danger, you fool. Can't you feel it?" She stretched up and stabbed him in the chest with a bony finger. "Forget about Zahra," she hissed. "If you love her."

Adir stumbled, falling backwards onto his doorstep. For a moment Junah stared down at him, then vanished around the corner in a swirl of dark skirts.

The council convened in the evening to receive Sayid's trade report. Adir slouched in his chair. His position on the council was a mere courtesy to his father, so he usually kept his mouth shut and admired the intricately-carved wall frescos. He watched Sayid's entrance through slitted eyes.

Sayid was light on his feet, always smiling and charming. He bowed to the Elders and nodded to his fellow council members, gaze skipping over Adir.

"What did the Gloam have to say about the poppies, Sayid?" Elder Tamam leaned forward and raised his grizzled brows.

"They were most pleased with our poppies. Results were unexpected and they have requested more of the same," he replied, displaying a smug expression.

Adir suppressed a frown. He cast a glance at the other men. Several muttered and shook their heads, while the rest appeared unruffled.

Can't you feel it? Junah's voice had snapped. Sweat beaded on Adir's brow as the air in the room became oppressive. Hatred, overwhelming—

"This is a difficult request to grant." Tamam looked at the other three men who shared the Elders bench with him. Zahra's father, Wadi, slanted his hand in a negative motion. Adir sucked in a deep breath as the pressure eased.

"We cannot continue with this practice," Wadi said. There were nods around the room. Sayid's smile slipped.

"The Gloam understand the difficulty faced by this village in providing poppies cultivated in such an *unusual* manner. To that end, they have proposed assistance in procuring what we need."

Adir sat up straight. "Stop speaking in circles, Sayid," he called. "What exactly are they offering?"

Sayid ignored him and spoke directly to Wadi. "Father-of-my-wife, I understand your concern. We do not wantonly sacrifice our innocent women for the sake of a few poppies. The Gloam will send us criminals from other villages."

Wadi glanced at Adir. *Is he regretting his decision now?* Adir shook his head, a tiny movement.

"I'm sorry, daughter-husband, but I must still oppose this." Wadi crossed his arms over his chest. "I am against the Gloam."

Sayid spread his arms. "The Gloam cannot be refused. Think of our traditional obligations."

"We are not obliged to kill our own for their unnatural desires,"

Wadi said with a growl. "What have we come to?"

Tamam clicked his tongue. "Sayid is right, Wadi. I vote with the Gloam."

The two remaining Elders shrugged. In unison they said, "With."

Tamam stood and faced the younger men. "Will we call a general vote, or will you submit to the will of the Elders in this matter?"

Adir felt Wadi's gaze on him, but he kept his demeanour calm. No one spoke.

Tamam nodded and spread his hands. "It is agreed, then." He put his hand on Wadi's shoulder. "None of our women have anything to fear as long as they obey God's laws."

Adir's cheeks grew hot. He ducked his head and inspected the tiled floor. When he looked up Sayid's stare met him head on. One corner of his mouth lifted in a mocking half-smile.

Does he suspect? Adir refused to look away and refused to blink, even as his eyes burned. With easy grace Sayid stepped back and broke his gaze.

A solid lump of fear lodged in Adir's throat. He left the squat building, avoiding the general mingling and talking that took place after a meeting. Sweet opium poppy perfume laced the evening air and filled his nostrils. He had to be careful.

• • •

Without warning Adir's father returned to the village. Asim knocked on Adir's door in the dark of night, slipping in without a word as Adir opened it.

"It's bad," he said without preamble. He sat at the fire, warming his hands. "The new poppies have stronger properties. The magic of the Gloamlings has become sharper, more dangerous. I assume it was previously tempered by the dull nature of sheep."

"But, women?" Adir sat beside him.

"Oh, I assume God-fearing women would make magic just as dull as the sheep," his father replied. "We're talking of women who have fire inside them, women who've defied God's laws. Do you have any bread left?"

Adir fetched him a flatbread and sat back down, contemplating his father's words. "What kind of power?"

"Their normal powers are amplified: healing, illusion, animal mind-control. More worryingly they have developed the power to shift objects and bend humans to their will," Asim said, around a mouthful of bread.

"Do you think Sayid was manipulated?"

"Most certainly," Asim said and sighed. "Sayid has always been fascinated by the Gloam. I think he wished he was born a Gloamling. He has chafed at his limitations. Your brother is a difficult man, but he is not a bad man."

Adir looked away and remained silent.

"I know you're angry, but you need to let it go. If you'd wanted the girl, you should have gone to Wadi. He wasn't going to refuse the prestige of the chief trader as son-in-law. It's your own fault for waiting."

"He did it to spite me."

"Maybe." Asim sighed again and stretched his shoulders.

"She was too young to marry. I was waiting for her birthday." Adir glared at his father, who raised his eyebrows.

"It's in the past, Adir. I wish you would make peace. There are other young women—"

Adir stood. "Did you feel it? When you returned?"

His father stared at him and chewed the last mouthful. "Yes. Darkness. Hatred. Something old and malevolent. Adir, there is more."

"What?"

"When I was in Farbec, I consulted their histories. There was no mention of a foreign invasion of Sharaz. None."

"They could have erased it—"

"But why? No, I believe the Gloam has been using us for their own purpose. We were once a nation of scholars, scientists and philosophers. Now we are peasants and poppy farmers. Why is that?"

Adir had no answer. Instead he asked, "Have you ever seen a red poppy?"

His father raised his eyebrows and shook his head. "No, son, poppies are only white."

Adir nodded. "We're feeding more than the opium poppies, father. Wadi may be an ally, but Tamam holds sway."

Asim nodded. "On the morrow," he said.

Upon rising in the morning Adir discovered his father already gone to meet with the Elders. He rubbed his eyes and splashed water on his face before treading the familiar route to the bakery.

• • •

While Sayid was in the village Adir stayed as far away from Zahra as possible. She always bought bread in the company of her sister, Fadwa, and numerous cousins, and they were both careful to remain polite but distant. The last two weeks was torturous for Adir, but Sayid was due to leave soon.

In the dirt near the door Adir noticed a crudely-scratched flower. His heart beat faster. The sign was Zahra's way of telling him that Sayid had left and she would meet him in the poppy field at midnight.

A memory of stern eyes brought the words 'forget about Zahra, if you love her' into his head. He kicked the dirt to erase the sign and went inside.

The fires roared to life. He stoked them, distracted, wrestling with his conscience. Life was meant to be simple. He loved Zahra and he wanted to be with her. Darkness swelled in his heart. Zahra should have been his. Sayid stole her. The shadows cast by the fire brooded, while Adir whistled as he imagined Zahra naked under the stars.

There was little light as Adir navigated the furrows between the rows of poppies. The moon was dark, but the stars provided just enough light to see by.

She waited for him in their usual spot, a little hollow created by the shift and movement of their bodies. He caught her to his chest, kissed her soft lips. She shivered against him.

"How I've missed you," he whispered. "I thought he would never leave."

"Adir, my love . . . " her voice was stilted. "We can't . . . I can't keep doing this."

He looked down at her upturned face. Shadows distorted the familiar angles. "What's wrong?"

In the silence that followed his words, his heart drummed anxiously in his chest. Slowly she replied, "I told Sayid I am pregnant."

Adir's ears hummed. He grasped onto the tiny thread of hope she offered. "You told him? But . . . ?"

"I am not."

Adir looked up at the stars, trying to understand. "Then why—?"

Zahra shifted away from him. "He is . . . different, since he returned. Unpredictable. Violent. I was scared."

His hands clenched by his sides. "Did he hurt you?"

"Sweet Adir," she said and laughed before reaching out and touching his face. "After tonight, I will be the dutiful, faithful wife. Do you understand, my love? Your brother is my husband. As much as I wish it were you, we cannot keep doing this. You must find a wife. Promise me."

He pushed her hand away. "No. I will not promise."

Zahra stepped back. "Do you feel it? The anger, the hunger? Adir, we are part of the problem. We must not give them any excuses." She waited for his reply.

He could think of none. His mind cried out for her. *Think, Adir, think.* But life was meant to be simple. "One last night, then?"

"Yes."

Adir buried his fears and pulled her to the ground.

It was too bright. The sun had already peeped over the horizon. Adir swore and scrambled upright. A cry went up and people rushed for the field. He glanced down at Zahra, who was rubbing her eyes in sleep-daze.

"Stay down," he snapped at her then ran, great strides taking him from her side in the hope she would remain undiscovered. A man rose from the poppies and tackled him. They tumbled to the ploughed earth in an awkward tangle.

More people joined the fray. The villagers swarmed; bodies heaving and bumping together, united in outrage. Adir caught a glimpse of Zahra's face. Dark eyes wide with fear as they hauled her from the hollow in the fields. Sweat slicked his skin. Hard fingers pinched him.

"Zahra!" he called as fear scurried through him. Small women hurled abuse at him, their familiar eyes narrowed in hatred. He heard a scream and fought to free himself from the mob. The many-fingered monster that held his arms pushed him out of the field and towards the village square.

"Zahra!" Adir called again. "Let her go!" His muscles flexed and heaved as he was shoved down the street. Someone draped an itchy sheet over his shoulders. His feet were numb from the cold.

Shadows still lingered in the village square, giving the whitewashed walls a blue tint. He saw Zahra. She was ashen pale as they prodded her; laughing when she stumbled on her bare feet. She had been wrapped in a sheet, covering her shame. Her black hair was wild and tangled. Her face bore scratches and trails of tears. She cast a glance at the wooden post and looked away with wide eyes.

"Murderer," a woman hissed at Adir. He glanced at her and saw Grandmother Junah's wrinkled face. "Your fault," she said.

"No!" he yelled and with a lunge he tore free. He ran to Zahra, shrugging off the grasping hands. Men appeared before him, barring his way. He roared and threw punches, but they tackled him, sat on him, ground his face into the gravel.

Someone grabbed Adir's hair and wrenched his head, forcing him to look up. Zahra was bound naked to the post; the sheet crumpled by her feet. He heard mutters and saw the anger on the faces of the women.

"Cover her," called Grandmother Junah. Gawky young Hassan hurried forward and hastily wrapped the sheet around her body.

Adir strained to move his head to see. Where were Asim and Wadi?

"A trial," he croaked the words out. "A trial," he said louder. Zahra's gaze pierced him, her eyebrows raised with hope. A trial was a slim chance, but . . .

"The whore was caught lying naked in the arms of my brother! She is guilty as witnessed by many. Adultery carries but one punishment." Sayid emerged from the crowd and strode to stand before Zahra. "Surprised to see me?"

Zahra looked briefly to the sky before bowing her head. Adir stared at his brother. "Then kill me too."

Sayid turned and spat in the dust. "She is my wife. I have this right."

Adir's arms cramped behind his back, his shoulders ached. He tasted blood and grit and Zahra.

"Friends," he said, raising his voice. "Can't you feel the darkness in the air? The Gloam wants blood poppies, not opium poppies. They're turning us into savages." A foot landed in his ribs. He grunted in pain. Where was his father?

"Enough of this," Sayid said. "Kill her."

"Wait! Without a trial, you have no right to call on the village to execute her."

Sayid paused. "You would like me to kill her with my own hands? You think I can't?" He turned and slapped Zahra across the cheek. She grunted, then glowered at Sayid.

Adir gasped as the air thickened and the menacing presence filled the village.

Sayid hit her again. And again.

"You are a coward, brother."

"I have no brother," Sayid replied as he pulled a long dagger from his belt. Zahra moaned and shook her head.

"Sayid! Our father—"

"Father is . . . indisposed." He held Zahra's jaw in his hand and forced her to look at him, then ripped the sheet from her body. "I bet the spawn in your belly is his, isn't it?"

Adir stopped breathing. *Stall, Zahra! Beg, grovel, convince him!*

The look in her hate-filled eyes turned his blood glacial. Her laugh withered his hopes. She said, "Oh yes. Never yours."

Sayid drove the point of the dagger into her belly. She screamed.

Breath returned in a rush. Pain squeezed Adir's heart tight and he shut his eyes. *Forgive me, Zahra.*

"How would you like to fuck her now?" his brother yelled. Adir clenched his teeth and ground them together. He wanted to grasp his brother's throat and slowly crush it.

Zahra's scream cut off with a gurgle.

Silence. A hush like the moments before a newborn takes its first cry. Tears forced their way from beneath Adir's closed eyelids. If he didn't look, she could still be alive.

Something in the stillness made him look. It was too quiet. Zahra—streaked with blood from a gaping wound at her neck— hung unmoving from the post and at her feet were a mass of red poppies. As Adir watched, a drop of blood fell from Zahra's breast. The ground stirred as the blood seeped in. A tiny green shoot surged forth, spindly and rapid. In seconds the plant reached full growth and the bright buds bloomed. Adir's eyes widened. He glanced around. Faces were slack-jawed, eyes filled with awe. Little Fadwa wailed and fell to her knees.

"A miracle," he heard. Cries of fear and sadness followed. He narrowed his eyes and tilted his head to look up at his brother. A flicker of unease crossed Sayid's face and he cast around, looking for someone.

"A whore," Sayid began, uncertain. "She was a whore! God wanted me to kill her. It is so!" He looked for support. Villagers shied from him. The hands that pressed Adir into the dirt eased and let go. He stood, letting the sheet fall. Naked, he confronted his brother.

"You are a pig."

Sayid recoiled. "How dare you—"

"I loved her. She loved me. I wanted to marry her, but you stole her from me. There is no shame in love. None."

His brother stumbled back, raising his hands. Adir glanced around at the villagers. Some were slinking from the square. At the edge of the square he saw a hooded, grey-robed figure. Sayid saw it too and a sudden smile bloomed on his face.

"Stop!" Adir urged. "This is not the end." Behind him Zahra was a macabre scarecrow in her growing field of red poppies. "This can never happen again. Love is not punishable by death." He pointed to the grey-robed figure. "The Gloam are using us." The figure stood unmoving as the frightened villagers watched.

"The poppies must be fed," someone called.

"The poppies have been fed! You have grown a crop of blood poppies, my friend. What darkness do they bring? Before, we fed the opium poppies with sheep. We must return to that practice. We have become little more than savage monsters."

Sayid's lip curled. "Whores make fine fertiliser, better to not waste the sheep."

The faces before him changed. Eyes looked past him, grew wide, fearful. Someone shrieked.

He turned. The crimson poppies were writhing, growing bigger, sending out tendrils formed of smoke and blood. More people screamed. The first tendril reached Sayid. Uncomprehending, he swatted at it. It curled around his wrist.

And then it curled around his neck and strangled him.

Chaos. Men and women ran back and forth, trying to escape the square, but the tendrils were everywhere—lethal snakes of death, hunting indiscriminately. "Mercy!" cried one woman as the tendril closed around her neck.

A wall of grief separated Adir from their terror and shrieks. Grief . . . and satisfaction.

Revenge.

One of the tendrils found a small boy, lifted him and threw him into a wall. Shock punched Adir in the gut. *No. Not the children.*

A vicious tug on his arm sent him sprawling. Junah stood over him, her face hard. "This is what they want," she said, pointing. He looked and saw the Gloamling walking undisturbed through the chaos, waving the tendrils away with a word. The face was shadowed but a thin smile could be seen. "You must stop it."

"Is it Zahra?"

She shook her head. "It was there before Zahra, but it is stronger now. She is part of it."

He got to his feet. The blood poppies grew tall as men, their colour dark as Muscat grapes. Tendrils thrashed. With a silent prayer Adir lunged forward and sunk his hand into the earth beneath Zahra's still form.

A vast pressure squeezed him; an ancient brooding presence woken to a frenzy by blood and hate. At the edges he felt Zahra's rage and terror. If he closed his eyes he could see them: the huge shadowy being, the women stretching in a mournful line behind his murdered lover. Adir breathed deep.

"Forgive us," he said to the ancient one. "This blood should never have been spilled, should never have woken you. Forgive us," he said to the women. "We are weak and cruel, but this slaughter is giving the enemy what it wants." He raised his arm with effort and pointed at the Gloamling, still untouched. "If they have their way, more women will die."

In the eye of the storm, Adir held his breath. The ancient one regarded him.

His mind was filled with a vision of what must be done. He nodded. The tendrils withdrew.

The ghostly women were unsatisfied. Adir sensed their anger and smelled burnt ozone. *Women who have defied God's laws.* He inhaled sharply.

"The Gloamling draws its power from your strength. You can take it away," he said, hoping it was true. The smell intensified, blistering his nostrils, before a zephyr blew the scent away. A sense of profound peace settled upon him.

The grey-robed figure stood beside him. The poppies had shrunk back to normal size and moved only with the breeze that ruffled their petals. Zahra's hair fluttered like a pennant. He reached his hand out and stroked a silky lock.

"You owe us your existence," the Gloamling said, its voice hissing and clicking simultaneously.

"Thank you," Adir said stupidly. He rubbed his face and discovered his cheek was wet.

The Gloamling turned and studied him. "Tell me what you did," it said.

Adir tensed his shoulders. He resisted the Gloamling's mind easily and relaxed. "It was their power. Never yours."

The Gloamling leaned down and touched a scaly claw to a red petal. It hissed in pain and pulled its claw back. "What is it?"

"I don't know. Some dark force, a being of immense power." Adir stared at Zahra through hazy eyes. He only half-listened to the Gloamling.

"That's impossible. We banished your Gods."

"There is but one God," Adir recited absently.

The Gloamling snarled and stalked away. Adir watched the grey-clad form retreat. He became aware of his surroundings.

The square was filled with sobbing people. Scattered around him was the wreckage of his village. Faces were swollen and black, tongues protruding rudely. As Adir turned, survivors scattered, but a small whimper made him pause. He stepped over corpses, careful of his bare feet. Trapped under the swollen body of Hassan he found little Fadwa. She wept silent tears, eyes shut tight against the horror. He knelt and touched her arm.

"Fadwa."

The girl covered her face with her hands and shook.

"Fadwa. Please. Look at me."

She slid her fingers from her face and stared at him with tormented eyes. He leaned forward, kissed her lightly on the cheek and whispered in her ear.

Mute, she nodded. He stood and picked his way back through the bodies littering the ground. Back to Zahra.

"Goodbye, my love," he said. As the rising sun broke through the dawn cloud cover, light turned the blood poppies from dark Muscat to bright crimson.

Under the combined gaze of the few survivors he bent down and picked a flower. He turned from his lover, back straight, and walked naked from the village. A sharp wail sounded behind him like a knife at his back. It was joined by another keening cry. And another. The remnants of the village mourned.

Adir walked into the field of white opium poppies. He placed the red poppy in the hollow that held so many memories and touched his fingers to his lips.

Junah approached, holding a blazing torch in each hand. Fadwa hovered behind. Adir took the proffered torch and stood side by side with Junah. She placed her free hand on his arm, then held the flames to a row of perfumed blossoms. They shrivelled and fire took hold.

Adir avoided her gaze as she turned to him. He watched the spread of the fire. With a nod she left him there, gathering Fadwa up as she went.

"Adir!"

He saw his father hurrying toward him, a grief-stricken Wadi trailing.

"Stay back," he warned. "This is the only way." He saluted Wadi. "For Zahra."

"Zahra would want you to live," his father cried in anguish. He started forward, but Wadi held him back. Adir turned his back on them.

Adir touched the flames to the poppies, swinging the torch slowly back and forth. He walked through the field, a harbinger of doom and hope. As the sun rose he found himself in the centre, surrounded by blistering heat. Fire burned him clean.

THE NINETY-TWO

CLAIRE MCKENNA

When the devil died (aged forty-five, heart attack from overtraining, keeled over on the Nugget's Crossing five kilometres into a ten kilometre run), he was wearing his number ninety-two guernsey, and even then nobody wanted to touch it, or him, because if there was ever a man averse to kindness or tenderness it was Beaufort Kinsey. So they stood in the middle of the road instead, eighteen dumbfounded men watching him die, and not one lifting a finger to help.

Only a passing motorist had the good sense to call an ambulance five minutes and thirty seconds later, but by the time the paramedics arrived Beaufort had passed on to the great beyond.

"Christ, it was quick," said one witness. "Died right there on the spot. Dead before he hit the ground."

A subsequent autopsy was confirmation enough of a cardiac arrest. A minor blood vessel in Beaufort's grotesquely scarred heart had pinched off like a highway after a five car pile-up, and the cascading trauma climaxed with a split artery and Beaufort hitting the concrete at the midpoint of haranguing a seventeen-year old kid about the correlations between sexual orientation and not being able to keep up with the much fitter pack.

What the report didn't quite mention was that a good ten minutes might have existed between the incident and the sweet hereafter. Nor was it floated that with CPR Beaufort might have been saved, nor did anyone want to mention the croaked, "Help me, you fucks," that constituted Beaufort's last words.

Two hundred people turned out for his funeral.

The event was woefully under-catered. Kylie Kinsey, Beaufort's long suffering wife, had calculated for the thirty members of the North Trafalgar Victorian Football Association and maybe the one or two drinking mates he had not totally isolated from years of using the Royal Arms Hotel as his preferred provider of maggoting volumes of spirits. In a last (and her first) moment of rebellion she catered the event herself with five loaves of stale supermarket bread and the cheapest sausages she could find, pre-cooked and left overnight in the too-warm fridge Beaufort hadn't replaced last month because it wasn't fucking broken you fucking bitch.

Like they said, the devil.

Kylie sat stonily through a service MC'd by the budget celebrant from several towns over, a man who had never known Beaufort Kinsey and gushed about how wonderful and respected and loved Beau was, and you could have heard a pin drop as everyone looked at their feet or the gaudy crying Jesus statues in the corner of the church. Kylie shed a couple of tears, but only out of relief that Beau was gone, and only from her left eye, because the healed orbital fracture in her right—the size of Beau's fist—had destroyed her tear ducts.

Seated next to Kylie was Beau's employer and North Trafalgar's main sponsor, Finnegan Torch. Sixty-year-old Torch was the owner of Torch's Meats, the regional meat and butcher specialists. Beau had been Torch's head abattoir manager, and Finnegan had loved him like his own delinquent and terrifying son.

Kylie Kinsey might have been stoic, but Torch wept like his heart had been broken.

When Coach O'Laughlin came to the lectern, he continued the fictional theme with a story of a man dedicated to his club, a father-figure who took his time in mentoring the younger ones, whose commitment had him becoming the oldest still-active player in the state.

Coach O'Laughlin didn't mention how Beau was meaner than a drunk on Good Friday, that his mentoring extended only to taking the over-18's on sex tours. Anyone who didn't go was immediately branded a flaming fucking poofter and not fucking playing in a Trafalgar North team. Heterosexuality according to Beau was measured in how many naked men could fit into a bedroom and service one unconscious local girl. He was that person both sad and too common; who found himself equally aroused by another man's shame as a stranger's breasts but would never admit it even privately lest the possibility of poofterism raise its judgemental and perhaps even purplish swollen head.

"He stayed with his team to the end. A legacy lasts longer than a memory, and his legacy will stay with us always."

(More than one mourner put his hand in his pocket and surreptitiously scratched his nuts, because on the last tour everyone contracted something red and weally and anitibiotic-resistantly itchy that also threatened to stay with them always.)

Beau had two daughters, eight and ten. Easy enough to feel sorry for them at the loss of their father, but they had the look of survivors who have just been airlifted out of a war-zone. Kylie's younger brother Scott flew down from Sydney and in a fit of defiance wore his pinkest and most flamboyant shirt.

"I would have brought my goddamn maracas if I thought I could piss that fucker off any more," Scott was heard to grumble to his partner later that evening. "By the way, don't eat the sausages."

Two weeks later, when everyone had recovered from the gastro epidemic that had run rampant through North Trafalgar's male demographic, Coach O'Laughlin convened a meeting with the rest of the football club.

"Well boys, we have to elect another club President, and we have to vote on shelving the guernsey."

North Trafalgar's clubhouse was longer than it was wide, and one long wall was completely covered in mounted Australian Rules football guernseys, each one bearing a photo of the man who had worn it last. The earliest jumpers were long sleeved and woollen, from the original style of the game where a player waited in Melbourne's wintry conditions for the ball to be kicked his way. Back then the men were small and nuggetty, hard working men from the inner city whose factories overlooked re-appropriated cricket grounds turned into mud-pits. As the game modernised, so too did the players. Poached from athletics clubs and other sporting codes, the players grew in stature, and a new style of no-sleeved parachute silk jersey replaced the wool-knit in the fast-paced marathon that the game had become.

None of the numbers were in use. There is a grand tradition in Aussie Rules, that a player who has lived an exemplary life, who is a hero and a mate and brave and true, all the qualities that are held in the highest regard, will have his number retired on his death. No other player will wear his guernsey, and it will join the wall of heroes and champions, a football Valhalla.

Being a little town, a lot of men had filled those criteria. They were men who had fought bushfires, rescued families from swollen rivers, had gone overseas to fight wars they knew nothing about and had still carried on a tradition. They were giants, and they were numerous, and there wasn't a player alive now who had worn a North Trafalgar number below eighty.

Beau had thought himself that sort of man. Two years ago, when he'd beat with extreme prejudice the cancer that lost him a testicle, he had begun to rearrange the Hero Wall so that the central space above the Premier's Cup was vacant. That space was going to be reserved for a single guernsey, a number ninety-two, and for the hero photo Beaufort Kinsey would be immortalised in the prime of his life, taking the spectacular mark that had shattered another man's collarbone.

"As you know," Coach O'Laughlin said, "We have to vote unanimously to have a guernsey retired. All those in favour . . . "

Beau's influence was so absolute that even after his death most of the hands went up in stiff, shuddering columns.

All except one.

"C'mon Darren," whispered one of the younger players to the malcontent who sat, legs spread and arms folded, refusing to vote. "Just put your hand up."

"No," he said. Now that Beau was dead, Darren Speaker was now the oldest player. As Beau's best mate since they were teens, everyone thought he'd have been Beau's biggest cheerleader.

Instead, one of his knees trembled. A doctor might say that the deep tremor was the remnants of a brain injury, a concussion when he was twenty and twenty-three year old Beau had beaten him up for rooting a girl Beau had had his eye on. But the others knew it was Beaufort's ghost pulling on strings he'd hooked into years before. Darren was waging a great and terrible war inside himself. When his words came out they came forced, through clenched teeth, as if his own body was trying to stop him from speaking.

"Beau was a cunt. To his missus. To me. To all of youse. What about Frankie, our best fucking player?"

"Frankie was a poof," a lone voice piped up hesitantly.

"Frankie had integrity. He wouldn't rape a girl when youse all did. Cause you were all scared of Beau, he turned youse into animals. Turned youse criminal."

The men looked at each other, waiting for the one person who would restore order by defending Beaufort Kinsey and make everything normal again. But King Beau had beaten, cajoled and threatened the balls off of them during his quarter century reign. Nobody could speak yup now.

Darren went on, his voice a metronome. "What about Josh? Josh had to move cause Beau threatened to kill his kids."

"Josh rooted Beau's missus."

"He took her to hospital when Beau caved her face in!" The anger made Darren's voice raise to a crescendo, and the memory-hooks snapped, allowing him to stand. "You go vote for that cocksucker, but if that guernsey goes on that wall I'm leaving the club. And I'm taking the fucking bus with me."

Darren stormed out and Coach O'Laughlin said in a faux-cheery voice, "Right, let's have a re-vote shall we?"

But when he made the call for *In Favour*, nobody put their hand up at all.

Thirty miles West of North Trafalgar and just over the state border was South Trafalgar, an inappropriately named and dying town that had been amputated by a Bicentennial Road Project and freeway bypass back in 'eighty-eight. Combined with the gut punch of legalised gambling in the state where most of the tourist busses originated, South Trafalgar was in decline. No longer did the hordes of senior citizens and sports clubs descend upon South Trafalgar to play the pokies. The conference rooms and motels emptied out and fell into disrepair. With unemployment at an all-time high, scores of young men fled the town to work the mines of Western Australia.

A decision was made to merge the struggling football teams together under the North Trafalgar banner. The number ninety-two guernsey went to Chris Fowler, their most promising young player. Tall and rangy, he had once qualified for the Olympic high-jump team before snapping his cruciate ligament and losing that tiny championship edge. They made him a ruckman, and with his half-foot reach over every other VFA player, the combined Trafalgar team won their first off-season game against the Nugget's Downs Lyrebirds. Fowler broke the record in marks, his own personal best in handpasses. Everything looked good.

• • •

"Fowler's out," Coach O'Laughlin said after a practice match made strange in the absence of their new Ninety-Two. "We had to replace him with Giraffe, which means there's a now a gap in the wing."

Everyone murmured in concern. The season hadn't even started and yet Fowler had more than made up for the offensive gap Beau had left behind. Beau's game tactics had primarily consisted of king hits, clotheslines and haymakers. Generally when he'd gotten the ball, most players had left him alone and let the mad bastard have the kick.

Any concerns that Fowler wouldn't match Beau had been quickly doused, as in a matter of months he had transformed from a gangly kid to a battering ram.

"Testicular cancer," the Coach continued. "I'm ashamed as a Coach to say that he was probably juicing."

"Bullshit," one of the Southie full-forwards shouted. He was a big ginger monster, claimed he was twenty-nine but was really closer to thirty-five. "Chris never took steroids."

"How do you explain him getting so big, Harris?" a North player retorted. "He wasn't going through puberty again."

"Didn't the last guy to wear that guernsey get cancer?" Harris demanded.

The Southie chorus of *fuckin' yeah*, drowned out the Coach's attempt to get the conversation back on track. He waved his liver-spotted hands as if flagging a goal.

"Settle down lads. Settle! We can bring another player out of reserves."

He chose Nicholas Coil, the part-time manager of the South Trafalgar Holiday Inn. Though there was the odd grumble that a North T player should have gotten a chance, none of those who had known Beau wanted to wear the number ninety-two.

Nikky was a decent bloke, a quiet man who was married with three boys. After the chaos that had been Beau, he restored a steady, strong order on the team.

North Trafalgar lost five matches in a row.

After sitting on the bottom of the VFA ladder for weeks, Darren Speaker prudently called a late night emergency meeting.

Since Beau's departure, Darren had been voted in as President, mostly because nobody else wanted the job. When Beau was alive Darren had lurked in the background, putting out spot fires. Now he felt that all dealt with was the aftermath of a disaster.

To make it worse, the sponsors were talking of pulling out.

"What the hell's happening with you blokes?" Finnegan Torch demanded. "I'm not going to have Torch's Meats associated with a losing side. What am I going to put on my advertisements now? Torch Meats—eat failure?"

"There's no failure involved, Torch. The other teams are finally putting on their best men," Darren barely managed to keep the annoyance out of his voice. "Before now anyone who played with us got injured, so we always got their crap players. We're just getting back to normal."

"Normal was when we had Bazza," Finnegan growled. "Like looking at a team of poofs, now."

Talking with Finnegan Torch made Darren grit his teeth. Torch had one of those florid, self-righteous faces with mean little eyes that plagued certain politicians and loud media personalities. Beau had loved Finnegan.

Darren might have retorted something sharp and mean, but was interrupted by a phone call.

As twelve pairs of eyes watched him, Darren's face drained of colour and he looked perilously close to passing out.

• • •

Sergeant Patterson, their reserve half-back and town policeman, told Darren that the chance of Nikky's court case being held before the finals was slim to nil. Besides, the preliminary magistrate had already denied Nikky bail on account of the seriousness of the crime. He was going to stay locked up until the trial.

"But he didn't kill anyone," Darren said hopelessly. "The hotel could have been a break-in. He could be innocent."

Patterson only shrugged. He'd already thought of every excuse himself.

"Nick Coil's got a wife and three kids in hospital, CCTV footage and witnesses. He's fucked, mate."

When Darren drove the bus past the motel, police tape still

blocked off the driveway. A lone reporter and TV cameraman lurked out the front, waiting for a local to venture too close and be ambushed for an interview.

Along the highway he passed a second crime scene, the place where they'd found Nikky, standing on the side of the road, bloody knife in his hand and his wife's finger in the other. A strange place to head off to, on foot and after a serious blue. The town was in the other direction.

Oddly, the first person who Darren thought of was Kylie, Beau's widow. She lived in the South now, having moved back in with her parents after Beau had gone into the soil.

Beau's two girls were playing in the yard outside when Darren parked the club bus under the wattle tree. He did not recognise the new car parked in the driveway. The pink car-seat covers with Playboy bunny-heads seemed an almost childish affectation, the car of a woman hanging on to a lost youth.

"Hello Uncle Darren!"

Beau's daughters ran up to Darren, smiling as if for the first time. He could not see anything of Beau in them and was glad. It would be too difficult to love anything that reminded Darren of him.

"Hey girls. Is your Mum in?"

He was pointed towards the kitchen at the rear of the house, where Kylie was rolling out pre-mixed cookie-dough on the kitchen table. Darren could have watched her rolling that dough all day. No doubt about it, but Kylie Kinsey was a looker, even with her droopy right eye. She wasn't even thirty. Beau had swept her up in a storm of romance and impossible promises, and had scared off any other man of her age with very real promises of pain. Kylie was too innocent back then to know a warning sign when it punched her in the face and then sobbed that it will never do it again.

"Hey Kyles."

"Oh, Darren, hi." She rubbed her forehead with a floury wrist, and wiped her hands on a dishcloth. Her wedding rings were gone. He wondered if they'd covered the down payment on the new Toyota.

"Just dropped by to see how you were going. Been a hell of a night."

"Yeah, I heard about Nikky on the radio this morning," she said absently, as if it was not Nikky she was thinking of.

"What's wrong, love?" Darren asked. Kylie did not know Nicholas or his family. Beau had been very parochial when it came to friendships. Anyone not from North Trafalgar might have been Al Qaeda.

"Oh, I don't know. Just some prank caller last night. Kept calling the house, grunting. My mobile too. We all went and stayed at the caravan park in Nugget's Downs."

"Funny, I didn't notice the full moon."

"Ha," she said.

"You just got back?"

She nodded, and the sunlight caught her blonde hair, and Daren felt a flutter in his chest that he'd not felt for a long time. He had been married once, far too young and only briefly. Now his kids were old enough to have kids. They lived in Melbourne, and he saw them once a year if he was lucky. Since then he'd been spare with girlfriends. Big bad Beau would come around with his intense gaze, his simmering aggression masquerading as passion, his silken words; as if some other, gentler man took over Beau's body for the short time it took for the seduction to play out.

"Hey," Darren said impulsively. "There's a show in the RSL tomorrow night. An eighties cover band and dinner. You want a break from all this?"

Her eyes lit up, then clouded over.

"I don't know. The girls."

"You can leave them with my sister and her mob. I think one of them's in the same class as your oldest."

Darren held his breath. He knew he was a good looking guy, a well preserved specimen even if he did have too many footy seasons under his belt, but Kylie was perky and pretty and young and Beau's wife. Any one of those would knacker his chances of seeing more of Kylie than occasional welfare checks.

Kylie could not think of an excuse to remain trapped in unhappiness, so she nodded instead. "I'd like that."

• • •

The band was not that great, and the sound system made each sound like a toilet, and the microwaved meat-and-three veg was served on plastic plates, but Darren didn't care because he couldn't help but looking at Kylie Kinsey as if she were a goddess.

She'd dressed sexy too, a red dress that left nothing to the imagination. Her blonde hair was newly frosted in a style he had not seen since he was a teenager back on the Sapphire Coast, where the girls smelt of salt and coconut oil, Juicy Fruit gum and deep fried Chicko Rolls. The scent combination always reminded him of sex, even now, thirty years later.

Their hands met and collided over the table as they reached for salt and pepper, or the carafe of pub squash. Her lips were painted as pink and shiny as cling-wrap over a pair of musk-sticks. Darren was caught up in a hot thrall of living memory, a nineteen-eighties summer, with A-ha singing *Take On Me* on the AM radio of his first car as he lost his virginity to an older girl called Fiona.

"Come back to my place," he said breathlessly.

"Yes," she said, and it was in a fog of horniness that they took a taxi back to his bachelor flat in North Trafalgar and they tumbled on the bed where Beaufort had had most of Darren's girlfriends, and there wasn't a goddamn thing the bastard could do about it because he was dead.

Afterwards, Kylie lay in Darren's bed and clicked her shellacked nails together in an anxious tic.

"You want a drink or something?"

"No, I'm fine, thanks anyway Darren."

"Okay."

"Do you read books, then?" She pointed at the shelf where some tattered copies of old schoolbooks obscured a punched hole in the wall.

"Um, I used to. I liked those old Greek legends, about the gods and stuff. They were always fighting, you know. Rooting and getting into trouble." He laughed self-consciously. He'd loved to read as a kid, but reading and heterosexuality were mutually exclusive, according to the masculine culture of the time.

"Is that you?"

She pointed at a faded poster on the wall. Nineteen-year-old Darren was taking a massive mark, having climbed a step ladder of three colliding bodies to reach the Sherrin.

"Yeah. I was just about to be picked for the VFL draft back then."

"What happened?"

He feigned an indifferent shrug. "Went drinking one night, played up. Got a month in Pentridge prison out of it."

"Beau," she said. One word, as if that was the explanation for anything.

He sat on the end of the bed, and felt the old snags on his ribs, that disappointment in himself.

"Yeah. Big B took me out that night. I told him I had training but he leaned on me and I had to go. Fuck, I was stupid. I should have told him no."

"Nobody says no to him."

"I guess not."

Kylie drew the doona up to her chin.

"I never knew what evil was until I met Beaufort Kinsey."

"Well, I don't know about that. A dickhead maybe, but wasn't exactly Charles Manson."

Kylie only shook her head. "You don't know the half of it. The things he said, the stuff he's done. He's killed people."

"Ah, I don't know."

"It's true. The Trafalgar Highway serial killer . . . "

"Now come on," Darren interrupted her. "James Duncan admitted to that."

"I went to school with James," Kylie sighed. "James knew nothing about skinning and slicing up bodies like they were pigs in a slaughterhouse. He couldn't lift a dead weight like those poor people they found. Reckon Beau just pinned it on James afterwards to teach me a lesson."

As Kylie spoke, Darren's vertebrae unhinged themselves from his spine and crawled in a millipedes shuffle. Maybe all the beatings had sent Kylie Kinsey loopy. All of a sudden he didn't want her in his bed anymore, telling her nightmare stories about Beaufort.

"Nikky," she continued, "He got Beaufort's guernsey, didn't he?"

"Yes. Why?"

"The night his wife and kids got beat up, it was Nikky that called me."

"I thought you said it was a prank call."

"It was him. His hotel number came up when I Googled it."

Darren was confused. "But you two don't know each other. Why would he stalk a woman he doesn't know?"

She set her jaw, and her droopy eye became flinty, as if the injury had made her see things that were not really there.

"He knew me as soon as my husband's guernsey number went on his back. He was coming for me, Darren. He'll come for you too now."

"Not in prison he won't."

"I'm not talking about Nicholas. It's Beau. We made him crazy mad and now he won't rest. Each time someone puts on that guernsey, he keeps coming through stronger and stronger."

Her words frightened Darren. She had completely lost it. Fortunately Kylie didn't want to stay in Darren's bed, not when Beau's face peered at her from team photographs on the wall. She made her apologies and got dressed, and the dress which had looked so stunning four hours earlier seemed to hitch and snag on her bony frame in all sorts of unflattering angles, and her pink-coloured lips were oddly shaped from the dermal filler shit all the young women used these days.

"I'm not staying in Trafalgar," Kylie said as she walked out the door to the waiting taxi. "Too many people knew him here. He's infected them all."

• • •

Several things happened at once after that.

Nikky's wife woke up from her coma, and described a stranger with her husband's face. All the bruises and her defensive marks were on the right hand side of her body, landed by a lefty with a powerful hook. Nikky was right-handed.

Beau's left fist had been a thing of might and terror.

The Trafalgar Highway serial killer case re-opened on appeal from James Duncan's lawyers, his family and on anonymous information received. On the Crime Stoppers adverts an appeal was made to the woman who had made the untraceable call. She knew details that were not public. She might know who really committed the crimes.

Then Finnegan Torch died after a police raid on his abattoir, a suicide by jumping into his own carcass skinner. He left a rambling note explaining how his company was tainted with false accusations, how his equipment had never been used for anything untoward. Shaved bits of garment identified as a football guernsey were found clogging up the machine's internals. Rumours said that

Torch had been sleeping with it.

Chris Fowler's cancer killed him within the month. "The only person who ever defeated such an aggressive tumour was Beau Kinsey," said one of Fowler's team-mates during the funeral eulogy. "He's got his name in medical books."

When the time came to pass on the number ninety-two, nobody would wear it.

"That number's fucking cursed," Southie Harris yelled out during the Annual General Meeting, and a chorus of yeses followed him like demented echoes.

"Well, what do you want us to do?" Darren said. "Burn the fucking thing in effigy and we all dance around it like ding-dong the wicked witch?"

"No," a quiet voice said, and everyone tuned to where Coach O'Laughlin sat in the corner. "That will just make Beaufort upset."

"Beau's dead you old fool," Darren said.

"He's a hero. Heroes live forever."

"You call him a hero?" Darren asked with a murderous whisper. The clubhouse remained silent.

The Coach was pretty old by then. There had been a seventieth birthday in his past, and the white shock of hair that was his trademark had finally decided to thin out. But his voice was still strong, not muffled by the years. What he said held weight.

"He was a good footy player, and he won our team more premierships under his Captaincy than anyone else. For that the mighty gods will elevate him to Valhalla."

"Christ Almighty, you talk bullshit."

"But!" Coach shouted. "But he was also a bad man!"

By then Darren had been about to walk off the lectern, but Coach O'Laughlin words made him pause. Hadn't Kylie said a similar thing?

"I say we retire ninety-two, no votes, no discussion. We put the guernsey up on the wall with the others like Beau planned."

"It's disrespectful to every single man on that wall to put him there!" Darren shouted.

Coach O'Laughlin shook his head.

"They'll keep him in line, those fellows. They also have a hero's immortality; they also sit at the table of the gods and the gladiators, the great warriors of history. Beaufort won't have any influence when he's got the big men of North Trafalgar surrounding him."

Any complaint Darren might have had was drowned out by ferocious clapping and hollers of support.

• • •

Darren tried to get in contact with Kylie Kinsey a few times, but as good as her word she had disappeared from Trafalgar with her two daughters. He travelled to Melbourne that next year, hoping she would be at the inquest that cleared James Duncan of the crimes he had never committed. He stood on the windy, leaf-littered street outside the Supreme Court and smoked an illicit cigarette. She never showed.

A week after the club AGM, a newly mounted guernsey had been sent from a memorabilia framing supplier in Mildura, with a brass plaque and a colour photograph of Beaufort Kinsey taken just before he died, arms crossed, glaring out at the camera. It wasn't the heroic action photograph they had ordered, but it suited, for Beaufort's presence was that of warning, a wicked Cronos locked up in Tartarus, buried in the prison of the gods.

All around Beau the other framed guernseys stood guard, and a casual observer might have noticed what others had not. Every face in every photograph was turned towards Beaufort Kinsey, watching him despite whatever else they were doing.

Beaufort's photograph seemed to glower in a barely restrained anger. His hands were fists. His power to hurt was taken from him. But he hadn't given up, Darren knew that. He was waiting, waiting for the day when the Trafalgar football team would run out of two-digit numbers and vote to begin guernsey numbers again from zero.

Then it was only a matter of time.

THE OBLIVION BOX

FAITH MUDGE

It is a white box in a black void. There were people once, she remembers, or believes she remembers; long enough alone and you might believe anything if only to slow the spreading gangrene of an unused mind. If the memory is real, there were hundreds of them, perhaps thousands, a long queue of the damned stretching behind and ahead of her to file down into the dark. When the grille slammed down behind each one it was like the chomping of vast steel teeth, and when it rose they were gone.

She, too, was swallowed. She woke up here.

Her name was Shaya. Stripped of her jangling jewellery and elaborate henna tattoos, she finds it difficult to recognise that woman in herself. The only colour left in her world is the cinnamon tan of her skin and the blue tracery of veins beneath. Everything else she sees is white or black. Muted white phosphorescence pulses from each side of the cube in which she is imprisoned; when she stands at the wall and squints against the light, all she can see beyond is unremitting darkness.

There are other cubes like her own. Shaya knows this the same way she knows there are stars and sunrises, intangible theory grown meaningless from too much contemplation. Sometimes she remembers faces from that day, that queue—a gaunt dead-eyed woman, a man heavily muffled in robes as though he thought he might get to keep them. She wonders whether they are still here, somewhere in the abyss. She wonders if they, too, are slowly going mad.

Food appears on a ridged circle in the middle of the floor. For a while she tried to judge time by that but she quickly lost track of how many times the food has come, and she has nothing with which to make a record—not even a knife to mark the tally on her own skin. Once Shaya coated her body in creams and studied it critically in the mirror with ideas for improvement. Given a knife now, she knows she would cut herself purely for something to do.

Sitting beside the circle, as she often is, she reaches quickly for the much-anticipated supplies. It is, as always, a small slab of coarse dark bread and two white nutrient bars, accompanied by a black enamel jug of tasteless dark liquid Shaya thinks is some type of water. Holding it up to take a gulp, she catches a blur of reflection: a pale oval of face swimming between shadow curtains of hair, punctuated by black blots for eyes. Her lips, her beautiful irresistible lips, which were once painted every shade between orange and vermilion, are too pale to be seen at all.

Her throat tightens. She drinks anyway. She will not receive more supplies until the emptied jug has been replaced and phased away, denying her the comfort of one small and useless object to break the emptiness of her cell.

With the food, though, she takes her time. She tears the dense grainy bread into small pieces and chews each to a fine mush before swallowing. The nutrient bars are hard and chewy with a sour tang. She does not need to invent tactics to make them last; by the time they are gone her teeth and jaws are aching.

On a full stomach it is easier to sleep, though she has never grown used to the inescapable light of the cube. Shading her eyes with hair, cushioning her head as best she can on her arm, she drifts into uneasy dreams.

• • •

The show was about to start.

The Royal East Pavilion was all old-world glamour: crimson glass walls swimming with shining fish, tasselled carpets patterned to look antique. Servitors in red robes glided between the private balconies in the treble-storeyed auditorium, bearing trays of sweet wine and decoratively shaped fruits to be picked over by disinterested patrons for whom this event was attended more as a display of wealth before their friends than for the formal entertainment. Teardrops of petrified oil dripped from the earlobes of beautiful women; tiger hybrids settled at their feet, growling softly as the servitors passed by.

Testosterone-enhanced men in gilded robes gathered in small groups at the balcony railings. They cast scornful glances through the curlicued wooden screens at the secondary seating below, teeming with an eager crowd. The Third Millennium Sultanate might be founded on co-opportunist philosophy, the new heart of modern democracy, but old capitalist feeling was bred into the bones of the urban elite.

Backstage with her zither strung across her back, Shaya tugged fretfully at her midriff-baring blouse until its fringe of bright bronze discs bounced and jangled a counter-rhythm to her many bangles. Rationally, she knew she was beautiful, but it was easier to take her nerves out on her looks than endure the wait peacefully. Running a fingertip over the cherry pink bow of her lips, she was suddenly certain she should have picked a different shade.

The gong sounded, a crystalline reverberation thrumming through her blood like electricity, and she swung her zither down into her arms, sashaying onstage as though she'd never possessed a doubt in her life.

The central podium was lit by a single golden spotlight. Shaya positioned herself on the stool provided and struck a pose there, fingers poised on strings, allowing her audience a moment to admire the picture. Then she struck the first chord, opened her mouth, and sang.

Later, Zali told her that was the moment he'd fallen in love with her.

"You must get a thousand proposals a night. God, your voice. You could make me believe anything. I hadn't cried since I was nine, until I heard you sing."

"Flatterer," she purred. "You'd never heard a balladeer before, that's all."

"You're not a balladeer, Shaya, you're a fucking hypnotist."

She bowed off-stage three hours later to thunderous applause. Laying the zither in its case, swaddled up in padding like a baby, she swapped her flamboyant costume for a light violet modesty robe and began the triumphant walk back to her apartment.

It was a sultry night. The street bazaar outside was fragrant with sizzling meat and aromatic spice, perfume, dust and sweat.

Shaya stopped at an imaginatively constructed booth with stacked tyres forming a bench and a shuttercraft wing for an awning. She tossed over a couple of brass sequins to the stallholder, who caught them deftly and passed across a lamb skewer. Shaya bit into tender meat, her tastebuds popping at the hot herb dressing, and strolled away through the crowd.

She liked this part of town. The street was a canyon of steel and glass, physical reminders of last millennium's disastrous alliance with the West Union, but the capitalist shells were not as abandoned as they seemed. The alleys between buildings were criss-crossed with treble-deep lines of washing, coils of jasmine trained around the concrete pylons of an underground carpark below. What had once been the domain of computer drones was now home to entrepreneurial families, many of whom held booths in the bazaar. This appropriation of property was not strictly lawful but the authorities turned a lenient eye, recognising the spirit of co-opportunism when they saw it at work.

Shaya didn't live here. Her apartment was a nice little pad in the residential zone of Aladeen three blocks away. In reality she'd never trade that up for what was essentially a modified squat, but her bohemian side sometimes indulged in a little wistful speculation. The bazaar looked at its most romantic at this time of night, lit by solar lanterns in a hundred colours strung overhead in the narrow laneways between booths. Music was playing nearby—tambourines, drums. *Dancing.*

Elbowing her way towards the sound, Shaya broke through a ring of watchers surrounding an improvised dancefloor where a bare-chested young man was doing handstands. He flipped back onto his feet with easy grace, snapping off a salute to the crowd, and bounded away, replaced by a trio of girls in matching headscarves performing synchronised pop-kicking.

Normally, Shaya was self-conscious about the way she danced. The Muslim Sisterhood school she had attended as a teenager had offered classes, but it had taken her rapidly growing limbs a long time to catch on and in the meantime two girls from her clique were putting everyone else to shame with their killer moves. They had gone on to join a dancesport company in the Ausasian Empire, but Shaya still felt stilted and slow when she danced in public.

Not tonight, though. She had wowed a pavilion of wealthy punters with just her zither and her voice—she could dance the world down if she wanted. The pop-kickers ended their routine to a flurry of applause and Shaya grabbed her chance, leaping into the emptied floor. A flute joined the drums and tambourines, a high sweet piping. Shaya swayed backwards until her spine arched, spun a tight pirouette, spun again—and nearly fell when a hand caught hers. A man had joined her in the circle.

She stiffened, astonished. Men and women didn't dance together, not in the Sultanate. He took full advantage of her confusion, spinning her neatly back into the crowd, and claimed the floor. Watching him, Shaya had to admit he deserved the spotlight. He seemed boneless, swinging his limbs at impossible angles, with moves that would have given Shaya's old friends a run for their money.

As he snap-footed past he flashed a bright white smile her way. Admiration re-ignited into indignation. She waited until he finally relinquished the floor and stalked over to intercept him.

"Hey, you. What was the idea? That was my turn."

He turned and grinned again. Dark-skinned and clean-shaven, he had a lean athletic body and chin-length black hair streaked with metallic gold at the temples. She could smell the incense of expensive cologne on him from a foot away.

"You're the balladeer," he said. "I was at your show. Maybe I just wanted an excuse to touch you."

Shaya felt her eyebrows brush her hairline. "*That's* your defence?"

She was charmed, though—she always fell easily to flattery. He swept her a flourishing bow and took her hand.

"Shall we start over?" he asked, and kissed her palm. "My name is Zali Scherade."

And that, she thought later, was the moment she had fallen in love with him.

• • •

The deluge comes.

Shaya is woken from her unsettled dreaming to a drenching spray of cold water jetting seemingly from every direction. There is no place inside the cube where she can move to escape; within seconds every surface is slick wet and her thin white shift is transparent, clinging to her body like a second, extremely ineffectual, skin. Knowing what to expect, she closes her eyes and endures.

The water stops. There is exactly a minute's pause before the heat comes.

Like a wind direct from the desert, warm air pumps through the cube, transforming it into a sauna. Shaya's hair and shift are still slightly damp when the heat shuts off and the temperature returns to its neutral standard. Throughout the entire business she has remained seated on the floor, not seeing the point in rising. Now she stands and looks upward.

The ceiling of the cube is exactly like every other side. For all Shaya knows it may not even be the ceiling but she calls it that to spare her sanity. She is sure there are sensors embedded into this cube to monitor her and that there is a warden somewhere out there in front of a screen, watching, so she tries to look strong. The resentment hot in her veins helps a little. She had been dreaming of home.

Anger feels good. It burns up her throat, stinging her apathetic brain into response. She must do something. There is nothing she can do. But she must do *something*. The two thoughts form an inescapable litany inside her head, triggering a surge of frustration and panic, until she suddenly flings back her head and screams.

The full power of her trained voice is unleashed in a raw siren of sound. It amazes her. She has not spoken aloud in so long she had almost forgotten she could speak or hear at all. As the aftershock of her scream fades from her ears, the silence falls again like a suffocating weight. Well, this she can change.

"My name is Shaya Scherade," she says. Her voice sounds raspy, her throat still sore from the screaming. "I am twenty nine years old. My father died from canine flu when I was three and I grew up with my uncle. He is the most honourable politician I have ever known. He fought to abolish the death penalty for thirty years. He's dead now too. I'm glad. It would have broken his heart to see me like this."

Her eyes blur with tears. Shaya rubs them away and keeps talking, pretending someone is listening, waiting for her to go on. She has never failed an audience yet. Even an imaginary one.

"He was awarded the Commendation of Service by the Sultaness herself before he died. I performed at the ceremony. I can play the zither, lute and mandolin. I know over two hundred traditional ballads by heart and wrote forty of my own. When I sing, grown men cry. I lived my life to the full. I was remarkable."

It does not sound convincing, even to her own ears. But it is true.

"I loved a man!" she shouts. "And he loved me. I know he did."

• • •

Zali was vain. Shaya knew that from the first time she met him.

He exercised religiously to maintain his gorgeous physique, adhering to a strict regimen of nutrient bars, protein capsules and power shakes, untempted by Shaya's diet of indulgences. She admired his dedication, but felt no need to emulate it—how he started the day without a strong Turkish coffee and a bowl of sweet, pitted dates, she didn't want to know. His apartment was a shrine to fitness and health and was possibly the blandest place she had ever been. She barely ever saw him there. Most nights, he came to her.

It was Zali who introduced her to genEx.

"It's no different from getting a skin rejuv or a hangover killer," he said persuasively. "It's great. You've already sampled the goods, I know you'll love it."

"What goods?"

He brushed a hand over his muscular chest in one of those extravagant gestures that were so *him* and Shaya laughed. They were in the sun swing on her balcony, watching the sun rise. The sky was streaked in vibrant pink, the tall palm trees lining the shady street below outlined with halos of gold. The winged silhouette of an ROC flew low across the city—one of the genetically engineered super-eagles used by wealthy risk-seekers for their joyflights. They scared the hell out of Shaya at close range, but from a distance filled her heart with an ache at their beauty. Dawn was the most peaceful hour of the day, she thought, the time when this overcrowded, overheated city of hers was at its loveliest.

"Just try it," Zali urged, breaking her reverie. Exasperated, she twisted to look at him. He was very attractive, it was true, but he would have to learn she didn't appreciate pressure.

"What improvements do you think I need?" she asked sweetly.

He shifted awkwardly, not stupid enough to take the bait. It won her nearly ten minutes of quiet before he found a comeback.

"Do you like this?" He held his arm against her nose and the faint fresh scent of citrus drifted into her lungs. "Is that cologne?" she asked. "It's a serious improvement."

He knew she didn't like his intense incense colognes but it would probably have triggered an argument anyway if he had not been so focused on persuasion. As it was, he laughed stiffly and drew his arm away.

"It's not cologne. The scent is a skin enhancement from genEx. Interested now?"

Shaya turned her face into his throat. The scent was there too, subtler than perfume, mingling pleasantly with the familiar smell of his skin. "Tell me more."

That was how two days later she found herself in the corporate sector of the city, in the pentagonal square outside the genEx building, with Zali a smug tour guide at her side. She had only been to this part of the city once before, joining a financial co-operative when she came of age at twenty. Her uncle had been with her, a big solid presence greeting every official they met by name in his deep slow voice.

It had still been unusual to see women in management positions then, despite the late Sultan's very specific equal opportunity decrees, but in the genEx lobby they were greeted by a stunning thirty-something in formal white business robes. Her hair was tucked demurely beneath a designer scarf, indicating her position as a second tier member of the Sisterhood. Shaya, in a thin azure modesty robe and glittering wedge-heeled sandals, was a third tier. She felt instantly overexposed. She had been lectured at school by women like this. *Men will try to objectify you,* she had been told. *They will ask you to wear sluttish clothes and demean yourself to please them. You must not allow that. Remember, you are a woman. You are precious as you are.*

Then again, she wasn't the one working for a cosmetic enhancements company.

The woman introduced herself as Yasmeen and ushered them into a modernist office furnished with 20th century antiques and white vinyl wall-liner. Shaya slid into an organically curved chair she'd swear was authentic plastic and tried not to stare. She was pretty successful for a musician, but this kind of luxury was way out of her league and spoke volumes for the popularity of genEx.

"You have to understand," Yasmeen said, sliding gracefully onto a lime green stool, "genEx is not really about looks. I know, I know—" she lifted one beautifully manicured hand to stall Shaya, whose eyebrows had soared upward. "That's how we're usually portrayed, but it's an unfair slant. What we do is enhance all that is wonderful about what you already are. We believe that everybody has the right to feel beautiful in their own skin."

Shaya thought about the delicate scent of Zali's sweat. She remembered friends who never put on weight or broke out, who swore by genEx and took shots of it in their coffee like sugar. She had always been comfortable with her own looks, safely ranked as the pretty one of the family by her younger cousins, but she didn't want to be left behind while everyone in her circle jumped aboard with improvements. What harm was there in an enhancement or two, anyway? A shot of antiblush and she would never be caught red faced again. A follicle augmentation and no more bad hair days, ever.

In the end she was uncharacteristically cautious, opting for a mild skin enhancement like Zali's. The procedure took less than ten minutes. She was then sat down by a smiling specialist who provided her with a pack of booster shots and instructed her to take one every six to eight days.

"Otherwise the augmentation stops activating," she explained. "If you're taking your boosters and you feel it's not working properly, though, come and see me. Some people do get reactions. Just sit quietly for a few more minutes, then you can go."

As it turned out, Shaya had to wait considerably longer than that, pacing around a stylishly spartan waiting room while Zali underwent some impulse augmentations of his own. She was beginning to suspect those muscles of his owed less to his health regime and more to some sneaky muscle stimulants.

He emerged almost hyper with energy, wanting to head straight out to a club. When Shaya quashed that one, he suggested some other forms of exercise involving the bed back at her apartment. She was still irritated at having to wait and kicked him petulantly in the ankle.

"Did you get a libido booster in there or something?" she snapped. "I want to go home. And no, not to get love drunk. I need to practice for tomorrow's show."

He jerked back, insulted. "You'd rather be with that string stick than me?"

"It's a *zither*!" Shaya shouted. "And right now, yes, yes I would!"

She didn't remember the rest of the fight, only that it was loud and bitter and very public. They ended up on the steps of the genEx building screaming abuse at each other. Zali grabbed her by the upper arms, gripping tight enough to hurt, and when she shrieked at him to let her go he shoved her away so hard she fell down the stairs into the square.

She landed awkwardly onto her elbow. The bone jarred numbingly; she made a sobbing noise of pain and shock and looked up in automatic accusation. Zali was white-faced. He started down the steps towards her, holding out his hands, saying her name, but she somehow scrambled to her feet, swearing at him, telling him to stay away *or else*. What exactly she would have done against him with one arm out of action, she didn't know, but Zali got the message. He fell back, watching her go without interfering.

Shaya caught a shuttercraft home. She was shaking the whole way. It was only when it dropped her off on a relay roof close to home and she was climbing down the steps into her street that she realised the sleeve of her modesty robe was ripped, stained with blood. But it didn't smell of blood. At some point during the flight, maybe even during the shouting match outside genEx, her enhancements had kicked in. Her torn skin smelled sweet, of sandalwood, and spice.

• • •

Shaya has always loved stories. That is why she became a balladeer in the first place. She remembers stalking a street storyteller when she was fourteen, ignoring his uneven teeth and the fifteen-year age gap, enchanted by the magic he made with his voice. He couldn't play an instrument; his accompaniment came from an eCord, plugged into a discreet speaker concealed by a fold of his robe. She thinks her uncle probably paid for balladry lessons just to end that particular crush. It worked. Shaya fell head over heels for the idealised hero of her favourite ballad instead.

It occurs to her like a bolt from the blue. She cannot remember the second verse of that ballad. She has forgotten.

Horror freezes her veins. She rifles rapidly through her mental catalogue of stories, wondering how many more are fading like ink-print left too long in the sun. A sob tears its way through her throat with an ugly ripping sound. Shaya rocks back and forth, her arms wrapped tightly around her knees, shuddering uncontrollably. She opens her mouth. She has to clear her throat three times before her voice emerges without cracking.

In a dead land beside a dead sea he was born
In the dying years of a century
The sky forever red, the ground forever black
But he was alive, alive as any man can be.

Halfway through the first verse she remembers how to begin the second. The melody flows from her throat, and she finds herself on the third verse, the fifth, the tenth. She has sung this ballad so many times but every time she seems to hear it anew—as though she, like the audience, has no idea what will happen next. How did Gashir end up in a robot-run junkyard, immune to the poisoned air of the radioactive wastes? Who is the beautiful girl imprisoned in the tunnels beneath the wrecking yard? Can he save her before she sickens and dies?

Shaya sings until her throat is dry and sore. By the fourteenth verse she has to stop, breaking off as Gashir falls into the fiery pit. Her panic has subsided, lulled by the familiar rhythm of a beloved story. She rests her forehead against her knees, chewing on her tongue to work up enough saliva to soothe her dry throat. When she looks up there is a jug of water in the circle at her feet.

She stares at it, nonplussed. This never happens. The water comes with meals, and unless she slept far longer than usual she is not due for more supplies yet. Is she really going mad, conjuring hallucinations from her wishes? But when she reaches out, the jug handle is smooth and firm to her hand, the liquid inside cool and wet. She tips it into her mouth, gulping gratefully.

"Finish the story."

Shaya drops the jug. It rolls away across the floor in a spreading pool, but she hardly notices; she is choking. Whether it is misdirected water lodged in her throat or her hammering heart, she can't tell. She has heard a voice. A voice. In this cube. Which is impossible.

"I said, finish the story. What happened? Did he fall?"

Shaya looks around wildly. The voice seems to come from everywhere, the way the light does; it is deep and husky, definitely male, completely unfamiliar. She is suddenly intensely aware of someone, somewhere, watching her. Listening to her.

Her throat contracts. "Who—who are you?"

"Just finish the fucking story!"

She has never failed an audience yet. Somehow, Shaya sings. She can barely hear herself through the pounding of her blood in her ears, which is a shame—she has always loved this part, when Gashir meets the cyborg queen in her timelocked citadel, the battle with her mechanised serpents. His return to Topaz, his love, only to find her dying from radiation poisoning.

She lay in his arms, the beautiful husk,
Of a beautiful heart, a beautiful love
Now just a dead woman beneath a dead sea
In a dead, dead land, in a dead century . . .

She falters again towards the end, and once more a jug of water appears at her feet. This time she snatches it up without hesitating. Her brain has done some quiet calculations without her and now clues her in. Someone out there wants to hear her stories; someone who is not only prepared to communicate with her, but perhaps reward her. Is this, the first turning point in God knows how long, really the right time to fall apart? By the time she puts down the jug, Shaya has pulled herself together. She sings the final verses with a return of some of her old flamboyance. Her fingers quiver, the music of her zither playing on the inside of her skull. In the final verse she reveals the denouement no one ever sees coming, and lets the final notes ring out triumphantly.

They fall to silence. She waits, but there is no congratulation, no response at all.

The silence lengthens. Shaya drums her fingers nervously against the sides of the jug, then realises she is still holding it and quickly replaces it in the circle. It disappears. She is left with no reason to believe that anything out of the ordinary has occurred, only the ramblings of an unreliable memory.

She runs her wet tongue over her lips. She's not giving up so easily.

She chooses another ballad. An older one, full of bloodshed and tragedy and evil warlords, and begins to sing. Five verses in, she breaks off and waits.

The silence is very loud.

"Go on. Keep singing."

Shaya feels the corners of her mouth tug in what feels like the first smile in a hundred years. She has stories. She has an audience. This is solid ground.

She sings.

• • •

They got married. Third tier Sisters were allowed to date a man for one year before making the decision to marry or move on, and for some reason Shaya stayed. The wedding was very elaborate and arranged entirely by Zali's mother, who had more than enough enthusiasm to power the project alone—perhaps a good thing, since the actual couple spent the four months of their engagement engaged in either violent feuding or passionate sex. Zali's mood swings collided with Shaya's hot temper and resulted in explosions.

"It's the stress, my love, he is about to be married!" Zali's mother insisted. "You must try to understand him. You are very lucky to be marrying such a handsome boy."

Shaya found it hard to think straight. It was true, her cousins swooned over Zali every time he flexed his biceps and kept calling the two of them a 'glamour couple', the most hackneyed phrase in the entire language as far as Shaya was concerned. She was equally to blame in most of their fights, if she was completely honest with herself. She had slapped him across the face on more than one occasion—what was so much worse about the times he hit her? She loved him, didn't she? She wasn't trying hard enough.

The wedding was a blur of congratulations drowned in alcohol. By the end of the night she and Zali were in a minishutter, on their way to their new home in a leafy, family-friendly corner of town. They were both exhausted and more than a little drunk. Shaya suddenly desperately wanted to be walking through the teeming bazaar to her own little apartment to spend the night alone. Zali seemed to read her thoughts.

"Too late to get out now, beautiful," he slurred. "You're my wife now. Mine."

Shaya didn't know whether to burst into tears or kick him hard with her gem-studded slipper. Instead her body took over and she threw up, twice. It was mostly bile—she had barely eaten all day—but Zali recoiled from her in revulsion. He, she remembered, had received an augmentation a month or two ago to prevent involuntary vomiting. It was getting hard to keep track of his enhancements; he seemed to be in at genEx every few days, like a piece of faulty machinery that needed constant alteration. He kept trying to convince Shaya to come with him but after that first visit she had dug in her heels and refused. There were times she even thought about removing her only enhancement, but then she would arrive late at a show one day, coated in sweat, and would be complemented by the backstage staff on her perfume.

Compliments had, after all, always been her weakness.

Shaya had back-to-back matinees for a week shortly after the wedding. Zali and his mother had briefly joined forces during the wedding preparations, trying to make her cancel, but she had steadfastly refused; she had never cancelled a show and wasn't about to start now. Every evening when she got home Zali was there, taking up space, demanding her attention, complaining that she was never there for him. He would either ignore that she had had a show at all or question her minutely on every detail.

"Who was there? Did anyone talk to you afterwards? Who? What did he look like? What did he say to you?"

"What does it matter to *you*?" Shaya snapped. "It's not like you ever come!"

The next day she saw him in the audience, close to the stage. He was waiting when she came down, fully assured of his welcome. Shaya stopped uncertainly with her hand against the curtain, a foot or so away from him.

"You came," she said, flatly.

"I have to make sure you don't run away with another man," he said. He used to make jokes like that and she would laugh, knowing he didn't mean it, but there was something off in his smile that night. She didn't laugh.

"What's going on with you?" she demanded. "I don't know who you'll be from one day to the next. This isn't you, Zali. This isn't the man I love."

He jerked as though she had cut him. "You don't love me."

"That isn't what I said—"

"You don't love me!" he shouted. "I knew it! You're a liar, a cheating lying cow!"

"How can you *say* that?" Shaya shrieked. "It's you who's lying! It's you!"

He grabbed her shoulders, shaking her hard. They were screaming things at each other, terrible things, and then she was just screaming, teeth rattling inside her skull with each time Zali shook her. A passing servitor saw them. He called for help and two men came running, dragging Shaya's husband away from her, asking her what was happening, was she all right. His hands were gone, but she was still shaking.

• • •

Shaya sings.

She is still a prisoner. The daily humiliations are even harder to endure knowing that every time the deluge comes and plasters her shift against her skin, every time she performs her ablutions over the phasing circle, there's a man somewhere watching. She wonders what he's like, the owner of this disembodied voice. What he looks like. Not for the first time, she hopes fervently he is not a pervert.

But in another sense she is powerful. She has a head full of stories, a voice to sing down the angels, an eager listener—and she can play her audience like she played her zither. She takes longer breaks between verses, claiming tiredness, testing her unseen listener's patience. She tantalises him with snippets of stories and asks him to choose the next for her to sing. She is frequently surprised by his choices. The warden of a deep-sea prison apparently likes tragic romances.

Shaya sings until her voice throbs with sorrow. Her listener never applauds, but one night after finishing an epic thirty-verser the jug of water arrives with a plump red pomegranate. It is the first time she has tasted fresh fruit since she was imprisoned. She savours every mouthful and sucks her fingers until they're sore.

She begins to venture questions of her own.

"What's your name?" No answer. "Oh, please. Wouldn't you be curious?"

More silence. Then, finally, when she has given up hope of a reply:

"Xever. My name is Xever."

Gradually she eases little details from him, greased with many anecdotes of her own. He soon knows everything there is to know about her childhood, her career as a balladeer, the foods and colours she likes. She learns he is an only child. His parents, like her own, are dead. And the year is 3044. The breath goes out of her when he lets that detail drop. She has been imprisoned for two and a half years.

"Why are you doing that? Shaya. Shaya, what is it?"

He sounds uneasy. He should be. She is doubled over on the floor, racked so hard with heaving sobs that she thinks she might be sick. It takes her a long time to drag herself back together. As she leans her back against the wall and draws her knees up against her chest, she realises that was the first time Xever has used her name. The first time he has asked a question not directly related to the story she is telling. She wipes her sleeve across her sore eyes and looks up.

There is a handful of dates in the middle of the circle.

A choked laugh cracks from her throat. Is he trying to *comfort* her? If he is, it works. The sweet flavour of the dates overwrites the bitter salty taste of tears on her tongue. She licks her sticky fingers clean and looks up. She does not know from what angle Xever is looking at her, how he sees her at all, but as a rule she has decided to look up when she talks to him.

"Thank you," she says softly. "You're kind."

Xever says nothing. He is not a talkative man, Shaya has learned. She wishes she could see his face. It is so difficult to judge a man from his voice alone. But she returns his generosity with the comic ballad *The Zero Hounds*, one of her originals, and is rewarded when, during the chase scene in verse twelve, he laughs, a startled bark of sound. It is only the professionalism of nine years performing that keeps her singing while her mind is wiped white with shock. She wonders how long it has been since her taciturn prison warden last laughed.

These days, when the deluge comes, she does more than endure it. Xever has provided her with soap, an insipidly scented scrubbing tube for which she is ridiculously grateful, and already her hair is less lifeless, her skin brighter. When her supplies arrive they include small treats—fresh fruit, honey. Shaya forces her limp limbs into a few star jumps to get her blood moving before settling to eat. She makes sure to thank Xever after each meal. She is being entirely political, cultivating his good will. That does not make her thanks any the less sincere.

"That was wonderful," she tells him, when he thinks to include coffee. It is an explosion of caffeine; her brain feels kicked into gear, buzzing and alive. She jogs on the spot, hops up and down on alternate feet. Xever laughs again. A little peeved, Shaya taps into her old dance training and smooths out her motions, spinning slowly, sliding her feet across the floor, swaying her spine backwards into an arch with both arms stretched above her head. She is very rusty, but it comes gradually back to her. Her delight is edged with bitterness, remembering a different dance, that night at the bazaar. Zali.

"Why did you stop?" Xever is still watching. *"That was beautiful."*

Shaya looks up. "I didn't want him to die," she says. "My husband. I loved him. I told everyone that and no one believed me, but it's true all the same. I wanted to help him. No," she corrects herself, and it's her turn to laugh, a mirthless sound. "No, I wanted to *save* him."

There is a long, long silence. She has never brought this up before, though as a warden Xever must know why she is here. Perhaps now he thinks about it, he no longer wants to be involved with a murderess—a manipulative, dangerous woman who will enchant him and lie to him. Shaya's shoulders slump. She sits down quietly, cross-legged, on the floor beside the circle, feeling suddenly drained. Then Xever speaks.

"What happened?" he asks. His voice is hard, guarded, but he asks all the same.

She tells him.

• • •

"Insomnia. Mood swings. Paranoia. It's more common than you might think."

Shaya stared at the journalist on the other side of the table, her cooled coffee clutched tightly between her hands. Months venting to family and friends had divided everyone she knew into two camps: the 'Be A Loyal Wife's and the 'Leave The Bastard's. No one seemed to understand what she was really saying. Zali was no longer Zali. It was like she was living with a completely different man.

Then she had stumbled on a small column in an indie news feed, the only anti-augmentation piece she had ever read, and she had v-mitted her questions to the contact tag at the foot of the article. A couple of days later, she was in a coffee den in South

Bezzir while Zali thought she was at a show. It was a reasonably safe cover; he had been banned from entering the pavilion where she staged most of her performances. She hated lying to him, but his obsessive behaviour gave her no choice.

"Three percent," she echoed. "Three percent of the population get this reaction?"

"So my research would indicate," the journalist said. He was an Ausasian expat with the distinctive accent that made his every statement sound like a question. "Not easy to be really specific, of course, because many people can't afford the augmentations or object to them on ethical grounds, but three percent is the rough figure."

"But why?" Shaya demanded, appalled. "Why weren't we told?"

The journalist patted her hand like she was a distraught toddler. "GenEx is in denial. They don't want to pay compensation so they say their enhancements aren't responsible for this strain of schizophrenia. Science is telling a different story. Sooner or later the government will have to step in, but in the meantime there is no mainstream recognition of the disorder."

"So what do I do? How do I help him?"

"That's a question better put to a medico. I'm afraid I can't offer you much advice. The first step your husband would need to take for any kind of recovery is the removal of his enhancements, but whether he will believe you is another matter. GenEx sufferers are often delusional and dangerous. I would advise you approach him carefully, if at all."

"I have to do something. He's my husband, I can't let him— *deteriorate* like this."

"It's up to you, of course." The journalist drained his coffee and cleared his throat. "Thank you for your time, Mme. Scherade, I appreciate you agreeing to this interview. Can I quote you by name in my next piece or would you prefer to remain anonymous?"

She remained at the table long after he'd gone, trying to think of a way to explain this to Zali. How could she make him believe her? The prospect made her stomach clench with fear, but she had to try.

It was late when she got home. She keyed open the door, steeling herself for indifference or inquisition, whichever she might find inside. She did not expect to be seized by the throat and slammed against the wall, a butcher's knife pressed against her jugular. Zali's face was contorted into a snarl. His eyes were red from crying.

"Whore," he hissed. Saliva flecked her face. "Betrayer."

"What are you doing?" Shaya wheezed. "Zali, let me go!"

"I saw you." He released her so suddenly she slid down the wall and crumpled on the floor at his feet, gasping for breath. "At a show, you said. Why did I ever believe you? I saw you with him. I saw him take your hand."

"No—no, Zali, you don't understand—" Shaya struggled to her feet. "Please listen to me. You're sick, Zali, but I'm going to help you—"

"*You want to kill me!*" He seized a handful of her hair, yanking her head back. The knife was a cold metal line across her exposed throat. "I know everything! You're turning everyone against me. You are a whore, a traitorous lying whore!"

He hurled her away from him as though it were she holding the knife, as if it were she threatening him. She collided with the couch, falling to the floor, scrabbled back to her feet as he advanced with the knife. She couldn't scream. She couldn't breathe.

"Zali," she rasped. "Zali, stop."

She backed away from him, through an open door; she realised too late it led onto the balcony. She was trapped. He was crying, she saw, tears streaking down his face.

"I loved you," he moaned. "I trusted you. How could you betray me?"

"I never betrayed you!" Shaya's voice was thin, breathless. He didn't seem to hear her. She was up against the balcony railing, and then he was there, grabbing at her, slashing at her, sobbing abuse at her. She grappled with him uselessly for the knife. He stabbed at her and her hands shoved with all their force.

Somehow they had got twisted around. He was the one against the railing. The old rusted metal gave way to his weight and he fell, screaming, into the street thirty feet below. Shaya heard his body smack against cement.

She didn't know how she got down there. She didn't remember using the stairs, although she supposed she must have done. All she remembered was falling to her knees beside Zali's beautiful, broken body, cradling what was left of her husband in her arms, screaming at the medicos who came to take him away. Someone gave her a sedative and called a cousin. She was led back to her apartment in the early hours of the morning and told to rest. Alone at last in a bed that smelled of sandalwood and citrus, she fell into a deep, drugged sleep.

She was woken to blinding mid-morning sun and a heavy pounding on her door. A pair of black-armoured demiGs were waiting outside. She had only ever seen them on guard duty at political functions before; she couldn't remember seeing them up close like this. They were huge, taller and broader than a human, and behind their dark visors burned eyes red as rubies. She and Zali had always argued over whether they were robots or cyborgs, pointless arguments that could never be settled.

Zali. Zali was dead.

"Shaya Scherade." Even the demiG's voice did not sound human; it was deep and booming like there was an amplifier built into his throat. "You must come with us."

As it turned out, someone had witnessed the fight. And so Shaya found herself on trial for her husband's murder.

From the start, everyone believed she was guilty. Even her cousins. They tried to excuse her, insisted Zali had been violent and deranged, but no one believed them either, held against his mother's tearful testimony. It took the jury—present in hologram to protect their identities—less than an hour to convict Shaya and sentence her. Fifteen days after Zali's death she was in a line of prisoners boarding the subcell penitentiary *Kraken*.

The *Kraken* was swallowed by the sea. Shaya was swallowed by the void.

• • •

"You didn't kill him."

Shaya can tell Xever doesn't believe her. There is open scepticism in his tone that reminds her of the aggressive prosecutors from her trial. She lets her forehead fall against her knees, her face hidden by a fall of dark hair, the only privacy she can claim.

"No," she says. "I killed him. But I didn't mean to."

Xever is silent for a long time. *"Like Gashir,"* he says eventually. *"And Topaz."*

Shaya looks up, startled. "What?"

"By trying to save her, he made her die faster."

Shaya's eyes sting with tears. She nods, not trusting herself to speak.

Xever says nothing more for a long time. She tries talking to him once or twice but receives no response, and she cannot tell whether that means he's no longer there or no longer wants to talk to her. She tries to sleep and can't. Eventually she gets up and circles her cube, rubbing at her arms. She turns around and there is someone there.

She screams.

It is a demiG. The carapaced black armour makes it resemble a vast black beetle, its red eyes emitting a hellish glow. It carries a scimitar longer than Shaya's arm. It steps off the phasing circle and advances towards her. She is still screaming.

"Shaya, it's all right. He won't hurt you. Go with him."

As though Xever's voice is a signal, the demiG sheaths its scimitar and holds out a vast gauntleted hand. Shaya is still trembling.

"Where will it take me? Xever, what's going on?"

"Go with him."

The demiG could rip her limbs from their sockets if it chose. Shaya gives in, accepting the proffered hand instead of waiting to be seized, and is drawn onto the circle. Blinding white light jets around her. She squeezes her eyes shut, throwing up her free arm to protect them against the glare, and when the light fades she is somewhere else entirely. It is a perfectly ordinary corridor, but the sheer size of it all is overwhelming. The wall to her right is punctuated with square portholes and through the nearest she can see the sea, the pale dawn sky. The *Kraken* is floating towards a cliff-edged coastline.

Shaya doesn't know why she has been brought here. A jailbreak? A retrial? She doesn't care. She has told the story that really matters and has been believed. This man she has never met knows more about her than anyone else in the world, knows tragedy when he hears it, and truth. And now Shaya is in a world outside her imagination, the world she almost stopped believing existed.

Light washes across her skin like liquid gold. Through the porthole the dawn sky is streaked in red and rose, dazzling her eyes with raw colour. The sun is rising. A black gauntlet lands on Shaya's shoulder, turning her from the porthole, but she twists her head back to catch a last glimpse and sees a winged silhouette launch from the cliffs.

She begins to laugh.

HARRY'S DEAD POODLE

DAVID KERNOT

They say Death arrives at the darkest hour of the night and shows no mercy. But Harry hadn't heard Death arrive that night. He'd been away in another country, fighting a war that people didn't support. It hadn't changed the fact that Kim had died, that his life had fallen apart. Perhaps more of him perished that day too? He'd enough troubles on his return without finding the love of his life gone.

Harry's nostrils flared with disgust. Freshly used toilet paper littered the floor among the flaking paint that fell from the graffiti-covered walls. He stood at the ceramic urinal and drunken laughter, muffled by thick stone of the hundred and fifty year old pub closed around him. A cool gust of wind burst through the half-opened window, and the room's solitary light globe swung from the long ceiling cable. Harry's heart rate climbed as shadowy images splashed the wall. He knew the dangers of looking too close, of letting his mind wander. He took a deep breath, and blinked away the dark spectres that swam across his vision.

To his left, somebody coughed inside the toilet stall. Harry froze, surprised he was not alone. He loosened his top button as another gust sent shadows across the wall. Harry fought an internal struggle as the images from his past formed within the shadows. The muffled drunken laughter took on an insistent tone. The cool evening air turned hot, suffocated. The pub's tiled floor beneath Harry's feet shifted, turned into hot desert sand. The sun burned on Harry's exposed military uniform.

A rifle shot rang out.

"Contact front!"

Harry jumped as the forward scout's machine gun fired. He dived for cover, and his camouflaged uniform blended against the stone building at Al Bahra. Hot sandy soil burned at his hands as he scrabbled forward. He released 'The Bitch's' safety and inched forward, careful not to get sand up the barrel. He glanced through her sights. Ahead several men appeared between two buildings, firing as they ran. Harry heard the smack of bullets, and fragments of the stone building fell onto him. He squeezed the trigger and 'The Bitch' unleashed her angry torrent of vengeful bullets. Harry watched with detached interest as the men danced around like puppets on strings before they fell.

The man in the toilet stall threw up. The decade-old images of Al-Bahra faded, and a new wave of nauseous aromas assaulted Harry.

"You alright mate?" he called out to the stranger.

"Yeah." The man in the stall coughed and then retched again.

Harry stepped back from the urinal, and reached into his pocket for a small bottle of pills. He shook them, contemplated for a moment, then shrugged and dropped them in the trash.

The pills didn't work. All they had done was steal a little more of his soul each day. Post-Traumatic Stress Disorder they said. His hand slid into his pocket and curled around the pocketknife. It gave him comfort. What did they know? It was time to forget about Desert Storm.

Harry returned to his stool at the bar.

"You alright?" Mike shot him an odd look.

"Yeah, I'm fine." Harry stared out the window to the gum trees that danced in the wind.

"Angie was here the other day. She looks happy."

"I'm sure she does." His lip curled. "Guess I'll have to stop coming here then."

"Take it easy." Mike half smiled. "You sure you're fine? You got that look in your eye again."

"I'm fine, better, I think."

"How's that?"

"I've just tossed away my pills." He sipped his beer.

Out of the corner of his eyes he saw Mike's eyes widen. "Is that a good idea?"

"It's done." Harry downed the rest of his beer in one gulp. "Maybe it'll cure my stutter. Anyway, I'm out of here. This place gives me the creeps."

The barman slid Harry's Icebox across the bar, and chuckled. "Some of my patrons say that you've got beer in here to keep you going through the day."

"That's my business. Thanks for taking care of it"

• • •

Harry woke when somebody banged on his front door. He reached for his gun. It wasn't there. This wasn't Baghdad. He took comfort in the early morning smell of dew outside his window, relaxed slightly and reached for his clock. "It's four in the morning!" He groaned.

"Police! Open up."

"What?" He climbed out of bed, half-asleep and his front door splintered.

A man in a crumpled tan suit appeared at Harry's bedroom door. He held up his warrant card. "Police. Sit on the bed, hands where I can see them." He called over his shoulder. "Check the house, Constable."

"Yes, Senior Constable," replied the officer in the other room.

Harry peered over the man's shoulder; to the uniformed police officer who's reply was crisp.

"It's Senior out here in the field, Lad. Understood?"

"Yes, Senior."

The man faced Harry. "Been here all night?"

Harry peered at the man, at one time, as a butcher, he would have known them all, but didn't recognise this man. But Whittleside Way had grown in recent years. Harry nodded. "What's going on?"

"Come out here."

Harry followed the plainclothes officer out to the kitchen and sat down at his table.

"Anyone vouch for your whereabouts tonight?"

"No." Harry frowned and his voice caught. "W-why? I-I've been here on my own all night. W-w-what do you w-want. W-w-what are you d-d-doing here?"

The police officer remained silent, and studied him.

"It's all clear," said the other policeman as he returned from Harry's bedroom.

The plainclothes officer shrugged.

"Tip off was wrong, Senior, there's nobody here."

"Doesn't account for the decapitated poodle on the doorstep, or the blood over the front door."

"Midge is dead?" Harry stood, and looked around the room. He felt hot. He needed to throw up. Midge and Mackenzie were all he had!

"Sit down."

Harry's mind reeled. Another one of his poodles killed the same way. She was the last of his four. He closed his eyes with regret.

"You need to come down to the station and answer some questions." He threw Harry a thin smile. "Help us with our enquiries."

"N-now?"

"Afraid so."

"N-no, I'm n-not going anywhere. I want to see to my poodle. You can't just break in to somebody's home. I haven't done anything wrong." He stood up.

The young uniformed officer grabbed his shoulder.

Harry froze, and pushed back an impulse to react.

"Sit down."

"Cuff him," said the plainclothes police officer.

"W-What for? I said I haven't done anything."

"Arms out."

Harry looked at the young uniformed officer, and thought about it. He held out his arms, and closed his eyes as the cuffs were put on.

"We had a tip off that you had a young girl in here and she was screaming. What do you expect us to do, and there's blood everywhere outside?"

"W-What? That's nonsense."

"You do know Mackenzie Tyler?"

"Of course. W-why?"

"You saw her yesterday?"

"She was here last night."

"A nine-year-old? Here? Alone with a grown man?"

"It's not what you think. She's always here. I look after her, for her grandparents."

"And you hurt her?" He watched the faces of the policemen, their eyes never left him, watched his every reaction.

"S-She's hurt?" His stomach lurched and he stood up. When Kim had died giving birth to Mackenzie, he hadn't been there. He didn't even know that she had given them a daughter. But her parents had taken her in, brought her to the small country town of Whittleside Way, and raised her. Harry followed.

The young constable closed his eyes and nodded.

A chill passed through Harry and he went cold.

"We thought that you might be able to shed some light on that," said the plainclothes policeman.

"H-how? W-w-what's w-wrong with her?"

"Young Mackenzie was found strangled nearby. Late last night."

"You're lying! She c-c-can't be."

"You're a sick pervert!" The policeman snapped. "And now she's dead!"

Harry felt sick, and he fell into the chair. Grief struck him, like a knife that twisted in his gut. Tears clouded his vision. He shook his head. His daughter was dead? "This can't b-be true."

"Very convincing. You can tell us about it at the station." Harry felt a hand on his arm, encouraging him to stand.

"I can't h-help you. I d-don't know anything."

"Then tell me why we found her less than 100 meters from here. Yours is the last house before the forest?"

A memory tugged at Harry, something important. "Not dow-n by the large oak?"

"Told you he'd know something, Constable," said the plainclothes policeman. His smile never touched his eyes.

Harry shook his head and tried to blink away his tears. "This can't be a c-coincidence," he said as his stutter cleared. "I'll come with you, but I need my icebox from the bedroom."

"Your icebox? What would you want that for?"

Harry stared at the plainclothes officer for a moment and shrugged. "I take it everywhere."

"I'll check it out, Constable." He walked into Harry's bedroom.

When he returned, he grabbed Harry's singlet, pulled Harry off balance and onto the floor.

"You're a sick man, Harry Mills." He yelled and poked his finger hard into Harry's chest. "I want that thing out of that icebox and buried *if* we release you. Understood?"

"What's in it?" asked the constable.

"Don't ask." He glared at Harry.

• • •

Harry sat in the back of the police car and clenched and loosened his fists in rhythmic fashion. Turmoil churned within him like malice. He didn't care about being handcuffed, nor was it the first time he'd been a prisoner.

He had forced himself to be still during the time they had put the cuffs on and walked him out to the car, but he had observed everything. He took in the 12 gauge in the boot of the police car. There would be shotgun cartridges in the glove compartment. The keys to his cuffs were in the left hand pocket of the plainclothes officer—another mistake—the man had chosen to drive and would be unable to stop Harry. And there was no barrier between the front and rear seat. Harry took a deep breath and exhaled, pushed away the compulsion to respond when he was restrained. He reminded himself that these men were not the enemy, that this was an honest mistake. To ensure that he could exact revenge for Mackenzie, he had to stay in control. There was something about that oak tree, the location of her death.

"Breathing a bit hard there," said the uniformed officer with a grin. "He's sweating too, Senior. I'd say that those were signs of a guilty man."

Both men laughed from the front seat.

"Anything you want to say to help make it easy for you?"

Harry leaned forward. "Tell me about what you found at the scene. How was she killed? Was there anything odd hit you about it? Was it ritualistic?"

"Shut up! We ask the questions, not you." The man turned to his senior. "Jesus, what is all this crap? I thought you said he was the stuttering bookseller from the main street?"

Mackenzie! Anguish like bile filled Harry's stomach. He turned away from the men's senseless chatter and looked out the window. Strobing from the passing street lights, a constant pull of light and dark created hypnotic shadowy images. Harry's skin tightened and his heart rate climbed. It was best to let his mind wander.

The image of a parade ground appeared. Harry smiled as he remembered how he felt, fresh and green, just out of school.

"You men listen up," said McNeil, their drill sergeant as he dusted off his army greens. He bent down and picked up a weapon. "This is the M60, air-cooled gas-operated open bolt machine gun. It's effective up to eleven hundred meters and can fire nine hundred seven point six two millimetre rounds in less than two minutes. The results are devastating. It's got a kick like a mule, and a bite like a snake. With a velocity of eight hundred and sixty meters a second it will penetrate six millimetres of thick steel plate at five hundred meters, or a flak jacket at one hundred meters. A round from this baby will pass through you like a hot knife through butter. From now on it's your best friend. Whenever you have a shower you give it a clean. If it gets a grain of sand on it or a spec of dust, you give it a clean. You don't eat; you don't sleep, shit or shave unless it's clean, cocked, and ready to be fired." He stopped and grinned as he put the M60 down. Then he picked up a rifle and lifted it into the air. "This is the L1A1 SLR, or self-loading rifle. Like the M60, it also takes the seven point six two millimetre rounds. If the M60's your friend, then this baby is your girlfriend. You kiss her at least once a day, sleep nice and close to her every night. You treat her well men, like your life depended on it." He kissed the rifle and then put the weapon down.

"Understand?"

"Yes, Sir."

McNeil's eyes bulged. "Don't call me sir! I work for a living! I said DO YOU UNDERSTAND?"

"YES SERGEANT!!!" cried the men in unison.

"Good. It might be the only thing between you and a body bag. Special Air Service Regiment use these weapons so don't think that they're for pussies. They got a cut down version they call 'The Bitch', so do the right thing by her."

Harry smiled over the recollection. It had taken a while to get his head around what he wanted to do in the service, but he earned his SASR badge and the right to carry 'The Bitch'.

The desert heat of Al-Bahra returned with the sound of machine guns. Harry smelled death.

"Grenade!"

He ducked as a dull thud reverberated around him. A man screamed. Harry tensed and—

The police radio crackled into life. Harry remembered that he was under arrest. At least the urge to harm had vanished.

"Sierra Vixen Two Three, this is Mitre One, over." There was static at the end of the stranger's voice transmission on the radio.

"Roger Mitre One. Send," said the plainclothes officer.

"Mitre One . . . " There was a long pause on the radio. "Tell me you don't have Harry Mills in the car with you right now."

"Yep! We got him good and proper, Mitre One. Bastard's on his way in for more questioning."

There was more silence on the other end of the radio transmission. Then the voice bellowed from the radio. "He's a decorated war hero for God's sake."

"Sorry, but he's all but admitted to killing Mackenzie."

"Idiots! You let him go right now. He won't say, and most people don't know, but Mackenzie is his daughter. Harry wouldn't hurt a fly."

Dust stirred as the car pulled up on the side of the road.

The radio crackled to life again. "Harry, it's Dave Randall. You still on that medication for your trauma?"

Harry nodded. He raised both arms so they could remove the handcuffs. "I t-t-told you that I d-d-didn't have anything to d-d-do with her death."

• • •

"I'm sorry, Harry," said Anne, a local poodle breeder. "I can't give you any more of my poodles. Four have gone missing in as many years. I don't know what's going on but I want my dogs to go to a good home." She turned to look at her sister, Mavis, standing nearby. "And before you interrupt, Mavis, it's not personal. Harry's a good man, but I just want them to go to someone I can be sure can give them a long and happy life."

"It's got nothing to do with poor little Mackenzie either," added Mavis. "We know that you loved her like a daughter. I don't know how the police ever thought it might have been you."

"I-I don't know how they d-did either. Bu-bu-but I wish they w-would hurry up and f-find out w-who did it. It's b-been months now.

Anne paused and gave Harry a mournful look. "You understand Harry. Don't you?"

Harry considered what Anne had said, while he tried to quell the nervous blinking. "Of c-c-c-course." He agreed, voice low and quiet. He understood completely, and turned away and walked off, head down, carried the icebox that went everywhere with him.

"He was a good butcher," said Mavis loud enough for Harry to hear as he traipsed back to his car, "but with that terrible business with his poodles and now young Mackenzie, it's taken a toll on the poor man. Your poodles are all he's got, Anne."

"I know," Anne said. "But I'm more worried about the dogs. I heard another of my poodles was slaughtered and left on his doorstep one night. It's all very upsetting if you ask me. They say that he carries one around in that icebox of his."

"No," said Mavis with surprise, "I've never heard such things!"

"Oh yes, but you're right about one thing Mavis. He hasn't been coping since Mackenzie."

Harry slammed the door of his car, and silenced the women's gossip. He looked in the mirror and waited for the nervous blinking to subside; something that began when he lost Kim, and yes, the women were right, it was worse with Mackenzie's death. It was as though he'd swallowed sharp knives. Military training that had helped him compartmentalise everything about her—so he could manage each day—but he was sure that the anxiety, the stutter, and blinking wouldn't go until he found closure.

• • •

Harry sat on his chair at the bookshop, and ground his teeth in frustration, until his jaws ached. A search around by the oak tree, where Mackenzie died, had revealed nothing. What troubled him most was the stir of a distant memory that failed to surface. He knew it was important. It would come to him, eventually.

The sound of a bus rambling down the main street interrupted his reading, and he pushed the chair back and stood nervously. It was half-past-three, and his pulse climbed. The nervous blink returned. School children invaded the Main Street, flooded into shops. Mackenzie had always showed up about now.

A small group tumbled into his shop—loud schoolkids—and scattered to the four corners. "Found your poodle yet Harry?" The taunt came from behind the safety of the tall, but narrow rows of bookshelves. Another boy stood in the open, behind an open comic, stuttering loudly to the cheer of a small group of adolescent boys. "Sorry about your p-poodles, H-Harry!" The unsympathetic comment was followed by sniggers as some of the boys ran out the shop.

Harry heard the groan of the door to the adult's book section. "G-G-Get out of there!" He raced over and opened the door. "You're t-too young!" For the boys it was the most interesting room in the shop. Men of all kinds would call, too, usually around lunch time, others just before closing; eager to get their fill of titillating, yet trashy magazines.

Gilbert Smyth stood in the doorway; he wore a smirk that screamed trouble. He was Harry's neighbour, in his final year of school, and his thick, dark hair was slicked down flat against the side of his face. He walked everywhere with his mouth wide open, shirt half out, and a sullen downcast eyes.

"G-G-Go on, g-get out! You're n-not eighteen yet!"

"Doesn't stop me from doing *anything* I want, old man."

"J-J-Just get out," said Harry. A few boys behind Gilbert laughed.

"What are you going to do about it, pathetic old man? Couldn't even protect Mackenzie from the cold."

"Ge-Ge-Get out!" Harry roared in a rage. "Ge-Get out of my shop, or else."

"Or else what? What will you do? St . . . st . . . stutter all over me?"

Everybody laughed.

"I'll s-s-speak to your mother L-L-Lyn!"

"Like she has a say in what I do. Don't you ever mention her name again—you lost that right a long time ago."

Harry nodded; he had dated Gilbert's mother, when she moved into the district.

Gilbert turned and looked around at all the books in the room, and leered. "Come on, let's have some fun somewhere else."

Harry locked the front door, turned off all the lights and crawled into the furthest corner of the room, fists clenched and held tight to his head. Armed combatants he could deal with, but nothing in the forces had trained him for this. The taunts about his poodles were more frequent. His beautiful fiancée, Kim, Mackenzie, and his poodles; they had been happier times. Four of his poodles had gone missing over several years, all had been decapitated.

He looked over to the icebox, to where Snoop, his most prized poodle was stored. Kim and he had bought him when things were better. Snoop had been their dog and they bought her a gold medallion to celebrate her naming ceremony. It had been a wonderful gesture, symbolic of their commitment to each other, just as much as Snoop's long life with them. They would each take turns spoiling her, as if she was their child. When he returned from theatre, after Kim's death, Harry put the medallion on Snoop's chain to remember her. That was the night he found Snoop dead by the oak tree, decapitated. Snoop symbolised everything that had been great about his life; Kim, a future together, that's why he'd had Snoop embalmed, why he carried Snoop around with him in the icebox, so he wouldn't forget Kim.

Harry pulled his fists away from his head and stood. That was it! His beautiful Mackenzie! A daughter he had not known about until he returned from the war. She had been found at that oak tree. All his dogs, Mackenzie, there had to be a connection. But what? Kim had died, and Mackenzie had moved to live with her grandparents. The town didn't harbour any resentment against him, Mackenzie, or her grandparents.

• • •

Harry sat in the park along the edge of the river, and put down his book and watched the ducks quack nervously around him. It was his favourite time and he enjoyed the warmth of autumn sun on his back. He threw some sandwich crusts down for the ducks and watched as they gobbled up the scraps.

The voice of a local tour guide whose name escaped him drifted past as he lectured a small group of children. This area was a regional boundary for the Kaurna and Peramak people. He followed the conversation.

"This was neutral territory and different groups met together for ceremonies and danced at the full moon—"

"Late lunch?"

Harry turned and faced Alice, the local proprietor of the furniture shop next door to his bookshop.

She smiled.

He liked Alice a lot, and shifted on the bench to give her room to sit. They'd been on a couple of dates together, and she had made it clear that if Harry wanted, their relationship could go a lot further. "You could say. A business proposition I couldn't refuse."

"Shop all locked up for a while?" She sat down beside him and rubbed his arm.

He nodded. "I was told to come back at three."

"Harry, I don't know why you do it, loaning the shop out like that. I think it's disgusting! A grown man and women having sex in your bookstore! It's just not right."

Harry nodded helplessly. "It's money. It helps pay the bills."

Alice sighed. "What's happened to you, Harry? Why do you put up with it? You could get a job anytime you wanted as a butcher again. You wouldn't be hiding out in that dark little shop of yours. You're a damn good butcher, if I remember. Go and take up that offer to work with Stripes Meat! Move if you have to, just grab hold of your life again. I'm here for you."

"I know." He squeezed her hand. "I don't know if I can be bothered. It's been a hectic couple of years, and now, Mackenzie. I just need some time to find myself again."

She patted his hand. "It's been hard for you, I'll be the first to admit that, but you just can't sit on your hands. You wonder why they don't have any respect for you. Stand up to them—all of them. The town, the students, the mayor and his dirty little secretary. Don't think people don't know what's going on right now in your shop."

"I suppose you're right." Harry nodded in agreement and found some more food to throw the ducks.

They sat there is silence, just enjoying the quiet day until Harry looked at his watch and stood up. "I suppose I should go and tidy up, before the boys visit, " said Harry.

"You mean Gilbert Smyth?" She shuddered. "There's something about that boy. He gives me the creeps."

Harry laughed. "I thought that he just had a thing about me."

"He's a nasty piece of work."

"What happened?"

"Nothing you need to worry about, dear Harry."

• • •

The shop was empty when Harry returned. He switched the sign on the door from back to 'OPEN' and then stepped into the adult books section. Harry pulled his nose up at the smell and cleaned the room. He arranged the magazines so that each shelf was neat and ordered again. Each book, every title, had a proper place and Harry was never happy until they were correct. He replaced the cover on the small double couch and went to pick up the money left on his desk. They always paid well, and it kept his business afloat, no matter how uncomfortable he felt.

He had a lot of customers and the men would always give him a wink if they saw him down the street. Sometimes the occupants lost track of time and they left more money, while the women buttoned their business suits again. It was another reason why he was uncomfortable about the school kids going near the room. Some of the boys must have known what went on and this only made the room more of a challenge to get into whenever they visited.

The front bell went off as the usual group of boys returned after school—minus Gilbert. His stutter returned. He sat in the corner with a book and struggled to quell his anger when the taunts commenced.

"Got to go," said one of the boys.

Harry stared into his book and listened to the boy's footsteps, waited for the door alarm to beep.

"Yeah, sorry about your poodles, Harry. I heard Snoop's tag was real gold too!"

Shocked by the comment, Harry stood. Like a percussion bolt closing on a smoothly oiled revolver, his hand flashed across the bookshop counter. The boy didn't have time to move. Harry's hand tightened around the boy's school tie, lifting him up onto the tips of his toes. Snoop's 'tag' had never been found. Harry had bought the medallion for Kim when they got engaged. He'd put it on Snoop to remember her. Only Snoop's killer would have known about the gold medallion. "W-W-Who told you about Snoop's gold t-tag?"

"Take it easy," the boy pleaded, in a high-pitched voice. He tried to free Harry's vice-like grip on his tie. "Everybody knows."

"W-Who told you?" Harry didn't give any ground and squeezed tighter.

"Gil told me. I don't know if it's true or not."

"Gil S-S-Smyth?"

He nodded.

Harry let go of him and sat down.

"Don't tell," he pleaded and ran from the shop.

Harry nodded absently. The accusation didn't make sense. Gill was Harry's next-door neighbour, and always offered to help look for the dogs each time they went missing. One evening as Harry was walking home after work he fell. Snoop's body tumbled out of the icebox onto the footpath. Gilbert had turned up out of nowhere, and helped Harry put Snoop away before anyone saw. He couldn't have been wrong about Gilbert all these years.

Harry sensed a change stirring deep within him, not anger, more like before he went into battle. He would confront Gilbert.

• • •

Harry stopped at the Symth's house after work. The small ramshackle house had seen better days and fallen into disarray after Lyn Smyth and her son moved in years before. The lawn needed mowing, and weeds grew between the cracks of the heavy flagstones that led to the porch. Harry stepped up and banged hard against the side windowpane. While he waited, he could hear a radio, and then footsteps creaked on the wooden floorboards inside. He took a deep breath and smiled as the door opened.

Lyn Smyth opened the door and glared at him as she wiped flour from her hands.

Harry's stutter returned immediately. "H-Hello L-Lyn."

"Hello, Harry," she said eventually. "You surprised me. I haven't seen you in a while."

Harry nodded. Lyn Smyth didn't step outdoors very often. Nobody saw much of her; let alone Harry, her closest neighbour. She was a short dour woman. It was common knowledge she believed that life had dealt her an unfair hand. Harry had contributed to that. "I've been r-renovating the back room," he said. "Keeps me inside most of the time." He paused and gave her another smile. "Um, is G-G-Gil in?"

"I think he's in his room." She frowned at Harry. "What's he done this time?"

Harry disarmed her with a smile. "Nothing, everything's g-good." He watched her relax.

"Gil! Visitor!" She hollered and waited by the door until Gilbert arrived.

"What's *he* doing here?"

"Gilbert, don't be so rude."

Harry began to blink and his stutter worsened. "I-I-I'm g-getting another p-poodle!" The lie was aimed at piquing Gilbert's interest. If what he had been told was true, then there might be a reaction.

"That's nice," said Lyn and stepped away. Her eyes widened.

Harry noticed she looked uncomfortable. Gil just stared into space disinterested.

"Yes I spoke to the b-breeders the other day, and they said I might be able to have one of their n-next litters." Harry watched Gil continue to stare into space. "Anyway I came over to let G-Gil know I have that b-book he w-wanted."

Gil frowned. "What book?"

"W-W-One of the boys m-mentioned you wanted it while they were in the s-shop this afternoon." Harry handed Gilbert a novel. "It's alright, I d-don't want anything f-for it." He looked at Lyn Smyth and gave her a smile. "I thought Gil might like to h-help me clean out the s-storeroom one day?" The storeroom was the name on the adult's book section door. Harry could tell that Gilbert had cottoned on because he raised his eyebrows and nodded slowly. It was enough. "B-B-Better go."

Harry walked away and Gilbert followed.

"Here," Gilbert said when they were out on the roadway out of earshot. "I didn't ask for this. What's going on?"

"N-N-Nothing's going on, Gil." Harry shook his head. "I'll keep the b-book then." Harry took the book from Gilbert and blinked nervously. "I just w-wanted to thank you for keeping an eye out for my d-dogs over the years, and hope that it can c-c-continue with my new one."

Gilbert's voice was strained. "Sure, I'll keep an eye out for your new dog." He licked his lips.

Harry noticed the subtle change in Gilbert. It was enough. "I wanted to thank you for keeping quiet about Snoop in my icebox. Come around to the shop just before closing this Friday and I'll let you take any books you like."

"Sure." Gils's voice was monotone.

"J-J-Just keep quiet about it. I don't want to g-get into any trouble!"

"Whatever. Don't come around again. I don't want you near my mother!" Gilbert swaggered off without another word.

Harry shivered and rubbed his hand through his hair to stop the tingling sensation. Something twisted in the pit of Harry's stomach. He felt uneasy. But one way or another he'd get to the bottom of it. Mackenzie deserved that much.

• • •

Gilbert came in right before closing; he wore his usual sullen expression, eyes downcast.

"Anyone s-s-see you c-come in?" Harry closed and locked the door.

"Of course not." Gilbert curled his lip, defiant.

"Anyone know you're h-h-here?" Harry pressed the question, eager to know whether anyone knew Gil was there?

"Think I'd tell anyone I was spending an evening with you?"

"R-R-Rooms all y-yours then."

Gilbert smirked. He marched straight over to the adult's book section. "Keep out until I'm done, or I'll tell everyone what's in your icebox!" He slammed the door shut.

Harry put the "CLOSED" sign up. He walked over to the icebox on his desk and took off the lid. He smiled down at Snoop's withered body. "Hello old girl." He reached in and moved her, pulled out one of his favourite butcher's knives. He slipped it behind him, between his belt and trousers. He pulled out a meat cleaver. His eyes sparked as he felt the weight of the sharp cleaver in his palm; he felt alive.

Harry strode to the adult's section and pulled open the door.

Gilbert turned in surprise and dropped a magazine. "Shit, you scared me . . . "

Harry had his hand around the boy's throat before Gilbert could utter another word. He raised the meat cleaver high in the air, and glared at Gilbert. His hand trembled as it hovered near the boy's head. "T-T-Tell me how you found out about Snoop's g-gold tags. Don't think about l-l-lying."

"Let go of me, stuttering freak!" Gilbert tried to pull away.

Harry's vice-like grip tightened.

"I don't know anything!"

"L-L-Liar. N-N-Nobody ever knew about the g-gold tags except Snoop's k-killer!"

"Let go of me, shithead." Gilbert tugged at Harry's hand.

"Tell me. I'll k-kill you if you don't." Harry raised the meat cleaver higher.

"All right."

Harry waited, eager for a confession, an apology.

"Shit, they were only dogs!"

"D-Dogs?" A chill ran through Harry. "You k-killed them? C-Cut their h-heads off?"

Gilbert shrugged an admission.

"W-Why?" Harry blinking worsened.

"They barked all the time. They kept me awake."

"That's your excuse?" Harry was bewildered.

"And they crapped over our lawn."

Something twigged and he frowned at Gilbert. "What about the string of animals behind my back fence? All of them decapitated, mutilated over the years. That was you? Why?"

Gilbert shrugged. "Seemed like fun at the time."

Harry felt himself go cold as he framed the next question.

Gilbert followed the cleaver as it rose above his head.

"T-Think c-carefully. W-What about-t M-M-Mack-ken-zie?"

"She deserved it. She was useless and wouldn't put out."

Disgust ran through Harry like a tidal wave. He closed his eyes as his throat tightened. A sob sprang forth and then tears poured from him over the senseless loss of his daughter, sweet wonderful Mackenzie. He opened his eyes and stared at Gil. "The police, you know they'll lock you up forever." He stepped closer, waved the cleaver around. Harry put his fists to his head. "Ahhh. How could you?" He shook his head. "You're going to pay for this." Harry let the meat cleaver fall to the floor as emotions overwhelmed him.

"It'll be your word against mine, and we already know what a freak the police think you are." Gilbert bent down and picked up the knife from the floor, tested the weight in his hand. "Not bad."

"W-Why d-do you d-do it?" Harry stared at Gilbert, numb.

Gilbert shrugged. "Because I can." His lip curled. "I feel good. I tell you what. I'll keep this knife." He looked around the room and pointed. "And I'll take those magazines. If you even think about calling the police, I'll use this knife on your Alice next door. What do you think of that?"

Harry nodded, sickened, and disgusted. All of his dogs were dead. Mackenzie had been slaughtered the same way at this animal's hand. The boy was right; nobody would believe him. He looked up at the light swinging gently, and glanced over at the wall to the shadows images that danced. He took a deep breath, and blinked away the dark spectres that swam across his vision, but stopped. Mackenzie! Then he let them come.

Harry snapped. A primordial cry burst from within him. Humanity needed protection from monsters like Gilbert. He pulled the knife from behind his back and lunged before Gilbert had a clue. It was as if he was back in the desert, fighting for his life once again, butchering the animals that killed their own kind in the name of war. He threw Gilbert down onto the ground and stood over him, lifted his head back like the animal at the slaughter yard he was, and twisted the knife in deep.

"That's for my daughter Mackenzie, and Snoop, all my dogs, and whatever you did to Alice!"

Harry held Gilbert down, felt years of tension slip away. Blood sprayed everywhere, covered the books, and spurted over the soiled two-seater couch where the mayor had frequented. Blood ran between the cracks of the wooden floor and then slowed, pooled around Gilbert's still body.

When it was done, Harry picked up the meat cleaver and hacked off both of Gilbert's legs below the knee, and then each thigh. His arms were next and then the head. This wasn't a person, this was a monster. Everything was placed neatly on top of Gilbert's torso; if nothing else Harry was still an excellent butcher.

There was a knock at the door.

Harry froze. He wiped the blood from him in a panic and strode over to the door.

Alice stood at the door.

"Alice, you can't come in. I'm busy."

Alice held up the buckets in her hands. Each was filled with gloves and cleaning liquids. She shrugged. "I heard everything through those thin walls. If I'd have been quick enough, I'd have helped you use the knife." She was trembling. "Let me in."

Harry unlocked the door and let her enter. "What did he do to you?"

"It doesn't matter. He got what he deserved."

He watched as she walked into the small back room.

She faced him. "You go and get rid of him. I'll clean up here."

Harry frowned in surprise. "This isn't your problem."

"It would have been."

Stunned, he nodded. "Alright."

"Then we have to talk."

"Yes," he said.

. . .

Harry went home and buried Snoop. He returned three times that night and filled his icebox.

Machines could be heard all through the night at Harry's, which was nothing unusual for the former butcher. Everyone had become accustomed to the noise of his bandsaw and mincer.

The following morning Harry went back to the shop. He took down the adult section. Put the sofa on the back of his trailer and took it to the rubbish dump. He removed the boards on the windows and let more light into his shop. He rearranged his books and placed stories of animals where the adult books were with a sign that read 'Snoop's Corner'.

. . .

"Harry, what a surprise to see you," said Anne when Harry went to visit again. "You understand that it's not personal Harry. I'm only thinking of my dog's welfare. I still won't change my mind about giving you another poodle!"

"No Anne, it's okay. I brought you a gift." Harry threw her a big smile. "You can have my icebox. I don't want it anymore."

"No, I don't think I can take it." She hesitated and put her hand to her mouth.

"It's not for you." He encouraged her with another smile. "It's for your dogs." He put the icebox down.

"I heard that you sold your bookshop, Harry, and you got a new job with Stripes Meat."

Harry watched as Anne's eyes darted down to the icebox. He nodded. "It was about time I sorted everything out. I start at the new butchers on Monday. I've moved in with Alice, too."

"Good for you, Harry, good for you. But I don't know if I can take your kind gift of the icebox."

"Of course you can. I'd better be off. Don't let the icebox stay in the sun too long, Anne."

"Any news on Gilbert Smyth's disappearance, Harry?" said Anne.

Harry shook his head.

"I heard he ran away," said Mavis.

"He's probably off tormenting other people. Nothing good will come of that boy."

"I'm sure you're right, Anne." Harry threw her a smile and strode to his car. It was true that the town didn't seem to care about Gilbert.

He stood by his car and watched while Anne stared at the icebox. Both women's voices were clear.

"Open it up for goodness sake, Anne." Mavis insisted. "Let's find out what his secret is, once and for all."

Mavis rubbed her hands together while Anne slowly lifted the lid.

"Oh Mavis, look. That Harry is such a nice man," she said. "It's full of mince for the dogs."

"Not like any mince I've ever seen," said Mavis.

"No, it's probably chicken or pork, but I'm sure that the poodles will love it all the same. All this time I was worried about this icebox." She laughed.

"I was too." Mavis admitted.

"I thought I'd find one of his poodles in it! After all that, it's just mincemeat that he has been carrying around while he pined over his lost dogs."

"Harry's a good man," said Mavis.

"The dogs will enjoy it."

"Did you notice that Harry looks taller all of a sudden? His nervous blinking is gone?" said Mavis.

Anne nodded in agreement. "His stutter's gone too. Whatever he's doing he should keep it up!"

Harry chuckled as he drove off.

THE CAMP FOLLOWER

TRUDI CANAVAN

Contrary to what the soldiers said, it was not after battle that Captain Reny enjoyed the services of the whore in his tent. After battle, he was too exhausted to do more than wash off the blood and gore, even if he only ever fought when the king decided to join the fight, or to protect his leader. Reny was too old for the victorious lustful celebration the soldiers imagined their commanders enjoyed.

It was during the time between battles, after long meetings to discuss strategy, that he made use of the woman. Aside from the physical release and the sensual pleasure, he gained something even more valuable—a time in which he was free from thought and care. The past and the future did not penetrate his mind.

But all too soon he would be lying awake, his mind starting to dwell on matters best forgotten or ignored. As he was now.

To delay the return of those memories, he looked down at the woman sleeping on the floor beside his narrow stretcher-bed, and thought about her instead. She'd told him her name was Kala, but he doubted that was her true name. It was too common among the camp followers. Apparently it meant 'lucky charm', which was far too appealing a name in a time of war to be a real one.

Her waist was narrow, but she widened above and below in ways a woman ought to. He guessed she'd joined the other camp followers not long before he'd noticed her, or she would have been as skinny and wasted as they were. Yet he hadn't chosen her for her body alone. Something in her eyes reassured him. It was an *awareness*, that told him she knew exactly what she was doing, despite her obvious youth, and wasn't tormented by it. It was the absence of desperation, loathing, horror or resignation in her face that had caused him to look twice, and invite her to join him.

All his doubts about her had faded as the days and weeks, villages and towns had fallen to the advancing army. She did not chatter, did not fawn or beg, and never complained. She was quiet, obedient and willing. She rubbed his sore muscles after battle. She had a skill with the cook pot that could turn the worst of rationed foodstuffs into edible fare.

Choosing her had been the best thing he'd done since joining the Conquest.

• • •

Looking down from the ridge, Reny felt the breath catch in his throat. Wavy, sinuous lines of trampled whetta ran between the forest and the farmhouse. A lot of people had passed this way. The sort of people who did not care if they ruined a crop. This could be evidence of their arriving or leaving. They could be gone or still in the farmhouse. Reny's anger at this careless destruction was overtaken by dread.

Then he was at the house. He tried to shout but could not make a sound. I don't need to see this again. *Though he knew what he would find, he started searching.* I'm dreaming; I must wake myself up. *There was nobody in the kitchen where he knew he should find his wife . . . doomed to die after agonising days of pain and fever from infection within.*

Better they had killed her than left her like this. *The rooms upstairs were also empty. He ought to be grateful to not see, yet again, what they had done to his daughter and youngest son, but instead their absence left him fraught and hollow.*

They're gone. Where have they gone?

In the distance he heard the sound of horns—

He jolted awake.

And remembered.

His homeland had been invaded by the Henelan. The Laxen, his own people, had offered their empty throne to a sorcerer mercenary, Dael, if he would defeat their enemy. Within a year the Henelan, to the last child, no longer existed. A secret agreement was discovered between other neighbouring lands, who had planned to carve up Laxen among themselves once they defeated the Henelan. So a greater war started, until someone came up with the idea that lands united were lands free of warfare. And so, the Conquest began.

A retired soldier and former strategy adviser to the king of Laxen, Reny had offered his services to Dael at the beginning. When he had told Kala this, she had asked how long ago it had been, and he could not tell her the exact number of years with confidence. More than ten. Not as many as twenty.

The horns in his dreams rang out again, but his time he knew them to be real: the signal that the army was to pack up and be ready to march. Reny cursed and got to his feet. The woman looked up at him, a question in his eyes.

"Packing time," he told her.

She got up and started moving about, opening the trunks that held his belongings and started putting what had been removed back inside them. He moved to the tent opening and looked out, then sighed heavily and turned back to see her watching him, her smooth brow wrinkling in mute enquiry.

"I should have been told about this," he answered. "Vorl is still punishing me for disobeying him."

She nodded and started folding the bedding, but her frown did not fade.

"It was something that happened before we . . . before I invited you to my tent," he explained.

The look she gave him was accepting, as if she didn't expect him to tell her anything more, but he thought he saw a glint of curiosity in her eyes.

He took a deep breath. "Vorl had just been promoted to General. He wanted to test his authority. In the wrong situation, that can make a man do needlessly cruel things. Or order others to do so. I refused."

She grimaced in sympathy and understanding. "Do you regret it?" she asked in her lilting voice. Her strange accent had been annoying at first, but now that he'd grown familiar enough to understand her he found it appealing.

He considered her question, looking away as he remembered the incident. "No. Besides, I don't think I could have managed it anyway. Perhaps Vorl guessed that and wanted me humiliated." He turned back to find her looking bemused, and smiled grimly in apology. "Sorry, that won't make much sense to you. Dael sent

Vorl to attack a place in the mountains. Though it was not directly in the path of the army, there was a risk people there could attack our rear if we didn't deal with them first. It turned out to be a temple run by women. Priestesses. No threat at all."

Kala went still, her face hardening as she comprehended the fate of the priestesses.

"And you refused to take part?"

Her voice was deeper and stronger than he had heard it before. It also had a tone of demand. Another man in his position might have punished her for that, he realised.

"Yes." He shuddered. To watch what had been done to his wife and daughter being done to others . . . He pushed the memory away and set his mind on packing. Kala, accepting his silence, said nothing more for some time; then, as the last tent rope loosened and the oilcloth collapsed on the ground, she glanced sideways at him.

"Dael hasn't got rid of you yet. You must still be valuable to him," she said quietly.

He shrugged, too astonished by her insight to be angry at her presumption. "Until Vorl convinces him otherwise."

"Vorl is a weapon, to be used and discarded when blunted. Advisers are like scrolls or books, to be consulted over and over. You don't hit your enemy with a book, then go consult your sword, do you?"

He stared at her in amazement, but she was walking away, stooping to take up one side of the tent and start folding it ready for travel.

• • •

The stink of sweat, blood and gut juices permeated Reny's skin and clothing. These last were of an enemy soldier who had managed to dash through the front line of soldiers and Dael's guards only to impale himself on the captain's sword. Reny suspected he'd never forget the expression of surprise and dismay on the young man's face.

He reached the tent, staggered inside and stood there, swaying in the lamplight.

I'm still alive. Another battle survived.

Two buckets of water waited next to a neatly folded pile of clothing, ready for his return, but something was missing. He frowned and cast his eyes about the tent. Kala was absent.

Probably getting more water. Or food. Or something. He shrugged and started cleaning himself up. Long experience had taught him to start from the top of his head and work his way down, so that gore that might be trapped within his armour, clothing or hair would not drip onto parts already cleaned. Each piece of armour was removed separately, the soiled clothing stripped off and set aside. It was not easy this time, without Kala's help, but he felt a perverse determination to do it himself. *Do I think that if I show her I can manage this myself, she'll make sure she's here next time in case I decide I don't need her anymore?*

Once he was clean, he donned fresh undergarments, then set about putting much of the armour back on. Fortunately the protective shell was not heavy. Most of it was hardened leather and when camped on the battlefield he avoided removing it as much as possible. The enemy might launch a stealthy night attack. It had happened in the past. The King's army had lost many good leaders.

Even though exhaustion usually overrode discomfort, it was torture to sleep in full armour, so Reny compromised by leaving off the back piece. When he was ready for sleep and found Kala still hadn't returned, something made him turn from the bed and replace the missing piece. He paced around the confines of the tent slowly, then went looking for her outside.

He trudged around the camp twice in the deepening night, even checking Vorl's tent. In the end, he found her, but only because he had overheard a watcher chatting to the man sent to replace him.

" . . . one with the yellow hair again."

"Same as last night. I searched her when she came back, but she wasn't carrying anything. She still out there?"

Reny had stopped to listen, his heart skipping at the mention of yellow hair. The two men were squinting out over the battlefield. His eyes followed their gaze. A thin sliver of moon lit a landscape that was far lumpier than it had appeared when the army had arrived a few days before. Figures moved about carrying lamps, bending and stooping over the dark mounds.

Reny had seen and watched this post-battle ritual many times before. Long after battle had ceased, the field remained a scene of activity. The wounded deemed to have a chance at recovery were carried from the field, but those considered unlikely to survive were given a quick and merciful death. Despite rules against the practice, whores also slipped out after darkness to take trinkets and small weapons from the bodies of the dead, though if they were spotted returning to the camp they risked losing the most part of their takings to the watchmen as bribes. Soldiers did not look favourably on those who stole from the dead—unless they benefited from it themselves.

Surely Kala was not partaking in this shameful trade? Reny had taken care of her as best he could, though admittedly hers was hardly a life of comfort and riches. Was she greedy for more? As Reny stared out into the darkness his eyes were drawn to a figure, familiar in the way it moved. Suddenly he did not want to know. *But if it is her and the soldiers hear I'm keeping a scavenger in my tent . . .*

Sighing, he set out onto the battlefield. As he approached the figure he felt his heart sink. It was Kala.

She hadn't seen him yet. He stopped, suddenly reluctant to approach. Perhaps he could try to pretend he didn't know what she had done. The thought of throwing her out and returning to an empty tent each night was surprisingly painful.

While he watched, she squatted beside one of the dark shapes. He heard a groan, and then a voice.

"Please. End it for me," the voice begged. "I can't . . . stand it anymore. *Please.*"

Kala reached out and touched the soldier's face gently. "I will give you peace," she said.

She moved her hand down and spread her fingers out above his chest. Reny could see that the man was shaking convulsively. The air between her hand and the soldier rippled, then her fingers slowly curled into a fist. The man gasped, let out a long breath and went limp.

Reny's skin pricked with cold. He felt the world shift around him like a wheel on a carriage slipping into a rut. He knew nothing would be the same again.

Kala got to her feet. She looked down at the soldier, then sighed and shook her head. Stepping away, she began walking among the bodies with slow and unhurried steps.

She is no thief, Reny realised. *She took nothing.* But he knew that wasn't true.

She had taken the man's life. Something within him *knew* this.

He considered the shimmering air he'd seen between her hand and the dying soldier. It would be so easy to dismiss it as a bit of air heated by a campfire behind her, shimmering around her arm as she made a gesture of sympathy toward the man. But there was no campfire nearby.

Clearly she was not just a whore.

I have seen Dael perform magic, both subtle and dazzling. To deny the possibility that she is a sorcerer would be foolish and dangerous. Kala was walking away from him now. She hadn't noticed him standing there. He waited until she was too far away to hear or see him, then he made his way back to the camp. As he reached the watchmen, two soldiers overtook him, carrying a wounded man between them.

"We found him!" they called out to two other soldiers, who hurried to join them. "He'd been knocked out." They set the wounded man they had rescued down beside a campfire. Reny paused to watch as the man sat up and groggily accepted some water.

"I've seen Lady Death," the man said, his eyes wide. "And she's beautiful."

The four soldiers laughed.

"Must have been a good knock to the head."

"Just like you to have visions of pretty women."

"Well, if you're going to have visions, why not ones of pretty women?"

"I saw her," the wounded man said. "She saw me. But she let me live. She said I would live."

They laughed again.

Reny shook his head and continued on to his tent. From such talk, superstitions and legends might spring. He hoped Kala knew what she was doing.

If she returned tonight, he wasn't going to ask what it was.

•　•　•

It must have been torment enough to be dragged, defeated and in chains, to face one's enemy. But to have been given the freedom to walk to meet his conqueror, and then waste that small gift of dignity by stumbling and falling onto his face in the mud, was too much humiliation for the prince. There were smothered sniggers among the audience of army captains, though not from the captive locals brought to witness the surrender of their leader.

He struggled to rise, but could not get his legs under him on the steep embankment. A low sob escaped him, then two guards came forward, hauled him back to his feet and half-carried him forward, forcing him to his knees before Dael. He sagged, all pride and fight gone, his head bowed.

Reny was surprised to find that, after the countless defeated men and women he'd seen brought before the sorcerer King, he still felt a stirring of pity for this particular man. Even in the fading light he could see that the prince was young, barely old enough to claim the princedom from his father, who had been killed in this nation's first battle against Dael.

"Your army is defeated, your cities have fallen," Dael told him. "Do you surrender your land and people to me? Do you give your remaining army into my hands, to fight in the glorious Conquest to unite the lands?"

The prince remained silent. He was still so long that Reny began to worry that the youth would not respond. Then suddenly the prince straightened his body and lifted his head. He glared at Dael with intense hatred.

"I do not."

Reny looked at Dael. The sorcerer's eyebrows had risen slightly. There was a strange, avid light in his eyes.

"You know that the penalty for refusing is death, for you and everyone in your land?"

"Yes." The hatred in the young man's face vanished and was replaced by a blissful, wide-eyed stare as he tilted his head to the sky. "The Goddess of Death will take us. She will bring us peace." His gaze dropped to Dael and his eyes narrowed again. "And she will avenge our deaths."

The Goddess of Death? For a moment Reny could not inhale or move, then his heart began hammering in his chest and his knees felt weak. Was this a deity these people worshipped? Or was it, as he suddenly feared, the whore in his tent. The woman who had returned to his bed and fallen asleep at his side, then prepared his morning meal as if nothing had changed. In the morning light, it was too easy to dismiss what he'd seen last night as an illusion, or a dream. He forced himself to stand still and breathe normally, not wanting to give any hint of the shock that the prince's declaration had given him.

Fortunately Dael was not looking at Reny. His gaze was fixed on the youth as he rose.

"Are you sure," he asked. "I wouldn't want it to be known that I didn't offer you a choice."

The young man's eyes filled with fear as the sorcerer approached, but his voice was steady. "I am sure. As are my people."

Dael paused. "How disappointing," he said quietly. He nodded to the guards, who hauled the prince to his feet. Then he drew a long knife and plunged it into the young man's chest.

As always, Reny made his eyes stay focused on the scene, but not his attention. He'd grown adept at not *seeing* in these moments, and thinking of something else. Usually the whore. But this time, something caught his eye. Something strange and yet familiar. Something he might not have noticed if he hadn't slid down the ranks of Dael's favour in recent weeks, and been standing further down the slope, rather than in his usual place nearer to the King.

For the first time, he could see the knife protruding from the prince's chest, and the hand holding it . . . and more importantly, the air surrounding both.

It was shimmering.

The movement was barely noticeable, and he might have again dismissed it as an effect of the twilight descending upon the battlefields, or the heat from a fire or torch beyond the sorcerer and the prince. Now he knew better, and he wished he didn't.

But I do know, and it is dangerous to pretend otherwise. I must do what I would recommend to another man in this situation: consider every possibility, no matter how strange—because it is better to be over-prepared than be caught out by the unexpected— then deal with the problem.

He wished he could do his thinking alone and in peace, but, as ever, he didn't have that luxury. Now, after the prince's corpse had been removed, the sorcerer King and his captains retreated to the big tent where battle strategy was discussed and decisions made. Several hours had passed before all were sent to their beds. But as Reny reached the entrance of the tent he heard Dael call his name.

"Stay a moment, Captain Reny. I wish to talk to you."

As the tent emptied, the sorcerer King regarded Reny from the battered throne that was always dragged from battle to battle.

"Vorl doesn't like you," he said when they were finally alone. One thing Reny liked about the leader was how he always got to the point.

"I know," Reny replied, shrugging. "*I* don't like *him*."

"Why not?

"He is needlessly cruel."

"He is ruthless." Dael nodded. "Killing is what he does, and he does it well."

"Women and children?"

Dael's gaze became hard. "This is war. Nobody should pretend that it is merciful to the weak."

Reny opened his mouth to protest, thought better of it and nodded.

"He wants me to get rid of you," Dael told him. "He says you have rebellion in you, and your scruples will lose us battles one day. What do you say to that?"

Reny felt as if someone had dropped ice down the back of his armour, and it was sliding slowly down his spine. *I have a sorceress masquerading as a whore in my tent; a woman who both this army—and the enemy—think is some sort of goddess of death. The last thing I need is Vorn putting further ideas of betrayal in Dael's head.*

"I'd rather you got rid of Vorn," he replied, frankly.

Dael smiled. "Why should I do that?"

"Soldiers are like weapons," Reny found himself replying, "more useful in battle than hung on a wall. Advisers are like scrolls. You keep them so you can use their knowledge again and again." Somehow it had sounded more eloquent when Kala had said it.

Dael grinned, his eyes bright with amusement.

"*I* like you, Captain Reny. And that's most important. You may go."

Reny bowed, and hurried from the tent.

• • •

Reny would have liked more time to think, but he suspected that time was something he didn't have much of now. When he entered his tent and saw Kala waiting for him he felt a wave of relief, but it was followed by one of dread. And, unexpectedly, one of lust. She was regarding him with relaxed expectation from the end of the bed, with a small welcoming smile, and he was reminded once again that it was after strategy meetings that he most often used her services.

He knew that he never would again. That filled him with regret, but also determination. He drew in a deep breath, let it out slowly, and then sat down on one of the chests.

"What are you?" he asked. "Are you really a goddess?"

She showed no surprise, but her expression became serious, almost sad, and then the smile returned. "I am no goddess. What do *you* think I am?"

Reny met her gaze. "What *he* is. What Dael is. A sorcerer and . . . something else."

Her eyebrows rose and she regarded him appraisingly. "You've worked out more than I expected—or hoped."

"I've worked out nothing," he disagreed. "I have no idea what is going on. Am I keeping an enemy in my tent? Am I following someone . . . some*thing* more than an ambitious and clever sorcerer mercenary-turned-King, with a love for war and a desire to unite the lands?"

Suddenly all trace of her smile was gone. She had that knowing, worldly look again, but this time there was anger burning in her eyes.

"I am from the temple," she said. "The temple Vorl attacked."

His stomach plunged to the floor. He stared at her and felt guilt and pity fill him all over again.

"I'm sorry—" he began.

"I lived there for over a thousand years," she continued.

Disbelief overtook guilt. He remembered the shimmering air between her hand and the dying soldier, and knew that he had to consider that something so incredible might be possible. If this was true . . . he felt the first spark of awe. *I bedded this woman . . .*

"But I am several thousands of years older than that," she added. She looked away, beyond the tent walls, and sighed. "When I was the age of the body you see before you, I developed more than womanly traits. I aged the same as other people, but then within a day or night I'd grow young again.

"Whenever I'd returned to youth, I found that I could heal from an injury in an instant, and I could use magic. But in time, I'd lose those abilities and start to age again. How could this be? I only worked out why when a sickness came and many of the local people died. It took many, many more years before I started to age again." She paused and looked at Reny meaningfully.

He frowned. "You . . . you can take magic from people who are dying?"

"I don't *take* it. It comes to me. When someone dies, magic is released and if I am nearby it flows to me. Or if there is someone else with the trait nearby, it flows to whichever of us is closest."

"So you are immortal."

She shook her head. "I am sure that, if I stayed away from death long enough, I would age and die like everyone else."

He thought about the temple, so isolated and only attended by a handful of young women. Healthy young attendees were less likely than older ones to die while serving the old woman they believed was a goddess.

"That's why you were there," he said.

She nodded solemnly. "I have lived too long. I am tired of it."

His mind took a leap of comprehension. "But if death gives you magic, why didn't you save the women in the temple?"

She blinked at the sudden shift in his questioning, then scowled. "It was their death that gave me magic. Once dead . . . " She sighed. "I cannot bring the dead back to life. I might have been able to heal one or two of them, if any had been alive after the soldiers left." There was bitterness in her voice.

"So you joined the camp followers of an army, which would surround you with a never-ending source of death and allow you to grow strong." He took a deep breath. "Is revenge worth delaying your release from this life?"

She smiled. "I am not seeking revenge. If I was, Vorl would have stopped being a problem for you months ago."

"Why are you here, then?"

She looked at him with an expression he could not name, and it sent a shiver down his spine. "All those years in the Temple, waiting for death. I felt boredom beyond what you can ever experience. One thought kept me there, and kept me from giving up and leaving. One question that I will never know the answer to myself." She paused, and then smoothly rose to her feet. "Where does the death magic go, if sorcerers like me don't take and use it? What do you think, Remy?"

He stared at her as she walked out of the tent, and disappeared into the night, her words repeating themselves unceasingly in his mind, and rousing a deep, undeniable horror.

Soldiers believed in souls. They believed there was a life after death. They might not agree about the form that soul took, how it was judged, or who ruled the place souls went to, but they all held onto the same basic hope.

If they knew what she did, nobody would worship the Goddess of Death. They would fear her.

And Dael. Reny shuddered. Now that he knew the truth, some of the sorcerer King's more destructive decisions made sense. Dael was not trying to unify the lands in order to bring peace to them. He was harvesting fallen soldiers, his own and his enemy's, and keeping the lands in a perpetual state of war so that he might have eternal life and unending power over the living.

Reny did not see Kala again that night or the next morning. He did not expect her to return. If her absence was noted, he planned to shrug and say he had grown tired of her, and sent her away. He considered finding himself a new whore to make this lie more convincing, but didn't.

He pretended to have an injury—a strain in his back—to avoid having to fight. It wasn't that he was afraid he would die and lose his soul to Kala or Dael. He simply didn't want to miss seeing whatever all this was leading to.

He pondered Kala's motives and her possible strategy to carry them out. She had all but told him she wanted to stop Dael, but was she strong enough to face him and win? He considered that perhaps she intended to lose, and achieve the death she longed for, but he doubted it. She would not have been gathering strength by walking the battlefield at night. Instead, she would have confronted Dael in a deliberately weakened state, ensuring her defeat.

At midday Dael led the army into the city to carry out his punishment for their defiance. To Reny's surprise, the king placed him among his personal companions, and sent Vorl ahead to rouse the citizens, who had not emerged to face the invaders.

Soldiers beat down a few doors before they realised all were unlocked. They emerged from the buildings, confused and pale, each group hurrying to report to Vorl, whose face grew darker and darker.

"What is wrong?" Dael called.

Vorl hurried over and knelt before his leader. "They're dead," he said. "All of them. Poisoned themselves, by the look of it."

Dael looked up, his eyes scanning the buildings lining both sides of the main city road. "Surely not all of them. I'd have . . . Keep searching."

Though soldiers roamed further and further afield, they found only corpses. Old men, women and children tucked in their beds or slumped in chairs. From the expressions on their faces, whatever poison they had taken had seemingly sent them to a blissful end.

It was then, in the silence of realisation, that a woman dressed in white stepped out onto the main road. Reny heard all the men around him draw in a sharp breath. She glowed faintly as she walked toward them. Her feet were bare. Her pale hair was long and unbound and much too familiar.

Reny could not believe this was the whore he had kept in his tent. She had been attractive, but not this vision of beauty. *She certainly never glowed like that when she was mine.* She must have gathered up the death magic of all the city's remaining citizens as they expired from the poison they'd taken. *Or did she poison them? Is this a part of her plan? Is she that ruthless?*

Unexpectedly, he saw through the glamour around her to a woman who must have suffered much in her long life, despite the magic that kept her alive and healed every wound. She was a woman who had not been able to escape the evils of the world, even when she had isolated herself in search of the peace of death. A woman who had no choice but to question if her own powers, over which she had no control, were evil, She must have cared deeply about the answer, he thought. Perhaps this was the true reason she sought her own death. *No, she did not kill these people.*

The soldiers shifted fearfully, muttering to themselves. Reny guessed they saw something else: the Goddess of Death. But Kala's eyes were fixed only on Dael. The sorcerer King was watched her, his eyes bright and smiling indulgently, as if watching children performing.

"Greetings, King Dael," she said, her voice echoing between the buildings.

"Greetings . . . who do I have the honour of meeting?" he asked in reply.

"I have had many names. You may call me Saeyl."

He gestured to the buildings on either side. "Well, Saeyl. Did you do this?"

"Poison all these people?" she shook her head. "No. They arranged that all on their own. I don't know if they guessed what your abilities are and decided to deny you the magic you gain from the moment of their deaths," she shrugged, "or if they hoped their souls would go to me instead."

Dael's smile faded. She slowed to a stop a few paces away.

"I have not met anyone with my particular skills before now," he told her.

Her lips twisted with distaste. "I have met plenty."

"Where are they?"

"Gone. Dead."

"So we *can* die."

Her eyes brightened at his ignorance. "Yes, but only at the hands of another of our kind."

"So . . . you killed the others?"

She shook her head. "Not all of them. Most fought and killed each other. The last one I met wanted to go. He was very old, and tired of living." She lifted her chin. "How old are you?"

"Two hundred and forty nine."

Reny's skin prickled with cold. *I have been fighting for, and been loyal to, a man who is more than five times my age!*

Kala's eyes never left Dael. "So young. And with such skill in sorcery. When I discovered my power, few could or would teach me. Now there are *mortals* who know more than I did at your age."

"How old are you?" Dael asked.

"More than four thousand years," she said. "Less than five. It is hard to keep an exact tally, when counting systems keep coming and going with the civilisations that invent them."

"What do you want?" he asked.

Her eyebrows rose at his bluntness, then her expression became serious. "I want you to abandon this conquest of yours."

"Why?" Dael asked, his voice low and dark with defiance and anger.

"You don't need it." She took a step closer. "Look at me: I am proof that you do not need to wage war in order to live forever."

"Do you think that is my sole mission? What of power? What of peace? If I unite the lands there will be no more wars. We can do good things with our magic. And there will be no risk that you or I will be killed in some petty squabble between kingdoms."

She took another step, reaching out but not quite touching him. "How will you gather the power you need? Will you resort to slaughtering more innocent people? Will you breed people like livestock, to be a steady supply of sacrifices?"

"There are always criminals to be executed. And those who die of natural causes. If that's not enough . . . I'll think of something. You could help me," he said, reaching out toward her. His other hand shifted to his waist.

The movement was familiar, and even as Reny choked back a shout of warning Dael's dagger plunged into her chest under the ribs.

Trust that she knows what she is doing, he told himself. His heart raced. He stared at her face, seeing the pain and shock there, holding his breath and daring to hope. She was staring at Dael, her eyes dark with hatred.

"You said 'only at the hands of another of our kind'," Dael reminded her smugly.

She shook her head. "I did. But you are far too simple in your thinking."

Taking another step forward, she plunged her hand through his armour and into his chest, as if metal and bone and skin were the thinnest of paper. Dael's eyes went round then, as she pulled her arm back, he looked down in disbelief at the bloody, pulsing mess of organs trailing from her hands back to his body.

Her heart held his heart, twitching and wobbling. Dael opened his mouth, made a faint, whimpering noise, then crumpled at her feet.

Kala waited until the first sounds escaped the watching soldiers. As the realisation that she had killed their leader sank into the minds of those watching, she raised her eyes and surveyed those standing closest. She gestured with the bloodied heart, beckoning them closer. Instead, all turned and ran, yelling and screaming their terror.

All except Reny. A movement in the air had drawn his eyes. The shimmer between Dael's body and Kala was so intense it was almost a sound.

Is it only her magic or does it come from all the souls he has taken?

He looked up and met Kala's eyes. Weariness and resignation had replaced her fierce grin of triumph. She grimaced as she let the heart drop to the ground.

"I can't stop myself taking it," she said sadly. "But I *can* do this . . . "

Then she turned and strode away, the rippling air stretching and slowly thinning between herself and the dead sorcerer until the effect was no longer visible.

• • •

When he left, Reny took nothing with him but a large pack and his sword. While he would rather have left the weapon behind, he wasn't stupid. The road home would not be free of trouble. It would be full of ex-soldiers like him, and some would resort to theft and murder to get food, shelter and other essentials. He'd pass through lands that the sorcerer King had conquered, who would not welcome the men who had followed him, bringing so much suffering and loss.

At the end of the long journey was his home—and the ghosts of his family. If he made it, he would live the remaining years left to him there, and concern himself only with the strategies of crops and animal breeding cycles and bartering in the markets. He resolved to forget the war, and let all tales of his part in it fade from the memories of others, even if they would never leave his own.

Every day Kala was in his thoughts, and every night she appeared in his dreams, and he never stopped wondering where she was, and if she still sought her own death.

DISCIPLE OF THE TORRENT

LEE BATTERSBY

The storm had turned the world into a swirl of broken lines. Jeronimus Cornelisz stood with his shoulder jammed against the slick wooden wall of the aft quarters and his opposite arm wrapped around the deck rail, and watched the water grab hungrily at the sides of the boat. He loved the storm, loved the way it destroyed the natural order of the Universe. The horizon was an unreachable ideal, the sky an enemy of life, the ordered hierarchy of the *Batavia* a maelstrom of shouting men and panicking women. This was June as Cornelisz wished the whole year to be. Back home it was a time of warm breezes, long summer days and picnics on the open lawns of Haarlem. But June on the far side of the world demanded rain and wind and the chaos of untamed winter. The Sun was low and weak, and fury ruled the elements. It was the torrent brought to life, and the perfect place to rescue his Master.

Above him on the upper deck, Pelsaert and the skipper, Jacobsz, were arguing again. Cornelisz grinned. Jacobsz had been a worthy ally on the long voyage south. Motivated by money, booze and sex, he was the perfect shield between Cornelisz' ambitions and the ascetic, nit-picking Opperkoopman, always willing to flood his fat face with angry blood, and argue the slightest command. Jacobsz was the dough that soured the batch. It was all Cornelisz could do not to break into a jig to hear him screaming back at Pelsaert while the ship listed and fought the watery demons hammering at its hull.

Cornelisz abandoned his fragile grip on the deck rail and squeezed himself below decks. As Onderkoopman of the *Batavia*, he was entitled to the third best lodgings, which counted for little more than a curtained off cupboard with a rough plank and thin blankets for a bed. He barely owned enough floor space to step around his steamer trunk. But there was room for what he had planned. He rummaged around in the trunk, drew out two candle stubs and a stick of chalk, and placed them on the bench. A quick check to make sure nobody was lurking outside his curtain, then he pushed the trunk as far under his rude bed as it would fit and sketched a rough circle on the floor. Five quick slashes of the chalk filled the ring with a star. Cornelisz knelt with one point between his knees, laid the candles in front of him, then placed a hand over each. There was danger in unguarded flames below decks, and he lacked the time to snuff out a taper and clean up should he hear boot steps approaching. Heat was necessary, to warm the air and soften the ether sufficiently so he could send his message through the gap to the world beyond. The warmth of his hands would have to suffice. He closed his eyes and bent over. Like a dog before its owner, he began to beg.

"Dark Lords, dark masters, bequeath me this gift." The air in the tiny room grew foul, drew itself down towards blackness. Cornelisz felt it at the rear of his mind, a welcome weight like the pressure of a massive hand upon his bowed head. "Bequeath me this gift."

A voice in his ears, like the crashing of waves upon a distant cliff face, the language unknown but the tone questioning. Cornelisz bent lower, opened his mind as far as he was capable. "Land," he muttered. "Bring me land to house my Master."

The waves receded. Cornelisz held his breath. The candles under his hands were hot, burning designs into his palms. His mind crumbled under the force of the spirits leaning upon it. He tried to exhale, couldn't, panicked for a moment before giving in to the airlessness and the odour of decay within him. The waves sensed his submission, confirmed his obeisance. They crashed once more against his mind, then just as suddenly, were gone.

Cornelisz retched as the salt-and-sweat air of the ship reasserted itself, then quickly removed his hands from the candles. They were cold, of course, the skin of his hands clear and unblemished. He stared at them for a moment, then rubbed them down his vest. A dozen times he had performed this ritual, a dozen grovelling requests to the beings his Master, Torrentius, had introduced to him. Still, he was unnerved. He took a minute to control his ragged breathing, then swept the candles and chalk back into the bottom of his trunk and rubbed out the pentacle with the sleeves of his shirt.

He had barely finished when the ship hit the rocks.

No sooner had the last swirl of black air dissipated than a great screech of rending wood echoed through the hull. Cornelisz was thrown onto his face as the 650 ton ship came to a shuddering halt, lurched forward a dozen feet, and stopped again. The world tipped, then righted itself, stopping partway to the horizontal so that the floor fell away from him at the gentlest of angles. Cornelisz felt blood on his mouth, wiped it away with the back of his hand, then licked at the rest. He could hear screams now, the sounds of panic in the dark around him. Boot steps clattered as men leaped to all corners of the boat. Cornelisz laughed like a madman set free. He dragged himself to his feet, and staggered to the nearest ladder, then hauled himself up to the angled deck above.

Pelsaert and Jacobsz still stood on the poop deck, but their argument had devolved into a yelling match that sounded shrill and hysterical above the crashing waves. Cornelisz fought his way to the ladder, climbed so that he stood next to them.

"What has happened?" he yelled, struggling to keep the smirk from his face. Pelsaert had two fistfuls of the bigger man's shirt. He loosened his grip to point out over the thundering waters. "This drunkard," he yelled, "This utter fool has damned us all. He's run us aground!"

"Not I!" The skipper was swaying under the older man's assault, or the uncertain footing, or the half-pint of rum he had been sneaking all night with Cornelisz's quiet encouragement. A line of blood ran from one nostril, and a red welt was already forming on the side of his face. *Gods*, thought Cornelisz, *had Pelsaert struck him? Could things be going so well, so quickly?* "They were your directions! *Your* directions, not mine!"

Pelsaert lifted his hand again and Jacobsz responded in kind. Cornelisz risked a grin, and looked beyond them to the cliffs rising out of the sea, the gift he had received from his dark Lords. His smile died, to be replaced by an uncertain frown.

"Aground?" he asked? "On what?"

There were no cliffs. No bluff. No land of any type to meet his gaze. Only the rain, and the black clouds, and the white crests of waves as they rose high and smashed back down onto the backs of their neighbours. Pelsaert dragged Jacobsz to the edge of the deck and pushed him against the rail. Cornelisz followed.

"There!" the Commander shouted, pointing to something barely visible off the starboard bow. "That there."

Cornelisz followed his gaze. Thirty feet away, barely poking through the angry waters, lay two long lines of pallid sand. He stared at them, and felt dark laughter curling around the base of his skull.

"Land ho," he muttered. Ignoring the murderous glares of his compatriots he backed away, and slid back down to his shelter beneath the deck.

• • •

It took eight days to abandon ship. Pelsaert was inconsolable. All his dreams of glory, of advancement within the East India Company, vanished with the waters that slowly snuck in through the broken hull and swamped the lower decks. Cornelisz stayed to the end, sticking to the pretence that he could not swim and was afraid of the rising sea. In reality, Pelsaert's glory was doomed the day Cornelisz had persuaded Jacobsz to separate the *Batavia* from the protection of its little fleet as they rounded the Cape of Good Hope.

Cornelisz cared nothing for swimming or rescue. He had assembled a tiny band of mutineers on the promise of piracy and riches. Now he sat above them, in Pelsaert's stateroom, in Pelsaert's red-lined chair, and gave them a benevolent gaze as they grew drunk on the fulfilment of his promise.

Wine, there was, and chests of silver brought up from the hold, and baubles ripped from the chests of panicked families as they fought to desert the broken ship and gain the meagre safety of the tiny atolls that surrounded it. While the human cattle panicked, Cornelisz and his pirates lived like Gods of a dying world. Then the ship broke its back during the night. The silver descended into the water below, along with the wine and the drinking water. Grudgingly, in fear, sneaking along the timbers like careful rats, even the pirates deserted.

Finally, Cornelisz was alone. He stalked the halls of his crumbling empire, listening to the dark voices of his allies as they smashed against the empty vessel. Now, he could talk to them without interruption. Now, he could ask them why.

Torrentius had been gaoled two years ago. The Dutch had ensnared him, caged him with charges of heresy and Satanism, stripped him of followers, power, and freedom. But Cornelisz had escaped. He kept his allegiances secret, and formulated a plan to remove his Master to a refuge beyond the edge of the horizon, where a ship filled with riches, women, and disciples-for-the-making could be his. All he needed was a land on which to place them. "Why?" he asked the black voices as they ate his ship, "Why would you betray my Master like this?"

But the waves only laughed, and crushed the ship in their grasp. After four days of solitude Cornelisz abandoned his frenzied questions. Gripping a broken spar he washed up on the nearest island, to be treated by the weeping survivors like a returning saint.

"The Onderkoopman is saved! God bless Mister Cornelisz." They hauled him from the surf, laid him upon sand-encrusted blankets and warmed him next to the most pathetic fire Cornelisz had ever seen. When he was sufficiently rested, and had a gathering of his faithful around him, he allowed them to explain his rapturous reception.

Pelsaert had gone. The news almost set him to laughing. He had taken Jacobsz and nearly fifty of the ship's crew, and abandoned the rest to their fate. The survivors were leaderless, panicking, reliant upon the shrinking goodwill of the company soldiers who crouched at the far end of the island like a pack of snarling dogs. But now a representative of the Company was amongst them again, and the civilians were crying that their prayers were answered. Cornelisz listened in open amazement, and when they were finished with their story, he leaned back against the soft sand and closed his eyes.

"Oh, my friends," he said, to the waves that licked powerlessly against the land. "Prayers have been answered, indeed."

• • •

All their water lay in the ocean. The barrels of drinking water had fallen with the rest of the supplies. Now people were dying of thirst. The pirates were bored, and beginning to fight amongst themselves. The soldiers were casting long glances in their direction. Cornelisz looked over his tiny empire and saw it divided. Then a fool named

Woutersz got drunk—there was always drink, stashed in flasks and bottles by morons who would have been better served to pour them out and dip them in the barrels before they were lost—and bragged about his role in the aborted mutiny, and the treasure that was to be his.

Cornelisz met with his lieutenants. And the braggart was killed, deep in the night, when nobody was awake to see the knife sliding across his throat, and the stein held beneath the cut filling with blood that bubbled and hissed as it struck cold pewter.

Cornelisz drew designs in the wet sand of the tide line, and poured the hot blood inside. The laughing voices accepted his offer. And ten days after he dragged himself upon the shore, rain came to the tiny islands.

The people danced, and fell to their knees in unconscious imitation of Woutersz's last moments. They thanked the God that Cornelisz knew had played no part in their deliverance. Pots and pans were laid out to fill with water, barrels were opened and left under the deluge. Hammocks and blankets and canvases were stretched between tent poles, to fill and sag under the weight of the deliverance they caught. Through it all, Cornelisz sat in his tent and watched through the open flaps, counting the bodies that ran back and forth through the rain.

• • •

No man dies without leaving questions. Woutersz was not missed, but his absence *was* noted. His story gained weight, and credence. Soon enough, the soldiers marched down in double file and stood before Cornelisz's tent demanding answers to questions of loyalty and fitness for command. He stood at his tent flaps and stared Weibbe Hayes, their leader, in the eye, then invited him inside.

"Water," he said, as Hayes gazed at him across the driftwood table he had erected within. "The problem is water."

"Explain." Hayes was a simple man in Cornelisz's estimation. A common soldier, not even the highest rank within the company, but ramrod straight in bearing, bluff to a fault, a company man from the toes of his scuffed boots to his rank hair.

Cornelisz mistrusted simple men. He held up his empty mug and tilted it so Hayes could see inside.

"We've water enough for how long, do you think?"

Hayes squinted at him. "Days, perhaps. A week."

"And what happens then?" The two men glared at each other across the broken strip of wood. When Hayes gave no response, Cornelisz answered for him. "People start dying."

"People have already started dying."

"Woutersz?" Cornelisz gave a contemptuous shrug. "Some men in this company do not share the breeding of you and me, Private. Men get desperate. Desperate men . . . " He shrugged again.

"You're saying you don't know who killed him?"

"I'm saying neither you nor I know he was even killed." Cornelisz indicated the world outside the tent. "A man like Woutersz? Who is to say he didn't get drunk and try to swim back to the *Batavia*? Or take it into his head to follow our beloved Opperkoopman . . . " The venom in his voice could not be hidden, " . . . and fall off whatever plank he chose for his boat? The point is . . . " He jiggled the mug, recapturing the soldier's attention. "Woutersz has gone, and a whole colony of thirsty people remain. People who will become much thirstier in days. Perhaps a week."

Hayes stared at him through narrow eyes. "What is your point, Onderkoopman?"

Cornelisz smiled. "When there is nothing for soldiers to fight, it is time for them to become explorers."

• • •

It was all so simple. The soldiers lined up, two by two like animals ready for the ark, on the tiny beach. Two by two, they climbed into the colony's remaining boats. Cornelisz stood on the sand and watched a complement of his men pair off and climb into each boat after them, two by two. Then they rowed off, past the shallow breakers and across the water towards the largest of the islands, some hundreds of feet distant. The soldiers were searching for water, he had told the civilians. They were off to find our salvation. He and Hayes had agreed: once it was found they would light a fire. The boats would launch once more, to bring them back and the new-found water with them. Hayes sat in the last boat, stiff-backed and still-faced, and watched Cornelisz as the boats pushed away. Cornelisz matched his stare until they were too far apart to distinguish the soldier's features. Then he turned away.

"What happens when they send up the signal?" Jacop Pietersz, his most trusted lieutenant, asked, as they trudged the short distance towards Cornelisz's tent. "What do we do then?"

"There is no water."

"How do you know?"

"The waves told me." Cornelisz brushed past Pietersz and into his tent, sealing himself away from the world.

The water *had* told him, on the beach, his fingers sticky with blood and sand and his head bowed under the pounding blackness of their presence. The islands were dry, empty, bereft. There was no life here, except that which he promised to sacrifice to the waves and which they would give him in return. That was why he had despatched the soldiers. His greatest threat, stranded on a rock with no water, no weapons, and only themselves to feast upon when hunger and thirst and madness brought them to the edge of death. Cornelisz smiled, and indulged in a long draught of precious water. Only two things remained: the civilians he had promised the waves, and the men who would carry out the sacrifice.

Cornelisz was ready to free his Master.

• • •

Heat is the source of all change in the world. It can bend and liquefy metal; turn sand to glass; crack stone; turn sprout to full-grown plant. Heat is the lingua franca of the universe, the element that makes magic work. It opens up the walls between the worlds and makes all things possible. The closer to the life force of the universe the source is, the more powerful the magic it makes. Fire is close. Small magics can be accomplished with fire. But for great feats, for opening up a tunnel across the ether between Holland and the edge of the world and dragging a man through, something greater is required.

In the hierarchy of magic, nothing is hotter than blood.

For the price of three lives, the waves gave him clear weather so his men could strip the *Batavia* of straight wood and metal for weapons. For a family of six, they weakened his subjects so they could not object when gathered all food and water and impounded it within the circle of his militia's tents. For a gaggle of sickly victims they directed his men to a tent at the far corner of the ragged colony, and served him up a concubine.

Cornelisz had lusted after Lucretia Van der Mylen from the moment he first saw her. Dainty little Lucretia, tiptoeing about the ship like her tits were too perfect for touching. Aloof Lucretia, keeping her tiny waist and long, white neck covered in preparation for her new husband, who loved her so much he had left her to make the journey alone. A husband who scurried ahead to Java to get his pego polished by Asian whores. Pelsaert's favourite passenger. His swan amongst savages. Cornelisz had watched from the *Batavia's* rigging as a group of his pirates-to-be attacked her in an effort to bring Pelsaert into disrepute. Cornelisz remembered her skin in the dim moonlight; her slim, white figure twisting, writhing as his men tore her clothes off; saw the swinging of her breasts and heard the slap of his men's hands against her firm arse cheeks in his daydreams.

The sacrifice of a herd of puking cattle was nothing to have her kneeling in the sand before him, head bowed so he could see the arch of her neck through her unwashed hair.

Cornelisz once smashed a vase worth a thousand guilder, just to know he could destroy something so beautiful and get away with it. It took a week— a week where she twisted away at his every approach and screamed every time he tried to touch her—before Pietersz held a knife to her throat and explained just how long it would take her to die if she refused to let Cornelisz break *her*. After that, he broke her whenever he felt like it.

His men took women too. Now the struggle was to get them out from their tents, to give them a sense of purpose. Cornelisz formed them into six teams of four and set them to work. They were the only ones who had weapons, water, direction. Everyone else was livestock, to be fed to the waves.

The island was small, perhaps a mile in length, but after so long pressed together in the Batavia's cramped quarters, the civilians had scattered across it as soon as they were able. Cornelisz sent his men among them in the dark, quiet as panthers. Every night, he sacrificed warm, fresh blood to the waves, until the beach smelled of offal and his fingers were never free of the sand that stuck to them. He returned to his bed after midnight, battling Lucretia's cold and unmoving body, until the only reason he had for digging his fingers into the sand was the pleasure of driving their gritty lengths inside her to hear her pain. Every night he fell to his knees in the tide line, bowed his head over the cooling bodies of his prey, and begged the waves to bring him Torrentius. And every night they slithered up onto the beach to whisper in his ears.

"More, more."

The men were beyond caring. They did not share his passion, or care for his cause. They were simply savages he had chained to his banner. So long as they could kill, fuck and stay drunk on the diminishing stores of rum, they were content to wreak carnage on the defenceless civilians. Soon, not even the darkness was enough. Killings began to occur during the day. Random, indiscriminate slaughter, with no thought for consequence or the magic that was lost. Cornelisz watched a pack chase a child along the beach before cutting it down with wild glee, passing around a flagon of rum as they each took turns to hack at the moaning body. He held his knuckles to his mouth as his carefully prepared altar became an abattoir, without ritual or request. Finally, as the child's body was dragged across the sand and thrown unceremoniously into the water, he set his face and sought out Pietersz.

"They need a lesson," he said. "Something to show they are not indispensable. They are servants to my cause, not free men."

"What do you want?" Pietersz lounged on a rescued hammock. His concubine, a girl of perhaps thirteen, sat in his lap, swigging from a bottle. Cornelisz turned his gaze from them, saw a tent alone at the far edge of the ridge upon which they sat. A hospital, of sorts, where sick children had been deposited to cough and moan in isolation.

"Gather the men," he said. "And find me a boy with a good arm."

• • •

Andries De Vries was twenty, and his only crime was to admire from afar the beautiful young wife of a trader on the voyage out from Holland. But nothing on the *Batavia* had gone unwitnessed. Now that wife was the chattel of the islands' ruler, his crime had returned to doom him. He knelt on the rough sand between the tents, surrounded by Cornelisz's men, while the Onderkoopman stood before him.

"Andries," Cornelisz said, as the young man tried desperately not to cry. He had already wet himself, much to the amusement of the ring of killers. Cornelisz leaned over and gripped his trembling jaw, raising his head so their eyes met. "Andries, I have to decide what to do with you."

The men sniggered. Cornelisz tensed for a moment, then turned to the nearest. "Walter, your knife."

The crony hesitated. Cornelisz clicked his fingers. Reluctantly, Walter passed it over: a sliver of sharpened angle iron tied into the end of a bone. Cornelisz contemplated it, turning it this way and that, then aimed the point towards Andries' eye. The young man squeezed his eyes shut, tried to turn his head away, but Cornelisz held his jaw tight, and he could not.

"Andries. Andries." Cornelisz gave his head a shake. "Look at me. No. Look at me." The young man did as he was ordered.

"You could be killed, Andries. I think we all acknowledge that." More sniggers from the surrounding killers. "But I need you to emphasise a point for me. Will you do that?" Cornelisz raised his gaze and took in his cadre. "Everyone here was selected for a purpose, and only that purpose." He looked back down at his young captive. "And now I have selected you." He turned the knife around, held out the handle. "Take it. Go on. Take it."

Andries stared at it in terror. Cornelisz leaned closer, pinched his jaw tighter. "If you don't take it, I'll have to tell them to kill you. This is the only way you live. Take it, my boy." Cornelisz reached for an unresisting hand. He placed the blade into it, and drew Andries up to his feet.

"There are only two classes on this island. Those who do what I tell them, and the dead. Is that clear?" He was addressing the whole group now, his voice strident, intense. He turned Andries towards the tent at the top of the rise. "Twenty children lie in that tent. Twenty useless mouths, eating our food, drinking our water, shitting and mewling and sucking up our diminishing resources with nothing in return. It is time we dispensed with this drain on our wealth." He looked to Andries. "Well?"

The young man stared from him, to the blade, to the tent, then back. He took a step away, staggered as he felt the pinprick of blades at his back. He made to drop the knife, but Cornelisz's hand was around his, clenching tight, trapping the handle inside his fist.

"They die, or you do, boy. I have no preference." He nodded to Pietersz. The older man took the unwilling conscript by the arm, frogmarched him to the entrance of the tent, and opened it. Cornelisz watched as he whispered something in the boy's ear. They matched stares for a dozen heartbeats. Then the younger man's head dropped, and he disappeared inside the tent.

By the time he returned, red-armed and weeping, Cornelisz had summoned Lucretia. She stood by his side, two henchmen behind her, while Andries staggered down the rise and dropped the knife in the sand at Cornelisz's feet. Cornelisz smiled at him.

"Now," he said, "tell her."

"What?" The boy could barely speak. His throat was swollen shut from grief, his eyes puffed and raw, streaked with blood where he had wiped tears away. Cornelisz glanced at his men. "Tell her what you have done."

"I . . . "

"Do it, boy."

Andries glanced at Pietersz, who had sidled into his range of vision. In short bursts, in words belched out rather than spoken, Andries confessed his task. Lucretia burst into tears long before he finished.

"What have you done?" she moaned, and it was not clear whether she spoke to the boy or his tormentor. "How could you? How could you do this?"

Cornelisz retrieved the knife from the sand and handed it back to its owner. The henchman dragged Lucretia back to his tent. He waited until they had returned, then addressed the group.

"Learn this," he said. "Anyone can be taught to do what you do. This lad is proof of that. I require only two things from you. Obedience and loyalty. That is your first lesson. As to your second . . . " He turned his gaze upon the sobbing murderer at his feet. "Stand up, boy." Andries did so. Cornelisz turned him towards the open beach. "Go on," he said gently, "Go on. You're free to go."

Andries staggered a few steps, righted himself. He began to walk away then, as sudden fear and repulsion overcame him, to run. Cornelisz watched him go, then turned back to his men. "As to the second," he said, his voice tight as a garrotte. "Disobey me, exceed your instructions, betray me, and I'll have you hunted down like vermin." He pointed to three men at random. "You, you, and you. Talking out of turn is an act of betrayal. Kill him."

The men grinned, and ran in pursuit of the fleeing Andries. Cornelisz sneered at the remainder of his group.

"Out of my sight until I need you again."

They went in silence.

• • •

Cornelisz crouched on the sand and watched the traitorous ocean. The sacrifices were not working. The waves had grown still. Torrentius lay in prison on the far side of the globe, and he, his most faithful servant, sat trapped on a lie of an island, surrounded by the smell of the dead. The waters were thick with blood. More than two dozen had fed them, and still there was no portal through which he could draw his Master, no deliverance for the man whose dreams he should be bringing closer with every killing.

"What do you want?" he asked the grey wash. "Why do you not reward my loyalty?" He scooped up a nearby stone and flung it. It skipped across the face of the waves, three times, four, then sank. "What do you want?"

A susurration at the back of his mind. A darkness that engulfed him in an instant, and pressed his face flat on the ground, filling his mouth and nose with sand.

"A King for a King," they whispered. "A King for a King."

And then they were gone, and Cornelisz was coughing and spitting sand and the waves were falling against the beach, laughing, always laughing.

• • •

"Come in, Father. Sit down."

Predikant Bastiaenz was a dithering old fool, but he had retained enough sense to keep his family as far from the centre of the whirlwind as possible. Cornelisz had no love of priests. It was priests who had declared Torrentius a heretic and a Satanist, who dragged him from his bed in the middle of the night and threw him into the dungeons of the Tuchthuis. Cornelisz was no friend of priests. But the old man was hardly kin to the hard-faced ascetics who tore down his Master's church. Cornelisz needed no enemies. All he needed were tools.

"Tell me, Father," he asked as the old man attacked his thin soup like a starving man, which, Cornelisz conceded, he was. "Do you consider Jesus your King?"

Bastiaenz slapped his lips together and frowned in concentration. "A complicated question, my son . . . " He eyed the loaf of hard bread in the middle of the table. Cornelisz pushed it towards him with a smile.

"Here, please, have some more."

"Thank you, thank you." He tore off a hunk big enough for two, plunged it into his broth, and sucked noisily at it.

"You were saying?"

"Yes, yes." He slurped down a gobbet of bread. "A complicated question. We are all under our Lord's rule—"

"Oh, certainly."

"But the Kingdom of Heaven belongs to any man who truly accepts the Lord Jesus as his saviour."

"Is that so?" Cornelisz leaned back in his chair. "We are all Kings in Jesus' eyes, then."

"We are all equal under his gaze."

"Good." Cornelisz smiled. "You have a big family, Father, all tucked away nice and warm in your tent, I hope. A wife and five children, is it? No, six. Six children."

"As warm as can be achieved." Bastiaenz paused, spoon halfway to his lips.

"And are they all Kings, father? All your children, and your big, homely wife, all cuddled together in your tent? Are they all Kings to Jesus?"

The old man laid his spoon down, and regarded Cornelisz with serious eyes. "Anyone who accepts the Lord into his heart, who works for the betterment of his Kingdom, is as a King in Heaven, Onderkoopman. All will be received to His Bosom as if they were Kings on Earth."

"Oh, that *is* good to hear." Cornelisz smiled and pushed the bread closer to his guest. "Eat up, Father. Eat up."

• • •

Cornelisz paced from one wall of his tent to another, then back again. A dozen steps, over and over. Lucretia hunkered down in one corner, too afraid to move lest he turn his rage upon her, but he was past caring. She was immaterial, now. He would kill her, just to be rid of the problem of her, but there seemed little point. Nothing was working. Nothing was having an effect. He had given the waves their Kings, a whole family of them, had performed the rituals and made the proper obeisances, and his only reward was an image, afloat above the water: not even of Torrentius, but of an ascetic Englishman with sad eyes and a perfumed collar, his thin pointed face turned towards Cornelisz as if momentarily interrupted from the task of governing his country.

"I know what a King looks like," Cornelisz muttered, kicking at the tent wall as he turned once again. He screamed through the open flaps towards the waves, unseen from this angle but hissing across the sand and into his ears, always hissing. "I know what a King looks like!"

"That's good." Pietersz stepped into the tent and gave his commander a quizzical glance.

"What do you want?"

"You might want to come and look at this."

"Don't bother me. I don't have time—"

"You should make some."

"Don't—" Cornelisz stopped. Something in Pietersz's manner made him pause, some nervousness or uncertainty he had not seen before. Cornelisz nodded towards the outside world. "All right. Show me."

The two men hurried down towards the beach. More of his men were gathered, gawking across the water towards a thin plume of smoke.

"The soldiers," one of them shouted, pointing towards it as if Cornelisz could not see it with his own eyes. "The soldiers."

Cornelisz stared at the smoke in disbelief. It had been three weeks since they abandoned Hayes and his men on the distant island. There could not possibly be water on that miserable rock, no way for the company to keep themselves alive. But there was the smoke, undeniable against the blue sky, shouting to any civilians who may care to see it: we have found water. We have found hope. Cornelisz turned to Pietersz.

"Who else has seen this?"

Pietersz shrugged. "Probably everyone on the island by now."

Cornelisz stared past him, to the water and the laughing waves. "A King for a King," they hissed as they slithered onto the sand and back again. "A King for a King."

"Kill them all," he said.

"What?"

"All of them." Cornelisz stalked to the tide line and began kicking the water as it reached for him. "Kill them all. Every one!"

Pietersz wheeled away and yelled to his men, the bloodlust in his voice like a blast of nausea in Cornelisz's ears.

"You heard the man!"

Cornelisz's cadre streamed up the beach towards their tents and weapons. Cornelisz stared across the water as they left him, watching Hayes's signal rise into the sky like proof of a burning world.

A King for a King. One leader of men for another. And he would provide, even if he had to kill the man himself.

• • •

For a week they slaughtered anyone they could catch, hunting down the weak and slow like a pack of hungry dogs. Cornelisz stuck close to his tent, allowing them full reign, consoling himself with mastery of Lucretia: one hand for dispensing punishment and the other to pin her tight while he gave himself over to whatever pleasure he wished. After five days he tired of her, and stepped outside to sneer at the carnage around him. Men lay in drunken disarray, their dissolute concubines laid out beside or beneath them as they rutted like animals in the dirt. From afar came the sounds of pursuit, high keening whistles as groups of predators chased their prey through the scattered gorse, and the occasional scream, abruptly cut off, as they ran their victims to ground. And above everything, the laughter of the deep waters, mocking his feeble massacre. He stepped between his debauched minions, and found Pietersz at the head of the beach.

"Ah, you've rejoined us." Pietersz eyed him sideways. "Figured you didn't leave any explicit instructions, so I let the boys enjoy themselves."

"How many done properly?" Cornelisz stared at the muddy sands. At the far end of the beach a body bobbed gently face down in the wash. Cornelisz did not recognise it. Just another civilian to feed the waves. He flexed his fingers and felt no warmth in them.

"Some," Pietersz replied. "Not many." He cocked his head as, somewhere towards the centre of the island, someone started screaming, high and hopeless. "Lot of trouble to drag them all down here."

Cornelisz wandered to the ocean's edge. The voices were stronger here, mocking him, pricking him with one word whispered over and over like a taunt. "King, King, King . . . ." He crouched and scratched a line of runes into the wet sand, watched the water wash over them and eat them.

"Soon," he whispered to them. "And then you give me what I want, or so help me . . . "

"The scurf licked at his fingers, cooling them, calming them. A promise from the edge of the darkness. He rubbed them together, feeling the salt on his skin. "Anything else?"

"Not much."

"The other island?"

Pietersz stayed silent. Cornelisz glanced up from his contemplation. The other man shuffled his foot through the sand, shrugged.

"Smoke went out a few days back."

"And?" Cornelisz rose, stood close enough to Pietersz to draw the remaining truth from his reluctant lips.

"A few escapees," the nervous lieutenant admitted. "Probably made it across. We couldn't get them all."

"Escapees?" Cornelisz heard his voice rising, saw the flush in his lieutenant's face.

"Yeah, well, you weren't exactly here to keep things in order, were you? It's a big island. Once they knew we were coming, they didn't stand around waiting to be caught, did they?"

"And how did they get across several hundred feet of open water?" This, to the waves. Pietersz, misunderstanding the nature of the question, providing a reply.

"Bits of driftwood, mostly. Some swimmers. A couple managed to build a raft."

"A raft? How long does it take to build a damned raft?" Cornelisz felt his hands curl into fists. Pietersz saw the action and hunkered down onto the balls of his feet: a fighter, expecting the fight.

"Long as it takes to keep out of the way of a bunch of leaderless men with drink in them, I expect."

"And what kind of leader are you?"

"One who follows orders." He measured Cornelisz with cautious eyes. "The Predikant is with them."

"They know, then. You've let them find out what we've been doing." Cornelisz quivered with anger. It would be a small thing, to attack this man. A small moment, giving in to the anger that threatened to turn his mind red. Instead, he forced breath through his nose, peeled his fingers back into single digits, turned away from his second-in-command and contemplated the hole in the horizon where the smoke no longer rose.

"No matter," he said through gritted teeth. "A smattering of hungry, ragged civilians. Let him have them." He inhaled deeply, let it back out again. "They've no weapons, no means of escape."

"You said that about the water."

Cornelisz let the words fall to earth unanswered.

"Get the men organised," he said. "Kick them sober if you have to. I want them armed and ready to man the boats by dawn."

"What about the rest of the civilians?"

"To hell with them." Cornelisz flexed his fingers. The itch for Lucretia had returned to them. "I have bigger sacrifices in mind."

• • •

They departed just after first light. Six boats, filled with as many men as were armed and willing to kill a soldier for Cornelisz: every one of his original cadre and a dozen more who had joined them since the first night of killing, drawn by the promise of rum and women and continued survival. They were back by midday the following day, their numbers depleted, one boat missing altogether.

"They've built a fort," Pietersz reported. "Piled rocks up into walls."

"You have the only weapons. You had superiority of numbers."

"They had the walls, and the high ground, and enough rocks to throw down on us all day and all night. And water."

Cornelisz dismissed him with a contemptuous flick of the hand. The men went back to their drinking and their women. The waves laughed silently against the shore. Cornelisz returned to his tent, and Lucretia, and his sand-stained fingers driving deep inside her while she wept.

They tried again, once the men had tended their wounds and replenished their bloodlust. And again, in the following week. The ground and the stone walls and Hayes's bloody-minded courage repelled them. Cornelisz screamed his defiance at the waves, and they, in turn, whispered in his mind as he slept, showing him pictures of his Master, buried deep within Government dungeons, waiting for rescue that never arrived. As the second week became a third, Cornelisz grew tired of their taunting, and gathered his men once more.

"Across," he ordered, climbing into the prow of the lead boat and setting his back to the shore.

"Are you sure about this?" Pietersz asked, as they crested the first line of breakers and pushed out into the channel between the islands.

"About what?"

"Well," Pietersz shrugged, "You've not been forthcoming in doing this sort of stuff yourself so far."

"Perhaps," Cornelisz favoured him with a sidelong glance that took in all his failures. "I should have done so much earlier."

"Perhaps," Pietersz replied sourly, "Perhaps."

Hayes' island was half the size of Cornelisz's, with the same low, scrubby vegetation that scratched at their legs and caught their trousers as they trudged out of the boats and up the well-worn paths they had followed during the failed assaults. Above them, on the single hill the island possessed, lay the ramshackle assemblage of stone walls that Hayes had fashioned for his defence. Cornelisz eyed them with distaste.

"They're tiny," he remarked.

Pietersz sighed.

"Small, but aided by the rise. All we have are our blades and poles. They can throw stones down onto us long before we get close enough to use them."

Cornelisz turned away from him.

"Attack," was his only reply.

• • •

They attacked, again and again, and were forced back, again and again. For every foot they pushed forward they fell back ten inches, creeping their way across the rise until they camped directly under one of the walls, protected from the falling rocks by a spur of sand and a thick covering of vegetation.

"They're running low," Pietersz reported as they crouched below their meagre covering.

"How do you know?"

"The rocks aren't as heavy as before. They're waiting until we get closer."

"Then push harder," Cornelisz shouted. "Push faster."

"We're exhausted. Half the men are injured. We've no supplies, and hardly any water."

"All the more reason to finish them now, don't you think?"

Pietersz opened his mouth to reply. One of the men behind him slapped him on the back. "What?"

The attacker pointed across the rise towards the tiny bay upon which their boats had landed.

"A sail," Pietersz whispered, then louder, "A sail!"

Cornelisz stared at it in mounting horror. A single white sail, a smudge against the grey-black of the ocean, no more than half an hour away.

"Pelsaert," he whispered. Pelsaert, who had abandoned the colony, had slipped out at night with nothing more than a boat and a handful of sailors, throwing empty promises behind him. Ragged cheers broke out amongst the soldiers in the fort. Cornelisz snapped back to the present.

"Get a boat." He pushed Pietersz. "Get out there, now!"

"And do what?"

"Stop Hayes getting there first!" Already, they could see soldiers scrambling down the far side of the hill, racing towards the beach. Cornelisz and Pietersz exchanged panicked glances. "Move, you fool!"

Pietersz slithered back down the rise, pushing subordinates before him as he went. Half a dozen of the men took off in pursuit. Cornelisz turned back to the wall above him. There was nothing for it now. All he could do was take the fort, kill Hayes before the ship arrived. Once Torrentius was summoned, the power of the Master and his allies in the dark would remove Pelsaert, the ship, and all who stood between Cornelisz and the new world.

"Move it, you rabble!" he shouted. "Over this wall and kill them all!"

· · ·

Cornelisz walked the line of shackled prisoners and stared down at them with undisguised contempt. Waves crashed against the sand behind him, their laughter loud in his ears. The captives kneeled on the hot sand, their heads bowed in abject misery and surrender. Cornelisz reached the end of the line, and turned to face the way he had come.

"Pathetic," he announced. "Utterly pathetic, each and every one of you."

"That will be enough!" Commander Pelsaert stood a dozen steps away, surrounded by the men of the ship *Sardam*. "Put that man on his knees."

The sailor who had hold of Cornelisz's shackles kicked his

knees out from underneath him. Cornelisz sank to the ground. The sailor grabbed his hair and yanked it back so he could look into the face of the Commander, and see the rough gallows that had been erected at the head of the beach. Behind Pelsaert he could see Hayes, unbowed despite the fury of the battle three days previous, and beside him, the gaunt figure of Lucretia, staring poison over the Opperkoopman's shoulder. Cornelisz grinned, and had it wiped from his face by the back of the sailor's hand. He tasted blood, and spat it onto the sand.

"For the act of mutiny against the rightful command of the ship *Batavia*, I find you guilty," Pelsaert began to intone. "For the crime of murder against no less than one hundred and twenty of the King's citizens, I find you . . . "

"Oh, for everyone's sake just shut the hell up and get on with it, you decrepit old windbag!" Cornelisz shouted his scorn across the beach. "Don't leave us out here in the sun to burn to death."

Pelsaert gazed at him like a child about to step on a bug. "Very well," he said, "If you wish." He nodded to the sailor at Cornelisz's back. The sailor tugged him to his feet. Cornelisz shrugged him off for a moment, but the sailor grabbed his wrist and twisted, grinding the bone hard against the metal of his cuffs so that he gasped with pain. He was dragged in front of Pelsaert and forced back to his knees. Hayes stepped forward, and laid a block of wood in front of him. Cornelisz was freed from his shackles long enough for two sailors to grab his forearms and stretch his hands across the block.

"What is this? What is this?" Cornelisz struggled, but his captors had the advantage of weight and angle, and held his arms rigid. He stared up at Pelsaert.

"The sentence is death."

"Of course it is. But what is *this*?"

Pelsaert smiled; a cold, thin little thing full of disdain. "I have been reminded by Mrs Van der Mylen of a clause in company law relating to the penalties for acts of treason. I am told that it is, in this case, particularly apt." He turned to Hayes. "Remove his hands."

Hayes stepped forward. He held a hammer in one hand and, in the other, a chisel.

Cornelisz screamed once after the first blow, then watched silently from a million miles away as the second descended. It took eight blows in all. Cornelisz stopped counting after three, and caring after four. The sailors to either side kept him upright as his hands were lifted from the block and carried down to the water's edge. Then they were thrown into the waves. The ocean ate them with glee. As if to thank him for this final gift, the darkness shut off his view of the world and accorded him one final vision.

His master Torrentius stood before him, brush in hand, a canvas sitting on an easel at his shoulder. On the far side of the board sat the same ascetic, sharp-faced King with whom the waves had once tormented Cornelisz, his shoulders wrapped in ermine, his neck and wrists dripping with jewels. A King for a King, the voices whispered. Cornelisz felt his blood dripping onto the sand, imagined it staining the water, and understood, at last, the sacrifice they required.

The waves had given him an island and he had made himself its King. And in return for his sacrifice, the King of another island would travel to Holland and free Torrentius, as Torrentius and his dark allies had desired all along.

Cornelisz laughed, and the spirits laughed along with him. They laughed as he was carried along the beach, his blood staining the sand with every step; as the noose was tightened around his throat; as he was hoisted above the sand, and the water, and the cares of the world.

They laughed, until the only sound in the entire world was the pounding of waves in his ears.

FLIGHT

ANGELA SLATTER

The feathers were tiny and Emer hoped they would stay so.

Indeed, she prayed they would fall out altogether. They were not downy little pins. Small, but determined, their black shafts hardened as soon as they poked through her skin, calcifying under her touch as she stroked them in dreadful fascination.

All day she'd felt something happening beneath the gloves hastily donned after her morning's escapade. The sight of those ladylike coverings had brought approving nods from both her mother and governess, as if they were a sign she was *finally* listening to their exhortations. *A princess does not run. A princess does not shout or curse. A princess keeps the sun in her voice, but off her fair skin. A princess sits quietly, back straight. A princess smiles at a gentleman's tasteful jest, but never laughs too loudly. A princess never furrows her brow with thought. A princess does not chew her nails.*

Emer had been determined that nothing untoward was occurring; that the healing salve she'd sneaked from her mother's workroom would put everything to rights.

But that night, when Emer closed her bedchamber door and finally peeled away the doeskin gloves, she found that the wound in her palm was sprouting dark fronds around its ragged edge. They looked like the collar of her mother's favourite cloak— except those feathers with their vibrant eyes were from the palace peacocks. A great ball of fear threatened to stopper her throat.

It had been the madness of a moment, to sneak away and run through the gardens with the sky so blue, the clouds so white, the grass such a vibrant green. Trembling in the breeze, the flowers shone like delicate gems: wine-dark amethysts, sun-bright topazes, heavenly sapphires, rubies red as blood, beryl the colour of a storm-tossed sea and, stranger still, the roses.

She'd danced and run, bounded and rolled like a child of five not a young lady of thirteen. Not like a princess on the eve of her fealty ceremony, someone who shouldn't frolic until her gown, once a triumph of pink embroidered with daffodils, had its hem torn and trailing, one sleeve held in place by four tenuous threads, and grass and dirt staining the pattern. Tradition decreed the heir—even if, to the regret of many, she was female—be left unattended this day, not so she could *play*, but so that she might stand vigil, alone, unsupervised and mature, meditating on her future life of state. Preparing to pledge herself to the land, to be its sovereign and its succour, now and always.

Leaving the manicured lawns upon which she was usually permitted a chaperoned stroll, Emer had wandered into unkempt areas where the demarcation between garden and myrkwood was little more than a rough boundary of aged briars. Smooth malachite stems spiked with roses' thorns—roses black as ebony!—entwined seamlessly with the gray and brittle barbs of the brambles.

A burning glow from the heart of each bloom had compelled her closer; an opalescent flash of green and red and gold, orange and azure and magenta had drawn her. She'd reached out to touch the nearest one, careful to avoid its prickles. The petals were like velvet. As she pulled away, she felt a stabbing pain in her upturned hand.

One moment the air in front of her was empty and the next, a raven, which had sat so still that it'd been invisible in the chest-high hedge, occupied the space with regal mien, its claws fixed tightly around the briar barrier. The crimson wound in the centre of Emer's palm showed where it had made its mark.

Emer stared at the bird; its feathers glistened tenebrous-dark, yet radiant as if moonlight had been woven into their undersides. The raven gave a harsh cry—if she hadn't known better, she'd have said it sounded apologetic—and Emer noticed its eyes burned with the same fire as the blossoms, colours flickering and dying, only to be replaced by the next brilliant hue. The creature took off, flying higher and growing smaller until finally it dove, plummeting straight at the girl, veering at the last second and shooting into the shadowy depths of the forest.

That was when Emer's nerve had broken. Hitching her skirts, she'd fled to her rooms, changed her dress and hid the destroyed one. She'd smoothed her hair and washed her face, slipped on the snug gloves, and spent the afternoon, heart aflutter, sitting in the solar. Feigning contemplation of the book on her lap whenever her mother or governess swept past, and hoping ever so hard that nothing would come of her misadventure.

Now, Emer removed her frock slowly, fearfully, wondering why she did not feel the cold. She stood in front of the mirror and turned. An inverted feathery triangle lay across her back and shoulders. At the nape of her neck were knots and twists where her tresses had begun to tangle into a kind of plumage. Her nails had toughened, lengthened and grown points. Her thumbs and little fingers were shorter.

Yet she did not call for help.

Emer knew the price of magic—something outlawed since the beginning of her father's reign. Herbcraft was acceptable; although leechwork was a gray area, its benefits were acknowledged; but witchcraft? Enchantments had enabled the Black Bride to bring calamity, to blind the King to the one he loved, to almost ruin a prosperous land, and to leave the Queen permanently scarred. Emer, transforming as she was, must be committing sorcery, even if it wasn't her choice.

No, she would not call for help. Surely it would go away. Surely all she needed was to apply more of her mother's lavender nostrum. Surely in the morning, she thought, upending the bottle of ointment and slopping it up her arms, surely by then this would all be gone.

• • •

At dawn, as the final act of her vigil the princess dressed all by herself for the first and last time.

A cream silk wimple, a veil of amaranthine gossamer, and a circlet of engraved gold hid the tight calamus cap her hair had become. Only Emer's un-feathered face remained visible. Her high-necked ruby robe had sleeves long and loose enough to conceal her glossy black body and her arms, which were rapidly knitting into wings. Stubbornly, she fumbled with gloves, but didn't bother with shoes—her legs had wizened, toughened with dusky gray skin, finished with pronged feet. Now three clawed toes *click-click-clicked* as she walked.

And so it was that the kingdom's firstborn, pride and joy (and occasional frustration) of her royal parents, entered the great hall with a strange new gait. Her eyes, once blue, were black, and her head moved this way and that, taking everything in with a darting gaze. She promenaded along the ermine carpet to where her parents sat, enthroned and enthralled by her terrible progress.

When she stood before them, dropping into the queerest curtsey ever seen, the Queen and King began to weep and wail respectively.

Emer's hands convulsed and the delicate gloves, which had been shoved onto the tips of her transmuting fingers, fell away as the flesh melded. The gown, too, was rent, and soon the princess was jiggling about on one leg then the other, kicking away the rags. Her head grew rounder, tinier, and her ears disappeared; the coronet slid down to sit around her neck like a collar. Wimple and veil hung loose until she shook them off. Emer's nose and mouth speared into a scintillating beak.

Ladies-in-waiting screamed and lords bellowed. The noise was astonishing; it swelled until the crescendo broke over the raven-girl and she tottered about, looking for escape. One of the high-reaching windows was open to allow the cool breeze in, and she half-ran, half-skipped towards it, shrinking, until the golden circlet slipped away and she leapt through the opening as if performing a circus trick. She hopped onto the sill, gave her parents one last look, and *caw-cawed*, a sound that echoed the whole sad length and breadth of the chamber.

With one swift beat of her new wings she caught an updraft. Her parents, released from their paralysis, ran to the window and watched as their daughter joined a waiting unkindness of ravens that greeted her with croaks. The sun kissed her wings and she and the birds were gone, faster than thought, faster than possibility.

• • •

They flew toward the horizon. Emer-that-was wondered how far they'd come—and when they'd stop—as they floated over fields and rivers, mountains and valleys, towers and turrets of rulers petty and great. But Emer-of-feathers did not ponder, merely obeyed instinct and followed her fellows. They flew for so long that Emer-that-was despaired of ever finding her way back.

When finally they began to descend, it was toward a huge granite edifice positioned astride a river, nothing like Emer's hilltop home of polished marble and clear glass. This was a castle fit for battle, with windows so slender they were suitable only for shooting arrows through, or sending out the occasional pigeon bearing a message to an attacking general, saying he may as well piss into the wind, for this bastion would never fall to the likes of him.

The flock aimed itself at the closed portcullis, winging precisely through the grille, Emer as lithe and light as the rest. They traversed a deserted courtyard, thence towards a great set of doors hewn from oak and banded with silver. The doors, as if sensing their approach, opened at the very last moment, but the winged host did not slow, did not hesitate, as if cooperation was to be expected.

They flew along hallways lined with threadbare tapestries and paintings of people who'd been obscured not by time but by the tearing and shredding of canvas. They flew through rooms lined with rows of weapon racks filled with rusting swords and battleaxes, unstrung bows, decaying spears and toothless morning stars. They flew through bedchambers so thick with dust they had to rely purely on intuition to navigate. They flew until at last they came to a hall as lofty and lengthy as a cathedral's nave, as cool and dim as one too, for most of the tall pointed windows were shuttered. At the farthest end sat a woman.

Bustling around the chamber was an army of servants. Here and there, valets and footmen, butlers and a majordomo, maids and ladies-in-waiting, some of them in the costume of courtiers and some of them in rustic attire, but Emer had no doubt they were all, without exception, slaves. No matter their garb, none wore human form. Each was canine, walking upright and wearing a motley mix of livery, using fans, carrying trays, bearing tea pots and saucers, one the lord of a samovar, another king of the canapés.

Emer glided onwards, unaware that her companions had dropped behind. She slowed, and descended, carefully avoiding the shifting mass of what appeared to be large rabbits—no, hares kicking at each other in occasional ill-temper. She alighted on the shabby red carpet leading to the dais upon which a cushioned throne was set. Three short steps separated her from black-booted toes.

Lifting her gaze, Emer took in the woman's face, gypsy-hued, marred with long-healed scars; her hair and eyes like jet, lips like a damson plum. And the features somehow familiar, yet Emer could not place them. The woman in a long charcoal dress, with carmined nails, smiled down at the raven who was a girl. Emer shuddered deep inside her hollow-boned body. She wished to fly, to flee, but her limbs would not obey.

The dark one limped down the stairs to gather up the bird. She tucked Emer under her arm as one might a chicken, and stroked her with a hand almost entirely curled in upon itself. Emer recoiled, willing her talons to lash out and tear, her beak to stab and shred, but her body was contrary. All she could do was shiver. Clicking her fingers, the woman produced a chain as fine as thread from thin air. The thing shone and shimmered as she twisted it twice around the raven's right foot. Emer watched as the metal fused. The other end was looped through the intricately carved rose-and-briar pattern adorning the top of the throne.

The woman's voice, when she spoke, was strange, a mix of the sweet and the discordant—only later would the girl realize it came of the scars at the base of her throat.

"Now. Now you are secure, my little one, the game has begun."

Emer, finding her own voice unaffected by whatever paralysed her body, gave an answering cry.

"Come, come—you want to help me, don't you? And if I take my fun at the same time, then what harm?" She laughed. "Would you like a story, my dear one? My sweet sister's darling child? Shall we begin thus? Once upon a time . . ."

And Emer listened as her unsuspected aunt told of two sisters, one swan-white, the other raven-dark. All the while the girl wondered how long she would be in this shape. How long before all she began to think of were bugs and beetles, worms and carrion. How long it would take for someone to find her. And Emer despaired because she knew her parents believed the Black Bride defeated and dead. They would never find their raven-daughter because they would never think to hunt for a ghost.

• • •

The girl spent many months feathered and tethered.

Each night she heard the Black Bride's version of the tale Emer's governess had told in hushed tones. Her mother had tenderly sworn it was no more than a story, and even though Emer pretended to believe her, she had seen the evidence on the Queen's very flesh: the blemishes around her neck where the gold band clutched too tightly, the left hand missing its smallest finger where her wings had been clipped so she would not flee the palace pond. By the end of her first month in captivity, Emer was acquainted with every cadence of the new account as surely as she was her own heartbeat.

How the Black Bride's mother had two perfectly serviceable husbands, one after the other, and produced one lovely daughter with each. How both girls were raised with equal affection, and how, when an exceedingly fine suitor—a king-to-be—came a-courting those very girls, this very same mother refused to choose between her daughters, so the dark girl had no choice but to make her own fate. How the prince had made his preference for the snowy girl known—and the girl of shadows had determined *her* will would prevail.

It wasn't as if she'd harmed her sister so terribly, said the Black Bride with a shrug. Turned her into a swan, certainly, but as she was sure Emer could attest, a few feathers never hurt anyone. And hadn't the swan-sister's revenge been a terrible over-reaction?

When she came to this point in the tale, the Black Bride always fingered the scars on her cheeks, neck, breasts, where spikes hammered into the barrel had pierced her as she was rolled up hill and down dale until that barrel had finally hit a tree and burst asunder, leaving her bleeding and dying, the tiny child within her withering as surely as an ice-lily on a summer's day.

How, when she'd thought her last breath was spent, she was found by a woman, a witch—not kindly—who mended her and taught her greater things than she'd ever imagined. Marvellous magics, legends of objects that might grant every wish, but none of this imparted fast enough for her wanting or wishing. There was still much to learn when the Black Bride held a pillow over the old woman's face and stifled *her* last breath, but the girl was simply tired of waiting for her to step aside and let a new order begin.

How, after years of plotting and planning, everything she'd worked for threatened to slip from the Black Bride's grasp. Though she'd schemed and marshalled her resources so she might yet play on, she had failed to get what her heart most desired: healing. It was tricky, balancing the time she had left between revenge and recovery, but she refused to relinquish one for the chance of the other. No matter how it taxed her, she could be—*would* be—whole once more, and all scores settled with her sister and the king.

Emer listened and watched, watched and listened, although no one spoke to her but the Black Bride. She paid attention to the comings and goings of the shadowed woman's pilfered court, noting the frequency and severity of the woman's wet cough, the sweet-sour dying scent of her breath. There were suitors—for her wealth, though stolen, though dusty, was not insubstantial, and the strength of her sorcery was of great value. Aside from these charms, in certain lights, the ravages of her punishment were not so obvious. So, the willing grooms came, though none of them ever left.

In the cold hours, after the woman had talked herself out, after she'd muttered at the windows *when will she come, when will she come?*, then gone to bed, Emer would work with her sharp beak at the deceptively fragile-looking chain, more out of habit than hope, but inexorably, insistently.

Peck-peck-peck.

Peck-peck-peck.

Peck-peck-peck.

• • •

"About time."

Emer, perched on the padded armrest of the throne, was enduring the Black Bride's caress, staring out the only unshuttered window. Normally, she divided her time between eyeing the roiling mass of canine domestics, the fluttering carpet of ravens who came and went at the Bride's bidding, and the hopping, kicking sea of fur that had once been the courting princes—all now transformed to fine, fat hares. This day, though, the sky had her undivided attention. She ignored the dark woman, assuming the remark was addressed to someone else. But the Black Bride's next words—and her tone, so soft and sad—dragged the raven-girl's gaze back to the room.

"Did you think yourself forgotten?"

Emer was startled—it was precisely what she was beginning to think. She had lost track of the days, weeks, months, but the turning of the season outside told her winter was arriving for what seemed the second time. She wasn't sure—speculations about bugs and beetles had occupied her mind of late. A tentative movement at the entrance of the chamber made her head tilt in curiosity.

The figure was willowy, dressed in white furs, a hood of silver fox framing her pale face. She moved with all the grace of a bird on the surface of a lake, effortless. She hesitated as if, unable to find whom she sought, she was unwilling to commit deeper to the room.

"You should know," continued the Black Bride, her touch stilled, "that she raised an army to find you. Your father failed and wept, wasted away—trust me, my girl, I have my spies. But she, oh *she* mobilized their vassals, rode at their head, slept in the saddle, scoured all the lands that could be covered by foot and sea. I'll warrant she'd have given her very soul to take to the skies if it meant she might find you that way."

Her hand slid to the black chain. She toyed with the liquid length, unconsciously worrying at the dent Emer's beak had made. She stared at the woman hovering in the doorway and seemed to realize that there would be no further progress without some kind of carrot.

"In the end, though, I sent for her. Reports of her mourning, her burning anguish, warmed my very soul. I could *imagine* it for I know her as well as I know myself. But there is no true joy in suffering that one cannot witness, child," the Black Bride said, then she snapped scarlet-tipped fingers, and the ankle chain evaporated. Before Emer could take advantage of this freedom and make it to the open window, the Black Bride wrapped both hands around the raven's trembling form. She held the bird as if intent upon stilling her heart, then kissed the top of her head. Whispering *flux*, she threw the girl—not upward, but forward.

The raven-girl's shape became fluid, like water tossed from a bucket. Her feathers disintegrated, her beak receded to a pert little nose, legs lengthened and grew feet with soft pink toes, the tips of her wings split into fingers. Emer plummeted like a surprised stone, landing half on, half off the fusty carpet, scattering canine courtiers and confused coneys as she went. Naked and suddenly cold, she sat up slowly, feeling sick, stunned. Her mother, as if released from a cannon, sped toward her, hands reaching, lips curving, focusing entirely on her child, drawn by that agonizing relief which makes caution flee.

The Queen's hands were not as Emer remembered; once soft as silk and pale as moonlight, they were now red, the skin split and dry, callused, coarsened from gripping sword and reins. But the eyes, silvery blue, the gaze wide and wise as an owl's—those were her mother's without doubt. Emer nestled into the embrace, feeling as much as hearing a *thrum* as the White Bride crooned her love.

"Oh, sister, how sweet!" The Black Bride teetered on the edge of the dais, shuddering with the effort of her magic. "What was lost is found. You didn't look for me like that, not even to make sure I was dead."

"A mistake I will not repeat, sister," said the White Bride as she rose.

"Now, now, sister, don't be too hasty. Didn't I give her back? Isn't she safe? Isn't she lovely and whole, unlike we who still wear our battle scars? Didn't I give you hope?"

"Only as one doles out breadcrumbs, sister, for without hope, suffering tastes flat," said the White Bride, which set the Black Bride off into peals of laughter.

When she calmed, wiping spittle from her lips, she looked fondly at Emer and the White Bride. "Didn't I say so, little one? That we know each other as well as we know ourselves? You should find *this* no surprise at all then, sister dear."

And the Black Bride clapped with a noise like a lightning strike and shouted something Emer couldn't quite comprehend, a word that slipped over her ears like oil across skin, and left nothing in its wake but a slight ringing. Where her mother had stood, half-buried under the fox fur hood, was a sleek alabaster she-hare with eyes of silvery blue. Emer could do nothing but stare through hot tears as the Black Bride hobbled down the steps and scooped up the animal that made no move to run.

"No feathers for you on this occasion—I do like variety. I would we had more time for thrust and parry—I could play this game forever—but you've taken so long to find us that my time is running short. Your child must be swift if she wishes to save you."

An iron cage, which had not been there moments before, appeared at the foot of her throne. The Black Bride urged the animal in and latched the door. "Best keep her here, though I'm sure she'd be terribly popular with the boys," she cackled, then shuddered into a fit of coughing that resulted in something nasty spattering on the stone floor. A spaniel footman hurried forward to lap it up. Emer shuddered to think of her mother at the mercy of the legions of bucks, whose noses twitched at the smell of a female.

Unsteadily, the girl picked herself up and wrapped her mother's cloak around her, clinging to the warmth left within. She worried at the hood between her fingers as she tried her voice, found only a raucous sound, tried again and managed, "Why? Why all this?"

The Black Bride gave her an astonished look. "For the sport, of course. The vengeance."

Emer looked at the hare, the Queen-that-was, and quivered. "If I was the bait, then she's taken it. You win. . . What use have you for me now?"

"I thought I'd have more time," the Black Bride murmured, not to Emer, but to the ghosts, the nobodies with whom she regularly conversed. Blinking, she looked down at the girl, as if calculating fitness for purpose. "You'll have to do."

"Do what?"

"You want your freedom, don't you?"

Emer nodded. The Black Bride mirrored the movement and went on.

"Retrieve something for me, and we'll see what we shall see about *that*."

"That's hardly a bargain," Emer said, surprised at her boldness. The Black Bride ignored her.

"I've sent that lot many times." She shrugged dismissively towards the milling crowd of ravens, "and all they've brought back are excuses and complaints about the loss of this cousin or that brother. What I need can be obtained only by someone with pure intent—and we both know that's not me—once it's taken, of course, it can be handed over to whomever the acquirer pleases. It seems a fair price to me, for your liberty."

"And my mother—her life, freedom, her true form," Emer said. She had listened for so long to the Black Bride's tricksy tongue, to conditions that seemed carelessly worded but were not, to deals she'd made with all those princes who now wore fluffy tails and pointed ears.

"Very well, clever little miss." The woman frowned, curious. "What did you think about? When you were bird-brained?"

"Worms. Sky. Flight." *Home. Mother. Father.* Emer's short life had been determined by the whims and demands of others; therefore, she chose to keep some truths for herself this time.

"Ah." The Black Bride seemed disappointed, and sat back on the moth-eaten damask cushions of her throne. "So. There is a castle atop a mountain of glass, almost a day's distance. Inside is a very special crown, which you will retrieve."

"And how do I climb slopes of glass? Will you give me wings again?"

"No, I can't trust you not to fly away. You said yourself, in that form all your thoughts were those of birds—you'll lose focus, grow forgetful." She shook her head. "In the stables, there's a horse—actually there are many, but you can't miss this one. A suitable beast, but with a foul temper." The Black Bride sighed. "You're a clever girl, Emer, so listen carefully: there are no second chances for you. If you do not return here before the turning of a day and a night with the crown, I will kill your mother. Understand? I'm sick with waiting."

"Is there a map?" Emer inquired stiffly.

"Follow the river—that'll be map enough."

"What's so special about this crown?" demanded the girl, her spirit growing the longer she stood on her own two fleshy feet.

The Black Bride's eyes slid to the animal in the cage at her feet. "Enough questions. Go, and be quick about it."

• • •

The bird had spent all the time since they'd left the castle pattering across the horse's broad shoulders, up and down its neck, and making occasional forays onto the saddle's pommel. In turn, the roan had not stopped whickering in irritation and shaking itself hard enough that both bird and rider were almost dislodged. The raven—Bertók by name—also kept up an unrelenting monologue.

"And *that*," he said with a meaningful look at the gingham bundle tied behind Emer, "if I'm not mistaken, is a loaf of bread and a flask of wine that will never run out. Purely magical, very valuable. The dog, I'm sure, was not meant to give you *that*."

A tired-looking Alsatian with sad eyes, green waistcoat, fawn breeches, and mauve frockcoat, had been instructed to find Emer clothes and food and send her on her way. He'd led her to a room decorated with colourful arras, furniture of pale honey wood, and brightly bleached linens. An alcove housed a tub; ancient copper plumbing rattled as the valet drew a bath. In all the past months, Emer had never suspected a room like this existed here.

She was provided with trousers and shirt, highly polished leather boots, and a worsted wool cloak, all in varying shades of black. Emer ignored the cloak, keeping instead her mother's fur and hood. When she was washed and dressed, her guide took her to the stables and pointed out her steed.

The Black Bride had been right—so many princes had left many, many horses—but this one stood out. At least twenty hands high and with a burnished hide, he wore no shoes for his hooves were of spiked bronze. When Emer knelt before him, his golden gaze was measured. She held out the apple she'd kept back from her own quick meal and he deigned to sink his sharp teeth in its firm flesh. The dog, noting the beastie's compliance, swiftly—and with palpable relief—saddled him, while Emer explored some of the stalls, patted the more biddable animals.

"Ahem. Excuse me, miss?" came a voice from the shadows.

At first, Emer couldn't find the source, but when her eyes adjusted to the gloomy corners she saw a withy cage hanging from one of the rafters. Inside was a defeated-looking raven. His eyes were dull until Emer approached. Then, a flare of recognition and something else: a fire within, a swirling conflagration of green and red and gold, orange and azure and magenta.

"You!" she'd screamed, rage rushing through her, and strode forward, intent upon throttling the bird. The raven flapped wildly, shouting, "Now, don't be hasty, I can explain!"

"This is all *your* fault, with your lying in wait and your pecking. Give me one good reason why I shouldn't wring your scrawny neck."

"Well, strictly speaking, you need to shoulder some of the blame—you were alone, wandering about outside. Well-behaved princesses—" he broke off as Emer began to shake the cage. "I'm sorry! Don't hurt me, I can help you."

The bird's terror broke through her fury and Emer suspected that the anger she felt was the sort of ire her aunt gave in to every day. She stepped back, shuddering with shame.

"No, I'm sorry I scared you." She reached for the latch and lifted it. "How is that I can understand you?"

"You were one of us for an age, it's bound to stick," he said, tentatively climbing out onto her proffered forearm. "If you're going where I think you're going, I really can help. Please let me come along."

It had seemed like a good idea at the time, but now Emer's head was fit to burst.

"When the old bat finds out what he's done he'll be a pair of slippers in the blink of an eye. Mind you, might come in handy," wittered Bertók.

"Why were you in that cage again?"

"Injustice! As always. 'Bertók, you talk too much. Bertók, you ate all the wild cherries. Bertók, you didn't bring me back that crown. Bertók, you're snoring too loudly.' It's getting so a bird can't fart let alone express an opinion without getting locked up."

In the brief respite while he took a breath Emer used the chance to change track. "You mentioned a giant?"

"Giantess. Always hungry—I don't know if they're all like that. I wonder –"

"So, this giantess lives atop the glass mountain and has the mysterious crown and eats everyone who comes to visit?"

"Well, except us—except the ravens—not enough meat. But it doesn't stop her using us for target practice."

"And the crown can only be gained by someone with pure intent? I don't imagine that would include you." The bird didn't answer. "Raven?"

He gave a shrug of sorts. "Well, that's what we told her—the part about pure intent."

"You lied?" Emer was less scandalized than delighted by this breathtaking bit of avian bravery. "You lied to *her?*'

"She doesn't know everything, you know," the raven squawked. "She's just so . . . We couldn't bear the idea of losing more of our number every time she sent us off on one of those quests. She's crippled but she's got everything and it's never enough. Imagine her with that crown, whatever it does, still demanding more, more, more! We—I—thought if we put her off long enough, maybe she'd run out of time, so we haven't been trying too hard to do what she's asked."

"Why are you helping me? After all, you were the one who started this whole thing." She waved at him so he could see the scar still marring her palm. The bird had the good grace to look embarrassed.

"It's not easy, you know. Disobeying her takes effort and it hurts. And I had no idea of what she was planning. I'm sorry for what I did. You deserve no more torment, nor does your mother. You saved me from that cage and I owe you a boon. I'll help you retrieve what you need; what you do with it after is something you must consider carefully."

• • •

The journey had been interrupted only by the raven's chatter. They had covered leagues and leagues, the line of the river easy to follow, the roan tireless and intent. Yellow eyes gleamed from shadows and thickets, hands gnarled against tree trunks as their owners peeked out. Emer heard snuffles and snorts, snarls and grumbles, but nothing came near them. Wolves and trolls, ogres, and things with no name watched as they passed, but left them unmolested. She wondered if the Black Bride's power stretched this far, or if these brutes simply sensed her touch on Emer. Or worse, she thought, sensed that they shared blood.

Their destination was less a castle than a single stout tower of ochre-coloured stone. Inside, the main chamber was topped by a stained glass dome that, on sunny days, showered the room with shafts of colour. The air was icy, however; it leeched the hope from Emer's bones and she wondered if she'd ever see the sun again. She could feel the raven trembling on her shoulder. He'd been silent ever since they set foot in the bastion.

The giantess, all big bones, protruding eyes and corkscrew auburn hair, was ensconced in a wingback chair, knitting, and giving Emer the same look one might bestow on a beef roast. Emer was glad she'd left the horse—who had taken the glass mountain at a canter and danced a kind of jig to show how pleased he was with himself—outside. Along the wall behind the enormous woman was a series of hooks, almost all hung with ill-made scarves. The scarf-free one held a huge bow of elm wood and a leather quiver filled with arrows longer than Emer's arm.

"How accommodating of you to arrive at lunch time," rumbled the giantess, who began to roll up her knitting. The door behind Emer shut with a *clang* and she rubbed sweaty palms against her trousers. She lifted her chin defiantly and wished she could fly away.

"My lady," she quavered and the giantess seemed taken aback to be so politely addressed. "I've come to ask—to beg with pure intent—for the crown."

They both looked to the crystal plinth in the centre of the room; it was topped by a primrose cushion that held a circlet of white and black feathers.

"Ask as purely as you like, my girl, you're still going to be eaten." The amazon nodded, rose, and reached for her weapon.

"Wait!" yelled Emer, and something in her tone stayed the woman.

"And why should I? I don't like to wait and I'm starving—always starving."

"I imagine it's hard to get enough food when you're stuck up here, madam," said Emer.

The giantess loomed and Emer quaked. She hurried on. "I do not ask your bounty for free. I offer you something most valuable in return."

"What could you possibly have to interest me, you little thing?"

"What if I were able to provide a loaf of bread that is never depleted and a flask of wine that never runs dry? Would that not sate your hunger, mistress?"

The giantess crossed her arms over her mammoth chest, contemplating. "And where would you find such a treasure, little scrap?"

"Outside, on my horse," answered Emer, hoping the stallion hadn't taken it into his head to go for a run elsewhere.

"Then bring it hither. I demand proof before I agree to consider this bargain. And I am not saying I will . . ."

Fifteen minutes later, when the giantess had attempted and failed to entirely consume the loaf and the wine three times, Emer thought her troubles were over.

"And so, my dame? Do we have an accord?"

"Let's not be hasty, little speck," said the woman slyly. "What's the point of eternal food and drink without companionship? It's been decades since I've had a chat—what with my tendency to eat my guests. Stay awhile."

"My lady—" began Emer, aware of the night's hours bleeding away.

"My lady, this young one is no fit companion for you—she has not lived long enough. What stories could she possibly tell? How she once wet her bed nightly, what frocks she has worn?" The raven began to wax lyrical. "I, on the other hand, am no mere bird."

Looking into the creature's swirling, sparking eyes the giantess admitted this fact. She seemed to nod more than was necessary. It was no wonder the woman normally shot birds out of hand; it was dangerous to listen to them. Bertók's voice swooped low, its ragged edges barely discernible as he promised hours, days, weeks, months, and years of conversations. The woman, Emer thought with a tinge of sympathy, had no idea what she was getting herself into.

By the time the raven had finished, the giantess leapt to her feet, removed the delicate crown from its cushion, and held it toward Emer.

"Thank you," Emer said, as she reached out. "Thank you."

"You're welcome," growled the giantess and snatched the crown away, while wrapping one meaty paw around both of Emer's wrists. "Did you think me a fool to fall for sweet words? Anyway, what's a sandwich without meat?"

Emer's heart hammered, and her mind emptied of all thoughts but these: feathers and air, lightness and flight. Just as her memory retained the language of birds, so too her flesh kept recollection of their form. This time the shape was *her* choice—no one else's to give or take or impose. She gladly shifted, shrank, sprouted plumes. Within seconds, the giantess clutched only emptiness, for the girl had slipped the fleshy bonds and snatched the crown of feathers with her beak.

The door to the chamber remained shut. Emer flew around the room, faster and faster, higher and higher, knowing the giantess was reaching for her bow. She heard the nocking of an arrow, curses thundering from the woman, the twang of a bowstring. She braced herself, heard a thud, but felt no pain. Risking a glance, she saw another black body hurtling downwards. Resolute and determined not to waste Bertók's gift, she raised her head and aimed towards the stained glass.

The raven-girl pierced the dome, raining coloured shards on the giantess. She shot upwards, a shadow against a pallid sky. With the dainty adornment gripped tightly in her beak, she flew on, tracing the snake of the river back to whence she came.

• • •

If the Black Bride had been surprised to see Emer feathered once more, she did not show it. The girl landed and transformed, steadfastly meeting her captor's gaze.

"Give it to me, girl," said the Black Bride, her tone limned by longing, and not a little desperation.

Emer shook her head. "My mother first. Restore her."

A brief, tense standoff took place while the Black Bride insisted her niece hand over the artefact before anything else occurred. Emer remained adamant. In the end, a rage-induced coughing fit tipped the balance in Emer's favour. The Black Bride was forced to concede that she did not have enough time left to indulge in a battle of wills.

When her mother at last stood beside her—shaking, dazed— Emer held the out crown. The Black Bride snatched at it greedily, turned it this way and that, held it up to the light, her eyes shining. Then she faltered, looked at her sister and niece and asked plaintively, "How does it work?"

And Emer recalled the story from her aunt's own lips, how she had done away with her mentor before full knowledge could be passed on; for all her power, the Black Bride was a half-written book—she might well know what an object did, but not *how*.

"Put it on, I'd imagine," Emer said, then asked quietly, "What does it do?"

In an equally hushed voice, the Black Bride replied, "It mends broken things," and, reverently slid the delicate diadem onto her blackavised brow. She waited, breath rattling, eyes wide and avid, a covetous child expecting a treat. Seconds stretched to minutes as she attended, with increasing impatience, for any sign of change, of *amendment*.

When it became apparent that no healing was forthcoming, the Black Bride's face seemed to split with rage.

"What have you done? Did you think to defy me?" She turned on Emer, stalking towards her, spitting out every horrible name she could muster. "I told you there would be no second chances! Both of your lives are forfeit."

Emer and her mother stumbled backwards, transfixed by the sight of the Black Bride summoning her power, watching as it coursed around her body, and sparked at the fingertips. Wanting, but not daring, to turn tail and run—for that would be certain death.

The dark woman drew back her unmaimed hand, and just as it seemed she would strike Emer down, the White Bride, in a flash of ash and silver, threw herself at her sister. The attack, so brutal and brave, so unexpected, knocked the Black Bride off balance and she retreated under each enraged blow her sister rained down. The firebolt-bright magical charge around her stuttered and snuffed, but she struck back, her nails tearing furrows along her sister's smooth cheeks. The White Bride snarled and leapt, not noticing how close they had come to the windows, and the force of her bound sent them crashing into one of the shutters. The wood, brittle and ancient, splintered like twigs and both women were oh-so-briefly silhouetted against the winter sky . . . then gone.

Emer rushed to the sill and peered down, too terrified to catch enough breath to scream as she watched them fall. She clung to the hope that her mother's flesh would remember the shape of wings, that she might fly; but it did not.

Flames erupted when the Brides hit the cobbled courtyard. Emer waited. The fire burned down quickly, leaving a cloud of dust and cinders that swirled and circled and, finally, found form.

Where two women had fallen, only one remained, unfurling like a lily, her hair a mix of light and dark, skin a creamy melding of the two extremes, limbs intact, unharmed. A single woman, lovely and *whole*. The mother-aunt raised her head, looked at Emer and beamed.

"Come home," she called. Emer stared, an uncertain smile on her lips, and she heard the echo of the Black Bride's voice: *She raised an army to find you.* She thought of her mother as she had always known her, the docile White Bride, so kind and loving; wise, but so bound by convention; always passive, meek and accepting— until the loss of her daughter. It had taken tragedy to give her the strength, determination, courage the Black Bride always had but used selfishly.

And Emer reflected on her entire life, on how it was moved by the ebb and flow of others' desires. She thought of her mother and aunt remade, all their chances given to them anew. She contemplated updrafts and thermals, swooping and diving. She looked at the sky, at the horizon.

"Come home," called her mother-aunt again.

Emer shook her head, only vaguely aware of the ruckus in the chamber behind her, of hares returned to the shape of men, and dogs released from servitude.

"I shall find my way there . . . some day."

Emer-that-was thought herself weightless. She thought herself plumed, skipped onto the sill and pitched out to spiral down and hover in front of the woman. The raven-girl memorized the new face, the familiar features, so she might recognize them later, then with a powerful flap of her wings, Emer-of-feathers rose towards the dawning firmament.

LA MORT D'UN ROTURIER

MARTIN LIVINGS

Juliette stood against the pastel-painted wall of the magnificent candlelit ballroom and watched disinterestedly as more than a hundred masked guests, mainly Parisians but with a few recently liberated Americans fresh from their French-funded revolution, each dressed in their finest clothes, danced and drank and gorged and indulged in any other *debauché* they could get away with in the flickering light of the chandeliers above, not to mention the numerous discreet shadowy corners they provided. Unfortunate servants all across Paris would be scrubbing unmentionable stains from the finery for days after this grand masquerade had ended. She was just deeply grateful that she wouldn't be one of them.

The windows of the ballroom were dark, midnight long since passed, though rain fell against the glass in a steady stream, and there were occasional distant rumbles of thunder that made Juliette shiver. Her costume was far less extravagant than those of the invited guests to this grand masquerade, of course, a simple dark blue masculine pageboy costume, her dark hair pinned up inside her cap. She wasn't there to be seen, not in the same way as these overweight nobles and other bourgeoisie. No, she was there for a far simpler function. The same function, she had to admit to herself with no small measure of reluctance, as the six drunken dwarves to her left juggling pigs' testicles tied with bright red ribbons while singing "Marlbrough S'en Va-T'en Guerre," and the raggedy stilt walkers who stalked the crowd, frightening delicate noblewomen by brushing spindly wooden claws across the backs of their corpulent necks.

She was an entertainment, a diversion, nothing more. She and Isaac. And clearly far less popular than the others, for obvious reasons. Those who partook in the . . . *demonstration* invariably walked away sucking their fingers and clutching a scrap of paper in their free hand, glancing time and time again at the writing there, working hard to look nonchalant and amused by the whole affair, but there was that disquiet in their eyes, a darkness that shadowed their mood.

Juliette smiled a little at that thought. You really shouldn't ask a question that you don't wish to know the answer to. They never learned.

"Mademoiselle Jaquet-Droz?" a light, effete voice spoke from beside her. She turned to face the speaker and recognized him immediately. Of course, she wasn't supposed to; the generous host of this masquerade made an ostentatious display of his anonymity, as he did of everything else in his profoundly entitled life. Nobody here knew who he was. *Everybody* here knew who he was. It was all part of the charade. The man was fat, of course, as were almost all the guests, and wore a flamboyant ball gown, his face half-covered by a deep purple mask. What flesh was exposed there was painted white, and his lips were stained red, as if he'd been eating mulberries. Juliette resisted the urge to look for his infamous wife, *la putain autrichienne.*

"*Oui, monsieur?*" Juliette responded as casually as she could manage. This man was her employer tonight. Her performance could mean considerable monies, or a swift exit to the shit-stained cobbled streets outside. The outcome was up to her. And Isaac, of course.

"You're not wearing a mask," the man pointed out, rather unnecessarily.

She smiled at him sweetly. "That remains to be seen. Do you wish to experience Isaac's wisdom?"

The man in the ball gown turned his attention to the incredible object that sat beside Juliette. A strange, crooked smile crept across his plump red lips. "*Ah, oui,*" he breathed.

Isaac was an automaton, his face and hands carved from delicate wax, sitting at a small mahogany writing desk. He was dressed from the waist up in the clothes of a peasant, rough-woven fabrics stitched together by hand. Below the waist he did not exist, his body merging with the desk and casings for the intricate machineries hidden within. On his shirt was a patch, sewed to his left breast, a coat of arms, two pure white crossed bones on a black background. One of his smooth hands held a quill, the feather dyed a brilliant red. The other hand rested palm down on the desk. His eyes were closed, his waxen face patient, implacable. Waiting.

"Incredible," the fat man in the gown said, his hungry eyes sliding across Isaac's mechanical form. He glanced back at Juliette. "It looks quite similar to *L'écrivain, n'est ce pas?*"

Juliette nodded patiently. "The Writer was a superb piece of engineering, *monsieur*," she agreed. "It could handwrite any twenty characters you chose, a marvel of intricate clockwork. It was, and still is, my father's finest creation." She smiled demurely. "Compared to my beautiful Isaac, though, it's a mere windup toy, a plaything for children."

He laughed at that, a surprisingly hearty laugh considering his reedy voice. His jowls vibrated with it. It made Juliette feel a little ill to see. "That's quite a claim, *mademoiselle*. We shall see." He walked in front of the automaton, examining it closely. On the desk, directly opposite the mechanical hand holding the quill, was an indentation, four fingers and a thumb. There were a few dark, wet spots near the groove for the index finger. "Place my hand here, *oui?*" he asked her.

"*Oui.*"

He turned his left hand palm upward and placed it in the indentation.

Juliette walked around behind Isaac. "You understand how this works, *monsieur?*" she asked him.

The man grinned. "Like clockwork?"

She nodded. "*Exactement.* Isaac is named after Sir Isaac Newton, and with good cause."

There was a snort of derision from beneath the blue mask. "*Un Anglais,*" he spat.

Juliette smiled. "Nobody is perfect, *monsieur.*" She looked down at the controls that jutted from Isaac's back through tiny holes in his shirt. "Newton showed us that the world, the entire universe, operates by a strict set of physical laws. These laws are consistent, and they are comprehensible, and, most importantly," she stressed, as she manipulated the automaton's delicate exposed gears with great care and practice, "they are *predictable*. As predictable as clockwork, in fact."

She placed one hand on Isaac's shoulder and pressed a metal button on his spine with the other. His eyes flicked open, and the man flinched at the sight of them. Juliette knew them all too well; they were the purest white, carved from ivory and shaped and polished for weeks until almost as clear as glass. "We are all automata, *monsieur*; you, myself, Isaac," she said. "Our bodies are mechanical creations, wound at birth, following our creator's will and purpose. And, as such, our inevitable conclusions are already written."

She pressed a second button, and with a faint whir, the automaton raised its quill into the air and moved it over the man's upturned hand on the desk. Juliette watched the fat man's eyes through the holes in his mask and saw that flicker of concern she'd seen so many times before there.

Then, in a single smooth motion, the point of the quill was plunged down into the fleshy pad of the man's index finger and out again. He released a yelp of pain and snatched his hand back, the finger going straight to his pouty painted mouth.

"Oh, *excusez-moi*," Juliette said, her expression disingenuous. "Didn't I mention that death is always written in blood? Your blood, to be precise?"

Isaac lifted the quill to its mouth, which opened, revealing a silvered tongue. The automaton pressed the point against this tongue three times, as if wetting it in preparation for writing, a crimson smear left on the shiny surface. Then its mouth closed again, and it lowered the quill to the desk, close to its other hand. That hand turned, revealing a small scrap of paper, and Isaac began to write upon it with the quill. In a matter of seconds it was done, and Juliette walked around to the side of Isaac and picked up the paper. She folded it in half without as much as glancing at it and offered it to the man with a small dramatic flourish.

"There you are, *monsieur*," she said. "Your future."

He hesitated only a moment before taking it, but longer before opening and reading the note. When he did, his eyes widened and he laughed. Then he looked at Juliette closely.

"You know, *mademoiselle*," he said, a nasty gleam in his eyes, "I know the Swiss clockmaker Pierre Jaquet-Droz quite well. I've enjoyed his company several times in court."

"Really?" she asked innocently. "You know my father?"

"I know Pierre Jaquet-Droz," he emphasized. "He is an old man. You seem terribly young to be his daughter," the man persisted.

She smiled at that. "I'm not as young as I look, *monsieur.*"

He leaned toward her. "How does it work?" he asked her.

"I told you—"

"No," he interrupted. "How does it *really* work?"

She looked at him carefully, glanced around the room, the other guests still oblivious to the drama unfolding, each caught up in their own private scandals. Then she sighed.

"The primary mechanism is the movement of the right arm," she said in a defeated tone. "Getting the quill to jab the finger without actually injuring it, moving it to the right place to 'taste' the blood, then down to the paper . . . everything else is smoke and mirrors."

"I thought so!" The host of the grand masquerade, the man paying her wages, clapped his fat hands like a child, thrilled with his own cleverness. "It doesn't actually write, does it? The casing is far too small for such an intricate mechanism."

Juliette shook her head. "The message is prewritten in invisible ink, a substance sensitive to light. Once the left hand reveals the paper, the text turns red. The movement of the quill conceals this."

"An excellent trick," he declared, and grinned. "Never fear, *mademoiselle*, your secret is safe with me."

"*Merci, monsieur,*" she murmured, head bowed.

He looked at her again, still smiling. "I was wrong earlier, wasn't I? You *are* wearing a mask."

Juliette shrugged. "This is a masquerade, after all."

"Just one suggestion," the man said. "Something to improve your act."

"*Oui?*"

He crumpled the piece of paper in his hands. "Be a little more creative with your death predictions. Almost everyone here got the same message. And perhaps make them less obscure."

"I don't understand," Juliette said.

He snorted again. "All we got was a name, child. One I recognize, incidentally, a doctor I happened to engage some years back to help investigate Mesmer's claims of animal magnetism. I doubt that's a coincidence." He winked beneath his mask. "After all, if your precious Isaac had proven to be genuine, I was considering employing him again to look into it." He laughed, then tossed the scrap of paper to Juliette, who caught it out of pure reflex.

"See Jean-Luc as you leave," he ordered her. "He will see to your pay."

"*Merci beaucoup, votre majesté.*"

"Hush now, child," he hissed, looking around with panicked eyes. "Mustn't spoil the mystery." He smiled again, took her bare hand, and bowed to kiss it. "*Au revoir*, Mademoiselle Jaquet-Droz, or whatever your name might be," he said, his fat painted lips unpleasantly warm and wet against her skin.

"*Au revoir,*" she responded with a curtsy.

Then he released her and was gone, back to the masquerade, immediately surrounded by lackeys and sycophants. Juliette watched him go, waited until he was lost in the colourful whirlwind of fabric and flesh. Then she opened the crumpled piece of paper and read it. It made no sense to her, but regardless, it filled her with a terrible foreboding. She turned to the automaton. "You know what, *mon amour?*" she asked it. "I believe it's time we left Paris." She glanced out of the huge windows of the ballroom, at a flicker of lightning in the sky there. "There's a storm coming, I think."

She wheeled Isaac toward the exit with some haste, past the blithely dancing nobles, who ignored her as she went. Behind her, on the tiled floor, the scrap of paper lay open, a single word on it, written in a splash of bright red royal blood.

Guillotin.

ON THE WALL

NICKY ROWLANDS

I was alone, willing the Queen to not return.

The Queen not only wanted to be beautiful, she wanted to be the only thing standing between her subjects and abject misery. So she created a hellhole for the sole purpose of rescuing them from it, to which I was an unwilling party. Anyone who prevented her was "eliminated", as she put it, even her own stepdaughter. That very morning she'd left, intent on doing just that. I couldn't bear to look for her.

So here I was, hanging alone, when that stepdaughter walked into the room, hand-in-hand with an exceptionally handsome young man. If I had eyes, I'd have cried for joy. I expected that they'd take a seat and begin reciting the many reason for their new-found love or, more gallingly, tear each other's clothes off and start grunting away. I was so happy to see her—and not the Queen—I was only a little disgusted by the concept.

They did neither.

The stepdaughter glanced around the empty room and almost straight away, her gaze fell where I hung silently on the wall. She tilted her head, bit her lip in contemplation. Then, with an almost imperceptible nod, she took a confident stride in my direction, grabbed my sides and said, "Let's get rid of this evil thing."

The attractive suitor mumbled in agreement. The Princess waved over a servant, who swiftly bundled me into a bag. I was flung up on some high place, where I waited for hours, only to be dragged over a bumpy dirt road, collecting bruises with each mile. Eventually, I was flung down again, landing heavily on top of something lumpy, with solid bits and squishy bits. It reeked to high heaven. Back in the garbage, I thought. Well, it was bound to happen, eventually.

Some days later, I felt a rustling. Tiny hands appeared at the opening of the bag. Small arms reached in to grip my sides. I was gently hoisted into the air. The bright of day was blinding. Details became clear slowly. First, I saw a patch of green below pale pink. Brown hair with green leaves threaded through it. Gigantic green eyes sparkling with pleasure. A mile-wide grin on a face lit up in childish glee. A glint of sunlight on delicate wings.

I was going to be owned by a fairy.

I hoped she wasn't evil.

• • •

The fairy let out a little squeal of delight, then covered her mouth with her hand. Her giant green eyes, peeking over the top, still sparkled with mischief. She placed me back in the bag, closed the tie and hoisted me over her shoulder (at least, I presumed it was her shoulder.) With a sickening lurch, in which my body felt like it rose quicker than my spirit, we flew into the air. I don't know how long we were airborne for, but I was glad to be in my bag—it meant I couldn't see.

Thankfully, I eventually fell to the floor with a gentle thud. I could hear her tiny feet pitter-pattering over what sounded like a hard wood floor. She whistled a merry tune to herself; I thought I heard the sound of a bird chirping. I could hear bashing and clanging. Occasionally she cursed or grunted in frustration. It sounded like she'd decided to remodel her entire home.

I heard her footsteps close by, then the sound of someone plonking themselves down in front of me. Now-familiar small hands came into view as my bag opened, bathing me in subtle, warm light. I was lifted out to see that we were in a small cottage, lit by a handful of mostly-melted candles. The messy abode was full of boxes that spilled over the rickety shelves and small wooden table. They were labelled with words like 'Trinkets', 'Doo-dads' and 'Thingummybobs'. I wondered how one distinguished between the three groups. I could also see a few trinket boxes without any labels, gathering dust next to some tacky ornaments. Days ago, I was owned by a Queen—today I was owned by the Queen of Pointless Objects. At least this one didn't seem evil, thus far.

And I'd been correct about the bird. In a small cage, a painfully yellow canary sat, chirping merrily. As I watched it sing, she lifted me up and placed me on a hook on the wall. The hook was a little itchy but at least I was out of the bag. The fairy stood back, looked at me and smiled. "Perfect," she said, with a quick bob of the head. She gave her little hands a clap, giggled, then turned to neatly fold the bag I'd come in and place it in a rickety cupboard.

For the rest of that first day, the fairy pottered around the cottage. She sang to herself as she sewed up a dress. She whistled as she stirred something in a pot. At one point she danced around the room to no music I could hear. Occasionally, she would glance at me, grin at her reflection, and then carry on. I wondered when she would decide to actually talk to me.

That night I watched her sleep in a small green hammock, snoring like a giant bee with a head cold, until I finally lapsed into blissful unawareness.

I was rudely awoken to the sound of pots and pans clashing and a small, angry voice screaming "Oh bubbletrumps!". *Bubbletrumps?* I wasn't sure I could handle such cuteness. I glanced in her direction to find her struggling with the mighty scrambled egg. Clearly, her magic did not lie in the culinary arts. Eventually, she triumphed and sat down at her rickety table to eat, using her magic to turn the pages of a trashy novel she was reading. Egg dribbled down her front, leaving yellow trails down her chin. Honestly, it surprised me that she had lived this long in such a cut-throat world.

After an exceedingly long time, the fairy flittered to the sink, and gave her plate a cursory swipe with a cloth. She popped over to her little bird's cage, replenished its seed and water, and made some silly noises at the creature. Then she began dressing for the day. For someone whose wardrobe consisted of shades of green, she took some time to select which particular garment to wear. After slipping her tiny feet into an equally tiny pair of shoes, she lightly danced over to where I hung on the wall, gazed at me and began fixing her fluffy brown hair. She worked meticulously, little pins sticking out of her mouth, while her tongue lolled from the other side. Once satisfied, she leaned forward, grinned, inspected her teeth for bits of egg—there were plenty—and then swiftly flew out of the door.

Could it be that this tiny fairy had no idea what kind of mirror I was?

• • •

I'd been watching her go through her evening rigmarole for at least an hour. Every time she glanced in my direction and treated me like some everyday looking glass, I considered whether or not I should shout, politely cough or let loose a demonic laugh. Which particular fantasy came to mind depended on how humiliating a particular behaviour was.

It was almost midnight when she flew over, a purple, sparkly pair of tweezers in her hand, and leaned forward to start plucking her eyebrows. Enough was enough!

"I'm sorry," I said. "But at any point are you going to speak to me?"

The fairy reeled back, her face a gargoyle of horror. She clutched her hand to her throat, her sparkly purple tweezers sticking out between thumb and forefinger. "D-did you . . . did you just *speak*?" she said.

"Well, yes." I said.

The horror in her face faded slightly, though her eyes were still twice their usual size. "Have you *always* been able to speak?" She glanced around as though looking for evidence of a spell.

"Yes, always."

"Why didn't you tell me when I first found you?"

"I suppose I thought a fairy would know what a magic mirror was. Before this, I've never had a master who didn't. I was waiting for you to decide to speak to me."

"Well," she said, sitting down on her chair with a huff. "I ain't never had a talking mirror before. Mama never told me about this!"

I waited patiently for her to realise the power suddenly in her hands.

"So, what can you do? Do you perform magic?"

"No, I see things. I show you things you want to see."

Her eyes lit up. "What kind of things?"

"All kinds of things. Anything you want to see, really."

"Just things or people too?"

"Anything includes people. Is there someone you want to see?"

She blushed furiously and looked down at her hands. "Well, actually, there is someone." She looked up at me, a dopey smile on her lips, her cheeks still flushed. "He's ever so lovely but I have no idea if he feels the same or even knows my name." She paused. "It's Fern, by the way. My name is Fern." She pointed at her little bird. "That's Tinchy." She looked expectantly at me.

"I don't have a name."

"Oh," she said "Well, *his* name's Ugra. He's, um, a dwarf. Did you hear about the Princess going missing and eventually turning up living with a bunch of dwarves? Well, Ugra was one of those dwarves. He's so brave and strong, though *some* people think he's just an old grumble-guts, hmmph." She raised her eyebrows. "Can I see him? Maybe then I'll know how he feels."

Swallowing the urge to groan, I drew a mist across my face, much like a person would blink an eye, and there, where Fern's reflection used to be, stood the object of her affection. She leaned in, enraptured. She studied every line of his dour face, every hair of his scruffy beard. She grinned widely when he spoke and templed her little fingers at her chin, not quite hiding that dopey grin. Here and there, she pointed out some insignificant detail, such as the way he furrowed his brows in concentration or the way he scratched his temple. It didn't take being a magic mirror to see that Fern was infatuated. Her behaviour bordered on the stereotypical, except that there was something almost ridiculous about watching a scatterbrained fairy making eyes at a dwarf who looked like a bearded potato.

This might be a long service.

Over the next few days, Fern whiled away many hours gazing at her beloved Ugra while he gallumphed around the cottage or through the mine. Despite the irritation of having to pander to her infatuation, I had to admit that Fern was not as bad as I first thought. Though her ditziness was tedious, it led to a kind and trusting personality. She actually took the time to ask how I was or inquire as to things that interested me. I wouldn't have called myself fond of her, but she was certainly more tolerable than I had pegged her to be. My masters still sometimes surprised me.

"So, what do you think?" Fern's merry little voice interrupted. "Can you show me that?" I stared expectantly, hoping for a clue as to what I'd missed. "Does he love anyone?" she pressed. At least Fern was easy to work with.

"This might take a little while," I said "Why don't you do something else while I investigate?"

I drew the mist again and looked for Ugra. I scanned his interactions with others, what he did when he was alone and, for the most part, there was nothing I hadn't seen before. Fern was growing impatient after an hour. It took me nearly six hours to find an answer, so you can imagine what state Fern was in by that stage. Unfortunately, I had no good news for her. I saw Ugra sitting in his room, a wrinkled picture of the stepdaughter clutched in his grubby hands. His face bore the same expression that Fern's did when she looked at him. Fern might not have been my favourite master ever, but I didn't relish having to hurt her. I braced myself and showed Fern her beloved gazing with longing at another.

Fern stared quietly for a long time. She scanned the image frantically, as though searching for some sign to suggest he wasn't really in love, that he was gazing at her picture for some other reason. A look of desolation passed Fern's face, then her pretty features crumpled into ugly broken heartedness and she lay on her cottage floor crying out her pain. It was times like these I wished I had arms to pat her back with or make her some tea. Having none meant I could do nothing but watch, as I am forced to do whenever a master's heart is broken.

Fern's sobs became more subdued until she lay there sniffling. Gingerly, she sat up and glanced at me tiredly. She let out her breath. With a stomp, she got to her feet, almost snapping her heels together, strode over to pick up her rucksack, then stood in front of me. "Show me the nearest witch."

"Fern, I've seen more people than you'd believe go through this. The best advice I can give you is to cry, eat a lot of baked goods, and find someone who returns your love. Time and distraction heals many things."

"I don't want your advice. I want a witch."

With a deep sigh, I located the nearest competent, reasonably ethical witch I could think of. Fern was out the door before my last sentence was even finished.

Another master I couldn't bear to look for.

The goblins were out on their nightly hunt by the time Fern returned. Instantly, I could see she had what she wanted.

Fern charged purposefully into the cottage, flung her rucksack on the table and began pulling out items. The first thing she pulled out was a deer's heart. As she continued unpacking, I saw the flash of blood on her hands. The poor, silly girl. Next to the deer's heart, Fern arranged a candle, some strands of her own hair and what appeared to be a gem from Ugra's mine. After a quick rummage through her cupboards and boxes of miscellany, Fern returned with more candles and a locket.

I knew this spell.

Tinchy flitted uneasily in his cage. Fern waved him into silence, without even turning to look at him. *Glad it's not your heart there, bird*, I thought.

Fern placed a circle of candles around the assembled items, then pulled out a little scrap of paper. With trembling hands, she held it to her nose as she read aloud, with surprising confidence:

Ugra, give me your heart
As gentle as this deer's,
As precious as this gem,
Burning as brightly as this candle
Ugra, give me your heart
Filled with love only for me

She tore off a hunk of the heart, then wrapped her hair around it and the other items, somehow managing to not break it, her tongue stuck out with concentration.

I bind these things with my own self
His heart to my heart
As my will is done, Ugra will be mine

With a grunt of frustration, Fern managed to shove the amateurish charm inside the locket. She placed it around her neck, clutching it to her chest reverently, eyes shut in raptured dreams of love. Turning her big green eyes toward me, she grinned. "I think it worked," she said. She swirled to her feet, twirled around the cottage and leapt into the air, letting out a little squeal of triumph. "My love is coming to me!" she cried, dancing around the floor. She raised her arms and began to waltz, humming the music for herself. "We shall be together forever, we shall. It will be a love story the ages will write about." With a dramatic swish, she faced me and declared, "And he'll never think of *her* again, either."

Or himself, I thought.

• • •

I could hear two pairs of footfalls on the gravel outside. Fern's light almost-dance-like step was familiar. Behind her came a plodding sound, which I assumed to be the unfortunate object of her misplaced affections. The door swung open with a bump, and in flew Fern, her wings fluttering madly at her back, her eyes bright and an almost maniacal grin of joy planted on her face. Ugra followed, more subdued but compliant.

So the spell had worked, then.

Fern flitted about her cottage, showing Ugra her collection of thingummybobs (not to be confused with her doo-dads), her sleeping hammock (they'd have to get a proper bed to share), where the food and tea was kept and a few random items here and there. Throughout, Ugra smiled benignly and gazed with glass-eyed wonder at his new-found love. Every so often, I noticed Fern glance at Ugra, eyebrows raised, as though waiting for a response. Ugra just smiled and Fern, with a mild pursing of the lips, continued to flit about the cottage. She even took Tinchy out of his cage and held him on her finger. Ugra patted the little bird's head, and it chirped merrily in response.

Once Fern ran out of things to show Ugra, she sat him down and began to fuss around the kitchen. She sang to herself as she prepared some tea. Ugra sat back in the chair, a blissful smile on his face. Slowly, in a resonant bass, he began to hum along to Fern's singing. Fairy and dwarf singing together was something I hadn't actually heard before and I was surprised at how well they harmonised. Fern came over to where Ugra sat, wrapped her arms around his shoulders and cuddled him as they sang. Tinchy's sweet chirping joined them. Ugra's blissful expression never changed.

I actually began to hope that things might turn out for the young lovers.

Those first few days, Ugra and Fern calmly went about their days together, not always singing but still somehow in harmony with each other. Ugra's clumsy slowness did not seem to hamper Fern's dancing gait: if anything, they complemented each other. As Fern made her way around the cottage, Ugra sat patiently and watched. As she became tired or bored, she'd sit by Ugra, lay her head on his knee and he'd stroke her hair. Ugra didn't seem to have any more personality than a pet rock, but his presence appeared to make Fern happy.

For those first few days, anyway.

By my estimation, Fern and Ugra had been going about this daily ritual, with some outings into a nearby village and around the surrounding forests, for about two weeks when things began to change. Fern's lips had pursed in irritation more and more frequently during the previous two weeks, but that was nothing compared to the outward frown she wore when Ugra answered her with "Whatever you like, dear," for the umpteenth time. She sighed, stamped her little foot and snapped "Do you not have *any* opinions of your own?"

Ugra glanced at her, slightly intrigued but not even surprised, then shrugged his shoulders and turned back to whatever he was doing.

Fern stood stock still and stared. She clutched the locket at her neck, as though willing it to give her an answer. As though one had come to her, she knelt by her lover's side and said "Ugra, darling, I keep hearing these strange noises at night. Maybe you should hunt down and slay the beast making them for keeping me awake?"

Ugra smiled mildly and patted her head. "It will be fine, dear."

"You aren't going to attack it for me?" Fern eyes looked the size of teacups. "But . . . but you hate beasts who disturb you! I once saw you swat a fly with a hammer! Ugra, can't you show me how brave and tough you are?" I admit I could barely resist the urge to chuckle at that last comment.

"I tell you, it will be alright, darling. If we're together, then what could a measly beast do to bother us?"

Fern sat back. She fixed him with a hard stare. "Say my name."

"Huh?"

"Tell me my name."

"The most beautiful name in the world, darling."

"Which is?"

"Why yours, my pet."

Her pretty face crumpled into that now-familiar ugly one and she flew out of the cottage, sobbing noisily. Ugra watched her go, shrugged and turned to an open newspaper, confident that his love for this unnamed fairy would solve all hurts.

The poor, dear girl.

To Fern's sorrow—and Ugra's cheerful indifference—things quickly began to deteriorate from there. Over the next few days, Fern quizzed Ugra continually. She asked him specific questions about her, to all of which he replied "Whatever is best for you," or "The most beautiful name/animal/kingdom/village/colour in the world, my dear." He clearly had no knowledge of Fern, other than that she was beautiful, that he was happy in her presence and that he was no longer grumpy. It didn't seem to even occur to him to wonder at his complete change in personality, circumstance, or even affection. But that last issue occurred to Fern. Oh, did it ever occur to Fern!

It was mid-morning when Ugra was sitting at the table, reading one of Fern's many insipid novels of forbidden but, miraculously, successful romance. He looked up and turned his glassy eyes toward the door as his beautiful love flew in, in an apparent rage. She held what looked like a crumpled piece of paper in her hands. "Hello, dear woman," he said "how is my love?"

"I don't know, Ugra. How do YOU think she is?" Fern flung the paper in her lover's hands and I saw that it was in fact a portrait of that hated stepdaughter. It was the kind the royal family would give out to peasants as a collectable. In fact, it looked like the exact one that the Queen had handed out to report her "beloved daughter" missing—to arouse sympathy, of course.

Ugra took it in his hands and looked at it, his face scrunched up in consternation. "This isn't my love." He held it out to Fern. "This isn't you."

"No, this is her, this is the person you love!" Fern began to cry. "This is the Princess. This is *Snow White*. I saw you crying over this picture of her. *This is your love!*"

Ugra shook his head. "No *you* are, my dear."

"Then what's my name?"

Ugra looked at her as though she were a small child asking what colour the sky was. "You know your name, darling."

"But *you* don't! Just like you don't know my favourite colour or what I like to eat or my mother's name or anything of any real importance to me—not even *Tinchy*! You don't know me and you don't love me."

Ugra stood up and closed the small space between them. "I do. I do love you."

Fern sniffled. Again she clutched that locket. She took a step closer and lifted her chin. "Then show me."

Ugra smiled, then threw his arms around her and kissed her

on the mouth. Fern immediately melted into his arms, apparently forgetting everything she'd just said. Ugra pulled back, lifted her hand and said "These are the arms I love." He kissed her again. "These are the lips I love." He gazed deeply into her eyes. "You are the one I love."

Fern smiled and threw him on the bed. They were noisy. Very noisy. Being a magic mirror certainly has its disadvantages. Watching couples, well, *couple* was certainly one of them.

It was not to last. Although Fern seemed content to teach Ugra about herself, thus helping him love her for her, not a spell, Ugra didn't seem to want to listen to her discuss her childhood, her dreams or any of the other endless things couples who are falling in love discuss. All Ugra wanted to do was gaze at her, to grin at her stupidly, and to make noisy love. To Fern's frustration, it wasn't enough.

Fern decided, for whatever harebrained reason, that she must test the reality of his feelings. Surely, if he loved her for her and not the spell, he would display some other emotion at some point? Surely, if she treated him badly enough, he'd initiate a lover's tiff?

She began by calling him names, slipping subtle insults into the conversation. Ugra glanced at her once or twice but did not respond. At one point, she even pushed him but he just became sympathetic, suggesting she'd had a rough day and that he'd irritated her. "Goddamn it, why won't you fight me? Where's the strong, tough Ugra I fell in love with?" she'd screamed.

I hoped the end would come soon.

It did, about two weeks after that. Ugra was making faces at Tinchy while Fern cooked their dinner. I was watching her closely for some reason. There was a look in her eye that I recognised. It's not something I can describe in words, but it's a look that signifies some serious misadventure, some ill intent that departed from what could be considered morally right. It was a look devoid of emotion. A look the Queen wore the day she decided to kill her stepdaughter. Today, my ditzy and gentle Fern wore it.

"Ugra," she called "There's not enough meat in this dish. Bring me Tinchy."

Obediently, Ugra opened the little cage. Tinchy innocently hopped onto his proffered finger. "Do you want him to look for food?"

"No, I want to cook him."

Oh no. Was my Fern gone for good? "Fern . . . "

"Quiet, mirror, we're going to cook him."

Ugra frowned. "That seems extreme." He took a step closer. "But I suppose you know best, my love."

Fern's jaw dropped. She didn't crumple or cry, she just stared. Then she screamed and threw her tiny boot into Ugra's stomach. He sprawled on the floor, a look of mild surprise and confusion on his face, yellow feathers briefly flitting past him as Tinchy made his escape. "You never loved me!" Fern roared. "You've killed me, Ugra, you've killed me!" She ripped the locket from about her neck, so violently little beads of blood smeared her throat. She threw it at Ugra, hitting him square between the eyes.

I couldn't tell you if the spell was broken because, without warning, she turned to me, her pretty face unrecognisable behind a mask of pure hatred. "And you, you did this to me! Had you never come, none of this would have happened!" I knew better than to argue. Fern took me in her arms and flew out of the cottage. She flew upwards, holding me aloft in shaking hands. "You can die, too!"

I fell.

. . .

Pain. Like being splintered in reverse. Darkness, giving way to blurry shapes glowing with ethereal light. Agony reverberated through me. If this was the afterlife, I was sorely disappointed.

Soon, my vision began to sharpen. I could hear tinkering and looked down to see a pair of hands confidently gluing shards of my broken body together with what looked like liquid glass. *So that's why I felt like I was shattering in reverse*, I thought. I was literally doing just that. I closed my eyes against the sight of my scattered self being handled by those unfamiliar hands.

I must have passed out again because, the next time I looked down, there were no more hands and no more shards of glass. I ached all over but that bizarre sensation of reverse destruction had left. Someone cleared their throat. I squinted my eyes, trying to focus.

"Mirror, mirror, on the wall," a voice said. "Does this mirror work at all?"

I tried to laugh but coughed instead. "That was a terrible rhyme," I said and prepared to meet my new master.

ALL THE LOST ONES

DEBORAH BIANCOTTI

"Ah, but no? You have not moved into a house of the Lombardi!"

"Temporarily," Francesca explained, "while my husband finds a residence."

The air in the cavernous salon of the Contessa Rossi was warm and dense with humidity. The furniture was at once plush and sharp. Ornate gold arms were fixed to plump black chairs, and heavy drapes blocked the sunlight. It smelled of the ocean as much as of the fat, perfumed candles that stood unlit and uneven in the candelabra around the room.

In the midst of it, Francesca in her simple blue silk felt almost infantile. Her hair was plain and dark and pinned back with none of the clasps of the Contessa's tresses, and she lacked for rouge and powders on her face, being too modest to buy such fineries. She admired the heavy lace and crinoline of her hostess's dress. The Contessa was as elaborately regal as the porcelain figurines that seemed to pin the room to its floorboards.

"*C'est bon à savoir,*" Contessa Rossi replied. She beat the air with a white, silk fan, a tracery of trees distorted by its folds. "It is not an adequate address."

"I have heard about some houses in Venice . . . " Francesca hesitated. She did not want the Contessa to think her entirely foolish. "I've heard many are haunted?"

The Contessa's eyes widened and the fan rose to cover the indelicate smile on her face. "*Alors!* It is true."

"Really?" Francesca leaned forward.

She'd been in this salon for less than an hour, with its heavy, closed air. She looked forward to breathing fresh air again. But the stories of the Contessa Rossi were proving too much of a delight to move.

"They call the city *La Serenissima*, but how serene is she?" the Contessa asked. "Have they told you, for example, of Biasio?"

"Did he live in the house of the Lombardi?"

"*The* house? *Mais, non.*" Rossi shook her head and sent her careful curls bouncing.

It was almost impossible to guess Rossi's age under the heavy rouge. Her hair—her wig—was carefully coloured a deep, unconvincing red and her décolletage was gently hidden behind fine lace.

"Who is he, then?" Francesca asked in a rush.

"A butcher."

"Is that all?"

Contessa Rossi waggled a finger. "The *murderous* butcher of Venice."

"Here?" Francesca leaned forward. "Now?"

"*Ah*, centuries ago. He served the finest meats in Venice. He was a favourite of the sailors of Venice, and his pies were much sought after. Until one—" here she leaned forward and whispered conspiratorially, with her fan to one side of her face, "one sailor discovered in the sausage he had bought, the tiny finger of a little child."

"No!" Francesca whispered.

"*Oui!*"

It took Francesca a moment to recover, to hide her face with her hand, since she lacked a fan, and to lean back into the awkward settee.

"What happened to this monster?" she asked.

"They cut off his arms," Rossi smiled, leaning in. Her voice dropped a full octave. "And they took him into *la Piazza San Marco* so they could behead him."

"Good," Francesca heard herself mutter.

"And they hung the pieces of his body from the four corners of the city."

"*Mon Dieu!*"

"*C'est vrai!*" Rossi leaned back with a satisfied look. "And then they named a street after him, can you believe? *La Riva di Biasio.* Where even the priests fear to tread."

"Also as a reminder?"

Rossi shrugged and clucked her tongue. "Who knows? The Italians! And they think us the savages."

"I see."

"This is Venice," Rossi sighed. "No place for innocence. Do you have children, Madame Branscombe?"

Francesca bit back on the gnawing sorrow that had followed her from London. There was something about the Contessa's bluntness that drew her in, after the mannered parties and dull dinners her husband liked her to attend. There was something about Venice, too, all that jewelled finery and the easy grace of her people.

"We did," she said. "But . . . "

She gestured, and Rossi nodded her understanding.

"Lost," the Contessa said. "So many lost. Mothers waking to stillness. Do you know, children have been snatched from Italy for many years."

"But, why?"

"To serve evil masters as slaves and street peddlers. Some go as far as England, even the Americas. You might have seen them in London?"

"Perhaps." Francesca nodded.

She'd seen those sad, unsmiling children, dark-haired ghosts obscured by layers of grime from the streets. She'd had them beg her for coins and offer to play incongruous melodies on harps and horns and violins that were bent and old, tucked beneath the points of their small chins. The sight of them had made her cry. Even before her own lost child.

"It is the scandal of Italy," the Contessa continued. "Garibaldi and his man, this *Generalissimo—*"

"Menabrea?"

"*Si,* they shall have to deal with it if they are to build a united Italy."

"Will they, do you think? Deal with the children, I mean."

Contessa Rossi shrugged and gestured to the heavens hidden behind her dark ceiling. "What is the future of Italy without *gli bambini?*"

When Francesca's baby had been lost, it had left something behind. She could feel it, restless, tugging at her. Sometimes when she was alone, she thought the child spoke to her.

She tried never to be alone.

The Contessa must have caught in her expression some of the grief she felt.

"Yes, yes," Rossi said in her deep, brooding tone. "I understand."

The Contessa seemed to forget Francesca was there for a moment, her gaze lost to the patterned walls.

"The house?" Francesca prompted her.

"*Oui?*"

"You were saying it was not appropriate?"

"Ah! The Lombardi have several other houses, it is the height of rudeness to put you in such a place."

"It is close to the *Ponte di Rialto*," Francesca replied. "I thought it quite fashionable."

"The *fashion* of the Lombardi is not in doubt." Rossi was almost crooning, waving her thick, silk fan in front of her, the tassel bouncing against her forearm. "It is because we are French, you see? And foreign, they give us the dreadful places. Venice is so unforgiving."

Francesca couldn't think what to say, so she stayed silent and rocked in her oversized chair and tried not to look at the Rossi family portraits that hung sternly above her. The salons of Venice, Francesca was finding, were at least as dangerous as the streets.

"It is better for me," Rossi continued. "At least I married an Italian."

"That must be a relief," Francesca muttered, more to herself.

"And to think! The Italians, they took Venice from Austria in this war of theirs. I ask you, why? Other cities would do better."

"Contessa," Francesca interrupted, "If it is not the fashion of the Lombardi house that is at issue, then what?"

"Oh, *ma chère, ma chère petite*." Rossi's fan thumped the heavy air. "It is because of the child who haunts it."

• • •

Francesca rose from the sheets, heavy linens twisted with sweat and sleeplessness.

There was, she thought, a terrible energy in the house tonight. The dark chewed through everything. It turned the red of the rugs to black and made the marble fireplace gape like a maw.

The heavy magenta curtains were held back from the windows in the hope of breeze, but whatever breeze was out there only travelled along the canal this evening and not up.

In the gloom, she tripped on the brocade bed cover they had kicked to the ground. She stumbled and stifled a cry.

Francis' voice was clear. "Have you hurt yourself, *mon amour?*"

"My pride, only," she muttered. "I thought you were asleep."

Francis sighed and stirred and kicked off the thick sheets. "I might never have slept. I feel I might not have slept in my entire life."

"You exaggerate so," she replied.

"It is the continental way," Francis replied. "I'm just fitting in."

The air was damp with canal water. Strands of hair stuck to Francesca's neck and forehead.

She pulled at her long nightgown. The lacemaker had assured her it was wrong for the season, but the lacework was so delicate— like rosebuds against spider's web—that she'd declared she must have it. And the lacemaker, shrugging, had wrapped it for her and then tried to sell her others that were, he proclaimed, just as fine. Nightgowns, he declared, you would be proud to wear even to your grave.

Francesca had thanked him sourly. But now she saw fit to curse him. Lace fell like a rash along her chest and lace clamped wetly around her wrists.

"Why did you agree to purchase this wretched nightgown?" she asked.

Francis twisted to look at her. "You insisted—"

"*Cette m'ennuie,*" she cut him off.

"I think it was this stifling Venetian air, it does things to one's mind."

"How is your fever?"

"Still as wretched as ever."

Francesca sighed. She crossed to the tall, arched window and stood side-on against the curtain, wrapping it around herself like a shroud.

Outside, Venice hung with its spires reaching towards Heaven, its colours like a muted carnival, all pink and grey and blue with cascades of flowers that were, by daylight, bright yellow and red.

There was still a buzz of activity, even this late. People were walking along the embankments, moving slowly, the best to show off their evening finery. The *gondole* that populated *il Canalaso* fluttered like black moths on the water. If she pressed the side of her face to the cool window glass, she could just catch a glimpse of Venice's most famous bridge: *il Ponte di Rialto*.

"It's only April," she said.

"Yes?"

"Already so warm. What will July be like?"

"Warmer, I should think." His tone was flat.

She rubbed her wet cheek on the sleeve of her nightgown. "There are still people outside."

"What are they doing?"

She gestured, the heavy lace dripping from her wrist. "Walking, mostly."

"Well, this is Venice."

She turned from the window and faced him. The moonlight gave him a ghostly pallor and his shadowed eyes seemed sunken in his head.

"You say that like it explains things. What does it explain?"

Francis sat up from the crumpled bed. He sighed. "They sleep in the afternoons. In the evenings, *loro fanno una passeggiata*. They walk."

She turned back to the window. "Contessa Rossi says I should have married an Italian."

"I don't see why, half the people in Venice aren't Italian."

"When are we leaving, Francis?"

"The house? Or the city?"

"The house would do," Francesca replied. "I can't sleep here."

"The heat will be the same all over the city."

"It's not the heat, it's the ghost."

"Ah," Francis sighed. "That foolish Rossi woman, she tells you stories of make-believe for what reason? Perhaps she despises the Lombardi and seeks to get back at them—"

Rossi was an old woman, and bored, and perhaps she had invented the stories to save herself from more boredom. But Francesca didn't believe it.

"You weren't there," Francesca said. "She was convincing."

"You were convinced, you mean," he corrected her. "You do

love these sordid stories the locals tell. You listen and then you let your imagination run away with you. And then you don't sleep. This Rossi, she sounds grotesque."

"She is quite macabre," Francesca replied, with feeling. "And honest, in her way. I like her. And anyhow, what about those drawings I found? The ones the servant Marzio snatched away."

The servants were so forbidding that Francesca had taken to spending her time in the rooms assigned to her for sleeping and dressing.

It was in those rooms where she'd been admiring the furniture, running her hands along the deep, lacquered wood, pulling out drawers and opening wardrobes. They were all empty and she assumed the rooms had been unoccupied a long time. The Lombardi, it was said, hardly ever returned to Venice. There was a sense of wilting to those rooms, too, and the kind of the neglect that comes from a too-long empty space.

She'd noticed, too, that the servants hadn't bothered to clean the rooms for their arrival. Now and then she'd find a scattering of dust and the marks where covers had been left on furniture haphazardly, exposing a corner to the thick air.

It was the wardrobe she'd been inspecting when she'd found the drawings. They were pressed up against a back corner, as if they'd been wedged there behind something else that had since been removed. Boxes, perhaps.

Francesca had reached for them and found two pages in a child's hand. Thick, colourful pencil traced the outlines of smiling figures in what appeared to be pink gowns and lace caps.

Images of Venice, she'd realized, the broad buildings behind the figures unmistakable with their repetition of windows, the doors so vast that smaller doors had to be cut into them so a person could come and go without three others to help open the door. The buildings in the drawings sat not on the ground but seemed to float on the dark, blue water that ate into their foundations. They were cheerful images, except for the consuming waves.

The pages were yellowed on one page, but the other, having fallen behind its partner, had remained better protected.

Francis said, "So you assume the drawings you found were done by a child who died, but you base that on nothing."

"You assume," she said, "that the drawings were *not* made by that child. But why else hide them away in a wardrobe?"

"If they *were* hidden," Francis sighed. His face was ashen with fatigue. "If they weren't, perhaps, simply forgotten. And this ghost, this child died how?"

"The Contessa wouldn't say."

"She didn't know."

Francesca shrugged and pulled back her wet hair. "Quite possibly. She doesn't seem the kind to hold back a detail like that."

"I should think she's not the kind to hold back any detail."

"She's been kind to me, in her way. She's invited me to her house. She's the only one."

"Give it time."

"Do you think we'll find somewhere to live as grand as the Lombardi's house?" she asked.

"We might find it, but we couldn't possibly afford it. I have heard of a modest place nearer the university."

"Beside *il Canalaso?*"

"I'm afraid not. But possibly there is some place other than the Grand Canal to take your heart away from me."

She smiled. "Is it far from the Rialto Bridge, then?"

"Nowhere is far in Venice," he said.

"Will there be other people there? Foreigners, like us?"

"Ah, you're lonely, my dear. That's all."

He held out a hand and she crossed to him, moving through the dark and the light of the window. She sat with her back to a bedpost and pulled her feet up under her.

"I didn't expect it to be so . . . different," she said.

"To France?" he scolded.

"Yes, to France, to home."

"*Ma chere*, all of Europe seems different to me, from England. And different, again, each city from every other." He clasped her hand with both of his. "Soon enough the offers from other Venetian ladies will arrive, the calls to private salons, the exhibitions, the . . . well, whatever it is you'll find to be of interest. There is music, art. The glass and the lace—"

"Come for a walk with me," she said.

"At this hour?"

"Why not? All of Venice is doing it. We may as well fit in."

She didn't add, *and get outside this accursed house.*

Francis raised a weary hand. "I have a meeting in the morning with *il Generalissimo*."

"*Bien sûr*, sleep, then, if you can." Francesca got to her feet. She pressed the back of her hand to his temple to feel the heat of his skin. Beneath her wrist, his eyes were heavy and dark. "Perhaps I'll see if there's any cool water to be had in the kitchen,"

"Don't fetch it yourself," he said roughly. "If you want something, call for one of the servants."

Francesca snorted. Her husband liked to pretend—if he had not forgotten—that it was not long ago she was a servant herself, and a scandalous woman for stealing a Lord's heart.

"I don't want to wake them," she said.

"You think they're sleeping?" Francis lay back on the bed. "They're probably all outside, taking the continental walk."

• • •

Francesca tiptoed into the hallway with her dressing gown pulled tight around her, lending heat and weight to her progress.

The house was huge, designed for a large family and all their attendant servants. A hall ran its length, rising through two stories, so that Francesca could grasp the balcony outside her bedroom and gaze down to the marble floor that led to the front door. She liked the unfamiliar openness of the place. But even here the air was stifling and clammy and the marble balustrades shone wetly in the gloom.

She left the hallway and crossed to the room adjoining the bedroom, where her trunk had been deposited. The servants hadn't unpacked it, but rather left it standing on its end with its contents crowded and falling. The dress she'd travelled in two days earlier was still laid on the bed where she'd left it. In the gloom it looked like someone had fallen there, angled across the bed in an attitude of neglect.

She moved to the trunk and pulled out a simple, grey gown. But she decided it was too heavy for the climate, even this late at night. She swapped it for a lighter gown in green, where the sleeves finished at her elbows. She dressed by candlelight and then slipped from the room towards the stairs.

She wouldn't go far, she promised herself. She would stand with her back to the front door and watch the people who walked the embankments.

She would take in the air that ran the length of *il Canalaso*.

All the way down the stairs she had to steel herself against the sound of her stiff silk dress and the whispers she was sure filled the air. She thought the stones of the building were talking amongst themselves. When one step creaked, she fancied she could hear soft crying.

She moved forward, through the dense air and the noises of sorrow.

The closer she got to the bottom of the stairs, the worse the whispering became. It was almost chanting, a soft susurration of noise that rose and fell, holding her up and bearing her down. Her heart thudded in unison. She felt she might be enclosed in the lungs of something warm and wet and alive.

She would have turned and run back to the room where Francis lay, probably still awake and fitful, except then she would have to explain to him her dress and why she'd been heading outside alone.

In the end it seemed the darkness at her back was worse than the gloom of the hall in front of her, so she kept moving. Though her hand stiffened on the railing and she had to drag herself forward.

Just above the well of darkness at the bottom of the staircase, she hesitated. The chanting had stopped, fallen away with a choking noise.

Instead, a sound hung in the air around her, a kind of hushing, hissing noise. More than a rush of wind through a half-closed window or the ocean against stone foundations.

The skin of her temple prickled and something seemed to crawl up her spine.

Something watched her in the dark.

She spun, fast enough that the candle she was holding faltered and almost went out.

"Hello?"

Her voice was sharp and too loud. In the cavernous space of the central hall she heard it echo.

No answer.

She waited with her heart pounding, hoping Francis wouldn't rise and find her in the wide hallway, dressed as if she intended to leave.

"Who's there?" she whispered hoarsely.

A face caught on the edge of the candle's light. *"Scusa, Signora."*

It was impertinent to use the familiar to address her. But it was a familiar impertinence.

"Marzio?" she said.

Only one of the servants, after all. She felt the relief roll from her temple to her toes, though her heart seemed to beat all the harder.

He loomed out of the darkness and stepped towards her. *"Prego."*

"Why are you here in the dark?"

But it wasn't quite dark. As he moved, she glimpsed a triangle of light behind him. It was coming from one of the sitting rooms, where a heavy brocade curtain had been pulled aside.

"Who gave you permission to light the lamps in that room, Marzio?" she asked. "That is not for servants."

She moved to go around him and Marzio blocked her.

"Pardon!" she cried. "You do not dictate where I may go in this house."

Marzio sneered and for a moment Francesca quailed and might have turned away, back towards the relative safety of the stairs. But then behind her she heard a door open and Francis' voice calling.

She turned, humiliated, and watched him come down the stairs in his nightshirt and dressing gown. His hair was untidy and he looked as far from a lord of any manor as she had seen. But she was glad he was there.

"What the devil?" he asked. "And who are those people in the sitting room?"

Francesca realized he was right, there were people in the room. Seven of them, wedged together around a dining table, their hands linked, their skin shining from the light of the lamps.

She recognized one of them—another servant, Knaus, a young man with pale skin and dark eyes. The rest were strangers. An old couple caught her eye, their skin the deep olive of the south. The woman's face was red and puffy with tears that still stained her cheeks.

"What is this?" Francis asked. "Marzio, explain yourself."

"Permesso." Marzio bowed stiffly. "We gather in honour."

"In honour of what, blast it?" Francis asked. "For the duration of our stay, I am the master of this house and I will give you permission or otherwise."

Tall as he was, Marzio seemed to cower.

Francis moved to the sitting room and she followed.

In the room, the strangers dropped their hands and turned with expressions of contrition or contempt. Gathered on the table in front of them, Francesca saw something familiar. A child's drawings of Venice.

"Where did you get this?" she asked at once.

Marzio turned to her stiffly.

"The family," he began, "the Lombardi, in their absence, we may borrow this room."

"They allow it?"

Marzio gestured with his hands, but he didn't quite nod.

"You should know your place," Francis said.

"These drawings," Francesca said. "These are the ones I found in the wardrobe."

To her horror, she felt the eyes of all the servants turn to her. The mournful look on the face of the old woman changed to something between wonder and horror. Her hands rose, twisted together in the shape of prayer.

"You see?" the woman asked. "You *see?*"

Francis interrupted, "I see that whatever you're doing here is unchristian. You must desist at once. Kindly take your leave!"

At first the gathered people sat still like they'd collapsed there, wilting in the heat.

But then the oldest man stirred. He rose to his feet, bobbing his head and uttering strange, accented apologies. The others followed, making their way to the front door of the house where Marzio bowed to each of them as they left.

"Francis," Francesca whispered, "They were trying to speak to the dead child."

"Oh, hang the child," Francis muttered.

She reeled. "Francis!"

His face twisted and something rose in his eyes, hot like the air. But then he righted himself with an effort.

"I'm sorry, *cherie*," he said. "The fever. And the servants! Where did Marzio go? I would speak with him first."

"I didn't see. Perhaps to the kitchens. Go," Francesca pushed him. "I'll take some air."

"Not alone."

"Knaus will accompany me," she said.

"See that he does. A house empty so long they think they own it, not just serve it. It's not decent."

Francesca wanted to say that the house wasn't empty, that even without the fact of the servants, something moved in here, wetly, through the hot air.

But she let Francis disappear towards the kitchen and watched his candle narrowing in the darkness of the vast hall.

Knaus had remained behind, putting out the lamps with a pronounced methodicalness. Darkness took over the room, spreading with slow certainty.

Francesca took a seat in the room where the drawings of the unknown child still lay on the table. "Knaus?"

"*Si?*"

"Your name isn't Italian. You're from Austria?" she asked.

"My family," he shrugged.

He shrugged like an Italian, she couldn't help thinking, that careless grace she was growing used to.

"These drawings are very old." She indicated where they lay on the table.

"*Si*, they are from a long time ago."

"Do you know of a ghost in this house?"

Knaus chuckled. "Only one?"

"Then there are ghosts here?"

"This is Venice." He gave that shrug again.

"Yes. This is," she said. "Who were you trying to contact?"

Knaus frowned. "What do you mean?"

"During the *séance*, what spirit were you hoping to raise?"

His frown lifted into something that looked like a grin. "You think we contact the dead?"

He threw his head back and laughed.

"Then, what?" Francesca insisted.

"That is not for me to say," he grinned. "How is this you say, a *séance*?"

"What, then?" Francesca gestured with both hands towards the tall ceiling. "Wait, don't tell me. That is not for you to say."

Knaus might have shrugged again, but by then she was on her feet.

"Come with me," she said, with as much insistence as she could manage.

Knaus looked at her as if she were mad.

But he followed when she marched to the front door, through the dark, the candles neglected on the sitting room table. She pulled open the heavy door and stepped out, and turned once to make sure he followed.

She found the old couple boarding a *gondola*. From this distance it looked like a floating coffin on the dark waters of *il Canalaso*.

She rushed towards them, crying out in whatever Italian she could manage. *"Aiuto!"*

It wasn't the right word. She pulled at Knaus' sleeve and urged him forward.

The old man in the *gondola* only looked confused, but the woman with the sad eyes, she stopped and watched and waited until Francesca joined them at the water's edge.

"I should like to know," Francesca breathed, "about the child."

"The child?" the old man muttered.

She could feel Knaus' stare burning into her back. Away from the overheated rooms of the Lombardi house and the overheated salon of Contessa Rossi, she didn't feel so afraid. Outside where the air moved and she could breathe at last. The *Ponte di Rialto* sat in canopied splendour across the Grand Canal. The breeze cooled her skin, soothing the strange ideas the house had put into her head.

The *gondoliere* spoke to Knaus in rapid, staccato Italian. Too fast for Francesca to understand.

She clambered into the gondola, feeling it rock under her feet. It was lacquered black, like they all were save for the official boats of the papacy. The small cabin where the old couple now sat was embossed with curlicues and shapes like swirling vines. Thin blinds let in slants of light across the couple's faces.

She turned to Knaus. "Please tell *signore il gondoliere* that I should like to be returned here when we deliver this couple to their home. And I will pay him handsomely."

Knaus sneered, but he spoke to *il gondoliere*. From what she could gather, the man seemed to agree.

They slid through the canal and the dark night. Francesca felt the air swell around her, cool and smooth, but still dense with seawater.

She settled into the rock of the boat. The push as the *gondoliere* levered the oar into the water from the stern was soothing, a steady press of boat through water with the night-calmed city around her.

Most houses featured a window or two where light still showed, but they seemed stilled, their broad facades and evenly-spaced windows calmer than the day. Even the spires didn't pierce, and the arches only beckoned. She realized she could surrender to this Venice, this softer place of night and dark.

"Il mio nome è Francesca," she said.

"Signore Neri," said the old man, *"e Signora."*

Francesca felt her way forward, as much into the language as the topic. "Tell me about the child."

The couple exchanged a glance.

For a long while, no one spoke. Francesca thought of Contessa Rossi's stories. She thought she should like to pay the woman back with stories of her own.

"I found drawings," she prompted, "in a child's hand. Drawings of Venice. What do you know about them? Were they your child's?"

The couple was silent, immobile as stone. As if they had been painted to the inside of the lacquered cabin.

"We used to work for the Lombardi," the old woman said at last.

Her voice issued hollowly from the cabin. The light from the blinds lit her brown cheeks and left her eyes dark.

"Yes?" Francesca asked.

"Our daughter would play in the rooms of the Lombardi. They indulged her. We thought they were . . . kind."

"Certo," Francesca said. "Where is she now, your child?"

"She is lost."

The old woman's voice broke and with it, something inside Francesca seemed to break, too.

"I lost a child, too," she said, in earnestness. Venice, she thought, could have all her secrets. "My child died."

Above her the sky was bright with stars, and the water dark at her sides.

The old woman said, "She did not die."

"Excusez-moi?"

The old woman leaned forward, out of the cabin and into the light. Her hair was silver and dark grey, and the lamp that swung from the bow of the *gondola* lit her face into masks of the *carnevale.*

She gave Francesca a piercing stare. "Our daughter did not die. She was taken from us."

"Ah!" Francesca said. "Is it so? What took her?"

She thought perhaps plague or cholera had claimed the girl, perhaps this was some great family tragedy from which the Neri, servants of the Lombardi, had never recovered. She thought, too, she could repay Contessa Rossi handsomely with this story.

The old woman continued, "She was *bellissima*. All who saw her could not resist. And so, they took her from us."

"They?"

"The Lombardi," she said.

"The . . . ?"

"The family," the old man interrupted, "who own the house you stay in. They took our *nipotina* to raise as their own."

"No!"

The couple only nodded, their expressions forlorn.

"But then," Francesca hesitated. "Why does she haunt the house?"

The couple reeled and turned to each other, their hands entwining in a motion that was practiced and perfect. Light bounced on the lacquered black finish either side of them, light slid along the carvings of vines that looked like serpents.

"Haunt the house?" the old man said. "She does not! She lives."

"But I was told a child haunts the house."

"Her memories, perhaps?" The wife explained. "They haunt all of us."

Francesca tried to understand. "The family, The Lombardi . . . they took her alive, then?"

"*Si.*"

It seemed so evil, but an evil so much more mundane than Francesca had expected. "Where is she now, your little girl?"

The woman gestured as if it were all the same to her. "She is grown to a woman in Innsbruck. But to us, she will always be our lost *nipotina*."

"Ah." Francesca was still. "But it's not the same. *Non*, it is not the same at all. To lose a daughter to a different life, and not to death."

She was ashamed of her disappointment. The child lived, after all. She lived.

"My child died," Francesca said. "She *died*."

Francesca wanted to explain that a child being raised in wealth and the semblance of whatever honour the Lombardi could bestow, that was not a child who had died. She was not truly lost as long as she still lived.

But when she thought of all those lost children, the ones stolen from Italy to beg, the children taken and dead, she wasn't sure herself if that was true. Too many children never found their ways home.

She saw now that to a parent, any missing child was a loss that broke them in half.

The old man eased back into the cabin, waving a dismissive hand in Francesca's direction. "Your child was chosen by God to return to Heaven."

Francesca didn't reply. She couldn't. Was the cruelty of the Lombardi anywhere near as bad as the cruelty of God?

Francesca blinked away tears. She caught the *gondoliere* frowning at her, so she turned to watch the progress of the houses and the people making their *passeggiare* in the lamplit streets.

"So, there is no ghost?" she asked softly.

Signore Neri let out a noise that might have been a sigh of disgust. "You long for ghosts? Life is hard enough."

"Life is very hard," she corrected him. "So I would like to know, for sure . . . if there is something more. For our children, at the very least."

No one replied.

The *gondoliere* made a sharp left into a canal.

They drifted past a white house with red roof and a cluster of short trees, their foliage black in the evening light, limned with moonlight at their untidy tops. The *gondoliere* pulled his boat to a halt beside a modest square.

The old couple moved to depart. *Signore* Neri alighted first, so he could turn and offer a hand to his wife.

Signora Neri leaned forward and squeezed Francesca's wrist. "You must leave the house. Bad things happen there. Cruel things."

Francesca felt a hollow open up in her stomach. She nodded and looked away quickly so the old woman wouldn't see her cry.

She heard the *Signora* heave herself from the gondola and felt the sway of the narrow boat as the other woman left.

Francesca did not watch them go.

The canal was too narrow to turn in, so the *gondoliere* navigated backwards to the entrance where it joined *il Canalaso*. He gestured at Francesca, almost like he was waving her away.

"You leave here," he said.

"I do not," she replied. "The understanding was to return to where you collected me."

"You leave here," he repeated, his voice neither insistent nor harsh.

Francesca made to argue. She'd had enough of the lack of respect in this city. But two men lumbered towards the gondola, greeting the *gondoliere* like an old friend. They stepped into the gondola, sending it rocking, and only then did they seem to catch sight of Francesca.

"You travel to Murano?" one asked.

"No, I return to *il Ponte di Rialto*," Francesca corrected him. She tried to keep the alarm out of her voice.

"It is the other direction," the second man said.

"We had an agreement—" she began.

The *gondoliere* waved her off. "Not with me! And not with your manservant, Knaus."

Francesca edged forward from the cabin of the *gondola*. If needs must, she could walk from here, back to the Lombardi house and the savage heat it trapped inside. But she had to get out now. If they took her to the island of Murano, there would only be the *gondoliere* to return her.

She stood and made for the embankment, ignoring the hand of the man who tried to help her alight.

They sniggered as she tripped and nearly fell. A hand reached out to shove her higher up the embankment.

With a splash the *gondoliere* pushed off.

Francesca watched them go. She stood under the darkness of the trees and tried to quell the anger that rose.

This would never happen in France! Never would a young woman alone be dumped onto a dark and empty street.

And then she realized that everyone who'd been out walking had, as if by mutual agreement, disappeared to their houses. The windows here were dark and empty, the houses looked abandoned like toys floating in a dark bath. She shivered despite the heat.

The canal where the Neri couple had exited was between her and home, and there was no bridge. Even had there been a bridge, the house on the other corner took up the whole block. There was no place to walk. It was the same when she tried to move from the trees and along the canal to her right. Everywhere she was blocked her.

Francis often spoke of how easy it was to lose oneself in the serpentine streets of Venice. Now she knew the truth of it. The only direction she could take was away from home, in the hopes she might find another bridge like the Rialto to carry her over to the other side and then, hopefully, back to a familiar safety.

She marched as fast as she could in the wrong direction, looking for a way back. She had no idea where she was, had never travelled this far alone. The houses that had looked so cheerful in the daylight now loomed tall, almost bending beneath the dark sky.

It was quiet, and her footsteps were too loud against the paved embankment. She began to tiptoe, watching her feet.

"*Aiuto!*" someone called.

Francesca froze.

The voice came again. *Aiuto! Aiuto!* Someone was calling for help. Softly, like they were far away. The sound echoed off the water and stone of Venice.

"Hello?"

Aiuto!

Francesca froze. The sound was coming from the canal she'd just left. She turned, but saw nothing except the shadows of the trees, almost solid under the moonlight.

The voice was fading, but something even worse than that occurred to her then. The voice was the voice of the child.

She stood, listening for it over her heavy pulse. The night was silent, even the faint breeze along *il Canalaso* seemed to have died completely.

Aiuto!

It wasn't a voice, she realized.

It was a group of voices, crying in unison.

It wasn't an echo. It was *children.*

"Where are you?" she cried.

She ran along the embankment, pulling at her skirts to free her knees, but even then she had a tottering gait, the dress clinging to her damp skin. She ran away from the sounds of the cries, away from home. She almost cried out herself, but she was afraid of rousing whatever was behind the blank Venetian glass of the windows around her.

She slipped, and skidded over the embankment.

She hit the canal with a splash and for a moment the moon was obscured by dark water. It was warm, warmer even than the air. Warm like something alive. Long skirts carried her down and she gulped water.

She kicked off her thin shoes and grabbed for a mooring sunken deep in the canal. She hauled herself up.

The stars danced in blurred patterns above her. She kept her head up, out of the water.

Something in the dark canal seemed to wrap around her, pinning her green dress to her body. Something hooked around her ankles, something pulled on her toes and knees and dragged her down.

Something was in the water with her, its small hands pulling her under.

"Help!" she called. She choked and coughed and spat sour water. "Help!"

No one was there to help her. It was as if the whole city of Venice had emptied out.

With a lunge, she made for the embankment and dragged herself, dripping, onto land. Her elbows shook as she raised herself from the water.

For a moment there was a tug-of-war between her hands and the hands that held her to the water.

Francesca pressed her palms to the stone and leaned forward until just her feet were in the water. Then with a roar she pulled her feet free of the water and rolled onto her side.

She spat up canal water and laid her forehead to the cold lettering of the street name embossed in the stone.

The cries she'd heard were gone. The hands she'd felt—Francis would never believe her—they no longer dragged at her. All was quiet.

She lay for a while in the cool of the dripping water and the cold moonlight, the lettering beneath her pressing into her temple.

Then at last she lifted her head and read the words embossed into the street.

And she cried for all the lost children for whom this street—*Riva di Biasio*—had been named.

GLASSKIN

ROBERT G. COOK

My lover comes to me at night.

He rises before me, coalescing, a bright star cooling into visceral flesh. But though his body is a transformed sun, the mind that moves it is, I think, of a more feminine cast. She teaches me about myself, even as he moves me to learn the glacial, melting contours of bodies met and wed.

He is always gone when I wake. My attic room faces down the alley to the old fishermen's docks, and as the sun rises far behind Tallinn over the hinterland, the roof's shadow shrinks towards me along the cobbles and I watch mist burning off the water in rising mandalas. Salt tangs in my nose and I taste copper. In my window's frost of salt stains I see fractured snowflakes, cancerous stars, each crystalline shape slipping in and out of the fog I breathe on the thin pane. I make tea, but watching my hands move carefully through the process of lighting the stove and pouring the water and stirring the leaves, I find myself remembering their movements in the night, their course across the smoothness of his body, the fingers splaying and contracting as her words speak his movements inside me; and the glass stands untouched in its baroque silver handle on the small folding table by my bed, the caramel liquid shifting with the movement of the floorboards and sending up curlicues of distressed steam as the tea steeps and cools.

By mid-morning the waters of the Finnish Gulf reflect an umbral green that is almost black, but by then I am downstairs in the workshop, the glory's heat tightening the skin on my cheeks and forehead while my grandfather leads the daily throng of tourists through the furnace-room to the temptations of the showroom and the gladdening ring of the bell on the old wooden till.

"The first oven is the crucible, the hottest of the three." My grandfather walks around to the other side of the furnace and opens the crucible's door with a set of insulated tongs. The billow of heat is fierce and instant, and the small crowd steps back almost as one. "Inside is the source—a pot of pure molten glass, our basic material." He swings the door gently closed. "The others are the glory, where my apprentice is working to reheat a piece between stages of work—" I look up briefly and raise a gauntleted hand in welcome, but don't bother smiling beneath the heavy visor "—and the annealer for gradual cooling and tempering, so there are no cracks in the finished work."

"Do you ever make mistakes?" someone asks. Someone always does.

"The artistry of the glasswright is as much in the use of extraneous materials as in the handling of the elemental glass." My grandfather smiles beneficently, apparently glad as ever to answer the same old questions. "We use many different formulations, gasses, acids and so forth. Rare essences, as it were. Fragments of time, distillations of the soul." His audience is rapt, the magic of his charm as potent now as when he opened this place half a century ago. He walks the length of a shelf along the far wall, brushing fingertips on vials and stoppered bottles. Stops and takes one in his hand, a small flask half-full of a moon-blue viscous liquid. "These do not always work as planned, though the end results are rarely uninteresting, as we'll see." He replaces the flask, gestures towards the heavy oak door at the far end of the foundry. "Now, if you'll follow me, I'll show you some of our finished work."

Our house, which is also our workshop and our showroom, is an old Lutheran church, a high, narrow antique of a building crammed indelicately between warehouses and processing plants and flanked along its ancient cobbled laneway by darkened empty cafes and half-abandoned tenements. My bedroom used to be the belfry, the long-gone bell still echoing faintly in the cross-beams. The vestry now houses the furnaces, a dying Saviour in a stained glass window the only sign of the room's former use, though the window backs onto a courtyard that has long been overshadowed by high-rise blocks and the only light the Saviour gets now is weak and stained itself. The showroom and shop inhabit the nave, its stone walls warmly yellow and the high rafters vanishing up into the night-black vaults. The showroom's shelving is made from artfully rusted iron rods and sheer glass flats, each shelf underlit by a high-watt bulb set into the stone floor. The wall lighting is gentle, directed: atmosphere to set off the floor lights' glare. And caught in the centre, filled with light, overflowing and bursting with luminescence as if it were liquid, is the glass.

Some days, the show-and-tell is my job: these are the off days, the *other* days, when my grandfather is feeling especially cantankerous, days when he objects bitterly to the whole notion of tourists and commerce and just about anything warm and human. Usually, days when he has been working at the furnaces in his cellar workrooms through the preceding night and into the dawn. On these days I know without asking that the daily round of babble and bauble is mine to perform, while he stays locked away from the world in his inner sanctum, his private workshop in the basement. I've never seen his workshop, though he has promised me any number of times.

I don't mind these days at all. Whenever he's a no-show, his small legend seems to swell a portion, and I'm free to embellish and provoke: the great Illar Kroos, glasswright extraordinaire, reclusive genius of the blow-tube. The showroom is my favourite part of the tour.

When my grandfather does the tour, he tends to wax lyrical. "We have a way here of making glass live," he says, "of making it breathe and laugh and weep and cry out in great gouts of colour and light. Estonian glassware is unmistakeable. It is a manifestation of dream, of bitter history, of triumphant spirit. It is visceral, it throbs with the dark joy of Northern blood."

When it's my turn, I prefer to stand back and watch in silence as the tourists wander through the displays, and I answer their hushed, reverent questions in the lightly bored and patronising tone of a museum guide. But it's a game, a fake jadedness: every time, seeing it through the eyes of others, I am as awed by my grandfather's art as I have ever been.

There are bottles, bowls, vases, drinking glasses: standard receptacles, certainly, but fashioned as if from dream-stuff, from faerie spells and princess magic, and always I find it hard not to laugh in delight at the sheer fantasy and trickery on display. The stoppered bottles are swirling full of richly veined smoke; others are subtly misshapen, surreally leaning. There are vases that look like columns of mist, jugs with handles and spouts that have an oddly pleasing intestinal quality to them; there are some unsettlingly phallic paperweights, others that look like weaponised prisms. There are half-dissolved plates, sea-green pyramids with melt-pools at one corner, pearl spheres cracked at the top like Halloween mouths. A dinner set is centred around a plate massed with droplets of bruised earthy quartz, like tender buttons of raw meat, and a carafe with the contours of an inverted human face.

And then, as ever, there is the mirror.

There is, I have found, an inevitable process to this—the moment of panic, the sharp look back over the shoulder, the jumping and waving of arms, the delighted laughter. The questions:

"What is this?"

"How does it work?"

"Are we all vampires?" (This usually from a child.)

"Is it for sale?"

"That's a blind glass," I say. "It's an arrangement of micro-facets in a highly complex system, so that almost every reflective surface points away from the viewer. No," I smile down, "it has nothing to do with vampires. It's a trick, that's all. And no, I'm sorry, it's not for sale."

"Why not?"

"Because it's the only one of its kind. My grandfather made it almost by accident, and hasn't made another one since. So it's essentially priceless."

When it's over for the day, and the last stragglers have wandered out through the arched doorway into the wet daylight, I always stand for a few moments before the blind glass, and wonder about the provenance of a mirror that cannot see you. A myriad of tiny, deliberate imperfections calculated (or as my grandfather insists, randomly fused) so that, for an average viewer standing at an average distance from the glass, it will reflect the viewer's background and surroundings but will leave a lacuna where the viewer would normally see themselves. It's a fairground trick taken one step further—you're not just fat or thin or tall or squat, you're not an impossible reflection of someone familiar but other; you're a reflection of no one. For the time that you look into the mirror, you're not there at all. Or you're there, but there's nothing to you.

But as with all tricks, it's easily tested. If the viewer is larger than average, for instance, or stands closer or further away, there will be a hint at the edges of the abyss, a barely discernible ghost image that is enough to warrant doubt and waive the spell.

For myself, I can never look into the blind glass for longer than a few seconds, a clutch of heartbeats. I can't bear what I can see.

• • •

You know there are things he's not teaching you.

My lover told me his name the first time he came to me, and every night I cry it aloud. *Mikus*, and as though it's a signal there comes a shift in mass, in form, in meaning, and while he lies inert beside me she grows inside my mind and ablates my senses.

He told me his name, but she does not tell me hers.

"I think he's teaching me plenty."

Not me. You know what I mean. You want to be as great a glasswright as he is, and he knows it.

"He'll teach me when I'm ready."

You've been ready all your life. That's one of the things he's not teaching you.

"He's my grandfather. He's a lonely man. I think he just doesn't want me to leave too soon."

He doesn't want you to leave at all.

I shake my head, try to find a point of slippage, of free space.

"How are you here? Why do you come here?"

For you.

"Where do you come *from?*"

She answers by receding, by folding herself away into an answer I cannot know.

That's something you should ask him.

• • •

"Too slow."

Illar's tone heralds the start of another off day, brittle and sharp.

"You won't get the colour all the way through how you want it if you're that slow in the shaping."

"How do you know how I want it?" It's a reasonable question, I think, and asked in a reasonable tone; but either the visor muffles my voice, or he just doesn't hear me. Or he pretends not to.

"You're too slow, I said!"

"I heard you." I sit back and raise the visor, dawdling the blow-tube in my gauntleted hand. "But I don't want the colour all the way through. I'm trying something new."

The air in the foundry stinks with heat, tinged with sulphur and burnt metal. Sitting at the large marble-topped bench in the middle of the room, I feel a flare of pride that I know is only arrogance, and revel in it nonetheless.

Illar stoops over me, tall and lean, long dark hair turning to grey, a slight beard. Skin leathered, eyes bright: he is young-old, a man in his long prime and in his element, even on a bad day.

"I've told you before, you learn the old ways first before you try anything new."

"So teach me."

"I am teaching you, for Saulė's sake!"

"Well you're teaching me too slow."

Around the edges of the room are open crates of various powdered substances: sands in a multitude of colours, silicate, crushed quartz. Arrayed on stands and smaller tables around the central bench are an infinite variety of blocks, jacks, paddles, tweezers, shears, sheets of paper. One stand holds nothing but blow-tubes; another holds two baskets, one of coloured glass rods of different thicknesses, the other of uniformly thick rods cut at different lengths and showing patterns in the cross-sections.

Illar straightens, rubs his back, paces over to the beaten metal bookshelf that is stacked like a tower puzzle with textbooks and monographs on glass art and glass-working, chemistry, materials science.

"Maybe it's you who's learning too slowly. Eh? Did you think of that, smart-arse?"

I look down at the bubble of yellow glass on the end of the blow-tube as it falls in a slow stretch towards the sawdust on the stone floor.

"Yes, of course, grandfather. It's my fault."

"I didn't say it was your fault." For the briefest of moments there is gentleness in his voice. "And stop wasting materials, for Saulė's sake!" Instinctively I jerk the blow-tube up and the elongated sphere of semi-molten glass folds into itself on the metal like a collapsing balloon. "It's not like you manage to sell enough of that crap out there to keep us in bread, never mind in glass."

He crashes through the connecting door into the showroom and I hear him grumbling aloud as he heads for the other door, the locked door, in the side-chapel. Then he's gone, the door sealed behind him, down into his private kingdom. He'll come back up later, for spiced tea and black bread, but we won't talk much. We never do on days like this. There's too much to say.

• • •

I have become a slave to injured sleep.

Glass can be like flesh. Mikus's voice is thick with desire. *Warm, supple, even yielding. Visceral.* His fingers curve and press where I am tender. *Strong as a prison, or frail as skin.*

"That hurts. A little."

It's all right. You won't break.

"Are you sure?"

I won't break you.

His own flesh is blue and translucent. Through his arm I can see his torso, an outline of sinew and muscle in empty skin. My hands glide along the surface of him, find drops of thick moisture on his back, strands of tangled fragility in his hair.

"Mikus." Not a cry this time, though, and he stays with me, moving and ever urgent.

You like my name.

"What if I didn't? Do you have another name?"

His movements slow perceptibly, and he shifts his head to look at my face, and for the first time I look directly into his eyes. The effect is unnerving, like looking into the eyes of twin hurricanes, and I realise with a twist in my gut that through a blue gyral mist I'm looking at the inside of the back of his head.

She hasn't told you hers, then. He smiles, and his lips sound out a soft grating, a susurration of glass on glass. *Not to worry, my little love. She'll tell you when you're ready.*

Angry heat blooms in my chest and in my face, and I twist sharply under him and push out. He rolls off but won't let go, and tries to pull me on top of him with the momentum. He has one cold smooth hand around my wrist; I raise my arm over my head and hit it down onto the iron bedstead. I hear a crunch and his grip is gone. I push at his shape and I am pushing at the bedclothes, waking up with a breathless and indignant shout.

Before I wake again, to the bitter light and the thin plane of ice on my window, the last thing she says to me is this:

Ask him about your grandmother. Ask him about Saulė.

• • •

The first round of tourists have gone for lunch and beer and sightseeing, to the King's Garden and Fat Margaret Tower or for a fake interrogation at the old Russian prison at Patarei. My grandfather is using an acid process to etch a design of nude female figures into a clear wide-flared vase—their bodies are a frosted flowing white, swimming upwards, arms outstretched and suppliant, faces subtly contorted with grief. While I sit at his side, the dutiful student, and marvel at his artistry, I also wonder at who might want to buy such a beautiful, terrible thing.

"No hesitation, you see. That's key to your success." He scrapes delicate contours into the surface, strands of hair, striations of muscle. Each stroke of his hand is solid and flowing, not the least tremor, each movement a smooth fragment of a greater line. "You can't stop and think about it while you're doing it. If you haven't thought it all through beforehand then you've no business putting hand to glass in the first place."

"Illar."

"What? Are you watching? You're supposed to be watching, not talking."

"I'm watching." I'm watching the minuscule eyes take shape in one of the undine faces, dark hollows above high cheekbones that catch an unearthly, invisible light. There's a photo on the mantel in his bedroom that has hints of that face in it, that face smiling beneath a bright summer hat and shards of light off Lake Harku in the background. "Who is she?"

The line doesn't falter, but at the end of that stroke his hand pauses and he flexes his arm out and back before starting on the next pass.

"You know perfectly well who she is."

"I don't know that grandmother would have liked to be imagined as a grieving nymph."

"Maybe not a grieving one, no." There is a sly grin on his face. "But Trüde was always only too happy to model for me."

He stretches his back, takes the acid pen into his left hand and reaches around to the wine cooler with his right, extracts the gothically moulded stein from the puddling ice and takes an enormous draft of clear cold water down his parched throat. Even on a winter's day with the crucible only idling and the other furnaces cold, the foundry is still the uncomfortably hottest room in the building.

"Tell me about her."

He crunches the stein back into the ice and settles the acid pen back into his working hand. Bends forward over the vase, begins his next stroke.

"What do you want to know?"

I think about what to ask, how to ask it.

"What did you call her?"

"Her name, what else? Trüde. You used to call her Nana Trüde yourself."

"What else did you call her?"

"God, I don't know! Darling, sweet one, Trüdelinde. Occasionally harridan or shrew." He pauses, squints at me. "Odd questions. You okay? Too cold up there to sleep?" He nods up towards my attic.

"Too hot, actually." I wait until he starts a new stroke of the acid pen, a perfect curved line over an elemental buttock, and say: "What about Saulė?"

The pen goes through both sides of the vase and into his left palm, taking a jagged shard with it and plunging a water wraith's outstretched hand into his own. Crimson spatters up the frosted whiteness of her limb. My grandfather howls, a sound of anguish as much as pain, and lurches forward. The remains of the vase clatter onto the marble benchtop, shattering and scattering into slivers and dust. I am rigid with fear and guilt. If I'd intended anything it was only to spoil the design, not to destroy, not to injure.

"Don't just sit there!" My grandfather is up and staggering to the big tin sink in the corner. "I need gauze and bandages, some sulfadiazine if we've got any."

"I'm sorry."

"Why are you sorry? I'm the one who cut my damn hand open."

"What I said—"

"What about what you said? God's sake, stop squawking and get me some bloody ointment."

I open the cupboard next to the sink, rummage for the first aid box.

"You should have been wearing gloves."

"I never wear gloves when I'm etching, you know that."

"You make me wear gloves."

"Yes, well. Do what I say, not what I do." Ice-cold water runs over the rip in his palm and sputters down the drain threaded with ribbons of crimson. His face is set against the pain as the acid from the glass and the pen burns the edges of the wound. "Gloves get in the way. Putting anything between you and the glass clouds what you're doing, stops you feeling your way through to the image, to the truth of what you're making." He glances at me, and for the first time his face looks truly old—accepting of its age, and bowed by it.

"We're the only ones left, you know," he says then. He tries to grin. "And I'm running low on material. All my deals are reaching their end date. Soon it'll just be you."

I take his wounded hand in both of mine and gently place the ointment-soaked gauze over the ravaged palm, then bind it with a crepe bandage.

"You've hurt your left hand, Illar, not lost your right arm. You've still got plenty of art left in you."

He shows me a grateful smile, but there's something hard now behind his eyes, an edge I've never seen before: a deliberation, a calculation. Something fundamentally cold. And I wonder then, thinking about the question that I asked, whether the wound in his hand is my fault at all.

Still, I insist that he goes to the Hambapol Clinic for proper first aid, a thorough investigation of the injury, a professional dressing. He, in turn, insists that I mustn't go with him, that an old wooden door and high windows aren't enough security for the showroom, that I must stay and look after the place. After the taxi drives away, Illar cradling his hand in a towel in the back seat, I walk back through the showroom and catch a glimpse in the blind glass of the side-chapel's archway, and a hint at the edges of the mirror's lacuna of something blue and sharp and cold.

• • •

"Mikus!"

But he's not there. I've fallen asleep fully dressed on the bed, and woken with his name in my mouth but no voice in my head. The clock says it's four in the morning. I'm thirsty and too warm, and make my way downstairs to the small kitchen behind the foundry.

I find myself instead before the chapel's archway and the locked steel door to the basement beyond. It's shut, as it always is, solid against the old stonework. I didn't get a drink, I realise, and turn to walk back through the darkened showroom, and there is the mirror on the far side, blind as ever, and in it the cellar's steel door at the back of the chapel is open.

Some part of my mind assumes this is a dream, and that therefore the contrary image doesn't have to make sense. But other parts, the parts that are thirsty and too warm and that saw the clock, make me look back again into the chapel. At the resolutely closed basement door.

"Oh, for Saulė's sake," I breathe, and stop and wonder why I said that. That is my grandfather's oath, not mine.

Ask him about Saulė.

I did ask him, and he ripped a hole in his hand and went to hospital. So what was the point of that?

Look again.

Her voice in the back of my head, and I turn sharply and am trapped again by the mirror. In the blind, unseeing glass, the door to my grandfather's private sanctuary stands open.

Remember, the mirror cannot see. So it cannot lie about what it sees.

"Mikus." I want the other dream. I want to wake up in the other dream with him beside me, with his impossible skin on mine. "Mikus, please."

No, not Mikus Auseklis. Not brother-lover, not this time. He found you, and led you to me. Now find me, and I will lead you to him.

The mirror cannot see, and so cannot lie about what it sees.

So what I see is a lie?

I step into the chapel. There is a memorial to one side, a stone sarcophagus mounted by the ruined effigy of some long-dead Teutonic knight; its feet are missing and half the face is gone, the noble features crumbling into pitted marble. I look closely at the door. Heavy steel, no handle, a smooth flush fit into the church's stone-brick walls. Impassable, to my eyes.

A lie.

I close my eyes and reach my hand forward to touch the door. My fingers touch nothing. To look now would, I know, be a mistake. I walk forward again, four, five, six steps, well beyond the door's barrier. I turn and open my eyes. The door is closed, sealed, solid. Or looks solid, at least. I think about testing it, and decide not to, decide to hope that it simply works the same way going back out. It's only a dream, after all. If it doesn't work, I can always wake up.

There are a dozen steps in front of me, old and worn and slippery with condensation. I tread carefully down them and find myself in a long chamber, a wide corridor in the earth lit by angled spotlights that leave irregular stretches of it in blackness. As I move through and down I feel the temperature drop. My breath skeins into mist in front of my face, and there is a faint odour of sulphur and old earth.

Lining the tunnel walls are the same iron-rodded shelves as in the showroom. Initially they hold more of the eccentric, glorious misshapes from the upstairs studio—Illar's signature melted forms and dissolute wholes, though more extreme in their deliberate imperfections. But further down the chamber there are other objects. Tall fronds of green glass set out in clusters along one wall: the first group all perfectly vertical, like the rods of glass in the foundry but with flared bases where they seem to be growing straight from the shelf; the next group beginning to bend, the merest undulation at their tips; the next group more pronounced, almost as if they are swaying in a non-existent breeze. And on down the wall into darkness, and then I look again and they are changed. The first group is now supplicant, bending almost to the flat surface from which they sprout; the group farthest away is upright, stiff as bamboo. And they change again, and I know, I think, that it is a trick of the light.

Looking hard away from the falsely swaying grass, I move down the line of transparent shelves. My gaze settles on another display, three curved semi-pyramidal pieces that look more like polished stone than glass—a lustrous golden brown like tiger's eye, with yellow fibres running through it. Each 'stone' is pitted in several places, adding a seeming element of decay to their beauty. On another shelf sits a clear glass paperweight globe with a partial opening in the top and striations in the glass that make me think uncomfortably of teeth. I stop beside a set of shelves replete with blood-red bowls interconnected with dendritic venous straws of blue-black glass. I look closer. There is a slight, slow pulsation, a peristaltic drift of current along the glass veins between each scarlet bowl.

All the days my grandfather spent down here—the bad days, the *off* days—brooding and grumbling and, so I always thought, pouring his little miseries into his art. But this isn't the artistry of the showroom, these aren't the modern relics of wonder that the tourists come to buy. I look back along the corridor. The thickly swaying filaments of green, like infected polyps or gangrenous muscle strands; the tiger's eye rocks like massive gallstones on a slab. This is an art of strange compulsion, of sacrilege and sacrifice, of offal and taint. These are vessels and organs rendered in infernal dust, viscera in glass.

I feel a hard binding in my own muscles, a tension that sets off an uncontrollable tremor in my upper legs and arms. I force breath into my lungs and movement into my feet, and walk on down the darkened corridor.

The tunnel opens out into a large circular chamber of rough-hewn stone, maybe half as big again as the showroom in the nave upstairs, lit by strings of arc lamps hanging from crampons hammered into the rock. Midway around on one side is an archway that leads to a narrow room—a small foundry, with three furnaces and all the necessary equipment carefully placed to make the most of the minimal space. The glory and the annealer are closed and cold, the crucible barely glowing. There are several large holes drilled into the roof of both the foundry and the main chamber, and I can feel a cool passage of air when I stand beneath them. As in the vestry foundry, there is a small bookshelf to one side, though this one is of ornately carved wood rather than workaday aluminium. But there are no technical manuals on these shelves; instead there are volumes of Northern mythology, scholarly texts on witchcraft and religion, and a battered cloth-bound pocket book with the title stamped in gold-leaf: *On The Malleability Of The Soul.*

In the main chamber, there are six display cases of iron and thick glass set into alcoves that have been chiselled at regular intervals around the walls. Each case holds an assortment of small objects—

plates, bowls, goblets, glass flowers. These objects are neither the fanciful meanderings of Illar's commercial output, nor the grimly beguiling chimaera from the tunnel, but are instead curiously flat in their effect, almost void of artistry altogether, like mismatched minor parts of a greater whole.

To the sides of each case are smaller stands holding altogether stranger objects, along with wall-hangings and individually mounted sculptures. There is a picture of a long beach, with the sand fused into glass. There is a carved wooden pole on which sits a glass helmet, smoothly rounded, a rococo design etched into the facade and a darker opacity where the eye-holes should be. Another painting, smaller, back-lit stained glass that looks sand-blasted, of a ghost-pale child looking up to Heaven. Another, a monotone face behind frosted glass, but part of the glass is torn away like skin to show black-and-white flesh beneath. I see silicate viscera displayed as if on a mortuary table, blown-glass filaments fine as hair, miniature quartz figurines caught in poses of agony and joy.

Beside what I at first take to be one more display case, though this one is taller and covered in a heavy black cloth, there hangs an entire glass body, flawlessly transparent, upside-down and held fast in an inverted pose of blessing. Its eyes are sightless, hollow sockets in an angelic face, yet it holds my gaze and tells me that I am here now beyond all measure of safety.

I reach for the cloth covering the case and pull.

• • •

I don't know how long I've been standing there when Illar's voice breaks through the wall of my skull and my consciousness spills back out into the world.

"Nietzsche knew what he was talking about, you know. You should look away now."

With more effort than I would ever have imagined necessary for such a task, an effort that costs me pain in my shoulders and behind my eyes, I peel my gaze away from the blind glass and look at my grandfather. His left hand is thickly bandaged, his arm raised halfway up his chest in a sling.

"How? How did you . . . ?" I move away to the side of the chamber and turn my back more fully to the mirror. The density of its pull, of its desire for my sight, recedes. "You said the one in the showroom was the only one."

"It was, for a long time. In a way, it still is, the only one of its kind, at least." He walks towards the glass but keeps his eyes on me. "This one is of an entirely different kind. It doesn't just not see you, it sees not-you. It's a spectacle of nothingness." He walks briefly into the foundry, brings out a folding metal chair, opens it next to me. "Sit down. You look exhausted."

I look at him for a long time. His face looks ragged in the arc lights' glare; his shoulders are slumped, and I can see by the way he holds himself that his back is hurting. I gesture at the chair.

"Maybe you need it more than I do."

He grins, but it's tired and fleeting. He nods, and sits down.

"What did you see, when you looked into it?"

I stare at him, and say nothing.

"No. Well, can't blame you, I suppose." With his good hand he reaches into his coat pocket and brings out a half-bottle of Polish vodka that's already nearly empty. "They gave me some painkillers, rather strong ones, so I probably shouldn't have drunk all that. You want the rest? No? All right then, they can have it," and he swings his arm and launches the bottle at the mirror. It misses, bounces off the wall without breaking, and finishes neck down against the corner of a display case, the dregs of alcohol dripping out and soaking into the dirt packed between the stones in the floor.

"These tunnels were here long before the church, you know. There are older places to worship than churches, older gods to pander to than God."

"Was Saulė a god?"

"Goddess. And is, not was. Gods don't die, you should know that. Goddesses even less so."

"Who is she?"

Illar sighs and stands—it seems to take him an age to stand— and he walks slowly around the display cases. Stops at one and gestures to the shelf beside it.

"You see this?" There is a book, the pages filigreed black glass. Illar gestures with his good hand and the pages turn with a sound like falling diamonds. "You think I'm *ragana*, think I'm a witch?" He laughs, a guttural bark of old bitterness. "I'm nothing. I'm an ungodly taxidermist, that's all I am now."

"Illar, please. I don't understand any of this." There is an acrid and bitten-down fear in my mouth, and a wild pulse racing through my head and heart, but I force myself to speak slowly and softly.

"Of course you don't. I made sure of that, didn't I? I had to, that was part of the deal. One of the deals. I don't know, I lose track. So many bargains, so many slices off my soul. It's amazing what a man will put himself through just to keep his line running." He picks up the bottle, stands it on top of a display case, leans hard against the wall next to it. "Saulė is the sun." He points at the inverted, transparent body next to the mirror. "She is your mother, your sister. My wife. Next to her," he indicates the glass helmet, "is Auseklis, god of the stars, her brother, her lover." My heart beats faster and I'm surprised Illar doesn't hear it. If he sees the shock in my face he doesn't register it.

Mikus Auseklis, brother-lover. He found you, and led you to me.

I feel my sense of reality beginning to unravel, and I tell myself to focus on what my grandfather is saying.

He is indicating each of the display cases in turn as he speaks a litany of names. The black glass book is Laima, goddess of fate; the quartz figurines of agonised joy are Pērkons, god of thunder. There are Kapu māte, the graveyard mother, and Smilšu māte, the mother of sands.

"These are your family, your kin and kind." He looks around the room, a bitter grimace on his lined face. "Fickle, murderous, in-bred bunch of egotists, every one of them."

"They're nothing to do with me," I say, and though I know as I say it that it's not true, still it seems as good a defence as any against the madness my grandfather is pressing on me. "Whatever this is it's yours, and I'll have no part of it."

"But you already have, child. I know it, I can see it, I've worked with these bodies of glittering dust for so long now I can see every little taint when they merge. They are a part of you as you are of them, they are your glass kin and you are glass with them." His eyes are wild now, and his voice is rising through hoarse belligerence to a half-strangled shout. "All of this is for you, don't you see that? You're the last one, the last of our kind and set in glass. All the things I've done for mercy, gratitude, forgiveness—all of it for love, for *you*." He coughs, retches, and staggers forward—

not towards me but towards the mirror. He reaches out a hand to steady himself, and looks up and into the blind glass.

The steadying hand falls to his side. His breathing slows. The ragged lines of his face smooth into an expression of cold bliss.

My grandfather stands between me and the mirror, but the one brief, searing glimpse that I catch is enough. *The mirror cannot see, and so cannot lie about what it sees.* This glass, I know, is truly blind.

I pick up the metal chair, step quickly around my grandfather's frozen thrall, and in one wide sweeping arc I hurl the chair at the mirror's shimmering, minutely faceted surface.

Illar Kroos screams as the blind glass crazes and shatters and slides in great shards and planes to the floor. But even as he cries out and brings his one good hand up to his head, his gaze is still fixed on the mosaic remnants of the glass; only now his eyes are filled with disgust and hate and fear, and the pull of the thing drags him to his knees and tethers his good hand to a spike of broken glass and wrenches his terrified face closer into the wreckage, and I run.

This is beyond me now. I don't know if I've destroyed something or unleashed it, and I'm too terrified of either possibility to stay and find out.

At the same time, I know there is one thing left to do.

He found you, and led you to me. Now find me, and I will lead you to him.

• • •

When I reach the chapel door, Illar, or whatever is left of Illar, is still screaming, but there's almost a rhythm to it now, like a chant, like a ritual. I don't stop, just close my eyes and run straight through the steel door. For the briefest of moments, the smallest portion of a second, I feel a drag on my skin, a coldness grasping at my bones, and then I'm through and colliding with the footless knight, bruising my head on the edge of his shield. Out of the chapel and into the old nave, the showroom, and there is the blind glass again, the first one—the only one, my grandfather said, the other one of an entirely different kind and now shattered but still blind, still seeing. In this one, I see the steel door open in the background, the empty doorway an escape for whatever chaos is erupting in that cold stone chamber below. *The mirror cannot see, and so cannot lie about what it sees.* So if it can't see an open doorway, then the doorway must be closed. I run to the mirror and heave it around on its ornate black-iron stand, then run back into the chapel, stand before the door, close my eyes.

Push.

Solidity resists my trembling hands. I push again, harder, and still the door refuses to give way. My eyes clamped fiercely shut, I throw my whole weight at the door, and nearly dislocate my shoulder.

I sob then, I cover my face in my hands and cry like a child in fear and relief. I feel slickness on my hands, on my lips; open my tear-filled eyes and see blood on my fingers, and a distant part of me tries to distinguish between the two different tastes of salt.

One thing left.

In a back corner of the nave there is a stack of shelves for the showroom, still packed in cardboard and thick paper. Next to this is a bundle of the semi-rusted iron bars used to support the display shelves. I draw one out, the scrape of metal echoing in the high space and jarring my teeth.

I walk slowly back to the mirror, to the singular, blind glass. When I stand before it and raise my eyes to see, what I see is only right, the only thing I could have expected. An invisible, impossible self rising before me, coalescing, a bright star cooling into visceral flesh. Not me, not my own body, but the body I have become.

I smile, and I smile back, and I raise the bar above my head, and I bring it down.

THE NEST

C.S. MCMULLEN

The walls were filled with ants—a seething, burrowing mass of them.

"Come in, come in!" the man said, sitting like a god in the middle of the room, grinning at me through broken teeth. He levered himself out of his chair, breathing heavily, and then tottered over to the wall and pressed hard against it. Under his hand, ants scurried frantically through their tunnels. "It's quite safe. Two solid sheets of Perspex, each over an inch thick, layered over the original house's walls. They've got a gap of about four inches between them, for the dirt, but the whole thing is completely sealed. There's no chance of them escaping."

I slowly inched my way further into the house, stifling a scream when I looked up and saw that the ceiling was part of the nest as well. There was an industrious hum in the background, almost a whispering; thousands upon thousands of living organisms working towards a goal. If that goal was to terrify anyone who was foolish enough to enter their domain—well, it was working.

"Are you Mr Marsden?"

He snorted, and gestured around him. "I don't know. Do I fit the description? Crazy old man, lives in a giant ant's nest?"

I had to concede that there weren't many other plausible candidates.

"You'd be the girl from the real estate agency then? Here to see about the house?"

After we had ascertained that, indeed, I was the girl from the real estate agency, and that I was here to see about the house, Mr

Marsden led me on a full tour of what he fondly referred to as "The Nest."

This was his home, and he wanted me to tell him how much it was worth.

Shit.

• • •

I had only been working a few months at my job. My pencil skirt was always neatly ironed, my buttons always undone to reveal just the right amount of cleavage. My boss had insisted that I take this home valuation, emphasising how Mr Marsden was a valued and loyal client.

But, as I got further and further into the house, I had a sneaking suspicion that this was the real estate equivalent of a hazing ritual.

According to Mr Marsden, "The Nest" had been under construction for over twenty years, and the original house had been gutted long ago. Only the walls and some of the kitchen and bathroom fixtures remained. In each room, the walls had been layered with two giant pieces of clear Perspex about four inches apart and filled almost completely with dirt. Large plastic tubes ran haphazardly from one room to the next. At the edge of the walls, where the Perspex met the plaster, there were thick lines of sealant.

And everywhere I looked—sealed up within every wall— crawled the ants. And while I tried to tune it out, under our conversation, disconcertingly, there remained that soft whispering, that pervasive sound of the ants in their nest.

I'd already been to quite a few house valuations, and I was getting used to how nervous people are; the covert glances at cracks in the walls, covered haphazardly with plaster, the assurances that their small, humble house normally looks a lot better than this.

This man wasn't nervous, though. He practically burst with pride as he led me from room to room in the small house, pointing out various interesting nest formations in the walls, or a particularly clever piece of mechanical ingenuity. In fact, he seemed to enjoy how I stayed half-crouched, terrified of the weight of the dirt above my head, and the ants that scurried within it.

Perhaps I was overwhelmed by the house, by the magnitude of The Nest, but I would swear that the ants followed us as we toured through—a murmurous rush of activity that poured into the walls of each room. They seemed small, malevolent entities, tracking us, and I felt judged and observed as I had never felt before. I somehow knew that The Nest itself was looking at me, and had found me wanting.

But then, I always do this.

I had realized early in my life that I had a tendency to become painfully anthropomorphic, assigning excessive personality to animals or things that wasn't there in reality. It was why I still had a collection of over fifty soft toys, packaged up in my basement. I kept even the most battered ones, the ones that should have been thrown away long ago.

And as I toured through this small, strange house, I knew that this was why I couldn't help myself, that this was why I gave this collective group of insects a personality.

But still, even knowing that it wasn't real, I could feel it. I could feel the weight of The Nest's mind upon me.

Judging me.

• • •

The Nest was huge, almost two hundred thousand individuals, Mr Marsden estimated, although it was impossible to know how many there were exactly. The entire house was kept purposefully dark for the ants to function properly, but there were small, muted lights in each room, which gave me just enough light to inspect everything. The walls seemed solid, as far as I could tell, and there was minimal furniture; just the walls, filled with tiny bodies moving constantly. There was haphazard electrical wiring throughout the house, going around doorways and through holes, following a logic that only this madman—presumably—knew.

It was like nothing I've ever seen, before or since then.

Mr Marsden seemed to enjoy showing off his house and its small inhabitants, and he had a well-rehearsed patter, spouting off interesting facts and bits of information about ants. He was surprisingly articulate, and I gradually felt myself relaxing as I listened to him.

"Each room acts as a different part of the normal structure of an ant nest," he explained, his fingers pointing to hollows within the walls. "There are several main chambers that we can see, and some we can't. Somewhere, deep within The Nest, is the Queen's chamber, where she lies, producing a seemingly endless supply of eggs." He grinned at this, and I found his eyes staring at me intently, his large frame filling up the room, his pale skin almost luminescent in the dim light. I had the urge to do up the buttons on my shirt; even tasteful cleavage suddenly seemed like too much.

Inside the Perspex, the material of The Nest was layered, beginning with large granules at the bottom, a mixture of sand and dirt for the main part of the nest, and then, right at the top, a section that was left to act as a pretend "topsoil." It gave each room a strange appearance, almost as if it was part of a living painting: a strange thesis about modernity, nature, and life.

The Nest had been built haphazardly, and Mr Marsden had worked around the light switches and pipes, cutting and sealing the Perspex with precision. A labour of obsessive love, his work was impressive in its thoroughness, as well as its complete impracticality.

It was hard to look at the features that I would normally focus on for a valuation: size and functionality of the dwelling, the acreage and location of the land. This clearly wasn't going to be a normal job where I was in and out in twenty minutes. I considered stopping it then; telling him that this wasn't worth my time, and leaving, going back out into the bright daylight, and relieved to be out of that strange place.

But my professionalism won out.

Well, that, and my crippling fear of failing this arcane rite of passage. I would not be known forever as the real estate agent that had cracked and fled screaming from the crazy old man who lived in a nest.

He took me down to the basement, where, bizarrely, it was lit up as bright as day. There were two large tanks on the floor, made of glass, that looked like aquariums. They had plants and rocks in them, and several pipes led down from the main nest into each of them.

"This room acts as the "surface" for the ants," he said, pulling on a pair of work gloves. "I put food into these tanks, and they forage along the ground and bring it back to the nest, like they would in the wild."

He opened up one of the tanks, and gently brushed the ground with his fingers, allowing several ants to crawl onto his gloves.

"*Solenopsis invicta*. More commonly known as fire ants.

Their sting feels as if your skin is on fire. They can sting smaller mammals to death, and carry their bodies back to their nests, piece by piece." I stared, horrified at the tiny creatures on his finger tips, and he laughed. "A fully grown human would be able to get away well before they were stung to death, unless they were sick or allergic to their venom. Or unless they were caught in a swarm of them, defending their nest." He opened the lid of the glass tank again, and gently blew the ants off his hand, and back into their enclosure. "See? They're perfectly safe."

"And you're allowed to have these?"

He paused. "I've got all the correct permits for them." It had the sound of a lie, and wanting to break the suddenly awkward silence, I looked around the room for something innocuous to discuss. "Why are there two of these tanks? Wouldn't you only need one feeding enclosure?"

He looked at me, surprised. "Not many people notice that." Lowering his voice, he asked, "Want to know a secret?"

I hate secrets between strangers. It breeds forced camaraderie, a sharing of something exclusive. He took my silence for assent though, and gestured to one tank and then the other. "The name "The Nest" is actually a misnomer. The house actually contains two nests; rival nests, in fact."

"There are two different types of ants in here?"

"No, no, they're the same species. They're both fire ant nests. But they're rival nests, with two different queens. That's why I have to have two separate feeding enclosures. When they encounter an ant from the other nest, they fight."

We watched the ants forage peacefully in their tiny habitats for a while, and then he led me back up into the main house, saying cheerfully, "There's just one more room to see now."

I felt as if the ants watched from all sides, wondering what I was doing here with him, with their emperor-god. I kept straining to hear what they were saying, even though I knew the whispers were just them moving, burrowing through the dirt. I could feel them around me, stronger than before, and I knew I wasn't imagining it as they swarmed from room to room, following us.

As he pushed open the final door, I prepared for the worst; perhaps the bodies of women from other real estate companies, who had been foolish enough to come here alone.

But it was just his bedroom.

There was a sad mattress on the floor, and almost no other furniture, except for the mess of wiring near the headboard of his bed. There were various switches and levers, and it looked as if he had rigged up a rudimentary climate control system. The walls on either side of his bed were part of The Nest, filled in with dirt and humming with activity, but the wall that faced the bed directly was empty; the only empty wall in the house. There was a small hatch in the middle of the wall, with a handle on it.

He said, "I don't usually take people in here. This room is the dividing line between the two nests." He looked over at me. "Maybe, next time, I'll show you why this room is so special."

This was exactly why I didn't like people sharing their secrets.

• • •

The tour complete, we went back to the living room. Mr Marsden sat back down heavily in his chair and put his feet up, gesturing to the flat-screen TV in front of him, inviting me to look closer. It was made up of regular lines of white and black sand, with the ants burrowing through to create "static." He laughed and said, "Whenever I turn it on, it seems to be showing the same program." It had the feel of a well-worn joke, and I laughed politely.

"So, Mr Marsden, you're interested in a full valuation of your current property. Is this with a view to eventually selling?"

"No, no, I'd never leave. This is my home. I've finally got the decor just how I like it," he said, laughing wheezily. "When I started, it was just a small nest in the basement, more of a hobby than anything else, really. I just like to get an update occasionally, check how much it's worth." He leaned forward, eyes intent on my face and said sharply, "It's priceless, you understand? There will never be another house like this."

I smiled reassuringly at him, and nodded carefully. I was on firmer ground here. This part of the conversation was the same as all the other valuations I had done. They wanted reassurance. Reassurance that the place that they lived in, that they had put so much time into, that it was worth something. That they were worth something.

"It certainly is an amazing house. I'll have to do some further research, if that's all right with you? Just to get a better idea of the house's value, in light of its . . . unique characteristics."

He nodded and settled back into his chair again, the sharpness in his eyes disappearing as if it had never been there, the genial-yet-creepy uncle once more. Clasping his hands over his large stomach, he asked, "Did you ever keep ants? When you were a child?"

"My brother did. Just one of those little farms, two clear bits of plastic, with some gel inside. You could light it up. We captured some ants from the garden and put them in, and they burrowed through the gel, making little tunnels."

As I spoke, his hands drifted down from his stomach to the front of his groin, scratching slowly. I looked away, but he didn't seem embarrassed at all.

"And the ants. How many days until they died?"

"They . . . they only lasted about five days. Will, my brother, was inconsolable. He thought he had done something wrong."

He snorted. "Little death camps, those plastic sets are. The ants have no way to nest, nowhere to go, no chambers, no rooms, the light burning them. They just burrow through the gel, eating it until they reach the edge. Then they die. No fun at all, them dying that way."

There was an awkward silence. In my head, I saw the ants, burrowing to nowhere, dying at the end of their small, sad tunnels. It was definitely time to leave.

I stood up, brushed off my skirt, and turned on my real estate charm. "Thank you so much for your time, and the tour. I'll be in touch next week." As I left, he handed me a small book, with the words *Facts YOU didn't KNOW about ANTS!!!!* on the cover. It had the feel of a vanity press book: all ugly fonts and cheap paper.

"Take this. It's all my own work. It might be good for research on The Nest."

Never question where they live, or how they live, my boss always said. That's not your job. Your job is to tell them how much their house is worth, and then to try and sell them a new house.

But it never was that simple. Just by being there, in dilapidated houses and small apartments, I was judging their lives, telling them their worth. And I had never been in a place that was so inherently personal as this house; this shrine to the many. I paused at the doorway.

"Why ants?"

He shrugged. "I just like them, I guess. Always have. Ants are just . . . ants."

I plastered a smile on my face and shook his hand, promising I would be in touch within the next few weeks.

• • •

I had no fucking idea how much this house was worth.

I did all my normal due diligence. Even if it was just a hazing ritual, I was determined to treat it like a real job for a real client. I researched how much the house had sold for previously, before it had metamorphosed into The Nest. I checked average property prices in the area, and what schools were nearby. Were there shops in the neighbourhood? A mall? What were the crime rates like?

But it was all pointless, really. Essentially, the question I was asking was: What was the value of a habitable roadside attraction?

I couldn't find any other houses made of ants. Or any other houses that were made of living organisms. There were Scandinavian turf houses that used grass as insulation, but they seemed sensible in comparison. There was a house in New York that had been nicknamed "The Mushroom House," but this just referred to the shape, and I found that I was disappointed when I realized that mushrooms didn't sprout from the walls.

There was nothing like The Nest. It was unique.

Although I hadn't planned on it, I read the book about ants Marsden had given me. I had hoped to get some insight into what had possessed someone to turn their house into a giant nest, but was disappointed. However, as promised, I did learn a lot of facts about ants. No one could accuse the title of being misleading.

There were nests in South America that were thought to stretch over several miles, thriving metropolises that made The Nest seem like a small village. I wondered if that was what he was trying to recreate, that god-like feeling of enormity. All those tiny lives dependent on him.

Ants emigrated from these nests, travelling across countries to create new outposts. Fascinatingly, ants from these new nests that were captured and reintroduced to the "mother" nest by scientists weren't attacked by the other ants; their scent smelled right, even if they had never been to that nest before. But, there were ants that lived within the same ten meter stretch that would attack each other instantly, simply because the other ant smelled like the wrong nest.

I continued to research The Nest for a few more weeks, and then told my boss I was going back.

"I thought you finished that job ages ago," he said, looking surprised. "Just do what we all did—tell him it's worth the average in the area. And next time he calls up, we'll give him to that new girl, what's her name? Sheryl? Sharee?"

But I was a professional. I was a realist.

I knew what it was worth.

• • •

Like before, he greeted me from his chair, wheezing heavily from the darkness. I attempted to get straight into business, but he insisted on showing me something first.

"I promised last time. And I never break a promise to a pretty lady," he said, going to the kitchen and returning with a bucket of rancid meat. The smell was overwhelming. He held it awkwardly in one hand. "This way."

The ants were as busy as last time, and each room almost boiled over with activity as we walked through. The whispering was louder than ever, and I found myself listening for words again, trying to piece them together.

"Do you hear it?" I asked.

"Hear what?"

"Nothing," I said, and he gave me a strange look.

It's never good when a man who lives in an ant's nest thinks you're the strange one.

This time, we skipped the full tour, and he took me straight to the bedroom. He gestured for me to sit on the mattress, but I politely refused. There were overtones and undertones to sitting on his bed that I didn't want to encourage, and, more importantly, there was no way that I was touching those sheets. He shrugged, seemingly unperturbed, and then walked over to the blank wall. As the only section of The Nest that had been left hollow, it seemed to hold some special significance, but I had no idea what it could be. He opened the small hatch in the wall, and tipped the rancid meat inside, before sealing it shut again.

"I haven't fed them in a few days now. I never do, before one of my private shows. Didn't think it would be for an audience of two, though," he said, winking at me.

He walked over to one of the many plastic tubes that were installed around the house, that acted as walkways for the ants between different parts of their nests. It led from one of the walls of the nest to the blank, empty wall in front of him, but there were no ants crawling inside it. He pulled up a small barrier within the tube, and I saw ants suddenly emerge into the small plastic tunnel, pouring into it rapidly. He did the same thing to the tube on the other side of the room, and then walked slowly back to the mattress, half-collapsing onto it, his eyes avidly watching the wall in front of him.

Nothing seemed to happen at first, but then I realized what he had done. Those two tubes meant that ants from both nests were now enclosed in the same area.

The wall in front of me was a battleground.

It began slowly at first. Foragers from each nest navigated along the sides of the glass, meandering slowly along the surface of the Perspex. The horrible significance of the blank wall was explained, and I saw now that the lack of dirt inside was to allow him to see this; to allow him to see the battle that he had orchestrated—an emperor on his throne.

I felt sick.

Soon enough, ants from both nests found the meat, and began to cluster over it. He pointed to a few specific ants, who had left the food, and were hastily navigating their way back to their respective nests.

"They're going back to warn their comrades, to tell them that the nest is in danger. Reinforcements will be sent, both to fight and to gather the food. Ants fight by wrestling each other, and they can cut each other in half with their jaws alone." He stretched back on the bed, the grin wide on his face. "Thousands of ants will arrive within the minute, the emergency signal spreading throughout the nest from individual to individual. Isn't it marvellous?"

I tore my eyes away from the mass of ants, my heart beating erratically. This wasn't why I was here; viewing this wasn't what I had come to do, but it was hard to think about house prices when such a stark struggle played out before me. The ants no longer frightened me, and their whispering no longer seemed menacing. Instead, I now felt almost crippling sympathy for them and their war, orchestrated by a manipulative god.

He watched silently for the next few minutes, his eyes darting from spot to spot on the wall. From where he sat, they were just a swarming mass of tiny moving bodies, and I realized he didn't view the ants within as significant at all, just toys to play with and break.

He didn't seem to hear the whispering.

Eventually, he reluctantly pushed himself up from the mattress. "I suppose we better get down to business then. Although, I do love a good show."

He gestured for me to go ahead of him through the door, but I paused and looked back at the wall, which was now almost black with tiny ant bodies, battling desperately for the food that would ensure the survival of their nest. There was a column, stretching all the way down to the base of the glass, a battleline of ants defending their territory. It seemed as if there was a particularly fierce battle right at the sealant at the base of the glass, ants from both nests swarming frantically.

"You're not going to . . . stop this? While we're gone?"

He looked back at the wall and shrugged. "It won't make much of a difference. One nest always invades the other nest through the tubes, then I seal the invading party in there. But I guess I can speed it up a bit." He walked over to each of the tubes, and pushed the small barriers over the entrance, completely sealing off the nests from each other once again. The ants still in the battleground were now on their own.

I watched in horror, suddenly unable to detach from their tiny lives, as he pushed a button next to his bed, and a stream of water came down from the top of the wall, washing away all the ants, as well as the meat, into a drain at the bottom.

It was clean again; pristine. As if it had never happened.

As I stood there, staring at the now empty wall, I noticed something strange. Right where the ants had swarmed at the base of the glass, there was a tiny drop of water that had seeped through, that must have come from the deluge that had just washed the ants away. The drop would evaporate within a minute or two, but before then, I should show him, tell him that there might be a crack forming in The Nest's walls.

Maybe it was because of what I had just witnessed, or maybe it was the whispering that still softly hummed through my head, but for whatever reason, I didn't say a thing.

• • •

I was tense when we sat back down in the lounge room, but he was relaxed in his chair, his face expectant and anticipatory. He waited to be told that his house was one of a kind, that my research had showed that it would go for millions, a priceless gem of natural architecture.

But unlike every agent before me, I planned on telling him the truth.

"The Nest is worth nothing," I said. "The only value of the property is the price that the land alone would bring, if the house was razed clean." His eyes bulged, and I could see him drawing breath to protest, but I carried on. "This entire structure is inherently unstable. You're subjecting the walls to intense amounts of pressure, and none of your 'modifications' would be attractive to potential buyers. The Nest has no value as an exhibit or otherwise, and the original house has been modified so heavily that it would be impossible to resell."

His face reddened with rage, and his hand raised from his side as if to strike, an unthinking gesture of anger, before he lowered it jerkily. I could see him struggling to choke words through his windpipe, his throat closed by the force of his denial. When he finally spoke, it was in a stream of invective. "You're wrong, absolutely wrong, you don't know anything about value or houses or worth, The Nest is priceless, I can't believe you'd even think to . . . "

I left him there, sitting in his chair saying the most horrible things, and was perversely happy. It felt like I had scored a victory somehow, struck a blow in the war against tyranny, although if you asked me to specify how exactly, I would not have been able to tell you.

As I left, the whispering of the ants seemed to follow me out the door and onto the sidewalk, from the dark cool of the house, into the hot summer sun. But it had a different tone now, and I imagined that it was a friendly one.

• • •

The destruction of The Nest wasn't long after that.

It had been declared a threat to public health and safety, an aberration in the suburban ecosystem that surrounded it. The council had hired exterminators from several different companies to help, due to the threat of the fire ants escaping during the demolition process. Mr Marsden remained in the house, his last-minute appeal working its way through the courts, convinced of his invulnerability until the end.

I had heard about the planned demolition on the news and through the local real estate grapevine. It was the end of an era, the agents said. I was one of the last people to get hazed in The Nest, and the only one that had ever gone back there a second time. I wondered if he had shown anyone else the blank wall and the ants fighting within it, or if it was a sacred thing.

The day before it was scheduled to be destroyed, I visited for the third and final time, as dusk fell. I couldn't tell you why I went there. Something to do with the whispering I heard wherever I went, just at the edge of hearing.

He opened the door suspiciously, frowning as he recognised me.

"I just want to see the ants," I said quickly, before he slammed the door in my face. I looked at his impassive expression, and, realizing that more grovelling was required, added, "I was wrong about The Nest and your house. It's priceless."

His face cleared somewhat, and he stepped back, gesturing for me to come in.

"Are you getting ready to move them?" I asked, looking around. Nothing seemed different. I had expected insect containers, some way to transport the ants to their new home, but everything was the same.

"They're not moving anywhere," he said, shortly. "If the government thinks they can do this to me, they've got another thing coming. I've got rights. The second appeal will go through, you'll see."

"But, what if it doesn't go through? The ants . . . they'll all die."

"They won't. I'm never leaving this house, and the ants aren't ever leaving, either," he said. "Not now, not ever."

I thought about the exterminator trucks that would arrive in the morning to kill his subjects, and the earth-movers that would knock down the borders of his empire. While he was an emperor in here, outside this house he was a peasant. A peasant with delusions of grandeur.

He would stay until the very end.

The ants didn't follow us from room to room this time. In fact, the walls were almost completely empty of any movement. As we entered the bedroom, I saw where the ants had all gone. They were here, and each wall of the walls on either side of the bed was thick with activity.

"I haven't fed them in weeks," he said, looking around. "I've shut off the tubes down to the feeding area. They know that this is their best shot of getting food."

The whispering was rising to a crescendo, and I wondered again how he couldn't hear it. It was hard to focus on what he saying, and I felt as if I could almost make out the words, if I strained hard enough. As he walked over to the small hatch in the blank wall, my eyes darted from side to side, looking at the ants swarming in the walls. It would be a massacre, the entirety of each nest fighting the other for the meat.

He tipped the meat out into the hatch, closed it, and then opened up each of the tunnels. He then walked to his bed, and lay back upon it, watching intently. His position on the bed was the same as before, and I wondered how many times he had done this, how many battles he had staged for his own amusement.

"Should be a good one this time," he said, his eyes bright. "I've never seem them as riled up as this before."

But, as the floodgates opened, the ants from both nests then did something strange. Instead of swarming towards the meat, they all poured down towards the bottom of the wall, where the Perspex met the floor.

To where I had seen the crack.

"What the hell . . . " he muttered. "One of the foragers must have left a trail for them to that point. But why would they ignore the meat?"

It was only as the ants from both nests rushed out of the gap in the battle wall, through the gap in the sealant that they must have expanded incrementally each time they fought, that Mr Marsden must have realized the answer to his question, and tried to rise, to flee.

Before he could even get off the bed, the ants swarmed over him, stinging and biting and fighting, crawling from the inside out, fighting over his meat: their emperor, their god.

I suspect it was then, for the first and last time, that he heard their whispering. That he heard what they had been planning all along.

I stood next to his bed, remaining very still. He must have been stung hundreds of times within the first few seconds, and when he lifted his hand off the bed, pleading for help, I stepped back slightly, not saying a word. Eventually, he stopped moving.

The ants from each nest didn't seem to be fighting each other, I thought, and it was clear why. They had been united against a common enemy, and as the first of the scouts reached my legs, I realized that I was probably an enemy too. A collaborator.

As the ants swarmed up my body, I tensed and stood very still, waiting for the stings to begin. But there were none, just the dry tickling of hundreds of ants crawling all over me, a dress of moving black bodies. They crawled inside my nose and ears, and I think they told me secrets then, messages from their queens, messages just for me.

It all seemed so clear, and with this strange garment over me, I slowly walked to the front door of the house, which had been sealed shut, and opened it.

And then, they were gone.

They poured off me, shedding like a second skin, and under the cover of darkness, they disappeared into the suburbia that surrounded The Nest. After I was sure that they were gone, I walked back through the house to his bedroom, and took one last look at his body. I then slowly walked back out, closing the front door and locking it behind me, leaving no sign that I had ever been there.

I think of that night as a revelation; as a benediction.

The news had been much more dry: "Man found stung to death, in bizarre 'Nest House' enclosure. More at eight."

• • •

A few weeks after his death, the bulldozers and the exterminators came to destroy The Nest completely. It had been delayed during the police investigation, but once the scene was photographed, there was no reason to delay it any longer. I went to watch, and it had the atmosphere of a carnival, people gathered up and down the street, waiting for the big machines to do their work.

In the end it was strangely anti-climatic; most of the ants had escaped on the night of his death, and there were only a few left inside. They had plugged up the hole once they found it, near his body, but it had been too late. The local animal control was still hunting for the new nest, but so far, it had eluded them.

The bulldozers knocked down the Perspex covered walls, and suddenly that was it. The Nest was no more.

But it stayed with me.

I watched and read commentary on the incident every day, finding out obscure facts about ants in forums or enthusiast sites, applying the same dedication that I had previously applied to my job.

I felt a small, almost electric shock, when I read something deep in the comment threads of a particular forum, that *Solenopsis invicta* means "The Unvanquished" in Latin. I wondered for days if he had known the secret behind their name, if that had been part of their allure, part of his desire to capture and control them.

I wondered if the ants from each of the nests still smelled wrong to each other, if they had formed one nest or two wherever they had escaped to; if the alliance between the two warring tribes had lasted beyond the confines of their jail.

I hoped it had.

I thought I might be going mad, thinking about the ants this way. They were just ants. Mr Marsden had been able to see that clearer than me.

But I find it so hard to think these days, to remember through the sound. Whenever I go into a new house, to try and evaluate its worth, all I can do is look at the walls, and think how bare they look.

And then I start to hear it again, no matter how much I try to drown it out.

I hear that whispering.

BY BONE-LIGHT

JULIET MARILLIER

"We need light," says Susie.

The power's gone off again; that happens a lot at Woodland Gardens. This place must have been named by a clown—instead of numbers, the floors have names, Chestnut Level, Willow Level and so on, a whole tower of trees. Woodland Gardens itself is a concrete high-rise with no redeeming features. Along with dodgy power it has blocked drains, creeping mould and lifts that make everyone use the stairs, even people who live on the top floor—Oak Level—like us. If something can break, you can be sure it'll be broken at Woodland Gardens. Down the bottom, outside, there's a sad playground with a metal swing and a climbing frame on dirty sand. In the daytime it's usually empty because mothers don't want their kids stepping on dog poo or used syringes. At night it's a meeting place for dealers.

We're sitting in our flat in the almost-dark, my stepmother, my stepsisters and me. Our torch batteries are flat, Susie's lighter is used up and we've managed to run out of both matches and candles. It's nearly dusk outside and the heater's gone off along with everything else electrical, so it'll soon be icy in here. But I know better than to suggest early bed. Susie wants our projects finished tonight, so she can get them in the mail first thing. Since it's already too dim in here for us to see our work, one of us will have to fetch light. It's not going to be Sophie or Miranda, because they're Susie's own daughters, her flesh and blood, and she never makes them go downstairs in the dark. I am my mother's daughter, and my mother is dead.

"Won't the shop be shut by now?" I say, hating the way my voice shakes. "I think they close at five on a Thurs—"

Before I can finish I'm hauled up onto my feet with Susie's fingernails pressing into the soft flesh of my arm. I sink my teeth into my lip; I won't give her the satisfaction of hearing me cry out. My heart's thumping hard.

"You think I'm stupid or something?" Her hand tightens.

"You'll have to go to the basement," Sophie says.

"Better hurry, Lissa," puts in Miranda. "It'll be dark soon."

There's a silence. I feel the weight of their gaze, the three of them, and I hear them thinking: *Go. Now. Before we make you.*

"That concierge woman's supposed to have everything," Susie says, and the hold on my arm slackens slightly. "You know, what's-her-name, the one they all talk about. Go down and ask her for candles and a lighter."

We haven't been at Woodland Gardens long. Susie got word that Dad's deployment was extended another six months, and almost straight away she sold the house that had been my home for all of my fifteen years. Home and haven. The house where my mother gave birth to me, her only child. The house where, only a year and a half ago, she gave me a gift, then died. Susie moved us so fast there was no time to ask questions. There wasn't even time to cry. It felt as if I blinked, then opened my eyes to find everything gone.

This flat is small. Two bedrooms: one for her, the other one for the three of us, with me on a trundle bed. Apart from my clothes, I got to bring one book—Grimm's Fairy Tales, which she had to let me keep because it was a Christmas present from Dad—and Mimi, who didn't get given to the Salvos because she was hidden in my pocket.

Susie had Wilmot put down. For that, I can never forgive her. She didn't have to choose a place with a no pets policy. She didn't have to move us at all. I thought I was going back to school at the end of the holidays and instead here we are in a completely different neighbourhood. When I asked about school—the kids at Woodland Gardens go to Westmoreland High—she said some stuff that frightened me so much I never asked again. Stuff about how screwed up in the head I was, and how much worse it would get if I was around people. Stuff about what she'd do to me if I told anyone what she'd said, ever. Miranda and Sophie never finished high school and now I have an idea why.

"Her name's Barbara," says Sophie, reminding me sharply of what's ahead.

None of us has ever been down to the basement. None of us has ever met Barbara the concierge in the flesh. But we've heard about her. Everyone at Woodland Gardens talks about her in the same way, hushed and scared like an olden-days person speaking of a witch. She's supposed to have lots of stuff down there, not only candles but old-fashioned oil lamps, fuses, all kinds of tools, probably matches and firelighters too. And weird stuff, so Kye told me. Kye is the only kid I've spoken to since we moved in here. Susie doesn't like letting us out, and we're not supposed to talk to anyone. Her reason is, the building's full of druggies and perverts. But doing the washing is one of my jobs, and that gets me as far as the communal laundry along the end of Oak Level. When I'm there I hear people talking. And I see Kye sometimes, not washing, just hanging around. He told me people go into Barbara's basement and never come out again. He told me she has a human bone for a door knocker. He said his uncle told him Barbara came from some country where they do voodoo, black magic, and that weird people are always visiting her to get spells. If that was true, if magic was real, I'd ask her for a spell myself. I'd get one to bring my father home right now. He probably thought he was doing the right thing when he married Susie so soon after Mum died. He must have thought I needed a mother, since we have no other family and he's away so much. And Susie wasn't so bad back then. Dad couldn't have known she'd turn into a monster the moment he was gone.

I've thought of asking Kye if I can make a phone call from his place, to . . . I don't know who, but there are welfare people who are supposed to help the families during a deployment, and I could look up their number. Or I could call my old school, speak to Mr Turner or Mrs Moss. I've thought of giving Kye a letter to post to Dad, because I suspect Susie rips them up, or Dad would have sent some back the way he always used to. Only Susie's so good at lying, and she's his wife now. She'd tell the welfare people I'm emotional and confused, and say she's getting professional help for me. And then she'd punish me. She's good at punishments. I have lots of bruises, the kind that show on my body and the kind that are deep inside where nobody can see.

"Off you go, Lissa," she says now. "Don't take too long about it. You're way behind with the orders; at this rate you'll be up all night getting that one finished." What we make, Susie sells online. Sophie's fine shawls; Miranda's Aran sweaters; my one-of-a-kind dolls. I make a lot of dolls, so I guess they're popular. Susie won't let us use the internet, so I don't see the customer feedback. No internet means no email either. Dad could be on another planet. He's been gone eight months, and in those eight months my whole world has changed.

"What are you waiting for?" Susie snaps. "Pitch darkness? Go! Now!"

There's no refusing. And with Susie standing over me, there's no getting a coat or gloves even though it'll be freezing in the stairwell. At least I have Mimi. She's about all I do have these days.

Susie locks the flat door behind me. Locks me out. When I get back with the candles I'm supposed to knock on the door three times, count to five, then knock three times again and wait for her to let me in. The two times three knocks are so she won't open up to some kind of crazy person. Though that's what she told me I was: crazy. A crazy girl can't go to school, but it's OK for her to sit at home making dolls for her stepmother to sell. I hope my dolls go to better homes than mine, homes where people love them and look after them and whisper secrets in their woollen ears.

The hallways in Woodside Gardens are long and grey. At this time of day all the doors are shut. There's still enough light from the tall windows down the end for me to see my way to the lift, and beside it the stair door. This door's broken, falling off its hinges. I step through and start down the twelve flights.

The stairwell stinks of wee. I'm hoping not to meet the perverts and junkies Susie talks about, though the shadowy landings seem like places where bad stuff might happen. I reach Willow Level, Aspen Level, Juniper Level, and the light's almost gone. I have to slow down or I might fall. There'll be no sympathy from Susie if I break my ankle, only a reprimand for being clumsy and costing her money for a trip to the doctor. I wonder if the doctor would believe me if I told the truth about my stepmother? For a moment it seems almost worth breaking my ankle to find out. I sit down on the top step of Juniper Level to stop myself from jumping. I take Mimi from my pocket and put her on my knee. There's just enough light left to make out her little face, her dark beady eyes, her snub nose, her mouth that's not smiling and not frowning but something in between. Her black embroidery-silk hair; her moss stitch gown in my favourite purple.

"I'm scared, Mimi. Scared of Susie and scared of myself. Scared of going down to the basement."

Give me a kiss, says Mimi.

I oblige with a peck on her knitted lips.

Give me a hug.

I press her against my cheek. My mother's last gift was teaching me how to knit. How to put love and hope and courage into every doll I make, so the person who gets that doll will have a true friend in good times and in bad. Mimi was the first doll I ever made, and knitted into her body is a strand of hair my mother cut from her own head as she lay dying. "When you are sad, Lissa, when you are lonely, when you are at your wits' end, she will help you," she told me. And it was true. I don't think Mimi is truly magic—how can she be, when I made her myself with wool and needles?—but when I speak to her in the right way, I can hear her speaking back to me.

Now let me fly!

I toss Mimi up in the air. She performs a triple somersault and I catch her on the way down, setting her upright on my knee again. She's only a little doll, ten centimetres from the top of her head to the soles of her knitted shoes. In the dim light it seems to me she's looking quite pleased with herself.

Why are we going downstairs in the dark?

"To visit Barbara in the basement. To ask her for light."

Mm-hm. Mimi seems to be considering this. *We'll need that if we're to find our way back up. Did you say you were scared?*

"I'm scared of Susie because she hurts me and I never know when she's going to be angry. And I'm scared of Barbara the concierge because everyone else is."

Mimi appears to be waiting for more.

"And I'm scared of myself. A moment ago I was going to throw myself down these stairs and hurt myself on purpose, and that would make what Susie says about me true. I wasn't crazy before she came, Mimi. I'm sure I wasn't."

Was your mother ever afraid of anything? Even at the end?

I remember Mum lying on the bed, hooked up to a drip, a skeleton with a fine layer of white silk for skin. Her eyes huge; her mouth stretched in a terrifying smile. Speaking words of hope. I shake my head.

You are your mother's daughter, Mimi says. *Get up, walk down, fetch light. I will help you.*

We go on down. Poplar Level, Cypress Level, Eucalyptus Level. I can hardly see the steps now. Ash Level, Elm Level. Somewhere below me a door clangs open, and I hear someone charging up the stairs toward me. I shrink back against the wall, stuffing Mimi into my pocket for safety. My heart's in my throat. A drug deal gone wrong, someone being chased with a knife, someone desperate . . . The person reaches the landing below me and comes straight on up. *Don't see me,* I beg. *Just go on past, please, please . . .*

It's a man dressed all in black, leather pants, hoodie, chunky Doc Marten-style boots. He hurtles past me. Either he's a top athlete or he's terrified of what's coming after him. His face is as dark as his clothes; there's a hint of gleaming eyes, and he's gone. I wait, making myself remember to breathe. Wait for whatever is coming next. I count up to fifty but nobody comes. Mimi says nothing, but I imagine her thinking, *What are we waiting for?* As well she might, because since the man ran past me, it's gone so dark I can't see my hand in front of my face. I pray that Barbara the concierge is home, and that she does give me light.

The lower levels, I navigate by touch. One hand on the iron railing, the other stretched out toward the concrete wall of the stairwell, I go down foot by cautious foot, hoping there are no broken steps, no missing stretches of rail. The dark's like a presence pushing at me, weighing me down. I feel as if I'm deep underground, though I think this is only Yew Level, third from the bottom. There's no reading the signs anymore, so I start counting the steps, counting the turns in the stairs. This stairwell comes out on the ground floor; I've been down here in the day time, when Susie took a risk and sent me to the shop on my own. Back then, I thought of running away, asking the shopkeeper if I could use the phone, asking someone, anyone, for help. I didn't. Susie's got a long reach. As I go down the last flight of steps to ground level, I start wondering if she actually doesn't want me to come back tonight. She might be hoping I run into a murderer so she can get rid of me with a neat explanation for Dad. It's not as if my dolls are making Susie a fortune, or we wouldn't be living here in Woodside Gardens. I wonder what's happened to Dad's Navy pay. What if he's sick or even dead and she hasn't told me? But that couldn't happen. Could it?

The stairs come to an end. I stand still, trying to get a sense of direction. Somewhere in front of me I know there's a door that leads out to the so-called plaza, where kids ride skateboards and do graffiti during the day and adults shout and smash bottles at night. Between me and that door there's utter darkness. I can't even see a line of light around the doorway, though surely there's at least one street light working out there. I creep forward with my hands outstretched, hoping I'm not about to fall down a flight of steps I've forgotten about. My heart's jumping around like crazy.

My hands touch the concrete wall. I work my way around till I find the door and pull on the handle. It's locked.

For a bit I just stand there, thinking of the long way back in the dark, imagining myself telling Susie I failed, guessing what might happen then. Susie making me stand in a cold shower till I'm blue and shivering. Susie making me stand out on the balcony in my underwear. Susie shoving my head into the wall. Susie has a great imagination.

I sink down onto the floor and get Mimi out of my pocket. I sit her on my knee. "I don't think I can go on," I mutter.

I can't see her face in the dark, but I hear her familiar voice.

Give me a kiss.

I touch my lips to her face.

Give me a hug.

I hold her to my cheek and find that I am actually crying a bit.

Now let me fly!

I flip Mimi up into the air and manage to catch her, blind.

So, we're down here in the dark. And you're curled up in a ball crying.

"I do try to be brave." I scrub a hand across my cheek. "But sometimes it's too hard."

There is a light to be found in every darkness. You are your mother's daughter. Find it.

"But—" I fall silent, because it seems Mimi's right. The blanketing dark has lightened just enough for me to see that there *is* another set of steps, leading not up but down, and from somewhere below a faint glow is coming. I thought you could only reach the basement by the lift or a flight of outside steps. But maybe there's a third way.

With Mimi in my hand I creep across to the steps, which don't have any kind of guard rail. We go down. The dim light gets a bit brighter. There are only seven steps, and here we are at another level, with a short landing and one door at the end. The door is painted in blood-red gloss, and on a shelf beside it is the source of the glow: a lamp made from what looks like a real human skull, with a tea-light candle inside. It makes weird flickering shadows all over the stairwell walls. And there, dangling beside the door, is that knocker Kye told me about. If it's not a human shin-bone I don't know what it is. Now I'm really cold.

There's a little brass plate on the red door, and on it is some lettering, only it's not the letters I know, but a foreign alphabet of some kind. It might say anything from 'Concierge' to 'Visitors will be eaten alive." I gather my courage, put my hand around the leg bone and rap on the door.

I wait. It feels as if getting downstairs took a long time, far longer than it should have done, and I wonder if Barbara has gone to bed already, in which case she won't be well pleased if I go on knocking. Maybe she's out. Maybe Mimi's instincts are wrong for the first time ever.

After a while I knock again, not too hard. I call out, "Is anyone home?"

The door opens so suddenly I yelp with fright. There's a woman in the doorway, long straggledy white hair falling out of a bun, little bright eyes, skin with a million wrinkles. She's wearing a knitted garment in exactly the same purple I used for Mimi's dress, and in her arms she's holding this humungous ginger cat. It is the biggest cat I've ever seen in my life and it has a mean look in its eye. I know cats, though. I see right through this one.

Barbara—who else could this be?—hasn't said a word, so I speak up before things get embarrassing.

"Sorry to disturb you. I'm—"

"Lissa from 1205. You'll be wanting light, yes?"

I gape, but only for a moment. Behind her the room looks dark and bright at the same time, full of changing light that shows me rich colours and elaborate patterns. Unlike ours, Barbara's place is full of interesting stuff.

"Come in," she says as if reading my mind, and steps back to let me go past her.

There are bones everywhere. Skulls with lights in them, their glowing eyes following me as I move cautiously across the room. Leg bones and arm bones and goodness-knows-what bones hanging from the ceiling like mobiles. Colourful pottery bowls full of tiny bones that must be from shrews or voles or something. There's a smell like incense, a lot better than the stink in the stairwell. I start to feel a bit dizzy and have to remind myself why I'm here.

"Our power's off," I say as Barbara puts the huge cat down on an overstuffed sofa. It settles on an embroidered cushion, looking at me through narrowed eyes. "My stepmother sent me to ask you for candles and a lighter. Please."

She just stands there examining me, her arms folded. I can't think of anything else to say, so I crouch down beside the cat and put my hand carefully out where he or she can smell it and decide to be friends or not. "Beautiful one," I whisper, remembering Winslow with his silky hair and lovely blue eyes. "Aren't you a fine cat, then?"

The giant feline deigns to sniff my hand, then gives itself a cursory lick. It raises no objection when I stroke it gently.

"She bites," says Barbara.

I don't think this cat's going to bite me. She's purring now. "What's her name?" I ask.

"Rory. Aurora."

I go on petting her for a while, and Barbara goes on standing there watching me.

"Sorry," I say eventually, remembering that it's late. "I miss my own cat. Is it OK for me to have some candles, please?"

"Ah," says Barbara, and I realise the door is shut and I'm alone with her and her house is seriously weird. I get to my feet and think about the twelve flights of stairs and the dark. "I have candles," she says. "I have lighters. I have all manner of things down here, as no doubt you've heard. They tell all kinds of stories about me."

"I don't get out much," I squeak. "But I did hear you have candles, yes."

"Can you pay?"

"Oh." My heart sinks. "My stepmother didn't give me any money." Stupid! I should have thought of this.

"Nothing's free, young lady. But there are other ways of paying."

I back away toward the door. If I can get out, if she hasn't locked it, I should be able to outrun her. She's a big heavy woman and she looks sixty at least, maybe even older.

"Can you cook?" Barbara asks.

I stop backing. "Yes," I say. I've been cooking since I was a little kid. Since Dad went away I've been doing pretty much all the housework, including preparing meals for four. If that's all she wants me to do, fine. Even if it takes until midnight.

Barbara flings open an inside door to show a dark old kitchen lit by more skull lamps. The stove is one of those ancient iron ones with a wood fire in a little compartment; there's a basket of logs sitting next to it. Bunches of herbs and onions and garlic dangle from the ceiling. In the middle of the room there's a wooden table and on it are a big bowl of fruit and veg, a basket of eggs and some little sacks that look as if they might hold rice or beans. In the corner stands a big red cupboard with a design of fruit and flowers painted on it, like something out of Grimm's Fairy Tales. *Then she shut her little brother in the red cupboard, and when she opened the doors again he was quite, quite gone.*

"I'm going out," Barbara says. "Work to be done. You'll make my dinner, three courses, each finer than the last. Lay it out on this table before I return home, and be sure it's a meal fit for a queen. If I'm satisfied I'll give you what you came for. But take care you leave my kitchen tidy. If I find the smallest thing out of place, I'll consider eating you for my dinner instead."

Seems as if she's heard most of the things the tenants of Woodland Gardens say about her and finds them amusing, not upsetting. I'm beyond being surprised by anything at this point, so I put on an apron, wash my hands and get to work. My gran had a wood stove like this so it's not too much of a challenge.

Making a three course dinner takes me a while. I put Mimi on the table, propped up against the fruit bowl. Rory the cat comes in at a certain point and hunkers down in a corner to supervise. As for Barbara, she's flung on a cape and gone off, slamming the front door behind her. It's pretty trusting of her, seeing as she's never met me before tonight. I wonder what work she could be doing at this hour.

I think about Susie, upstairs getting angrier and angrier in the dark. The doll I was working on will be lying on the table up there, all lonely, waiting for me to finish embroidering her face. Like all the dolls I make, she has in her a hair I plucked from my own head and knitted in with the wool. Someone's out there waiting for that doll, and unless I get this job finished and take the candles upstairs they'll have to wait a day longer, and Susie . . . I can't let myself think too hard about that; I have to concentrate. I dare to open the red cupboard and find it's a pantry full of useful ingredients. It's a long time since I've had so much good stuff to work with.

For starters I make a tomato and basil soup, with shaved parmesan and a herb scone on the side. I put together a spiced fruit compote and vanilla custard—there's no fridge in Barbara's kitchen, but the bottle of milk in the pantry is still OK, and so is the chicken waiting to be jointed and cooked. The main course will be breaded chicken pieces on herbed couscous, with vegies baked in olive oil and rosemary. In herb lore, rosemary means a strong woman, so it seems a good choice. I hope the meal's substantial enough for Barbara. She looks like she might be a big eater. I wonder who would have cooked her dinner if I hadn't been here.

It's starting to feel as if midnight might have been and gone, and my eyes are gritty with tiredness. The meal is pretty much ready, with only the couscous to steam. I make myself coffee, give Rory some chicken scraps in a bowl that looks like it might be hers, and sit down at the table for a bit. The kitchen's full of good smells; even with those skulls staring down at me, it feels safe in here. The coffee should give me enough energy to clean up, then I only need to set the table and I'm done. If Barbara likes the meal, I can grab the lighter and candles and head on upstairs, and I'll still have time to finish the doll before morning.

I find crockery, a glass, knives and forks. I check the kitchen: bench wiped clean, dishes washed, dried and put away, floor swept, fire made up, kettle steaming on the wood stove. Everything's ready. And I hear noises from outside the front door—Barbara's back.

Whoosh! Rory leaps onto the table, sending the open bag of couscous flying. Around two kilos of the stuff spill out all over the floor, the tiny granules rolling and scattering into every corner. I jump up and they crunch under my shoes. Rory has terrified herself; now she's standing on the table with one paw planted on the clean plate, fur on end, yowling. There's a rattle at the front door as Barbara sticks her key in the lock. What was that she said about eating me for dinner?

I scramble for the red cupboard where there's a dustpan and brush, and I slip over on the carpet of little grains. I land on my hip, putting new bruises on the old ones. I want to curl up on the floor and cry. Instead I look at Mimi, who's still standing beside the fruit bowl.

Give me a kiss, says Mimi.

The front door squeaks open. I struggle to my feet, reach out for the doll, kiss her embroidered mouth.

Give me a hug.

Quick, quick, I will her as I lay my cheek on hers.

Now let me dance!

I throw her high; in the few seconds we have left before fate catches up with us, she may as well enjoy herself. She twirls, tumbles, falls back into my waiting hands. Dear Mimi, my true friend in good times and bad.

Sit on the chair, close your eyes, lift your feet and keep that cat out of my way.

I manage to gather up Rory, who weighs half a ton, and sit down at the table again. I can hear Barbara walking about in the other room, muttering to herself. There's no way this can be cleaned up before she comes in, no way.

Somewhere near my feet there's a little sound like rats scuttling about. In my arms Rory tenses, making a deep-down whining noise. My body feels like it's strung on a wire, every bit of it jangly and terrified.

Hold on to that cat and keep your eyes shut.

Something small and woollen brushes against my ankle and is gone. The scuttling moves around the room, from cupboard to table, from table to bench, from bench to stove.

How much couscous does your recipe require? asks Mimi.

"A cup." This is crazy.

The scuttling moves up onto the table; becomes more of a pouring sound.

Done.

I open my eyes. The floor looks completely clean. Mimi is exactly where she was before, regarding me with her woollen gaze, and the couscous is back in the bag, most of it anyway. The enamel cup I had ready for measuring is filled precisely to the top.

The door opens and there's Barbara, tall and imposing, her dark eyes taking in the tidy kitchen, the neatly laid table, the various serving dishes waiting. I put the cat down, then move the couscous over to the bench and measure a cupful of water into a small iron pot.

"Please, do sit down," I say a bit shakily. "Are you ready for the first course now?"

She sinks weightily onto the chair. "I could eat a horse," she says, sounding as if she actually means it.

Barbara eats the tomato and basil soup, the parmesan and the herb scone without saying a word. While she's getting through that, I steam the couscous, which seems none the worse for its stint on the floor.

"Good." Barbara wipes her mouth with a large hand. "What's next?"

I serve the couscous, the chicken pieces and the baked vegetables: creamy potatoes, golden pumpkin, ruby-red beets, glistening onions. My mouth is watering, but she doesn't suggest I sit down and share her feast, and I don't either.

When she's eaten about half the main course, she sets down her knife and fork and stares at me. "I need entertainment," she says. "A story. Think you can manage that?"

I'm OK at cooking and I guess I'm OK at stories too, thanks to Grimm's Fairy Tales. I start to tell her a story about a girl who goes into the woods to find an old witch who lives in a hut on hen's legs, only Barbara keeps interrupting and asking questions, and it turns into a story about a girl whose stepmother takes her away from everything familiar, until the only friend she has in the world is the little doll her mother taught her how to make. A girl who only gets let out when her stepmother wants something; a girl who's lost touch with the good things of her past, and only sees the cruelty and loneliness of her future.

"Is this the doll?" Barbara asks, looking at Mimi, who stares back boldly from her spot by the fruit bowl.

I tell her. I explain about the other dolls I make and how Susie sells them as fast as I can get them finished. I don't tell her about the strands of hair; that feels too secret, even though Barbara's listening with interest and her expression's quite kindly. She's finished the main course, a meal big enough to go around all four of us at 1205 with leftovers to spare.

"Ready for dessert?" I ask politely, wondering what the time is and whether Susie will have given up on me and gone to bed by now. Maybe I can sneak in without waking her up.

"Mmm." Barbara stretches, moves her chair back a bit from the table. "Who taught you to cook, Lissa?"

"My mother."

"She did a good job. You could be a chef someday."

I say nothing. You don't get to be much at all if you haven't finished high school. I bring out the fruit compote and the custard, and I make a pot of tea.

"Sit down," Barbara says at last. "Fetch yourself a cup, a bowl and a spoon."

We eat the dessert course together. It tastes wonderful; each mouthful reminds me of summer and sunshine and being safe. It reminds me of Mum and Dad and the way things used to be.

"Well, then," says Barbara when the compote and custard are all gone and we're sitting over our cups of tea. "You've told me your story, and a fine one it was, full of joy and sorrow, good times and bad. Now it's your turn. I'm sure you have plenty of questions for the old woman in the basement with her voodoo spells and her cantankerous familiar. Go ahead, ask them."

My mind fills with questions. I'd love to know about her past, and what brought her to live at Woodland Gardens, where she doesn't belong at all. I'd like to know what the brass plate on the door says, and what language it's in. I'd love her to tell me what work she does out there at midnight. And I want to know about spells: whether there's one that will rescue me from Susie.

Suddenly it seems dangerous to ask much at all. It feels like prying into something best left alone.

"I only have one question," I say.

Her eyebrows go up.

"Is magic real?" I ask, hoping she won't laugh her head off.

She doesn't say anything, just looks at me, and I remember the thing with the couscous. I think of the hair I put into my dolls, as if that might somehow make them as real to their owners as Mimi is to me. Of course magic is real. But then I remember Susie and my bruises and how I've never been brave enough to ask Kye if I can use his phone, and I think no, it can't be.

Barbara goes on looking at me and sipping her tea, and I think she isn't going to answer at all until she gets up, goes to the red cupboard, opens a little drawer at the bottom and brings out something that looks a bit like a melted candle. When she shows it to me I see it's like a doll, with arms and legs and a head, but blobby and crude as if someone got tired of making it halfway through.

"What if I told you this was a voodoo doll?" she asks, and a shiver runs through me. It doesn't take much to imagine this little thing with pins stuck all over it, or being held over a lighter flame until it drips away to nothing. "What if I taught you how to work a curse?"

Now the room is bristling with magic, the Grimm's fairy tale kind where girls try to hide terrible secrets and wicked stepmothers dance in red-hot iron shoes. I take a deep breath, then reach out and pick up Mimi. "No," I say. "Not even if it gets me out of trouble. Not even if it fixes up the future the way I want. It'll cost too much. That kind of thing always does."

Barbara smiles. She reaches over toward the stove, opens the iron door with her bare hand and throws the wax thing inside, where it sizzles, making a vile smell. She clangs the door shut. "You'll be wanting that light, then." She stands, takes one of the skull lamps from the shelf and hands it to me. There's a wire running through a couple of holes on the top, so I can carry the skull. The tea-light candle inside has been burning a while; this lamp may be out before I even get to Oak Level. Perhaps the power will be back on by then. Perhaps Susie won't hurt me. After the voodoo thing, I can't seem to make myself ask for more.

"I'll see you out," Barbara says, leading me through the room with the embroidered cushions to the red front door. When she opens it, Rory streaks out, quicker than her bulk suggests is possible, and darts up the steps to the ground floor.

"Thank you," I say. "It's been interesting talking to you."

Now she does laugh, but in a good way. "And you," she says. "Hasten upstairs, Lissa. Dawn is breaking, and a new day comes."

A new day? Already? I see that she's right, because up the top of the seven steps the door to the plaza is open, and as Rory sprints out, the darkness starts to lift. Out there, it's nearly dawn, and upstairs in 1205 Susie's going to wake up and find I've been away all night. Can I really have been talking for as long as that? Did I somehow fall asleep and not even notice? Either way, this is a disaster.

"Farewell, Lissa," says Barbara softly, and the door closes behind me.

Grimly, I start the long climb. Pine, Cedar, Yew. Beside each painted name there's a little silhouette of the tree; nice idea, wrong place. Beyond the stairwell windows the sky turns violet, pink, gold. Elm, Ash, Eucalyptus. Let her be still asleep. Let me get inside and be sewing before she wakes up. But that isn't going to happen, because I have to do the twice three knocks on the door. She's going to kill me. Cypress. Poplar. My legs are on fire; I have to stop and catch my breath. I sit down on the steps with Mimi on my knee, and look out the window as somewhere beyond the concrete towers the sun edges over the horizon.

Down below, the stairwell door opens. The guy who walks through is not much older than me. His hair's the colour fairy tales call golden, and he's wearing snowy white overalls with a logo on the pocket, a smiling sun with Day and Son, Fresh Food Deliveries underneath. The guy's carrying a little crate, and in it are loaves of bread and bottles—old-fashioned glass bottles—of milk. Like the one in Barbara's pantry. "After you," he says politely.

We go on up, me first, the milk guy—Day Junior—second. I wait for him to ask me what I was doing sitting on the stairs at what must be about five in the morning, or to comment on the skull lamp, but all he says is, "Going to be a lovely day."

"Mm," I say, my mind full of Susie. Why am I so stupid? Why didn't I ask Barbara if she'd let me use her phone to call the welfare people, instead of cooking her a giant dinner and asking her about magic? No wonder I'm in so much trouble.

Day Junior and I climb through Juniper, Aspen and Willow. Outside, the sun comes up and proves him right; weather-wise, at least, it's shaping up to be a beautiful day. Seems as if he plans to start his deliveries at the top. When we get to Oak Floor, he balances his crate on one arm and uses the other to hold the broken door back so it can't fall on me as I go through.

"Thanks," I say, and head off toward 1205, not looking back to see who on Oak Floor can possibly afford a fresh food delivery.

The hallway is full of light; outside, the sun's climbing. I reach our door, knock three times, wait, knock three times again. The door flies open. She's been waiting. Her face is all squeezed up with rage. Her arms stretch out to drag me inside.

"Here," I say, holding out the skull with its pitiful, flickering candle inside. Too little, too late. Susie takes it, and the look on her face makes my flesh crawl. My fingers move to touch the comforting shape of Mimi in my pocket. She's not there. Somewhere on the long climb up, I've dropped her.

No time to think. I turn my back on Susie and bolt for the stairwell. Day Junior hasn't got past the first doorway, and when he sees me rushing down the steps he comes after me.

"Hey! Slow down or you'll hurt yourself. What's wrong?"

I gasp out an explanation, and instead of laughing at me he helps me search. As we go down, Willow, Aspen, Juniper, checking every step, I do wonder why Susie hasn't come after me, but nothing's as important as finding Mimi. Without her, a bit of me's missing, and I don't have a lot to spare.

It's Day Junior who locates Mimi, wedged between concrete step and iron railing on Poplar Level. He gets her out carefully, dusts her off, hands her back to me. "Safe and sound," he says. "Must have jumped out of your pocket."

I'm just starting to say thanks when there's a massive *Boom!* from somewhere up above. The two of us shrink back against the wall, Day Junior acting like a fairy tale hero as he spreads out his arms and shields me. The noise is over quickly, but now there's a strange light from up there, not the rising sun or a little skull lamp but a big, hot, hungry light. And people shouting. *Fire!*

Day Junior takes my hand. "Downstairs, quick!"

I hesitate for about two seconds, then people start streaming down the stairs from the floors above us, and the only thing we can do is go down with them. There's an alarm woop-wooping, and smoke starting to fill the top of the stairwell. People are in their nighties and pyjamas, with kids wrapped in blankets and old folk clinging onto the dodgy hand-rail, but nobody's panicking, and we all make it down to the ground floor and out onto the plaza where the Day and Son delivery van's parked, gleaming white in the sunlight.

The fire fighters arrive and we get moved away from the building. The fire's on Oak Level. I can see smoke billowing out of the windows. I look around for Barbara, but I can't spot her or Rory in the crowd. Still, the fire's a long way up; in the basement they should be safe. Firies head up the stairs; down here on the plaza there's a truck with a massive extension ladder and hoses being screwed onto water mains and lots of activity. Someone asks Day Junior to move the van. He asks me if I'm OK and I say yes, so he hops in and drives it away.

I haven't seen Susie. I haven't seen Sophie or Miranda. But Kye's here with his mum and his little brother, and they live on Oak Level. I can't make myself go over and talk to them. My head's gone muzzy and my legs feel weak. I collapse onto a bench with Mimi on my knee, staring up at the thickening smoke and thinking about that lump of wax Barbara threw into the stove. How it sizzled and burned. How it filled my nostrils with a smell like death. I want to say a prayer, but I can't think what should be in it, so I put my head down on the bench and press Mimi against my cheek and close my eyes. Magic *is* real, just like in Grimm's fairy tales.

The day after the fire, I'm leaving Westmoreland Hospital, where they've kept me in overnight for observation. A social worker from Defence Welfare is letting me stay at her place until Dad gets home on compassionate leave. Her name's Siobhan, she lives near my old house and she's told me she has three cats called Winken, Blinken and Nod. Siobhan seems to know a lot about what's been happening to me, even though I've hardly said anything. She tells me a Mrs Barbara Jaeger rang the office and told her where I was and that I needed help. And Mrs Moss from school rang too, a while ago, asking why I hadn't come back this term and if I was OK. I ask Siobhan if Mrs Jaeger is the concierge at Woodside Gardens and she says yes, and that Barbara said to pass on her best wishes for the future.

Before I go home with Siobhan, I visit my stepsister Sophie, who's in a different ward getting treated for smoke inhalation. Miranda's in surgery this morning—her hands got burned—so I can't see her. Sophie looks terrible, hospital-sheet-white with big bruises under her eyes, but she scrapes together a smile.

"Lissa. You're OK," she whispers.

"I'm OK. And you will be, too." I know the next thing I should say is that I'm sorry about Susie, but the words won't come out. I'm sorry it happened the way it did. But I can't be sorry she's gone.

"Look in the drawer," Sophie says on a rasping breath. "Got something for you."

I open the drawer in the bedside table, and there's the little doll I was making before Susie sent me down to get light. She's unharmed, just waiting there quietly for me to fetch her so I can finish embroidering her face. She's lying on the lacy shawl Sophie was knitting, and under that I see Miranda's Aran sweater with the fancy cables. I want to laugh and cry at the same time.

"Our Dad's coming," Sophie says. "They let me call him. He cried when he heard my voice. All this time, he didn't know where we were."

I start to understand why my stepsisters were sometimes unkind to me. I guess they were every bit as lost and afraid as I was. I feel strange, sort of sad, sort of relieved, but mostly just very tired.

"Miranda stopped to grab our work as we were running out." Sophie's looking at the doll, which is on my knee now. "That's how her hands got burned. I'm sorry we couldn't save your book, Lissa. I know you loved it."

A book is only a book. It's the stories in it that matter. "Thank you," I say, putting my hand on hers.

"Mum," Sophie whispers. "She threw that skull thing across the room, and suddenly there was fire everywhere. I don't know how it could . . . I don't understand . . . " Her voice fades to nothing.

"They think it may have been an electrical fault," puts in Siobhan from the doorway.

There's a silence, then I say to Sophie, "Let me know how you're getting on, OK?" When it's finished, this doll will be for her, and I'll make another for Miranda. Companions for a new life.

Siobhan comes in to put a little card on the bedside table, with contact phone numbers and addresses so Sophie and Miranda can find me if they want to.

"I have to go now," I say. I look at Sophie, and she stares up at me with her shadowy eyes, and the thing unspoken between us looms as huge and dark as the monster in every child's worst nightmare. "It'll be all right," I say, which is the best I can do at the moment.

Before she closes her eyes, Sophie whispers something. Maybe, *sorry.*

On the way to Siobhan's house, we drive past Woodland Gardens, where the clean-up is still happening. I don't look up at Oak Floor. An old woman in a purple dress is walking across the plaza, with an enormous ginger cat dawdling along behind her. I fish Mimi out of my pocket, hoping Siobhan's too busy driving to notice. I have a big question for my doll, a question about right and wrong and magic and responsibility. It's a question that's too big to be put in words.

Give me a kiss! demands Mimi.

I touch my lips to her woollen mouth.

Give me a hug!

I hold her against my heart, hoping the faceless doll in my other pocket won't get jealous. Her time will come.

Now let me dance!

One flip is all she gets, and not a very high one. I stand her on my knee, gaze into her knitted eyes and ask my question.

"All right?" asks Siobhan, giving me a sideways glance but keeping her hands firmly on the wheel.

"Fine," I tell her. "Could you drive around the block before we go home, please?"

Being a social worker, Siobhan is probably used to people acting weird. At the next corner she turns left and we begin a circuit of Woodland Gardens.

Start working on it now, Mimi says, *and by the time you're an old woman with white hair, you might know the answer to that question. Now can we go home, please?*

As we come around the plaza again, Barbara's still there, waiting while Rory does her business in a patch of dirt. I don't open the window and shout. I don't ask Siobhan to stop. I just look across at the two of them and mouth the words, "Thank you." Barbara turns and looks straight back at me. She lifts her hand in a sort of wave. Her mouth is not smiling and not frowning, but something in between. We drive on past, leaving Woodland Gardens behind us.

ABOUT THE CONTRIBUTORS

LEE BATTERSBY is the multiple award-winning author of *The Corpse-Rat King* and *Marching Dead* (Angry Robot Books, 2012 and 2013 respectively) and the upcoming *Magit and Bugrat* (Walker Books, 2015) as well as over 70 stories across Australia, the US and Europe, a number of which are collected in the collection *Through Soft Air* (Prime Books, 2006). Winner of the Writers of the Future, Aurealis, Ditmar and Australian Shadows Awards, he lives in Mandurah with his wife, author Lyn Battersby, and a pair of insane children. He is obsessed with Lego, Nottingham Forest Football Club, Daleks and dinosaurs, and blogs at the Battersblog **battersblog.blogspot.com**

DEBORAH BIANCOTTI is best known for her collections *Bad Power* and *A Book Of Endings*. She has been nominated for the Shirley Jackson Award, the William L. Crawford Award for Best First Fantasy Book, the Aurealis Award and the Ditmar Award. She is currently working on too many projects.

TRUDI CANAVAN lives in Melbourne, Australia. She has been making up stories about people and places that don't exist for as long as she can remember. While working as a freelance illustrator and designer she wrote the bestselling *Black Magician Trilogy*, which was published in 2001-3 and was named an 'Evergreen' by The Bookseller in 2010. *The Magician's Apprentice*, a prequel to the trilogy, won the Aurealis Award for Best Fantasy Novel in 2009 and the final of the sequel trilogy, *The Traitor Queen*, reached #1 on the UK Times Hardback bestseller list in 2011. For more info, visit **trudicanavan.com**

ROBERT G. COOK is an Anglo-Irishman from Kent, who lives in Brisbane, is a Registered Nurse, and writes fiction that nearly always comes out weird. "Glasskin" was his first published story. In late 2014, Brisbane publisher Tiny Owl Workshop will be publishing his flash fiction in a world-building project (*The Lane of Unusual Traders*) and in a Christmas cracker (*Krampus Crackers*). He can be stalked on twitter at **@robgcook**.

ROWENA CORY DANIELLS writes the kind of fantasy books that you can curl up with on a rainy Saturday afternoon. She has been involved with SF fandom for almost forty years and has served on the state and national management committees of several arts bodies. Her best-selling trilogy King Rolen's Kin, was released in 2010. *The Outcast Chronicles*, was released in 2012 and was a finalist in the Hemming Award. Her gritty-paranormal-crime *The Price of Fame* was also released in 2012. *King Breaker* (book 4 of KRK series) was released in 2013 and her original trilogy will be re-published as an omnibus in 2015: *The Fall of Fair Isle*. rowena-cory-daniells.com

TERRY DOWLING is one of Australia's most respected and internationally acclaimed writers of science fiction, dark fantasy and horror, and author of the multi-award-winning Tom Rynosseros saga. The *Year's Best Fantasy and Horror* series featured more horror stories by Terry in its 21-year run than by any other writer. Terry's horror collections are *Basic Black: Tales of Appropriate Fear* (International Horror Guild Award), Aurealis Award-winning *An Intimate Knowledge of the Night* and the World Fantasy Award nominated *Blackwater Days*. His most recent books are *Amberjack: Tales of Fear & Wonder* and debut novel, *Clowns at Midnight*. Terry's latest short stories include "The Four Darks" in *Fearful Symmetries* and "Corpse Rose" in *Nightmare Carnival*. terrydowling.com

THORAIYA DYER is a three-time Aurealis Award-winning, three-time Ditmar Award-winning Australian writer based in the Hunter Valley, NSW. Her short fiction has appeared in *Clarkesworld*, *Apex*, *Cosmos* and *Analog*. She has stories forthcoming in *War Stories* and *The Mammoth Book of SF by Women*. Her award-shortlisted collection, *Asymmetry*, is available from Twelfth Planet Press. Dyer is represented by the Ethan Ellenberg Literary Agency. She is a member of SFWA. A lapsed veterinarian, her other interests include bushwalking, archery and travel. Find her online at Goodreads, Twitter (@ThoraiyaDyer) or thoraiyadyer.com

MARION HALLIGAN AM is one of Australia's most prolific authors. She was born and educated in Newcastle and worked as a school teacher and journalist before publishing her first short stories. She has been awarded the Age Book of the Year, the ACT Book of the Year (three times), the Nita B. Kibble Award, the Steele Rudd Award, and the Geraldine Pascall Prize for critical writing. She has been shortlisted for the Miles Franklin Award, the Commonwealth Writers' Prize and the Nita B. Kibble Award. Halligan has also served as chair of the Literature Board of the Australia Council and in 2006 received an

AM for service to literature. She lives in Canberra.

DMETRI KAKMI is a writer, editor and presenter. His book *Mother Land* was shortlisted for the New South Wales Premier's Literary Awards in Australia; and is published in England and Turkey. He edited the acclaimed children's anthology *When We Were Young*. His essays and short stories appear in anthologies and journals. He lives in Melbourne.

DAVID KERNOT is an Australian author living in the Mid North of South Australia and when he's not writing, he's riding his Harley Davidson through the diverse local farmlands. He writes contemporary fantasy, science fiction, and horror, and his stories have been published in a variety of anthologies, magazines, and e-zines in Australia, the US, and Canada, including the *Year's Best Australian Fantasy & Horror (2011),* and *Award Winning Australian Writing* (2012). More information can be found at **davidkernot.com**

MARGO LANAGAN is a four-time winner of the World Fantasy Award, in the novel, novella, collection and short story categories, and her work has won many Aurealis, Ditmar and other Australian awards, and been shortlisted/honoured in the Tiptree (twice), Shirley Jackson (twice), Hugo, Nebula, Sturgeon, Bram Stoker, International Horror Guild, *Los Angeles Times* and Printz awards, as well as several British awards. She's written fantasy fiction for children, young adults and adults. Her most recent full-length works are the novels *Tender Morsels* and *Sea Hearts*, and her most recent story collections are *Yellowcake* and *Cracklescape*. Margo lives in Sydney.

S. G. LARNER is a denizen of Brisbane, Australia, where she complains about the heat, wrangles three children, and explores the dark underbelly of the world in her writing. You can find her at *http://foregoreality.wordpress.com* and on twitter **@StaceySarasvati**.

Perth-based writer MARTIN LIVINGS has had over eighty short stories in a variety of magazines and anthologies. His first novel, *Carnies*, published by Hachette Livre in 2006, was nominated for both the Aurealis and Ditmar awards, and has recently been republished by Cohesion Press. **martinlivings.com**

KIRSTYN MCDERMOTT has been working in the darker alleyways of speculative fiction for much of her career, with many critically acclaimed and award-winning short stories under her authorial belt.

Her two novels, *Madigan Mine* (Picador, 2010) and *Perfections* (Xoum, 2012; Twelfth Planet Press 2014) both won the Aurealis Award for Best Horror Novel, and a collection of short fiction, *Caution: Contains Small Parts* was published by Twelfth Planet Press in 2013. After many years based in Melbourne, Kirstyn now lives in Ballarat and is pursuing a creative PhD at Federation University. She can be found online (usually far too often) at **kirstynmcdermott.com**

CLAIRE MCKENNA is a Mebourne writer who has been writing spec fic for far longer than she cares to admit. She is a Clarion South Writer's Workshop graduate and a general lush. "The Ninety-Two" is based on a true story, when an AFL player got into some strife with his local clan over a football jumper that allegedly gave folks cancer, just like its predecessor. The story presented itself during the funeral of a very loved and respected writer friend, Paul Haines, a completely staunch bloke, and the complete antithesis of Beaufort Kinsey!

CATHERINE S. MCMULLEN is a writer and film & TV professional, currently living in Melbourne. Her fiction work has been published in *Nightmare Magazine*, *Aurealis Magazine*, *Dark Tales*, and others, and her non-fiction work includes articles for *Non-Fiction Gaming* and *Reading for Australia*. She was the youngest person to ever to sell a story to a professional science-fiction magazine, selling to *Interzone* at age 10. Her short story "The Nest" was nominated for an Australian Shadows Award from the Australian Horror Writers' Association, and her short story "Monday-child" was voted by *Aurealis* subscribers as Best Story of 2013.

JULIET MARILLIER was born and brought up in Dunedin, New Zealand, and now lives in Western Australia. Her historical fantasy novels and short stories for adults and young adults have been published internationally and have won a number of awards including the Aurealis, the American Library Association's Alex Award and the Sir Julius Vogel Award. Her lifelong love of folklore, fairy tales and mythology is a major influence on her writing. Juliet has two new novels out in 2014: The Caller, final instalment of the Shadowfell series, and Dreamer's Pool, first book in the Blackthorn & Grim series for adult readers. When not busy writing, Juliet tends to a small pack of waifs and strays. Her website is at **julietmarillier.com**

Born and raised in Adelaide, DAVID THOMAS MOORE has been a committed genre fan and writer his entire life. Now living in the UK,

David has recently celebrated five years working in the publishing industry, and is commissioning editor for Abaddon Books. He has a handful of short-fiction credits to this name, including in *Stories of the Smoke* and *Book of the Dead* (Jurassic), *Raus! Untoten!* (KnightWatch Press) and *Grimm and Grimmer* (FringeWorks). He lives in the UK with his wife, Tamsin, and daughter, Beatrix.

FAITH MUDGE is a Queensland writer with a passion for fantasy, folk tales and mythology from all over the world – in fact, almost anything with a glimmer of the fantastical. Her stories have appeared in various anthologies, the most recent of which include *Kisses by Clockwork, Kaleidoscope* and *Phantazein*. She also posts regular reviews and articles at beyondthedreamline.wordpress.com. Somewhere in the overcrowded menagerie of her mind, there are novels. She is even writing some of them.

RYAN O'NEILL's short stories have appeared in numerous journals and anthologies. His collection, *The Weight of a Human Heart* is published by Black Inc. He lives in rural NSW with his wife and daughters.

ANGELA REGA is a belly-dancing school librarian in love with folklore, fairy tales and furry creatures. She drinks way too much coffee, often falls in love with poetry and can't imagine not writing. Her stories have been published in Ticonderoga Publications, FableCroft Press, CSFG, Crossed Genres and PS Publications. She keeps a very small website at **angierega.webs.com**

TANSY RAYNER ROBERTS is an Australian fantasy author, blogger and podcaster. She won the 2013 Hugo for Best Fan Writer. Tansy has a PhD in Classics, which she drew upon for her short story collection *Love and Romanpunk*. Her latest fiction project is *Musketeer Space*, a gender-swapped space opera retelling of *The Three Musketeers*, published weekly as a web serial. Tansy also writes crime fiction under the name Livia Day.

NICKY ROWLANDS lives in Canberra with her wife, son and dog. In 2009, she left her job in the community sector to return to university, completing her Masters in Creative Writing in 2010. Since then, she's worked at home as a writer and stay at home mum. She has a keen interest in fantasy involving magic and mythical creatures, though story ideas that include neither come to her frequently. She's also worryingly addicted to stationery, books and tea. She can be regularly found on Twitter at **@Nicky__Rowlands**.

CAROL RYLES submitted her first short story to the Inaugural Katharine Susannah Prichard Speculative Fiction Award in 1998. To her immense surprise, it was awarded Highly Commended. Since then she has gained a BA in English and a PhD in Creative Writing focussing on steampunk, has graduated from Clarion West (Seattle), and has worked as Editorial Consultant and Project Manager for *Trove*, The University of Western Australia's online creative arts journal. Carol's stories have appeared in over a dozen small press anthologies and she is currently working on her second novel. You can read more at **carolryles.net**

ANGELA SLATTER is the author of the Aurealis Award-winning *The Girl with No Hands and Other Tales*, the World Fantasy Award finalist *Sourdough and Other Stories*, Aurealis finalist *Midnight and Moonshine* (with Lisa L. Hannett), as well as the 2014 releases *Black-Winged Angels*, *The Bitterwood Bible and Other Recountings*, and *The Female Factory* (again with Lisa L. Hannett). Her short stories have appeared in Australian, UK and US *Best Of* anthologies. She is the first Australian to win a British Fantasy Award, and was an inaugural Queensland Writers Fellow. She blogs at **angelaslatter.com** about shiny things that catch her eye.

ANNA TAMBOUR's novel *Crandolin* was shortlisted for the World Fantasy Award. Her next collection, *The Finest Ass in the Universe*, will be released by Twelfth Planet Press in July 2015.

Bram Stoker Nominee and Shirley Jackson Award winner KAARON WARREN has lived in Melbourne, Sydney, Canberra and Fiji. She's sold many short stories, three novels and four short story collections. Her latest collection is *The Gate Theory*. You can find her at **kaaronwarren.wordpress.com** and she tweets **@KaaronWarren**

JANEEN WEBB is a multiple award winning author, editor and critic. She is the recipient of the World Fantasy Award, the McNamara SF Achievement Award, the Australian Aurealis Award and is a three-time winner of the Ditmar Award. She is internationally recognized for her critical work in speculative fiction, and holds a PhD in Literature from the University of Newcastle. A collection of her short stories, *Death at the Blue Elephant* (2014) was published by Ticonderoga Press.

RECOMMENDED READING LIST

Ali Alizadeh, "Snow White and the Child Soldier", *Griffith Review 42: Once Upon a Time In Oz*

Pete Aldin, "The Whipping Tree", *Niteblade Fantasy and Horror Magazine #23*

Joanne Anderton, "Mah Song", *The Bone Chime Song*

——"Fence Lines", *The Bone Chime Song*

Liz Argall, "Blunt Force Trauma Delivered By Spouse", *This Is How You Die*

Peter M. Ball, "From Tuesday To Tuesday", *Daily Science Fiction*

Lee Battersby, "The Canals of Anguilar", *Review of Australian Fiction Vol 5 Issue 5*

Alan Baxter, "Roll the Bones", *Crowded*

——"It's Always the Children Who Suffer", *Midnight Echo #10*

Deborah Biancotti, "Indigo Gold", *One Small Step*

Tony Birch, "The Ghost River", *Griffith Review 42: Once Upon A Time In Oz*

Jenny Blackford, "The Quiet Realm of the Dark Queen", *Dreaming of Djinn*

——"Dream Hunt (Poetry)"

James Bradley, "Catspaw, Or the Rakshasa's Servant", *Aurealis #60*

O.J.Cade, "Burning Green", *Aurealis #66*

Anna Caro, "The Character of 82 James St", *Baby Teeth: Bite-Sized Tales of Terror*

Jay Caselberg, "Elephant's Graveyard", *Unnatural Conditions*

——"Sandals", *Unnatural Conditions*

——"Collage", *Dark Visions: A Collection of Modern Horror Vol 1*

——"The Axe", *Unnatural Conditions: Collected Short Stories*

——"The Track", *The End of the Road*

David Conyers and Brian M. Sammons, "Romero 2.0", *Undead & Unbound*

Matt Cowen, "Blood Sisters", *Baby Teeth: Bite-Sized Tales of Terror*

Thoraiya Dyer, "Seven Days in Paris", *Asymmetry*

Joanna Fay, "The Twelfth Hour", *Daughters of Icarus*

Jason Fischer, "Everything Is A Graveyard", *Everything Is A Graveyard*

John Paul Fitch, "Nip, Tuck, Zip, Pluck", *Diabolique*

Elizabeth Fitzgerald, "Phoenix Down", *Next*

Stephen Gepp, "From the Forebears", *Midnight Echo #9*

Lisa Hannett and Angela Slatter, "By Blood and Incantation", *One Small Step*

Lisa L. Hannett, "Another Mouth", *The Dark*

———"The Coronation Bout", *Electric Velocipede*

———"Morning Passages", *Shadows Edge*

———"Snowglobes", *Chilling Tales: In Words, Alas, Drown I*

Richard Harland, "Here's Glory for You", *Next*

Gerry Huntman, "The Cutpurse From Mulberry Bend", *Penny Dread Tales: Volume III: In Darkness*

Gerry Huntman, "Dom and Gio's Barber Shop", *Lovecraft Zine #21*

Gerry Huntman, "In Arcadia", *The Dark Bard*

Julie Kearney, "Light Dawns", *Griffith Review 42: Once Upon a Time in Oz*

Cate Kennedy, "A Glimpse of Paradise", *Griffith Review 42: Once Upon a Time in Oz*

Richard L Lagarto, "The Wild Hunt", *Next*

Chris Large, "The Red House", *Aurealis #58*

———"Girl Finds Key", *Next*

Sharyn Lilley, "Caleb's Chair", *Blood and Roses*

Martin Livings, "Stillgeist", *Midnight Echo #10*

Tracie McBride, "Wooden Heart", *Next*

———"Late For Eisheth", *The Demonologia Biblica*

———"The Oldest Profession", *Horror Library Vol 5*

Kirstyn McDermott, "What Amanda Wants", *Caution: Contains Small Parts*

———"Horn", *Caution: Contains Small Parts*

———"Lost and Found", *Review of Australian Fiction Vol 5 Issue 2*

————"The Home For Broken Dolls", *Caution: Contains Small Parts*

Ian McHugh, "The Canal Barge Magician's Number Nine Daughter", *Clockwork Phoenix* 4

————"Vandeimansland", *Next*

C.S. McMullen, "Monday-Child", *Aurealis Magazine*

Sean McMullen, "Acts of Chivalry", *Tales of Australia - Great Southern Land*

Robert Mammone, "Blood and Bone", *Midnight Echo* #10

Paul Mannering, "The Skulkybunking Wurld Champyon of the Hole Woorld", *Baby Teeth: Bite-Sized Tales of Terror*

Juliet Marillier, "The Angel of Death", *Prickle Moon*

————"Prickle Moon", *Prickle Moon*

Sophie Masson, "Restless", *Aurealis* #61

Eileen Mueller and Alicia Ponder, "Ahi Ka", *Northwrite Competition*

Faith Mudge, "Winter's Heart", *One Small Step*

Fi Michell, "Shoeless", *Andromeda Spaceways Inflight Magazine* #57

Charlotte Nash, "Parvaz", *Dreaming of Djinn*

Anthony Panegyres, "Oleander: An Ottoman Tale", *Dreaming of Djinn*

A.S. Patric, "Memories of Jane Doe", *The Great Unknown*

Dan Rabarts, "Remnants", *Aurealis*

————"All the Ghosts", *Baby Teeth: Bite-Sized Tales of Terror*

Angela Rega, "The Bellydancing Crimes of Ms Sahara Desserts", *Dreaming of Djinn*

Tansy Rayner Roberts, "The Minotaur Girls", *Glitter & Mayhem*

————"Cold White Daughter", *One Small Step*

Guy Salvidge, "Blue Swirls", *The Great Unknown*

Leife Shallcross, "A Little Warning", *Next*

David Schembri, "The Blackfather of the Night", *Eulogies II: Tales From the Cellar*

Angela Slatter, "By My Voice I Shall Be Known", *The Dark*

————"By the Weeping Gate", *Fearie Tales*

————"Cuckoo", *A Killer Among Demons*

————"The Burning Circus", *The British Fantasy Society Horror Anthology*

————"The Song of Sighs", *Weirder Shadows Over Innsmouth*

Darian Smith, "Recession", *Baby Teeth: Bite-Sized Tales of Terror*

Chris Somerville, "The Rift", *The Great Unknown*

Cat Sparks, "Scarp", *The Bride Price*
——"Beyond the Farthest Stone", *The Bride Price*
Grant Stone, "White", *Baby Teeth: Bite-Sized Tales of Terror*
Anna Tambour, "Marks and Coconuts", *Postscripts* 30/31
Kaaron Warren, "Sleeping With the Bower Birds", *Shivers* 7
——"The Human Moth", *The Grimscribe's Puppets*
Jen White, "The Family Is Gathering", *Andromeda Spaceways Inflight Magazine* #57
Kim Wilkins, "The Lark and the River", *The Year of Ancient Ghosts*
——"The Year of Ancient Ghosts", *The Year of Ancient Ghosts*
Suzanne J Willis, "Number 73 Glad Avenue", *One Small Step*
Danielle Wood, "The Good Mother", *Griffith Review 42: Once Upon a Time in Oz*
Damon Young, "Art", *The Great Unknown*

AUSTRALIAN & NEW ZEALAND FANTASY & HORROR AWARDS

THE AUSTRALIAN SF "DITMAR" AWARDS

BEST NOVEL

Fragments of a Broken Land: Valarl Undead, **Robert Hood (Wildside Press)**
NOMINEES
The Beckoning, Paul Collins (Damnation Books)
Trucksong, Andrew Macrae (Twelfth Planet Press)
The Only Game in the Galaxy (The Maximus Black Files 3), Paul Collins (Ford Street Publishing)
Ink Black Magic, Tansy Rayner Roberts (FableCroft Publishing)

BEST NOVELLA OR NOVELETTE:

"The Home for Broken Dolls", Kirstyn McDermott, *Caution: Contains Small Parts* **(Twelfth Planet Press)**
NOMINEES
"Prickle Moon", Juliet Marillier, *Prickle Moon* (Ticonderoga Publications)
"The Year of Ancient Ghosts", Kim Wilkins, *The Year of Ancient Ghosts* (Ticonderoga Publications)
"By Bone-Light", Juliet Marillier, *Prickle Moon* (Ticonderoga Publications)
"What Amanda Wants", Kirstyn McDermott, *Caution: Contains Small Parts* (Twelfth Planet Press)

BEST SHORT STORY

"Scarp", Cat Sparks, *The Bride Price* **(Ticonderoga Publications)**
NOMINEES
"Not the Worst of Sins", Alan Baxter, *Beneath Ceaseless Skies 133* (Firkin Press)

"Cold White Daughter", Tansy Rayner Roberts, *One Small Step*
 (FableCroft Publishing)
"Mah Song", Joanne Anderton, *The Bone Chime Song and Other*
 Stories (FableCroft Publishing)
"Air, Water and the Grove", Kaaron Warren, *The Lowest Heaven*
 (Jurassic London)
"Seven Days in Paris", Thoraiya Dyer, in *Asymmetry* (Twelfth Planet
 Press)

BEST COLLECTED WORK

The Bride Price, **Cat Sparks (Ticonderoga Publications)**
 NOMINEES
The Back of the Back of Beyond, Edwina Harvey (Peggy Bright Books)
Asymmetry , Thoraiya Dyer (Twelfth Planet Press)
Caution: Contains Small Parts, Kirstyn McDermott (Twelfth Planet
 Press)
The Bone Chime Song and Other Stories, Joanne Anderton (FableCroft
 Publishing)

BEST ARTWORK

Rules of Summer, **Shaun Tan (Hachette Australia)**
 NOMINEES
Cover art, Pia Ravenari, for *Prickle Moon* by Juliet Marillier
 (Ticonderoga Publications)
Cover art, Eleanor Clarke, for *The Back of the Back of Beyond* by
 Edwina Harvey (Peggy Bright Books)
Illustrations, Kathleen Jennings, for *Eclipse Online* (Nightshade Books)
Cover art, Shauna O'Meara, for *Next*, edited by Simon Petrie and Rob
 Porteous (CSFG Publishing)
Cover art, Cat Sparks, for *The Bride Price* by Cat Sparks (Ticonderoga
 Publications)

BEST NEW TALENT

Zena Shapter
 NOMINEES
Faith Mudge
Jo Spurrier
Stacey Larner
Michelle Goldsmith

AUREALIS AWARDS

FANTASY NOVEL

A Crucible of Souls, **Mitchell Hogan (self published)**
 NOMINEES
Lexicon, Max Barry (Hachette Australia)

These Broken Stars, Amie Kaufman and Meagan Spooner (Allen & Unwin)
Newt's Emerald, Garth Nix (Jill Grinberg Literary Management)
Ink Black Magic, Tansy Rayner Roberts (FableCroft Publishing))

FANTASY SHORT STORY

"The Last Stormdancer", Jay Kristoff (Thomas Dunne Books)
NOMINEES
"The Touch of the Taniwha", Tracie McBride (*Fish*, Dagan Books)
"Cold, Cold War", Ian McHugh (*Beneath Ceaseless Skies*, Scott H Andrews)
"ShortCircuit", Kirstie Olley (*Oomph: a little super goes a long way*, Crossed Genres)
"The Year of Ancient Ghosts", Kim Wilkins (*The Year of Ancient Ghosts*, Ticonderoga Publications)

BEST HORROR NOVEL

Fairytales for Wilde Girls, **Allyse Near (Random House Australia)**
NOMINEES
The Marching Dead, Lee Battersby (Angry Robot Books)
The First Bird, Greig Beck (Momentum)
Path of Night, Dirk Flinthart (FableCroft Publishing)

BEST HORROR SHORT STORY

"The Year of Ancient Ghosts", Kim Wilkins (*The Year of Ancient Ghosts*, Ticonderoga Publications)
NOMINEES
"Fencelines", Joanne Anderton (*The Bone Chime Song and Other Stories*, FableCroft Publishing)
"The Sleepover", Terry Dowling (*Exotic Gothic 5*, PS Publishing)
"The Home for Broken Dolls", Kirstyn McDermott (*Caution: Contains Small Parts*, Twelfth Planet Press)
"The Human Moth", Kaaron Warren (*The Grimscribe's Puppets*, Miskatonic Press)

BEST COLLECTION

The Bone Chime Song and Other Stories, **Joanne Anderton (FableCroft Publishing)**
NOMINEES
Asymmetry, Thoraiya Dyer (Twelfth Planet Press)
Caution: Contains Small Parts, Kirstyn McDermott (Twelfth Planet Press)
The Bride Price, Cat Sparks (Ticonderoga Publications)
The Year of Ancient Ghosts, Kim Wilkins (Ticonderoga Publications)

BEST ANTHOLOGY

The Year's Best Australian Fantasy and Horror 2012, **Liz Grzyb and**

Talie Helene, eds, (Ticonderoga Publications)
One Small Step, An Anthology Of Discoveries, **Tehani Wessely ed.**
(FableCroft Publishing)
NOMINEES
Dreaming Of Djinn, Liz Grzyb ed. (Ticonderoga Publications)
The Best Science Fiction and Fantasy of the Year: Volume Seven,
Jonathan Strahan ed. (NightShade Books)
Focus 2012: Highlights of Australian Short Fiction, Tehani Wessely ed.
(FableCroft Publishing)

BEST CHILDREN'S BOOK)

The Four Seasons of Lucy McKenzie, **Kirsty Murray (Allen & Unwin)**
NOMINEES
Kingdom of the Lost, book 2: Cloud Road, Isobelle Carmody (Penguin
Group Australia)
Refuge, Jackie French (Harper Collins)
Song for a Scarlet Runner, Julie Hunt (Allen & Unwin)
Rules of Summer, Shaun Tan (Hachette Australia)
Ice Breaker: The Hidden 1, Lian Tanner (Allen & Unwin))

YOUNG ADULT SHORT STORY

"By Bone-Light", Juliet Marillier (*Prickle Moon***, Ticonderoga
Publications)**
NOMINEES
"Mah Song", Joanne Anderton (*The Bone Chime Song and Other
Stories*, FableCroft Publishing)
"Morning Star", D.K. Mok (*One Small Step, an anthology of
discoveries*, FableCroft Publishing)
"The Year of Ancient Ghosts", Kim Wilkins (*The Year of Ancient
Ghosts*, Ticonderoga Publications)

BEST YOUNG ADULT NOVEL

These Broken Stars, **Amie Kaufman and Meagan Spooner (Allen &
Unwin)**
Fairytales for Wilde Girls, **Allyse Near (Random House Australia)**
NOMINEES
The Big Dry, Tony Davies (Harper Collins)
Hunting, Andrea Host (self published)
The Sky So Heavy, Claire Zorn (University of Queensland Press)

BEST ILLUSTRATED BOOK/GRAPHIC NOVEL

Burger Force, **Jackie Ryan (self-published)**
The Deep Vol. 2: The Vanishing Island, **Tom Taylor and James Brouwer
(Gestalt Publishing)**
NOMINEES
Savage Bitch, Steve Carter and Antoinette Rydyr (Scar Studios)
Mr Unpronounceable Adventures, Tim Molloy (Milk Shadow Books)
Peaceful Tomorrows Volume Two, Shane W Smith (Zetabella

Publishing)

BEST SCIENCE FICTION SHORT STORY

"Air, Water and the Grove", Kaaron Warren (*The Lowest Heaven,*
Pandemonium Press)
NOMINEES
"The Last Tiger", Joanne Anderton (*Daily Science Fiction*)
"Mah Song", Joanne Anderton (*The Bone Chime Song and Other
Stories*, FableCroft Publishing)
"Seven Days in Paris", Thoraiya Dyer (*Asymmetry*, Twelfth Planet Press)
"Version 4.3.0.1", Lucy Stone (*Andromeda Spaceways Inflight Magazine
#57*)

BEST SCIENCE FICTION NOVEL

Lexicon, **Max Barry (Hachette)**
NOMINEES
Trucksong, Andrew Macrae (Twelfth Planet Press)
A Wrong Turn at the Office of Unmade Lists, Jane Rawson (Transit
Lounge)
True Path, Graham Storrs (Momentum)
Rupetta, Nike Sulway (Tartarus Press)

PETER MCNAMARA CONVENORS' AWARD

Jonathan Strahan

AUSTRALIAN SHADOWS AWARDS

NOVEL

809 Jacob Street, **Marty Young** *(Black Beacon)*
NOMINEES
Undead Kelly, Timothy Bowden (Severed Press)
Topsiders, Scott Tyson (Legume Man Books)

LONG FICTION

"The Unwanted Women of Surrey", Kaaron Warren (*Queen Victoria's
Book of Spells*, **Tor)**
NOMINEES
"Soul Killer", Robert Hood (*Zombies Vs Robots: Diplomacy*, IDW
Publishing)
"The Home for Broken Dolls", Kirstyn McDermott (*Caution: Contains
Small Parts* (**Twelfth Planet Press)**

COLLECTION

The Bone Chime Song and other stories, **Jo Anderton (FableCroft
Publishing).**

EDITED PUBLICATION

Baby Teeth: Bite Sized Tales of Terror, **Dan Rabarts and Lee Murray eds (Paper Road Press)**

NOMINEES

Midnight Echo 9, Geoff Brown ed. (AHWA)

A Killer Among Demons, Craig Bezant ed. (Dark Prints Press)

Star Quake 1, Sophie Yorkston ed. (IFWG Publishing)

SHORT FICTION

"Caterpillars", Debbie Cowens (*Baby Teeth: Bite Sized Tales of Terror*, **Paper Road Press**)

NOMINEES

"Nip, Tuck, Zip, Pluck", John Paul Fitch (*Diabolique*, no publisher details)

"Fence Lines", Joanne Anderton (*The Bone Chime Song and other stories*, FableCroft Publishing)

"The Nest", C.S. McMullen (*Nightmare*: September 2013)

"The Dead Way", J.C. Hart (*Baby Teeth: Bite Sized Tales of Terror*, Paper Road Press)

SIR JULIUS VOGEL AWARDS

BEST NOVEL

Heartwood, **Freya Robertson (Angry Robot)**

NOMINEES

Journey of Shadows, Sam J. Charlton (self published)

A Cold Day in Hell, Sharon Hannaford (self published)

Night's Favour, Richard Parry (self published)

Chrystal Venom, Steve Wheeler (HarperVoyager)

The Wind City, Summer Wigmore (Steam Press)

BEST YOUTH NOVEL

Raven Flight, **Juliet Marillier (Pan Macmillan)**

NOMINEES

Talisman of Vim, Robert Wainwright (Makaro Press)

Pratibhashali (The Talented), Sanjay Joshi (Silver Leaf)

Fountain of Forever, K.D. Berry (Bluewood)

When We Wake, Karen Healey (Little Brown)

Wizard's Guide to Wellington, A.J. Ponder (Coombe House)

BEST NOVELLA / NOVELETTE

"Cave Fever", Lee Murray (Regeneration, Random Static)

NOMINEES

"Wings, Fangs and Shadows", Cindy Hargreaves (self published)

"In a World Full of Birds", I. K. Paterson-Harkness (*Regeneration: New Zealand Speculative Fiction 2*, Random Static)

"This Other World", Anna Caro (*Crossed Genres*)
"At the Bay of Cthulu", Matt and Debbie Cowens

BEST SHORT STORY

"By Bone-Light" by Juliet Marillier (*Prickle Moon*, **Ticonderoga Publications**)
NOMINEES
"Waking the Taniwha", Dan Rabarts (Wiley Writers website)
"Ahi Ka, Eileen Mueller and Alicia Ponder (NorthWrite 2013 website)
"All that Glitters", Dan Rabarts (*Ministry Protocol – Thrilling Tales of the Ministry of Peculiar Occurances*, Imagine That Studios)
"Love Hurts", Jan Goldie (*Baby Teeth: Bite Sized Tales of Terror*, Paper Road Press)
"Lockdown", Piper Mejia (*Baby Teeth: Bite Sized Tales of Terror*, Paper Road Press)

BEST COLLECTED WORK

Baby Teeth: Bite Sized Tales of Terror, **Dan Rabarts and Lee Murray eds (Paper Road Press)**
NOMINEES
Beyond This Age, Lee Murray and Piper Mejia eds (Oceanbook)
Twisty Christmas Tales, Eileen Mueller, Alicia Ponder and Peter Friend (Phantom Feather)
Regeneration: New Zealand Speculative Fiction 2, Anna Caro and Juliet Buchanan eds (Random Static)
Prickle Moon, Juliet Marillier (Ticonderoga Publications)

BEST PROFESSIONAL ARTWORK

Cover art, Emma Weakley, *Regeneration: New Zealand Speculative Fiction 2* **(Random Static)**
NOMINEE
Cover art, Samara Kirkham, *Beyond This Age* (Oceanbook)

BEST PROFESSIONAL PRODUCTION/PUBLICATION

Wearable Art **(Craig Potton Publishing)**
NOMINEES
The Hobbit: Unexpected Journey, Chronicles: Creatures and Characters, Daniel Falconer (HarperCollins)
The Hobbit: The Desolation of Smaug, Chronicles: Art and Design, Daniel Falconer (HarperCollins)

BEST DRAMATIC PRESENTATION

The Almighty Johnsons Series 3, **Mark Besley, prod. James Griffin and Rachel Lang, creators (South Pacific))**
NOMINEE
Eternity, Simon Bennett, written, dir, prod. Alex Galvin (Eternity Productions)

ACKNOWLEDGEMENTS

"Disciple of the Torrent", copyright © Lee Battersby 2013. First published in *Tales of Australia: Great Southern Land*, edited by Stephen C. Ormsby and Carol Bond, Satalyte Publishing.

"All the Lost Ones", copyright © Deborah Biancotti 2013. First published in *Exotic Gothic 5 Vol I*, edited by Danel Olson, PS Publishing.

"Camp Follower", copyright © Trudi Canavan 2013. First published in *Fearsome Journeys: The New Solaris Book of Fantasy*, edited by Jonathan Strahan, Solaris.

"Glasskin", copyright © Robert Cook 2013. First published in *Review of Australian Fiction Vol 5 #6*, edited by Matthew Lamb.

"The Ways of the Wyrding Women", copyright © Rowena Cory Daniells 2013. First published in *One Small Step*, edited by Tehani Wessely, Fablecroft.

"The Sleepover", copyright © Terry Dowling 2013. First published in *Exotic Gothic 5 Vol II*, edited by Danel Olson, PS Publishing.

"After Hours", copyright © Thoraiya Dyer 2013. First published in *Asymmetry*, Twelfth Planet Press.

"A Castle in Toorak", copyright © Marion Halligan 2013. First published in *Griffith Review #42: Once Upon a Time in Oz*, edited by Julianne Schultz AM FAHA and Carmel Bird.

"The Boy by the Gate", copyright © Dmetri Kakmi 2013. First published in *The New Gothic*, edited by Beth K. Lewis, Stoneskin Press.

"Harry's Dead Poodle", copyright © David Kernot 2013. First published in *Cover of Darkness Magazine*

"Black Swan Event", copyright © Margo Lanagan 2013. First published in *Griffith Review #42: Once Upon a Time in Oz*, edited by Julianne Schultz AM FAHA and Carmel Bird.

"Poppies", copyright © S.G. Larner 2013. First published in *Aurealis #65*, edited by Michael Pryor, Chimaera Publications.

"La Mort d'un Roturer", copyright © Martin Livings 2013. First published in *This is How You Die*, edited by Ryan North, Matthew Bernardo and David Malki, Grand Central Publishing.

"Caution: Contains Small Parts", copyright © Kirstyn McDermott 2013. First published in *Caution: Contains Small Parts*, Twelfth Planet Press.

"The Ninety Two", copyright © Claire McKenna 2013. First published in *Next*, edited by Simon Petrie and Robert Porteous, CSFG.

"The Nest", copyright © C.S. McMullen 2013. First published in *Nightmare Magazine #12*, edited by John Joseph Adams.

AVAILABLE FROM TICONDEROGA PUBLICATIONS

TICONDEROGA PUBLICATIONS LIMITED HARDCOVER EDITIONS

TICONDEROGA PUBLICATIONS EBOOKS

THE YEAR'S BEST AUSTRALIAN FANTASY & HORROR SERIES
EDITED BY LIZ GRZYB & TALIE HELENE

WWW.TICONDEROGAPUBLICATIONS.COM

THANK YOU

The publisher would sincerely like to thank:

Elizabeth Grzyb, Talie Helene, Lee Battersby, Deborah Biancotti, Trudi Canavan, Robert G. Cook, Rowena Cory Daniells, Terry Dowling, Thoraiya Dyer, Marion Halligan, Dmetri Kakmi, David Kernot, Margo Lanagan, S.G. Larner, Martin Livings, Kirstyn McDermott, Claire McKenna, C.S. McMullen, Juliet Marillier, David Thomas Moore, Faith Mudge, Ryan O'Neill, Angela Rega, Tansy Rayner Roberts, Nicky Rowlands, Carol Ryles, Angela Slatter, Anna Tambour, Kaaron Warren, Janeen Webb, Cat Sparks, Donna Maree Hanson, Robert Hood, Pete Kempshall, Karen Brooks, Jeremy G. Byrne, Kim Wilkins, Marianne de Pierres, Jonathan Strahan, Peter McNamara, Ellen Datlow, Grant Stone, Sean Williams, Simon Brown, Garth Nix, David Cake, Simon Oxwell, Grant Watson, Sue Manning, Steven Utley, Lewis Shiner, Bill Congreve, Jack Dann, Lucy Sussex, the Mt Lawley Mafia, the Nedlands Yakuza, Shane Jiraiya Cummings, Angela Challis, Kate Williams, Andrew Williams, Kathryn Linge, Al Chan, Alisa and Tehani, Mel & Phil, Jennifer Sudbury, Paul Pryztula, Helen Grzyb, Hayley Lane, Georgina Walpole, Rushelle Lister, Nerida Fearnley-Gill, everyone we've missed . . .

. . . and you.

IN MEMORY OF
Eve Johnson (1945–2011)
Sara Douglass (1957–2011)
Steven Utley (1948–2013)

Liz would like to thank Talie Helene, Helen Grzyb, Angela Challis, Shane Cummings, Amanda Pillar, Tom Bicknell, Kate Dunbar-Smith, Kate Williams, Andrew Williams, Debbie Wilson, Jacinta Rosielle, Ambre Hillier, Michael Hillier, Tasmar Dixon, Kylie Dainton, Mel Barbarat, Mel Donald, Phil Ward, Angela Rega, Annie Backshall, Alan Baxter, Carol Ryles, Anthony Panegyres, Jay Caselberg, Chuck McKenzie, Ruza Foster, Lina Piscitelli, Jacintha Bell, Nikki Irwin, Andrea Orlowsky, Anna Frankie Bertolini, Hilary Donraadt, Angie Irwin, Kim Astle, Rachel Randall, Jane Hebiton, and of course the Department of Fabulous.

Talie would like to thank Liz Grzyb, Russell B. Farr, Adam Calaitzis, Charmaine Calaitzis, Julia Svaganovic, Kirstyn McDermott, Jason Nahrung, Leigh Irwin, Josephine Wilson, Samantha Escarbe, Stacey Palfreyman, Felicity Dowker, David Trzcinski, Rocky Wood, Jack Dann, David Conyers, Deborah Crabtree, Satima Flavell, Lezli Robyn, Oliver Holm, Chuck Chainey-McKenzie, Sean Bowley Kramer, Wendy Rule, Ellen Gregory, Claire McKenna, Michelle Goldsmith, Sarah Endacott, Jamie Reuel, Lucy Sussex, Julian Warner, the SuperNova Writers crew, Martin Livings, Mariangelina Macaronne, Paddy O'Reilly, Helen Stubbs, Jessica Steele, Sonia Tamarri, Deborah Tamarri, Cynthia Tamarri, Fiona Trembath, Nalini Haynes, Dean John Anderson, Alison Goodman, Karen McKenzie, Narelle Harris, Janette Dalgliesh, Geoff Brown, Andrez Bergen, Craig Bezant, Linda Brucesmith, Jenny Blackford, Alan Baxter, Jodi Cleghorn, Jason Franks, Jason Fischer, Robert D. Grixti, Richard Harland, Catriona Sparks, Robert Hood, Trent Jamieson, Earl Livings, Gillian Polack, Yaritji Green, Sharyn Lilley, David Schembri, Mark Smith-Briggs, Guy Salvidge, Kyla Lee Ward, Marty Young, Lee Battersby, Deborah Biancotti, Terry Dowling, Thoraiya Dyer, Marion Halligan, Dmetri Kakmi, David Kernot, Margo Lanagan, Stacey Larner, Catherine McMullen, David Thomas Moore, Ryan O'Neill, Tansy Rayner Roberts, Angela Slatter, Anna Tambour, Kaaron Warren, Janeen Webb, Robert Cook, Jay Caselberg, Stephen Ormsby, Danel Olson, Alisa Krasnostein, Jonathan Strahan, Tehani Wessely, Jared Shurin, Angela Meyer, and Shelley Slater.

www.ingramcontent.com/pod-product-compliance
Lightning Source LLC
Chambersburg PA
CBHW020824030726
47496CB00001B/86